NORTH STAR

AMARANTH BOOK 2

DAVID M. SNOW

FLAME ARROW PUBLISHING

To my best friend Kim Archambault,
The star that guides my writing projects
As crazy they might seem

FREE BOOK

To thank you for purchasing this book, you can read the prequel to the
Amaranth series *for free!*

Get my free book by visiting www.davidmsnow.com

1

SKYLER

Water pulses through the tubes like the beating of a slumbering mechanical heart. A bluish shaft of light pierces through the foam and makes Tessa's silhouette shimmer as she inches forward, gun in hand.

Things have changed since the commander's death.

The lies nurtured in the last decades have crumbled, and the scents of a bitter victory are burning. Neal's hard-won control of the Ark to reach the Promised Land is not enough to forget the terrible desolation that still prevails in the Great Ocean one hundred and fifteen years after the Flood.

The abandoned vessel that Skyler and Tessa are exploring is yet another wasted opportunity to find salvation.

Skyler tightens his grip on his pistol. He didn't expect to get on a lifeless metal carcass, a true relic of a bygone era. But they should brace themselves if something or *someone* has stood the test of time.

The metal walls gurgle to the rhythm of the bubbles that spread through the network of glass tubes. Hypnotized by the squeaking rubber of their boots, Skyler almost ends up stuffing his nose into Tessa's sweet braids.

"Did you find anything?" Skyler says in a whisper, lest they be heard.

"Well, not the Promised Land," Tessa replies nonchalantly.

"This is a waste of time."

"Keeping control of the Ark is no small task. With the Archeans' distrust, Neal must prove he is fit for the role." She has avoided his gaze until now. "Your brother trusts us."

The play of light may be deceptive, but a strange glint shines in her eyes. After falsely borrowing the Farrell name and hiding her connection with the Brotherhood to get closer to him, Skyler doesn't know whether to believe her anymore.

"As soon as we locate the source of the signal, we get the hell out of here," says Tessa who breaks eye contact to keep moving.

Skyler doesn't follow her right away. Their first trip outside the Ark, the only place he's ever known, highlights the widening chasm between them. And yet, she has the audacity to talk about trust. He knew from the start it was a bad idea to go on a mission with her.

When she's out of sight, he finally decides to join her. As much as he hates to admit it, he is vulnerable without her protection.

"The people who used to live here may have died long ago," says Skyler, whose voice echoes off the vast ceiling of the great hall. It looks quite similar to the skylight in the Ark's dining hall.

Rotting dishes are still scattered on the perfectly aligned tables, decomposition having claimed its due. But what piques Skyler's interest is the gigantic tube in the center, where a diffuse light cascades over a school of multicolored fish swirling about. The resemblance is striking: This place is a true replica of the Ark.

The Amaranth, however, is unique; it is the only known vessel to have weathered the Flood, sheltering the last survivors of humanity. This place is probably a wreck, a relic of the past century.

"If only we knew how long the signal Neal intercepted has been on a loop," Tessa muses aloud as she walks the aisles.

Skyler moves closer to get a better look at the strange, dimly lit aquarium from the inside. A cluster of pink coral stands to the fish's delight. They swim through a mass of greenish thready algae wriggling under the water jets, the way the trees of the Gardens of Humankind sway during the occasional seaquakes.

Skyler bites his cheek as he realizes how the Amaranth could meet the same dark fate as this abandoned vessel. This is a stark reminder that the Sacred Fire has died. It is only a question of time before the ocean that saw them born consumes them.

Tessa lets out a strained sigh and mutters, "Why haven't we come across any dead bodies yet?"

The fish swim around giddily in their secluded watery world, unaware of what is happening outside their tank. If they knew there was an ocean beyond these walls, would their destiny be any different? Or would they lose heart knowing they are trapped in a cell contained in a vast prison?

"What if they could escape?" offers Skyler, resting his hand against the surprisingly warm glass.

"To where?"

The bluish glow emanating from the tube outlines Tessa's stubborn expression. She is absorbed by the upward movement of a bright yellow, dark-finned fish. It is more energetic than the others and looks out of place among its lethargic counterparts.

If this wreck dates from before the Flood, its passengers could have reached the nearest city. A mechanical failure beyond repair could have forced them to abandon the ship. And yet, the air is still breathable, and these fish seem to be doing well. Even the multiple branches of glass piping converging to the hall still have water flowing in them.

Skyler can't help but brood: What if the Commander of the Amaranth hadn't died? If his brother had not disappeared and their mother had not struggled with depression? Dylan would still be alive, and Emily would never have gone to the Sacred Fire with Milo.

"There's no point in staying here," says Skyler as he walks away from the aquarium, flush with annoyance.

"Wait. Let me explain—" Tessa's eyes waltz back and forth, the words slipping from her grasp.

"I don't think this is the time or place," cuts Skyler.

"I know it will never be the right time." The faces are too vivid in Skyler's mind, looking at him accusingly. "I shouldn't have kept my true identity from you, but I had my reasons to do so," she continues, pursing her lips.

"Good enough to betray me?"

She flinches, then looks down. "It's not that simple."

"Stop avoiding the question."

The ship's pulsing slows down, as if the system had failed. Then a hiccup sends a jet more powerful than the others through the aquarium in a swirl of bubbles. The fish quiver, then dart upwards vigorously.

"I did what I had to do for everyone's good," Tessa says in what sounds like a whisper after the ship's sudden hiccup.

"You knew my brother was still alive, but you chose to manipulate me."

"I couldn't jeopardize the Brotherhood's plan. It wasn't my decision."

"We always have a choice, Tessa."

Commander Hawk and Yasmina would not be dead if Skyler had not given in to Laurene's threats in the infirmary. The Ark would not be shutting down right now if he had persuaded the commander to cooperate. He could have talked some sense into his brother to keep Hawk on duty under the Brotherhood's supervision. Hadn't Neal wanted to preserve Hawk's life, anyway?

Skyler feels mired in a downward spiral, all thanks to his being a coward.

"I did what I thought was right, and I still think it was," squeaks Tessa, her eyes shining.

"Yeah, right. So now it was your decision to lie to me, not my brother's."

Stealthy footsteps in the corridor behind Skyler stop him dead in his tracks. He and Tessa exchange a questioning look. They step into the forking hallway with their guns raised. No one is around.

"I'll look this way," says Skyler eager to be alone.

This time, she doesn't hold him back. Why does Tessa have to make things more complicated than they already are? He's always been upfront with her. Why can't she do the same?

The slow throbbing in the background blends with the grinding of the shipwreck weathering the rough undersea currents. A storm must be raging on the Surface and thundering down into the abyss. Or is it something else? Or someone?

Why did he insist on coming? He should be treating patients on the Ark, not poking around a shipwreck with a rogue Paragon rebel. When did he change so much?

The lighting wavers and Skyler flicks on the flashlight on his pistol to get his bearings, his back brushing against the wall when the shaking gets too strong. The whitish light refracts against the water oozing in several places, droplets splashing on his face with the roll.

Skyler coughs violently, his throat dry from the strong smell of brine, worse than the fish smell that can linger for days in the Ark's dining hall. The cracks between the metal plates are filled with greenish moss which must be releasing harmful mold spores.

When the hallway splits, he instinctively takes a left. The

light from his pistol reveals the blocky outline of two elevators with out-of-order indicators. Skyler uses the adjacent stairwell and climbs. The place is eerily empty and silent, but for his footsteps scraping against metal.

How long has this place been deserted? Assuming it's an old military vessel and they all managed to escape, why does the signal keep playing on a loop? More importantly, why did they abandon ship?

Skyler coughs again and finally puts on the mask he brought. The rubber sucks in his nose and mouth, as he inhales deeply to suppress his cough. Skyler checks the oxygen levels via his wristband, which are slightly lower than normal. Someone must have been maintaining the air filtration system; otherwise, the air would be unbreathable. If their system is anything like the Sacred Fire, it requires maintenance every month or so.

Skyler runs his fingers along the wall: The familiar texture brings back vivid memories of exploring the nooks and crannies of the Ark with his brother when they were teenagers. Allen would have liked to carry out this kind of mission. Though Allen and Neal are one and the same, Skyler sometimes finds himself longing for the Allen he remembers. Neal decided to burden himself with his self-imposed, inconceivable mission: ideals he should have given up long ago.

This lifeless ship is alarming. The crew and its passengers simply cannot have disappeared. In an emergency, they would bunker up in the Refuge or, at least, its equivalent.

Of course!

Skyler hurries back down following his hunch. With each turn, the sense of familiarity grows stronger. Who are they? What happened to them?

What if they're on an Ark like the Amaranth? The Refuge should be located under the atrium.

His heart is racing at the thought they might not be alone.

Skyler sobers up as he passes a hallway that shouldn't be

here. He shouldn't have jumped to a conclusion without enough data. Did he take a wrong turn? He retraces his steps and notices his mistake: a fork that his torchlight had missed. Exhilaration bubbles in his stomach. He strides along in the darkness which sucks in the wavering light.

Skyler freezes, a strange shudder running through his body. He looks around. Nothing.

The gunstock rubs against his tingling sweaty hand. He doesn't want to have to use it. His skills cannot compare with Tessa's training, and his brother didn't bother to train him properly before sending him out on this mission.

A red-dotted eye is staring at him. Motionless.

It flashes.

Shit.

The red glow located on top is less than a meter away from the ceiling. A series of small blue dots light up on each side as if awakening. Skyler holds up his pistol, its beam of light reflecting off a jointed metal piece. He cautiously steps back to get closer to his destination, but suddenly, a purple flash dazzles him.

He covers his eyes by instinct and shoots blindly. The bullets ricochet off the walls. Why don't the simulations teach them self-defense?

He should be a doctor! Not a hunter or a secret agent of the Paragon! Especially not a member of the Brotherhood for that matter. Preparing an IV drip, administering antibiotics, and filling memory spheres he designed himself with consenting patients' memories. That's what he's made for.

An electronic noise snaps him back to the present; he lost the only chance he had to shoot down that thing. Skyler does what he does best: He runs, with a buzzing sound tailing him. A drone! Bullets riddle the metal walls behind him, as he pushes harder.

His breathing is shallow. He takes off his mask, and the

dirty air chafes his throat immediately. He takes a left at the fork under the thunder of bullets that rumbles around him. A large portal ornate with incomprehensible gilded symbols looms before him. He taps away at the console which won't open.

The killer drone is getting closer. Skyler throws himself to the ground as a shower of bullets lodges into the door. Eyes shut, he shoots a few rounds, out of rage or desperation he can't tell. The ship pitches, and he has no idea if he hit that hellish metalhead.

When he runs out of bullets, he drops the gun. His fingers hurt, and the horrible feeling of having been momentarily possessed creeps in. Powerless, Skyler waits for the killing blow to take him out.

Nothing happens. He opens his eyes and gets up carefully.

Lying on the ground, his pistol casts a beam over the crackling thing that nearly killed him. Its ghastly lights flicker out in a wisp of smoke. Skyler retrieves his weapon and crouches down to get a better look at it.

The propellers are motionless and probably the source of the strange buzzing sound. Before the Flood, authorities used drones like this for surveillance, but for some reason this technology is not widely used on the Ark. Tessa would know why.

He leaves the heap of junk behind to go back into the main corridor. If any more of those killer drones show up, he'll need new ammunition. The Refuge is his only chance.

The large door with the golden symbols has mysteriously opened. He steps in with hesitation and grabs the frame just in time as the seaquake worsens. If this storm keeps on, going back to the Amaranth will be difficult and *very* turbulent. An electronic voice startles him,

Welcome to the auditorium. There are no performances scheduled for tonight. Sedna works relentlessly to make the transition to the New World the experience of a lifetime.

The auditorium? That must be the atrium. And Sedna? Another mystery.

Fresh air is leaking out, like the cold that gets into a Strahl during a ride. The smell of decay is stronger here, but Skyler doesn't bother to put back on his mask. He walks down a hundred rows of seats where he would expect to find a platform which isn't there. He sweeps the darkness glittering with white dust particles.

Shots burst out in a deafening echo. Another drone? No, more like a gun. Tessa? Should he go back to her?

The pistol's light disappears down a cavity, about ten steps away. Skyler goes down the stairs.

At the bottom, a hatch that should be sealed is open. The rancid smell becomes so strong that Skyler's eyes fill with tears. A sensor activates as he enters a room as large as the Ark's atrium. The lights gradually flood the room and… Skyler is transfixed by the vision of horror.

There are heaps of bodies. Hundreds of them. No, thousands.

Dead bodies. Everywhere.

He retches violently and vomits against the wall. He remembers Dr. Nazar's advice when he saw his first body. He must detach himself from the present and analyze the situation objectively. Back when he thought his brother was dead, he panicked, but now it's different. He can do it.

He glances around, still overwhelmed by his moment of weakness. He holds his breath for fear he will be sick again. Those bodies could be the Ark's passengers if he doesn't do his job right. That is why he is here and why his brother trusts him.

Once the wave of nausea passes, Skyler wipes his mouth with the sleeve of his uniform and puts on his mask. He must find out the cause of their death or find a clue about their identity.

Their strange uniforms are tight-fitting, something relic

hunters would wear. Some have cloth fins sewn on their elbows and backs, like a wetsuit. The corpses within sight have puncture wounds in more places than he can count. Even the walls of the antechamber are riddled with holes.

"Look who I found."

At the top of the stairs, Tessa holds up a girl at gunpoint. The stranger's hair is black as ink, tied in two braids with orange cords tangled in her strands. She is wide-eyed, her eyelids almost invisible. As for her clothing, it is unlike anything Skyler has ever seen. It is not a uniform; she wears a seemingly handmade orange top with a plunging neckline, and short, puffed sleeves. Odd-shaped necklaces intertwined with some toothlike, pearly white stones cover her neck. Two rings droop down her ears, swinging furiously.

It may not be the Promised Land they had hoped for, but…

Who are these people? What happened to them? What is this world they live in?

"Who are you?" asks Skyler as he gets closer.

Then, realizing that he is wearing his mask, he takes it off.

The girl stares at them with a bewildered look before answering in a trembling voice, "I don't know."

2

NEAL

Neal presses on, not knowing what to do with what Dan has brought back. As if he needed that. Shouldn't they be happy they ended a rule of lies? Isn't that what they wanted, the power to choose for themselves?

The doors to the command center slide open as he approaches, Dan at his heels. The two guards greet him with a smile, and Neal mechanically puts up two fingers on his forehead.

Merely three months ago, Nora and Derek lost their younger brother in a food raid in the Delta sector. They had sworn to protect him with their lives, and his death devastated them. Neal offered them the opportunity to join the Brotherhood's cause, so they would channel their grief into training hard. They rose from their ashes and are now the trusted allies Neal sorely needs.

He beckons for them to follow him, and others take their place.

"The dining hall," Neal tells them, in a voice meant to be friendly.

"I can handle it," Dan grunts, bringing the shoulder strap of his large-caliber pistol forward to have a better grip on it.

"I know."

Neal's mind resumes its frantic race as soon as they reach the central corridor where the galvanized crowd closes in around them. His guards swiftly push any reckless people out of their way. Neal could do it himself, but what would people think of him? Anything could lead to the Brotherhood's downfall.

The rescue mission they swore to fulfill could become no more than a broken dream. It took five years to restore the Brotherhood to its former glory after losing their invaluable collaborator, Tyna Bates. Although she never pledged her allegiance, she played a key role in rekindling their spirits since the former Brotherhood disbanded. Tyna Bates was wrongfully convicted for treason, the injustice of it all sparking outrage that filled their minds with sinful thoughts. Despite the Commander's warning—it had to be!—, the Mavericks promised to never bend.

Mavericks. What a phony name! Their community is close-knit, even more so than those families who swear by their reputation. They might be given a bigger cabin, better food, or a one-hour visit to the simulator, but what difference does it make? Death knows everyone's name from the moment they take their first breath.

As humanity faces its greatest challenge since the Flood, the Commander only managed to divide them by stoking tensions. The Brotherhood's founder claimed they kept a leash around their necks to better control them. But this cunning trick never worked on the Mavericks, who resisted with all their might, even if it meant leading a life of misery. What a shame she didn't live long enough to witness their success.

Tyna Bates wanted things to change on the Ark, too. The Commander made decisions behind closed doors and shunned the Mavericks who wouldn't yield to the Paragon's influence—another problem! These generations of outcasts whose very existence is blasphemy to the other Archeans suffered in their solitude. This woman was able to breathe new life into the silenced Mavericks. Now, Neal only hopes to be right-minded enough to save them all.

As they take a sharp turn, shouts of protest rise from the dining hall. The stream of onlookers tries Dan's patience, and Nora and Derek help push them out of the way. Heavy humidity hangs in the air, and Neal wishes he could take off his lined uniform for once, but that would be pure madness. Without protection, he would be an easy target. All it takes is a distraction and a single bullet.

The Paragon agents rattle their electric prods through the crowd, and Neal grips his pistol. Two mixed groups of Mavericks, Archeans, and the Paragon are duking it out.

"Can't wait to see what this shitshow will look like in the Refuge," Nora groans.

"The Paragon has been divided since their leader Duke and his son Chris got arrested," says Dan, absently scratching his beard. "No one said a change of leadership would be easy."

"Will they ever learn?" complains Neal, clenching his fist.

"Most don't even think about the consequences. How could they share a room for a month? They're just a bunch of kids."

"They have their own battle to fight," Derek says in a low voice.

"They could've picked a better time for this," says Neal, craning his neck to get a better look at what the fuss is all about.

It would be madness to give access to the Pods to people who haven't shown loyalty to the Brotherhood. For now, strife in the Paragon's ranks work in their favor, but the tide could turn against them as soon as they move over to the Refuge. Living in a confined space can send the human mind back to its most animal instincts. All their lives, the Mavericks have had to deal with this reality, scraping to survive. The privileged Archeans, with their all-inclusive canteen, have no idea what it's like to do without.

Dan puts a hand on Neal's shoulder, his body shielding him from an odd character glaring at them a few steps away.

"How do you want to handle this? We need a plan."

"Is it that bad?" His question is stupid, Neal knows it, but it's too much to juggle. What will it take for the Archeans to realize that their lives are at stake?

Distractedly, Neal rubs his largest tattoo, the sharp prick of the needle and the ink seeping through his flesh still vivid: a lesser pain to remember the sacrifices to come. The network of ink branded into the furrows of his scarred skin is a memory he will never forget: a constellation of promises, a wave for change.

He must honor his commitment to the Brotherhood, the Mavericks, but also to himself. The life he has always dreamed of is so close that he can feel it at his fingertips.

"No fighting," says Neal to his watchful companions. "Or else there will be a mess in the Refuge. We're vulnerable until the Paragon switches sides."

Dan opens his mouth, as if to say something, but finally lets out a sigh. Neal raises his eyebrows.

"What?"

"Try not to get carried away this time." Neal balks at Dan's words.

"Do I have such a bad reputation?"

"I have a good memory."

If he's referring to Valdez, that doesn't count. Valdez blew his cover by pouring his heart out to his pretty partner after drinking too much. Walker had toiled away for weeks to get him into the Paragon. Thankfully, Tessa knew better, and kept her mouth shut, so at least they were able to keep their mole in. She did a good job of cleaning up that mess. Without her, the

Paragon would have found out about the Brotherhood. Neal's anger had been more than justified.

"I'll do what's necessary," Neal tells Dan, who nods. "Whatever is necessary."

"Be careful."

Dan is a gruff-looking man with a soft heart. Since the Brotherhood's inception, he's been tending to their every need, even before Neal came into the picture. But sometimes he has trouble minding his own business, like right now.

Walker has dimmed the lights, plunging the dining hall into an eerie gloom typical of the lower levels. The skylight is now a seething pit, with people perched on the upper floors watching the factions eye each other like old enemies in an arena.

The tables are overturned, and spoiled food is plastered all over the floor and walls. How many Mavericks could have fed themselves? Unsurprisingly, Fiona is in the middle of the ruckus with a group of rogue Mavericks who support the Brotherhood. They joined in when they heard that some Archeans loyal to Commander Hawk wanted to seize the Ark.

Neal heaves a deep sigh as he watches the morons wasting their only chance at survival.

"We need to stick together, not kill each other," he roars, glaring at Fiona.

The Mavericks are cooling down, but the disgruntled Archeans don't relent. As for the Paragon agents, they lower their weapons, some more willingly than others, with a few admiring glances at Neal. Is that respect? It's a start.

"We want to see the Commander now!" bellows a middle-aged man Dan must hold at bay.

He's an Archean dressed in a dull purple tunic with straight shoulder pads and an obi fitted around his waist which means he's a member of the Sigma's secret division. Few people know what they actually do for the Sigma Foundation, but they look strangely like martial arts masters. Could it be a superhero complex gone wrong? Many young Mavericks who were too proud of their successful supply missions tended to have this problem as well.

The fake superhero points a finger in their direction and vociferates, chin up. His hands should be calloused, but instead, his golden skin bears not the slightest imperfection, and his freshly manicured nails shine despite the poor lighting. A polished ring set with an aquamarine stone adorns his middle finger. Aquamarine can only have been recovered on a relic hunt. Making such jewelry requires resources that have not been available on this ship for a long time.

"My family has struggled for years to gain respect," he thunders, as the semidarkness casts an uncanny sheen over the hollows of his eyes.

"And what exactly did you do?" asks Neal, stubbornly.

Everyone holds their breath, looking horrified. This man enjoys a special status reserved to only a handful of families. Neal approaches him with as much nonchalance as possible, aware of people watching him intently. Isn't that what they wanted, a show?

Fortunately for him, Dan stands between them, one arm pushing against the seething man's chest.

"You think you're above the rules? You think a rat like you can decide what we do on *our* ship? You have no idea what is good for us in line with the plan."

Neal gives a wry smile at the man's caustic tongue. "*Our* ship as you say is now under *my* control."

"You're a self-proclaimed commander now?" jeers the foolish master with a grating laugh. "And then what? The century-old rules that govern the Ark can't simply be thrown out."

"*I* make the rules."

"Shouldn't Commander Hawk himself come and tell us? The official procedure is clear: There must be a handover ceremony presided over by the Paragon. As far as I know, none of this has happened."

"Obviously, you care a lot about maintaining procedures. You said you're speaking for your family but rest assured that the change in command doesn't erase your contribution. Every passenger on this ship will be fairly compensated for supporting the Brotherhood. I don't see what the problem is."

"The Commander should tell us himself. I think I made myself quite clear. Our reputation takes precedence over those rats!"

"It's just about your family's reputation, isn't it?"

Unease gnaws at Neal's chest, his nostrils flaring. He sorely misses the electric surge simulating the impact of flesh against his fists during his virtual fights. When was the last time?

He takes a deep breath and adds *talk to Walker* to his to-do list.

"You don't know what it's like to be an outcast looked down upon all your life."

Those years spent among the orphans hiding away on the lower floors were … miserable. There were so many of them. Most have no memory of their family. They were abandoned, left for dead. Instead of glorifying their reputations, these goddamn Archeans should treasure their loving families.

"You've always had it easy," Neal spits, his cheeks going numb. "We didn't. Now you'll listen to us." Dan makes a face that says he just screwed up at controlling his emotions. Easier said than done.

"They killed the Commander, that's why!" shouts an Archean barely younger than Neal. He's wearing the medical bay's Omega uniform. "Stowaways! That's what you are! Our problems started with you, and you made it worse by taking over our Ark. You killed the only qualified commander we had."

The Brotherhood's supporters cheer at that while Hawk's followers' shouts of protest thunder up into the skylight.

"Did we sacrifice our lives for nothing?" presses the fake superhero as Dan hold him tighter. "There's no way my family will be sharing the Refuge with those … terrorists!"

They're just words, but they pierce through Neal like the tattoo needle that stabbed his skin for hours on end until he couldn't bear the pain anymore. He's hardened up since then. The feeling is familiar, almost welcomed.

He should have foreseen the unfortunate death of the Commander resulting from Laurene going rogue on them. They took her out before she busted their plans and now, she's rotting in her cell until Neal decides her fate. Had Hawk given them the code willingly, they would've avoided getting into their current mess. The only thing they can do now is damage control.

The man in the tunic breaks free of Dan's grip and melts into the crowd, furious.

"What's your name?" Neal curtly asks the young Archean who exposed Hawk's death.

Neal had been meaning to announce the Commander's death himself as soon as the situation stabilized to quell the uproar, but it's too late for that now. He ducks ever so slightly, pondering in frustration.

"What difference does it make?" taunts the Archean, the brilliant skin of his neck gleaming under the orange lighting.

Neal feels like he's seen this boy before, but his memory fails him. Was it on a surveillance camera? With Skyler perhaps?

"I speak in the name of all those who, like me, want to claim what is rightfully ours," continues the young Archean, his mouth half-opened as if getting ready to bite. "Do these words remind you of anything?"

He has recited these words for the past five years, a daily ritual to remind himself not to squander this new chance to resurrect the Brotherhood. He knows them all too well.

Neal lets his anger run a little deeper into his veins and feeds off it. His credibility depends on how he will react. He's all too aware of the stares skewering him. His scene with the ludicrous superhero was not his greatest achievement.

He stays put, refusing to give in to his emotions.

"I guess you're the leader of this Brotherhood?" adds the young Archean in a scathing tone. "How does it feel to be a murderer?"

"The Commander is responsible for his own death," says Neal through gritted teeth.

The Archean snorts and raises his voice. "You are no less a murderer. How many bodies were cremated today? The most important person in my life was among them because of your stupid rebellion which doomed us all."

Personal motives it is then. Neal makes note of this valuable detail and replies, "I'm not responsible for your misery. I've also lost many loved ones, but I don't blame anyone just to ease my pain. I've come to accept it."

"I've seen dozens of patients die from the Fairy Syndrome. You must've heard about it."

Several Mavericks have also been affected, and Neal thought it was a weapon to purge them—an efficient way to destroy them from within. The Syndrome had sown the seeds of revolt in their hearts, and quickly became the catalyst for reviving the Brotherhood.

Command must have miscalculated the true power of their biological weapon. When you open Pandora's box, you can't guarantee it won't consume its master. Friend or foe, it knows no mercy.

"I thought those Fairies were the worst evil this world created by luring the weakest among us," continues the young Archean, still not getting any reaction from Neal. He takes an almost theatrical pause. "I was wrong."

He meets Neal's gaze, weariness in his eyes.

"There's something much worse and much more real. You and your gang of criminals."

Neal swallows a bitter retort, fists clenched. The young Archean retreats and shoves past the onlookers gathered around him.

Comparing the Brotherhood to a disease! Neal closes his eyes momentarily to calm himself down. Why can't he shake off the impression that Skyler was speaking directly to him through that boy?

Neal stares at Fiona. "How did this mess happen?"

"They were blocking our way to the dining hall," Fiona counters while gathering her thick hair in a braid that falls on one side. "There's no way in hell we're gonna skip lunch for a bunch of morons."

Derek and Nora scatter the crowd with those who decided to switch over to their side. Neal takes Fiona aside and whispers, "What exactly did you do?"

"I forced my way in! I couldn't stand idly by." By the looks of it, he's not the only one who needs to learn a thing or two about controlling his emotions.

"Next time, let me handle it my way before it gets out of hand." She clicks her tongue, clearly displeased.

Neal turns his attention back to the crowd of worshippers who have remained in the dining hall.

"These are tough times, but freedom comes at a cost." A hush settles, and Neal continues, energized by the show of respect. "But we can share this cost. Together."

He meets their eyes which gleam with fear. They try to conceal it behind a veil of confidence, but the fear is still there, waiting to pounce on them. Its potency is such that it can wipe out an entire civilization. Neal's job is to defuse it while there's still time. Without these people, a change of leadership cannot happen.

"This burden is too heavy for one person to bear.

Commander Hawk learned this the hard way by paying with his life. He kept us in the dark although we could've found a solution together."

Neal pauses to let his words sink in. They're afraid, but at least they're listening.

"Either we die knowing that the Promised Land exists, too afraid to peek out of our jail, or we do our best to find it. I choose the latter without hesitation. When doubt creeps in, when you're holed up in this doomed ship, remember the life that awaits you, and hope for a miracle. The miracle is here, and it is the Promised Land."

He takes a deep breath, the colossal task of the next few weeks weighing on his shoulders and pushing against his chest until it hurts.

"The Commander was afraid. But now that the Ark is ours, we can decide for ourselves."

"You're not the first to inveigle us. My father told me about the Embarkation and the real story, the one they don't tell us. The Farrells's."

Most people don't know what it refers to, but he does. By combing through the Archives with Walker's uncanny hacking skills, Neal has absorbed more knowledge than anyone living on the Ark. He knows the truth, and he won't repeat their past mistakes.

"I won't make you believe in the Creator's redemption unless you decide to. What I can promise you is that I will do everything I can during the remaining thirty-three days to get us to the Promised Land. But I will need your help."

The girl doesn't say anything, but she nods in approval. Neal turns his attention back to everyone else who still needs to be convinced, or at least reassured.

"You can help now by showing solidarity and collecting anything that might be useful for the month we will spend in the Refuge."

Keep them busy. The best way to divert their attention and preserve a semblance of order. This will do for now.

People are slowly nodding around him. Good. He gives his instructions to Derek and Nora, who take over, divvying up the crowd into separate groups assigned with specific resources to look for food, water, sleeping bags and whatnot.

Dan ruffles his hair with a smile. "For a moment I thought it was too late, but—"

"Yeah, right. I got it." Neal shoves him away affectionately and heads back to the Pod, Dan following behind.

The Mavericks are his family. They've always supported each other, just like what the Archeans need to do to get through what lies ahead. Hopefully, they'll understand before things go south.

The change of commander should delight the Archeans who can finally learn the truth. Neal staked everything on the Promised Land now that they're free. He thought he could reassure them. He thought he had succeeded in giving them a goal, an unshakable hope.

Never has he been so wrong. He took in the Mavericks' ideals when leading the Brotherhood, but he forgot to hear out what the Archeans had to say. If he fails to reconcile the two, he will pay dearly.

"Dan, I need you and Walker to take care of the Paragon tomorrow," Neal says once they're back in the former commander's cabin. "Update their wristbands so we can track and disable them if they fail us. Walker said it's possible, even for that many people."

"Didn't you say you didn't want to use any drastic measures?"

"They'll just have to thank the young bastard who rubbed me the wrong way."

NIGHT HAS FALLEN. At least, the ship's smart light display does an excellent job at keeping up the illusion. Neal woke up with a start in the middle of a nightmare. Another. Unable to fall back asleep, he exits the Pod. The Ark is eerily quiet. Just a few hours earlier, his failings blew up in his face. Nora calls him out, coming over to escort him as a precaution.

"I won't be long," he replies. "Go get some rest." She protests, but Neal finally gets the better of her.

He rubs his eyes, his head buzzing with thoughts as he walks in the bluish darkness of the corridor. Someone jerks his arm, forcing him to turn around.

"Leander," says the young bastard who challenged him in the dining hall, threateningly. "It's my name."

His eyes shine with palpable animosity. How long has this Leander been stalking him? Is it an ambush? A look around tells him it isn't. That bastard came alone. He's got guts.

"You'd better remember it," adds Leander. "Because if you don't keep your promise, *I* will take you out before you kill us all."

Neal clenches his jaw and breaks free with a tug. He stays still long after Leander's gone.

The future scares him. Without the Promised Land, they will die. Slowly.

3

NEAL

A suffocating heat radiates around him. He covers his face, blinded by the leaping flames. The blackening ivory walls are warping under the heat in a dance of pain. He retreats into a corner of the wall, crouching as the hungry fire melts onto him, his body shaking. A screech escapes him as the ruddy blaze chars his naked flesh.

Neal awakes with a start, panting. The sheets stick to his skin, and he dabs his dripping forehead, still in shock. His fingers instinctively run over his tattoos burning with life. He stares into space, unable to move. The images are so clear they hurt, as if his gut had been ripped apart.

He sniffs as he gets up to shake off the lethargy. His diary. He must hurry. The details of his nightmare dim as he grabs a pen lying on the desk and begins to scribble furiously.

The flames were hotter this time. I think I even saw a faint glow over the fire and heard a voice, but nothing that made sense. Or maybe it did? Fear. Dull, visceral fear. I screamed again and again. Was there someone else in there?

The jerky sway of his pen tracing the curves of each letter is a sensation beyond words. Powerful, relaxing, linear, and orderly. His mind is busy and his muscles tense along his quickening heartbeats until his fear finally subsides to reveal some deep, contemplative understanding. His thoughts spill onto the paper like a stream of light piercing through the fog, sealing the cracks of his feverish mind.

It was that same nightmare, but I know it's only a question of time before it drives me crazy. It was so real. Walker's repeated simulations must have something to do with it. They straight up messed up with my brain.

His pen leaves a shapeless blotch on the period. His memory fogs up, as it does every time that he's about to uncover the nature of his dreams. Despite his best efforts, his night terror is no more than a mere impression. He leans back against the wall, feeling the sheer exhaustion of those sleepless nights crushing him. Why can't he sleep through the night like a normal person?

He laughs bitterly at the thought. Could a normal person take over the Ark with a bunch of forsaken Mavericks?

Neal snaps his diary shut, his sweaty hands slipping under the tooled leather of the binding. His fingertips brush over the same wave-shaped reliefs of his tattoo.

The Commander's cabin is not what he expected. Nothing could ever replace his good old cabin, but especially the Brotherhood's hideout where their wildest dreams materialized. They have no happy memories here, but anger and fear only. He used to covet this cabin with all his might. So why does he want to run away every time he wakes up?

He wipes his cheek and locks his diary away in a small cabinet under the former commanders' portraits glaring at him accusingly. Come to think of it, revamping this place wouldn't be such a bad idea. He takes down the paintings one by one and throws them into a jumbled pile. Even the sound of canvas being punctured can't stop him.

It's stuffy in here. Neal turns the air conditioning down and gets back to work. His muscles warm up quickly as he pushes the sofa with a grunt. Dan would laugh his head off if he saw him milling around like this.

THE COMMAND CENTER is bustling with activity for the first time since they stormed it. A handful of Mavericks trained by Walker stands at the control screens, trying to reroute the ship's power before transferring to the Refuge. The air is so thick with moisture that they've covered and sealed the windows to prevent unnecessary heat loss.

With Derek and Nora's help, Walker binds the Paragon defectors' wristbands one by one. There are about twenty of them, more than Neal expected. At least, their crew is growing despite the shadow of a revolt chasing them. Neal should be relieved, but his muscles refuse to relax.

The formal screening Walker have them go through looks like joining a cult: voice recording, fingerprinting, wristband resetting, and, to top it off, the official Mavericks' uniform with a distinctive insignia. No one seems to care about the formalities. Either they really believe in the Brotherhood, or they want nothing to do with Duke. With the carnage at the Atrium under his command, which wouldn't be surprising. No one could possibly vindicate this act of madness.

"Please welcome Master Neal, your new Commander," Dan croons while trying to keep a straight face as they enter the Command Center. "All the secrets of the world will be revealed to you, only if you believe in his power. If you are worthy of his might, a place of honor will await you on the Promised Land where a lush estate for you and your children will be provided."

"Stop messing around," Neal snorts, elbowing him in the ribs.

Dan ruffles Neal's neatly combed-over hair that was supposed to help him make a good impression. His heart sinks when he hears people chuckling around. There you go! Now they'll think the Brotherhood is just a bunch of overgrown kids.

"What will the Paragon think of me?"

Neal shoves Dan, who hardly flinches, and grumbles as he runs his fingers through his tousled hair to fix the mess. A crowd has gathered around some newcomers glancing away at the surveillance cameras. They exchange nervous smiles as Neal joins them.

"Defectors. Not exactly the Paragon," rectifies Dan in a whisper, back turned so the others can't read his lips. "The hangdog look on your face won't help you get their good graces."

Neal forces a smile, and he feels utterly stupid. "You bet! You know that your full beard gives them chills, right? If I remember correctly, Skyler's friend called you … what was it again? The big bully!"

Neal laughs at Dan's murderous look.

"What? If I'm going to look more cheerful, it might as well be natural."

Dan is about to retaliate, but Walker comes to Neal's rescue. He owes Walker a treat.

"Twenty-two have shown up so far," Walker says, rubbing his eyes.

Derek and Nora take over to welcome the newcomers. Nora looks in her element, chatting away with each of them while they wait for their turn. Meanwhile, Derek is fumbling with the equipment, and Walker darts over to him before he breaks anything. Walker must be losing his mind by the way he shakes his head frantically.

"More will join us once they understand that the Brotherhood is giving them a fair chance at starting a new life," Dan says.

"I wonder what convinced those guys," Neal muses aloud, scratching his nape.

"Your little speech from yesterday worked its magic," says Walker, who came back in the meantime.

"See? Your hair has nothing to do with it," says Dan. Neal glares at him.

"Will that infuriate Duke Kay?" inquires Walker, arms crossed.

"He probably doesn't give a shit about double agents," says Neal, who remembers with disgust the recordings they found of him sentencing people in the Atrium. He even used to abuse his recruits during the Paragon training simulations. "He'd rather see them go or die."

"That's one way of looking at it," Walker agrees, deep in thought. "Who's to say he's not just vying for absolute control? He's the contender for Commander, after all."

That's true. He *is* the legitimate successor, but that doesn't mean he has to be.

"What harm can he do in his cell, honestly?" says Neal with a shrug.

"His most trusted agents visit him occasionally," Dan grumbles. "They might coordinate an attack."

"Why are visits even allowed? Isn't there someone to check their communications?"

"We can't break the Archeans' trust."

"Shouldn't there be an exception for a criminal who killed innocent people?"

His question is left hanging when a defector dressed in his new uniform joins them. Fiona and he could be cousins with his swarthy complexion and black hair. He greets them the Paragon's way, then awkwardly pulls himself together.

"Agent Miles was the first in the Paragon to comply with our demands," cuts in Walker. "Thanks to him, the others followed along."

"Thank you for your trust," Neal greets him, offering a handshake and squeezing his shoulder. "I hope your family won't give you trouble because of your decision."

Miles gives a nervous chuckle and absentmindedly smooths his wrinkle-free uniform.

"They didn't agree when I decided to join the Paragon. My family always said they caused problems on the Ark rather than fix them. Turns out they weren't wrong—Duke killed my parents."

"I'm sorry," Neal apologizes, clenching his fist.

"I was Tessa's partner," Miles says, not seeming to mind. "I could've helped her better if I'd known she was part of the Brotherhood."

"I have only good things to say about Agent Miles."

That voice! Neal's senses go into overdrive. When his eyes meet hers, Tessa gives him a wink. Her dark braids look wet, and her amber skin is reddish, as if coming out of a hot shower. Her wide, bright eyes search his to tell him something he can't quite understand. The soft, warm feeling stirring inside him is too overwhelming. She finally came back.

"Glad to see you're okay, Miles," says Tessa, who meets their little group.

They exchange a complicated handshake by striking their open palms and backhand, then fist bumping, up and down. The next moment their back is turned, while they repeat the movements backwards, then face each other for the finale. Tessa's pealing laughter fills the room as Neal, Dan, and Walker watch, stunned.

"I needed this," Tessa says once she catches her breath, her arm over her stomach.

"No doubt we *are* a bunch of kids," says Neal, a hand resting on his forehead, disheartened.

"Catching criminals, tracking down Mavericks and routinely scanning wristbands are not the only things the Paragon does,"

Miles adds. "Alcohol flows every night. Do you remember Tessa, that time when...?"

Neal switches off from their drunken debauchery and pulls Walker aside. Thinking about the happy times that he spent with Dan and the others before moving forward with their plan is painful.

"Good job," Neal says. "There's one more thing I'd like you to take care of—the surveillance cameras."

Walker rubs his eyes again before answering, wearily. "Right, I wanted to talk to you about it. They take up a lot of energy that could be used to—"

"We don't need to turn them off. Quite the opposite. We must secure them. People are watching."

"Oh." Walker snaps to attention as he peers into the electronic eyes. They might have been useful to take over the Ark, but they could also lead to their fall.

"Be more subtle about it," Neal whispers, keeping his attention on Walker's wan face. Things will have to end quickly before he burns out.

"I'm sorry. I should've thought of that. The entire system crashed because of the Sacred Fire, and I—"

"It's okay, you don't have to explain. The surveillance system can be accessed from the Paragon HQ, right?"

"Shit."

That's bad. Really bad. Any hotheaded moron like that Leander could know their every move. What if Duke's visitors have been coordinating an uprising with his loyal supporters?

"The Paragon server runs independently," Walker groans. "I should've thought of that before."

"Walker. We need to take over their headquarters and disable their access to the main system. Have Fiona and Milo organize a group with the defectors. There's something else I need to take care of."

He glances at Tessa talking with Dan and that defector

Miles. She hasn't taken her eyes off him, he's certain of it. What was she trying to tell him earlier?

"Are you sure you want to put Fiona and Milo together? They're kind of … on bad terms right now."

"If they've got something to deal with, let it be quick," Neal says angrily. "Their bickering is the last thing we need."

"I'll pass on the message."

Neal smiles thankfully before heading over to Tessa, who wraps up the conversation to follow him. Good.

Outside the command center, a breath of fresher air filled with the homey smell of simmering vegetables greets them. Aunt Sheyla must be concocting her stew recipe for tonight's dinner. Now that the Paragon defectors have joined in, it's a special occasion worth celebrating. But first…

Neal pulls Tessa into an empty hallway. Her fit and slender body matches his perfectly, sending a shiver down his spine. He runs his fingers through her braids and draws her mouth against his, hungry for her warmth. He steals two kisses at the corner of her lips, but then she backs away, and the magnetic pull between them fades. Neal pouts, slightly annoyed.

"What's wrong?"

"I must show you something." Her back is turned, as if wanting to hide her feelings from him.

"Can't it wait? We haven't seen each other in a while." His attempt at flirting leaves Tessa indifferent. "Come on," he insists.

Despite Neal's longing, he has no choice but to give up. Perhaps his nightmares will leave him alone tonight.

THE COMMAND CENTER's clinic is better fitted than he thought. Whenever there were casualties among the Mavericks, they had to improvise. Luckily, their contact among the divers would steal medical supplies during her shifts to help them, or else they wouldn't even have had anything to clean their wounds. Having Skyler with the Mavericks would've changed everything. They could've lived long enough to see their children grow.

As expected, the lights in the clinic are dimmed, and the lingering stench of chemicals smothers Tessa's fruity smell. Neal has the horrible feeling that something nasty is lurking around. Could there be a vengeful spirit stalking them? The crew members were killed a few days ago already, including the Commander and his girlfriend. Isn't this where Laurene killed her too? What if it had something to do with it?

What is he talking about? It's ridiculous. Those nightmares *really* have messed up his head.

"Why can't you just tell me if you found the Promised Land?" he asks. Tessa has been refusing to speak the whole way. Why is she sulking when they haven't seen each other in days?

"That signal must have come from somewhere," Neal insists.

"She's asleep," Skyler shushes them.

They walk to a remote corner of the clinic for more privacy so the other patients—probably victims of the run-in in the dining hall—don't peek in. A cloth curtain is drawn around the bed, where Skyler sits. His brother moistens the awfully chapped lips of a chalky-skinned girl lying asleep. Her necklaces made of white stones oddly look like what the Mavericks bring in during their free parties, a time to socialize and mingle with some bold Archeans who flout authority. The only time when they're all equal.

"Severe dehydration," says Skyler, working methodically. "Lucky we found her."

Skyler glowers at Tessa, looking upset. Did they interrupt anything or what?

"Actually, she found me first," says Tessa standing at the foot of the bed, a hand leaned against the drawn-up sheet.

The supernatural feeling is stronger here. Neal rubs his neck, uncomfortable. Something doesn't feel right about this girl. Even her breathing seems irregular.

"Something I should know?" asks Neal, not hiding his annoyance.

"We're not alone. We've never been," says Skyler, who gives him a hard look.

"So, the Promised Land...?" Neal presses, his heart squeezing.

"Doesn't exist," Skyler completes between gritted teeth. "Forget it."

Neal opens his mouth and closes it again, dumbfounded. "Meaning?"

Skyler gets up on his feet to rid himself of the wet cotton ball he was holding tightly between his fingers. Tessa adds nothing more. Neal turns to her, raising his arms. "What happened in there?"

The strange girl mumbles something in her sleep. The marks on her skin—some kind of tattoos?—shift in the gloom, like the cogs of an invisible clock. Neal frowns and moves closer to get a better look. The symbols are brownish with a hint of reddish orange. He straightens up when he realizes that the drawings are merely swirls and some gibberish writing that melt into a mosaic. They're not shifting; it was a simple optical illusion. He feels his forehead to check whether he's coming down with some mysterious disease. No fever.

"Killer drones and a bloodbath," Tessa finally says with a sigh. "The people who lived there are all dead. These drones must have been responsible. Well, one thing is certain: That ship was not the Promised Land."

"You're kidding!" Neal swallows a curse.

"She's the key," says Skyler, who's returned without Neal realizing it.

"A survivor?" Skyler nods, the pieces of the puzzle falling into place one by one in Neal's mind.

"It was an Ark," Skyler continues in a strange voice. "Like ours."

"Of course, it was," confirms Neal, trying to remember his research, which dates to a few years ago, when he was drawing up the first plans of the Brotherhood.

Tessa gives him an interested look and Skyler watches him.

"It was only suspicions. Nothing concrete," Neal brushes away.

"Like the Promised Land," Skyler replies matter-of-factly.

"Sky, we don't know that yet," says Tessa.

"Precisely." The strange girl flinches at Skyler's accusing tone. Neal comes over to grab his shoulder, but his brother abruptly steps away instead.

"Why are you overreacting?" says Neal indignantly, watching him throwing open a drawer and pretend they don't exist. "Just because—"

"She needs to rest," says Skyler, clinking bottles as he snaps the drawer shut. "I'll take it from here."

As Skyler turns away, Tessa beckons Neal to follow her. Despite his protests, she takes his hand and leads him outside of the clinic, while the ghosts of his mind stay behind to watch them leave, satisfied. On the doorstep, Neal is about to head back to reason Skyler, but Tessa's disapproving glance stops him. Dan would be proud of him for once.

They stroll silently through the empty command center. It's time for dinner, and Neal wouldn't say no to a serving or two of stew. Too bad he left his appetite in the clinic with his sulking brother.

Skyler has been acting weird lately, being on edge and all. Couldn't he be happy to have his brother back? Skyler should be supportive, not trying to undermine his plans. Either his brother is up to something, or his memory can't be trusted. It's a serious problem either way.

"What's up with everyone for God's sake?" says Neal once they are far enough from the clinic.

His voice shatters the stark calm that had settled in the timeless hallway. Neal can feel a vise squeezing his head; he feels hot. So much for not losing his temper. Tessa slows down as he catches up.

"Time," she says. "That's what people need right now."

Then she dumps him in the middle of the dark corridor and slams her cabin's door shut.

4

SKYLER

A NUTTY AROMA OF ROASTED COFFEE TICKLES HIS NOSE. SKYLER grunts, tries to ignore it, but then the squeaking carts roll in along with the morning whispers. With his throbbing headache, there's no way he can go back to sleep. He rubs his still numb face with a groan. His reflection in the small mirror stuck on a cabinet above the sink shows him a vision of horror: The folds of his sleeve have sunk deep into his flesh which looks badly bruised. He gets up, his body aching from sleeping sideways in a chair.

Pills. His head is about to split in half.

He shuffles to the cabinet to grab two white pills, then downs a glass of earthy-tasting water. The carts are filled with baskets of small muffins and other petit fours being served to the Maverick patients staying in the clinic. Their faces light up despite their wounds and speak volumes about how tasting this kind of food for the first time must feel.

Skyler gulps down his second glass of water and sets it down on the serving counter. He dozed off while keeping watch over the strange girl all night. He was so exhausted he couldn't muster the strength to return to his quarters in the Pod, his new home since his old cabin was severely damaged by the explosion.

Even though the girl's hydration level has stabilized, she hasn't woken up yet. Perhaps he should consider running more tests.

A maid offers him breakfast, and he nibbles on a muffin, his stomach still churning from his bad night's sleep. But as the carts roll out of the clinic, he rushes over to grab a piece of marbled cake, then stuffs it into a napkin for later.

His patient is whining in her sleep and mumbling incoherently. Her condition is stable, but it doesn't mean he can leave her unattended. He learned that the hard way not so long ago.

Near the entrance, Skyler asks a Maverick to keep a close eye on the girl. Thankfully, he accepts without asking any questions about her.

Skyler's body aches with nausea as he walks down the hallway. He crosses the main corridor leading to the service stairwell; the elevators were cut off to save what little energy they have left. He enters the empty reception area of Med Bay which feels oddly foreign to him. His old life was put on hold when he decided to take part in this senseless mission.

The throbbing headache finally lifts as he walks past patients' rooms abuzz with the ECG's intermittent beeping, a nagging reminder that life hangs on a fist-sized organ pumping blood to the brain.

Several rooms are already vacant, which means they have started to move some patients over to the Refuge where medical equipment is limited. Moving vulnerable patients who need constant monitoring requires a lot more preparation.

Med Bay feels empty without the usual chatter. Since Skyler has been running the Command Center's clinic, staffing is greatly reduced. Dr. Nazar and the others must be overwhelmed. Skyler trained some Mavericks to ease the patients' transfer to the Refuge before going out on a mission with Tessa.

But soon enough, Neal will have to acknowledge Skyler's failings, starting with Yasmina's death when she was under his watch.

Skyler knocks gently on the half-open door, his heart pounding. Will Murielle recognize him this time?

His mother looks healthier wearing lip gloss and makeup on her face. She combed her hair today, something she would never do when she was deep in depression. She is eating in bed with Dinah Farrell keeping her company. He decides to watch them silently from the doorway.

Dinah is dressed in her flared-sleeved priestess's robe. She holds up a censer burning off sage, a smell which sends Skyler into a deep nostalgia. His eyes sting.

"Before the Creator and our Elders, I cleanse this sacred chamber from the dark energy that lingers. This pure soul demands to be heard and receive His wisdom."

The priestess gestures to follow her movements. Facing each other, they clasp hands, their fingertips pressed against their chins. In their silent prayer, Dinah gazes at his mother's eyes jerking beneath her eyelids.

After a moment, his mother opens her eyes, smiling.

"Your connection with Him is even stronger than your grandmother's."

"Thank you, it's very..." the priestess replies with her voice breaking as she stares down to her feet. "Thank you very much."

Dinah lifts her head with sparkling eyes. As she stands up, her royal purple dress cascades gracefully in slow motion.

"Elaine would be so proud of you," says Murielle on her feet with a polite bow.

Eyes shut, Dinah dips her finger in a small metal container strapped to her garment and traces the sign of a cross on Murielle's forehead, her lips moving indistinctly.

"May the Creator guide you to your next destination," Dinah says with a soft yet powerful voice once the ritual is complete.

Dinah's surprised gaze falls on Skyler who steps in.

"Skyler," she says, smiling.

"Do you know each other?" asks his mother. A strange glint flashes through her eyes, and she adds quickly, "I won't be long. Well, not too long." Then, she hurries out to the floor's common restroom.

The energy that drives her is astounding. Since Neal's return, she's a completely different person.

"It was good," Skyler stammers, his cheeks on fire. "You know, the blessing. Sorry, I didn't mean to interrupt."

"I know. That's nice of you to say."

Skyler's gaze falls on a curious object hanging on the wall above the headboard. Cool colored beads and feathers adorn the faux leather straps ends hanging limply. The white strings in the hoop's middle are made of the same coffee-colored faux leather and woven into a beautiful canvas. The pattern is vaguely familiar. Does Dinah craft relics from the old Earth in her spare time?

"My brother Philip chose the materials," says Dinah, who noticed his interest. "His obsession with painting always leads him to unusual places for inspiration. I couldn't resist. This dream catcher is very powerful, perfect for your mother. That is if you believe in His power."

His mother must have told her he stopped praying long ago, so he changes the subject.

"Do you often come to Med Bay? I don't remember seeing you here."

They met just a few days ago, yet they had never crossed paths before. Something he has learned over the years is that living on the same Ark does not guarantee chance encounters. The possibility of a Creator and his grand design makes sense, but perhaps some things are best kept secret. Ignorance has its advantages.

"You should visit her too, you know."

Dinah realizes what she said a second too late and fidgets nervously. She is careful to avoid his gaze, while her too-large dress seems to swallow her whole.

"Is she…" starts Skyler scratching his neck. The words dry up in his mouth, and his breath becomes shallow.

Why is it so hot in here? The ventilation must be failing with the Sacred Fire being out.

"Not yet, but that doesn't mean she can't hear you," Dinah replies with renewed energy. "The Creator will know."

"I don't think it's a good idea. Not right now. It's too…" Too early? Too late? Dinah senses his hesitation and bends over to pick up her wicker basket she left on the ground.

"Sis, are you coming?"

Standing in the doorway, Philip Farrell looks more disheveled than ever. His clothes are streaked with dried paint and his hands smeared with a riot of colors. He looks much better than the last time they met when Mrs. Farrell suddenly passed away. Philip sought Skyler out to crystallize her memories in a memory sphere.

Skyler greets him with a smile.

"I've got to go," Dinah apologizes, and pulls her hand away from her basket. "Take some time to think about it."

She bows to him and scurries over her brother's side in a rustle of fabric. Philip is already walking down the hallway.

"Thank you," Skyler says to her on the doorway. "For my mother."

"Despite the darkness, the Creator knows where to find His children."

Her words hang in the air and expand like they have a life of their own. Skyler ponders over what Dinah meant until Murielle emerges from the bathroom with a quizzical look on her face.

"Is she already gone?" she asks, disappointed.

Skyler quickly nods and offers her the chocolate bread he wrapped in the soaked-through napkin.

"I thought you might like some," he says shyly. "You haven't had these in a long time."

She snatches the napkin and unwraps it unceremoniously. Her movements are a bit jerky like tiny electric shocks tickling her nerves, which might be a side effect of her medication. She sits on the edge of her bed and crumbles the bread with her fingers.

"Where's your brother?" she asks awkwardly between two bites that smear chocolate on her chin. It reminds him of when he was only nine and she scolded him for his bad table manners. He used to eat with his fingers which horrified her. How things have changed.

"He's busy," Skyler replies, hands behind his back, embarrassed.

Their family reunion was brief and awkward. Skyler had insisted that the three of them get together, though he had to coax his brother. Neal argued that the safety of the Ark depends on him, and that their family obligations can wait. Perhaps he was still struggling to come to terms with their father's death during the Ark's takeover? It's hard to say. Over the years, Neal has learned to hide his feelings from Skyler who used to read them easily.

Since their mother saw Neal, her depression has improved greatly. She emerged from an endless nightmare, barely aware of the lost years. Given her vulnerable condition, Dr. Zanya oversees her recovery, which means keeping her hormone levels in check, especially her serotonin. Skyler doesn't want to get involved for fear his emotions would make him do something reckless.

"When will I get to see him again?" she asks, distressed. "What can possibly keep him away from his own mother?"

"He has new responsibilities, Mom. You know he must organize the transfer to the Refuge."

Skyler should be happy his mother is finally showing encouraging signs of recovery, but she's not like she used to be. Only his brother's name hangs on her lips. But if that makes her happy, it's all that matters.

"I feel like I woke up in a bad dream," she says thoughtfully after taking a sip of water. "Both my son and my husband avoid me." Skyler swallows hard.

"They'll come. Give them a little more time."

She doesn't know about Dylan. Until her condition stabilizes, she could relapse and Skyler refuses to take any chance. He's sacrificed too much to get her back and have some semblance of normalcy.

"I always knew your brother was alive," she says with a strange, icy smile on her chocolate-smeared lips. "I can't believe you didn't tell me sooner."

The guilt he used to feel has subsided, but every time his mother talks to him accusingly, a sting prickles his insides, and the pain returns in a flash.

"He had gone dark," Skyler says, his voice breaking. He takes a seat beside her, and the bed buckles under their weight. "What else could I believe?"

Murielle gets up, and the crumbs that have left ugly greasy stains on her blue nightgown spill onto the floor. Her mouth twitches, the pasty skin of her face looking too old for her age.

"You should have trusted him," she says lowly. "His potential is unparalleled. He could become the next Commander, I'm sure. Such a waste that you didn't follow his example."

Skyler suppresses a sigh. Is this really what matters most to his mother? Even years of living miserably have not worn off her obsession.

Her inquisitive gaze pierces him, and the lie leaves him with the familiar taste of bitterness.

"I'll come visit you before the transfer," he states matter-of-factly, eager to leave.

Lips pursed, she says, "Bring your brother next time."

Skyler looks away, and steps out of the room, shutting the door behind him. He coughs until the sage filling his lungs is out. Grateful for the quiet the darkness provides, he slows his pace. When he was arguing with Allen, he would find refuge in the dark to clear his mind from the buildup of emotions threatening to burst.

The assault of images playing on a loop in his head is dizzying, but his first meeting with Dinah Farrell in that same hallway is clearer than the rest. She came to him as he couldn't forgive himself for what happened to Emily. Dinah also left him part of her grandmother's inheritance: Amaranth Bellerose's lost journal.

He finds solace in wondering about what he might discover inside. That is if he can retrieve it first. He was so confused when Dinah offered the journal to him that he can't remember where he left it. In his new cabin in the Pod, maybe? Reading will do him good, just like back in the days when he perused the old Earth's archives. That will make for some welcome distraction during the next few weeks in the Refuge.

"There you are!" says Dr. Nazar, striding across the reception as Skyler was making for the exit. Every time they meet, Skyler must look up to avoid getting distracted by the tuft of hair peeking out from the collar of his unbuttoned Omega uniform. His thick unibrow makes him look like he's constantly deep in thought, pondering over how to eradicate the next disease.

"Patient Valdez needs a dose of morphine now. His injuries are severe, and he needs to hang on until his next surgery." The doctor hands him a tablet glowing in the dark with the patient's profile on the display. "Just follow the list."

Skyler quickly scans the chart, and hesitation creeps in. His commitment to Med Bay takes precedence over the rest. His brother's return has put Skyler's obligations on the back burner. Although Neal is technically in charge of the Ark now, Skyler still feels bad throwing away everything he's ever known. Who he is.

Dr. Nazar notices his indecision and cocks half his unibrow.

"All right," Skyler finally says.

With a nod, his mentor returns to his urgent business, and Skyler hurries back down the hallway he just arrived. The journal will have to wait.

5

SKYLER

Skyler is lying in bed, something he hasn't done in a very long time. The ceiling of his new cabin is a dull gray, but his imagination is vivid enough to bring it to life with the many faces of today's patients. The next few weeks of isolation portend a difficult future. Their Ark will take years to recover, if ever.

His bedsheets smell of dust, dirt, and fear. They could use a wash, but time is slipping through his fingers. He rolls over to the side and looks at the flowers he stole from the park. Most are wilted but for three chrysanthemums, the same they offer to patients in recovery at Med Bay. On difficult days, the sick need something to keep their dark thoughts at bay. What better thing to do than to look after these flowers and see with their own eyes that they too can regrow and heal?

Skyler gently prunes the mums with small scissors, and their herby aroma fills the room. It will be a good addition to the bleak Command Center's clinic, which is a far cry from Med Bay's warm atmosphere.

The other flowers have retreated, robbed of their beauty.

Without the Sacred Fire's energy, they won't ever grow again. It is dreadful to think that life can be so fragile.

Skyler lets himself drift into a restful sleep filled with dreams of lush gardens and earthy scents. Upon waking up, he fumbles by his bedside table for a glass of water, but grabs something leathery instead.

It's Amaranth's journal.

"WHO ARE THEY?"

Skyler is suspicious of the Paragon agents who have stormed the Command Center's clinic. After the massacre in the Atrium, it's hard to trust them.

"They're on our side," says Dan. Skyler assumes he must be his brother's right hand. He stands out with his full beard he strokes now and then. Strangely, whenever he is around, a waft of something burning streams along. Does this have anything to do with his fire dancing he performed at the free party, or is it just his body odor?

"Since when?" wonders Skyler, who inhales the mums he brought to cover the strong smell.

"Your brother can be convincing." The Paragon is busy restocking the clinic and cleaning up, something Skyler never thought possible. He wouldn't want to disturb them in their work.

"In that case, I'd better get going," Skyler apologizes, and Dan grunts his assent.

Skyler hastens over to the Maverick watching over his patient still sleeping soundly, and thanks him for the help. The Maverick's gaze falls on the mums, his face filled with wonder, and Skyler promptly offers one to him.

"My sister will be thrilled," says the Maverick, scrutinizing every detail. "Skyler, right? Let me know if you ever need anything."

"I'll remember that."

As soon as he is alone, Skyler pours tap water into an unused jar and dips the two remaining mums into it. He sets the jar on the counter beside his patient whose vitals are stable. As he changes her fluids, he makes sure that her blood sugar and hydration levels are good.

Skyler sighs. Everything looks fine. What could be keeping her in limbo then?

He sits in the uncomfortable chair on which he fell asleep the night before and pulls the leather journal from the inside pocket of his uniform. The cover is warm under his fingers; he instinctively strokes it from one end to the other and feels the uneven ridges of the yellowed paper. He considers himself lucky that Mrs. Farrell thought of him, even after her passing. She would always make jokes about his uncanny interest in the elderly and their past, but she was also grateful to have him as her caretaker.

He flips through the paper quickly, barely containing his excitement. The spidery handwriting is almost illegible, and Skyler must squint to decipher the cursive, upset at the Academy for not teaching them handwriting analysis. What little Skyler knows is thanks to his curiosity, which led him to pore through rare texts confined to the Archives when he worked on the Memory Spheres project.

After several unsuccessful attempts at reading, he finally manages to make out a few words here and there. The first one he recognizes is *Paragon*. Some things don't change, it seems.

"You should try it. It's Aunt Sheyla's specialty." Dan is towering over him, holding out a dish that looks tiny in his large hands. He almost looks gentle behind his tawny beard.

"Is it for me?" asks Skyler, unsure.

"Neal's brother has to eat too," he replies in a low voice.

"Did he send you?"

"I know how to make myself useful." Dan gives him a mischievous look, then sets the container down on the nearby counter before walking away.

Skyler grabs the fork jammed in creamed potatoes and pokes at the greasy sautéed vegetables in the sauce. The taste is better than what he could find in the dining hall. Between two bites, he skims the journal he pulls open with his free hand. The fine ribs of the paper rubbing under his fingers contrast with the usual smooth surface of the tablets they normally use. He can feel himself connecting with Amaranth Bellerose through the inky pages where her innermost thoughts are recorded.

His gaze jumps from one word to the next, but the flourishes of the cursive make it difficult to read. He stops at what looks like a series of strange names: Bavera, Jeyrial, and Sedna. The journal is quite thick and Skyler wonders if he should just read it from cover to cover. He could use the same technique he used during his foray into the Archives: Create a reference table containing each letter of the alphabet according to Amaranth Bellerose's penmanship, then perhaps transcribe it. Given his lack of expertise, this will be unconscionably time-consuming.

Skyler sets the journal aside, appalled at the daunting task it represents.

The strange girl stirs in her bedsheets, and a second later, her eyes flutter. She sits up abruptly, disoriented, with panic filling her eyes like poison. Skyler quickly reaches around the bed and stops her before she rips out the wires connected to the heart monitor and her IV.

"You could hurt yourself," Skyler says quietly as he gently puts back the displaced catheter. "You were dehydrated."

The coming and going of the Paragon draws her attention. When her eyes land on their weapons, she starts to pant and writhe in panic. Skyler is caught off guard and awkwardly pulls the curtain shut in a whoosh. She freezes at the metallic sound, taut as strings.

"No one wants to hurt you here," he speaks while pouring her a glass of water. "I'm Skyler, a doctor. We'll get you back on your feet. But first, you need to drink."

He offers her the glass, and her distrust seems to subside a little. With shaking hands, she grabs the glass to her lips. Her skin is bruising in shades of purple where the catheter was inserted.

"Can I see your hand? I need to clean your wound before it gets infected." He holds up some gauze and sprays it with alcohol, then waits patiently for her reaction.

She examines her hands before letting him carefully dab at the angry wound.

"Not everyone is as lucky as you are. I thought we were going to lose you." Her breathing calms at the sound of his voice, so he continues. "People here will welcome you. You might even be able to help us understand what's going on outside."

She yanks her hands back and buries her face in a pillow. Skyler picks up the gauze that has fallen onto the sheet.

"Are you feeling any pain?" he asks worriedly.

No response.

"Do you want to leave?"

The young woman's stomach rumbles loudly, and Skyler relaxes as he begins to smile. He cleans the fork with soap and water and reaches for his half-full plate of food.

"I'm not that hungry anyway," he says, offering her the food tray. She lets go of the pillow and stares at the food with yearning.

"May I?" she asks in a hoarse voice. Skyler gives her a friendly smile and nods.

She first tastes with her lips, then takes another bite. "Do you like it?"

As if on cue, she gobbles the vegetable stew vigorously, every bite faster than the last. It seems like she can at least understand their language. For a moment, he had doubts.

Once she has scraped off all the sauce, he clears it away and rinses the dish in the sink. The young woman mumbles something—a prayer perhaps?—and feels her tattoos one at a time in what seems like a specific pattern. Skyler watches her from the corner of his eye, fascinated. When he used to practice with his family and the Believers at the Sanctuary, they had to perform some simple rituals for praying or cleansing, but nothing like this.

His patient springs up and scurries over behind him. She brings her face closer to the mums and takes the loop in the hollow of her hand. A petal comes off with an almost inaudible crack at the brush of her fingertips and Skyler winces.

"Careful. They're frail," he says breathlessly.

"I don't know." She purses her lips and frowns, lost in her thoughts. With the petal pinched between her fingers, she sits back on the edge of the bed, sorely perplexed. "I'm going to sleep. May I?" She asks with a flinch.

"Hold on."

He retrieves the journal he left on the nightstand. The old paper is soft and opens on the page he was reading. The strange names he deciphered earlier glow with mystery in the faint light coming from the cabinet's framing. A familiar word jumps out at him on the next page: Ark. His gaze wanders from the journal to his patient, who is reciting yet another strange litany. A name flashes through his mind, one he has already heard somewhere, he is sure of it.

"Sedna," he breathes. The stranger's whispering fades, and he repeats, searchingly, "Sedna?"

She stares at him intently, her finger hovering over a spiral tattoo in the hollow of her neck. Somehow, he feels like she is using a language he knows.

"Sedna's Ark," he continues. "Does it sound familiar?" She perks up, as if listening to someone else. Many victims of the Syndrome show similar symptoms when the elusive Fairies torment them.

"Uki." With a sigh of frustration, she adds a slur of incomprehensible words, speaking to herself for a few moments. Agonizing over how to make sense of her gibberish, Skyler is about to make her stop by talking over her when she cuts him right off.

"My name is Uki."

6

NEAL

In less than a day, they will seal the Refuge.

But this is the last of his worries right now. He wants to enjoy the last moments of their newfound freedom on the Ark without feeling the need to save everyone in selfless devotion.

He's not in his new office of the Command Center he once ardently coveted. Never did he hate a place as much. It will never replace the old Brotherhood base, where his shared madness became reality. The base is anything but special, but their memories permeate every bit. This is where the Brotherhood's ambitious ideals were born and where he spent most of his time planning his return to the upper levels.

"Those were the good old days," he mumbles to himself, etching every detail of this haven in his mind.

Despite ditching the base for the last few weeks, most of it remains unchanged. The untouched cushions are scattered and dusty; the sentences he scribbled away during his many sleepless nights are strung along the walls. There's nothing compromising, of course, but it gives him the strength to carry on with his ambitious plan. This labyrinth of words, of meanings and thoughts that led him to this day feels like home.

He sees himself giving the green light to their infiltration plan, surrounded by the members of the Brotherhood: Dan, Walker, Fiona, and Milo. They thought they knew what they were getting into. Soon enough, they found out how wrong they were.

Neal coughs on a chug of alcohol burning down his throat, and the glass bottle meets the metal of the musty floor in a hollow thud. Someone just came in, but he couldn't care less. He'd rather wallow in nostalgia until he drowns.

"I knew I'd find you here," says Tessa as she plumps herself down on a cushion which sends a cloud of swirling dust. "You shouldn't drink so much."

"It's a three-century-old whiskey. What a waste it'd be if no one were to drink it, don't you think?"

Neal straightens up, takes off his jacket, and tosses it a little further. The throbbing coldness of the lower levels slowly gives way to a gentle warmth that curls up his spine.

"Want some?"

He waves the bottle under her nose. Tessa gives a faint pout before grabbing it. She drinks a good mouthful and represses a wince, tears in her eyes.

"You could've told me before you needed to drink so bad," he says with a cocky smile.

"Just enjoying." She puts her braids back in place. "Wouldn't want to miss this once-in-a-lifetime chance."

"There she is!"

Neal stretches out to his full length and props himself on his elbow. With his free hand, he traces distractedly the outline of his tattoo etched on his forearm: an inky tree with its branches and roots entwined. The Promised Land. Will they find this tree of life they teach Maverick children about? It is said to be the Creator's source of life. Could it be real?

The image of the girl Tessa and Sky brought back flashes through his mind, and the pervading feeling that she comes from a mythical place won't leave him. Isn't anything outside of their Ark fancy, anyway? Hope lives on the mystery and the unknown, the very things people on this Ark can't live without. Could this girl be a sign sent by the Creator himself? The old lady Farrell would gladly tell them so from the comfort of her little makeshift chapel.

He frowns and asks, "You didn't really find this girl by chance, did you?"

"Does it matter?"

"No. Not tonight." Neal mindlessly drinks away his sinking feeling, hoping it will be enough to forget how stupid he was.

In the meantime, Tessa leaned closer to him. The bottle of whiskey wobbles dangerously on the ground before finally settling down.

"It's been too long," Neal says, tempted by Tessa's intoxicating warmth, "since we were alone together."

If he wanted to, he could gently slide his arm behind Tessa's back and feel her braids coiling around his fingers.

The whirring of the air vent dies down and every sound in the room is amplified: Tessa's slow breathing, the cushions shifting between them, his own heart racing away at the liquor coursing through his veins. It's only a question of time before the oxygen levels drop. He should be in his office making sure everything is going according to plan. Walker should be sending a group of new Paragon rebels to disable their system, and Dan coordinating the transfer … but something keeps him still.

"Whoever sent this message cannot be trusted," Tessa says flatly. "Better keep it to ourselves."

"As if this person existed! We can't know for sure. Like everything else for that matter."

He feels like he's been fooled all these years by his foolproof plan. The Promised Land is drifting away from them, and their future looks grim. He might as well steer an Ark for the rest of his life.

He desperately searches for the whiskey, leans over to grab it, but ends up kissing the bottleneck awkwardly.

Everyone relies on him. But what about him? Who can he count on?

"That's not true," Tessa says bluntly, which startles him. "We're not in the dark like we used to. We know for a fact that other arks exist."

"Any news from Sky by any chance?"

"That girl is still comatose if that's what you're asking."

The Creator's emissary is still unconscious? Neal sighs in resignation; he must have really screwed up for Him to send them this kind of sign.

"She should recover soon," Tessa adds more gently, pushing the bottle of whiskey away.

The faint luminosity sprinkles her face with gold specks, and he finds himself staring, speechless. She gives him a sidelong glance and bites her lips, as if to suppress a laugh. What would he do without her?

"Thank you," he finally says. "I mean it."

"Infiltrating the Paragon was interesting," Tessa replies with an amused smile. Neal can feel his face flush with heat. Eyes closed, he rests his head against the wall, feeling heady and dizzy.

"Not just for your mission. Without you, I would've never gotten Skyler back. My brother."

Saying these words is satisfying; his one true desire was finally granted.

"And obviously the success of our operation," he adds, mesmerized by the lights dancing in Tessa's irises.

"I wasn't alone. We wouldn't be talking about it if it wasn't for the crew's weakest link."

"Laurene? She wasted an entire crew. If that's your definition of weak—"

"Is that why you're keeping her jailed?"

Laurene was key to their plan's success, and she was right there when they needed her. But what she had to gain from their agreement still eludes him. What could she truly want?

His mind is spinning, and he shuts off his nagging thoughts. Not tonight, please.

"Can't we talk about something else?"

He searches Tessa's face which seems to come straight from the stars. What he would give to be able to let himself drown in it every single day. Feverish, he musters every ounce of will to control himself.

He reaches for the bottle, and Tessa's fingers brush against his. She's drinking, too.

"How are things going with your family?" she asks, passing over the bottle.

"With everything going on, I haven't really had time to see them. I'm hoping to catch up soon. How about yours?"

Tessa lowers her head and remains silent for a long moment. The fabric of her uniform bunches up in her fist.

"Sorry," he says, rubbing his eyes. "I forgot."

"It's fine."

Driven by his burning desire, Neal's lips meet Tessa's, his breath hot and shallow. He kisses her hungrily, the intoxicating contact of their skin like a whispered prayer. Why were they separated for so long? Cheeks flushed, Tessa lets him guide her.

Neal half-opens his eyes at the familiar tickle of tears rolling down his nose. Their lips part hesitantly, and he embraces her tenderly. He presses his hand gently down her hairline and rests his head against her shoulder as she sobs softly against him. Neal remains silent, his own pain heightened by her grief.

For a moment, he can almost smell the stench of burned flesh stinging his nostrils and hear the deafening roar of the flames eager to devour them. He should know by now that his nightmares will never leave him alone.

Neal repeatedly punches the air, grunting and sweating profusely, engrossed in the combat simulator.

Tessa was already gone when he woke up, a habit of hers when they spend the night together. She might be going through a tough time, but he would at least appreciate a little more attention from her.

Breathless, he takes off his goggles, puts them back on the base, then sheds his haptic suit. Coming up with a flawless plan to win against the Paragon would've been time-consuming or downright impossible without Walker's genius. They were able to borrow, *not* steal—Walker would insist that technology should be made available to all—the special program the Paragon uses to train its agents. Due to a lack of equipment, Walker was only able to develop a simulator that can host up to three players. Hacking the Paragon's quarterly simulation just came naturally after that. It was the best way to make an entrance and be taken seriously. The thing is, neither the Commander nor the Paragon wanted to negotiate, though they knew the Brotherhood had become a threat to their absolute control. Their thirst for power was too strong, it seems.

Neal catches his breath and runs a hand through his wet hair. He was never the best at these simulations, far from it. Their many nights of friendly competition weren't glorious either. How many times did Milo blow him out of the water? Walker had known better; he took his fight elsewhere, through unraveling the secrets of electronics and engineering.

Neal moves away from the console, still a little woozy from last night's drinking and the rush of adrenaline from the fighting. He heads to the nearby timeworn public showers unused since the last Archeans lived around these parts. The cool air sends a chill along his spine, and he slips into a shower stall in a remote corner with the icy jet hammering his back nicely.

It's unclear why the Commander deliberately abandoned this part of the ship. They say the Mavericks took over when it was flooded. Others argue that the Mavericks banded together to claim the lower levels during the Furies. But if this is the case, why didn't the Paragon simply get rid of them? Perhaps maintaining the status quo was good enough for them. The Mavericks had been disappearing one by one without a trace for quite some time already. Later, the Brotherhood discovered that the Paragon was testing new technologies. Their subjects of choice were, of course, what they considered to be the dregs of their microsociety.

If only he could get his hands on the data from these experiments. Time is running against him, and they will remain out of reach so long as Duke and his followers are alive. Neal has a hunch that the answer to the Promised Land may be lurking there. The only way to find out is to take complete control of the Paragon. His time in the Refuge will be ideal for planning, establishing his authority, securing the Ark, finding a new lead and, in the meantime, defeating death hanging over their heads herself. That should be a walk in the park, right?

He rinses off and shuts the water, satisfied with this plan. That'll have to do for now.

The darkness swallows everything and he must grope around for a towel. He knocks over a pile of towels that drops to the wet floor. He picks one up, but from the smell of it, it hasn't been washed. That's something he didn't miss from the lower levels.

Once dressed, he walks through the empty maze, his eyes perfectly adapted to the bluish emergency lights. The years spent here have accustomed him to the poor lighting. His muscles are still warm from his virtual training, and he stretches his arms as he walks to his cabin.

A strange rotting smell lingers in the passageway leading to the antechamber where corpses wait to be cremated in the

Incinerator, still warm from all the dead that were burned to ashes. He's never seen the place himself, but the countless crazy stories about it are enough to guess what lies inside. His heart rate quickens like every time—the few times—he's around. Things have changed, though. He no longer has to fear the Paragon lurking around these parts.

His unease fades once he is a little further down, where he comes across Sofia who decided to wear her long hair in a bun. The smell of death, however, is unmistakable.

"You came back too," she says, unsurprised at finding him here.

They exchange their usual greeting: two fingers on the forehead. Sofia has finally decided to wear her wristband. Considered as a sign of submission, she had sworn to never wear it. Now that the Brotherhood is in control, she has no more reason to resist.

"The prisoners didn't give you too much trouble, I hope?"

She scoffs. "Not as much as my rebellious daughter. How's Fiona doing?"

"The usual," Neal says casually. "I found her facing a mutiny among the Archeans. They didn't like her attitude."

She laughs.

"If her father were still here, perhaps she would learn to hold her tongue more often. It would save her a lot of trouble." Sofia pauses. "At least Milo is there to keep her in line."

Their many fights over the past few days have reached new heights. Milo, who usually keeps to himself and broods in his corner, has lost his temper more than once. He even stormed out in the middle of dinner when Fiona asked him what he was doing in his spare time. Their quarreling has been affecting their work according to Dan, which is something they can't afford.

"I wouldn't count on that too much," he says, pursing his lips. "It's not crazy love between those two right now."

"They'll get over it and love each other more passionately than ever. They always do."

Normally, Neal would ask Milo to put their romance aside, but since they're like brethren, he won't. They all have their share of drama, some more galling than others.

Sofia sighs. "Fortunately, her sister is as docile as a lamb. She's not the type to fall for the first guy who wants to spend time with her."

"How's Mara?"

"She tailed me like a shadow during the Ark's takeover," Sofia says with a satisfied look. "She's a good fighter. You can tell she has it in her blood. I can see her building her own army on the Promised Land. A queen in the making, no less."

She puts back the shoulder strap of her large black bag that Neal hadn't noticed in the half-light, and the crease above her brows deepen.

"People are getting hot under the collar these days. Especially since the inmates get a lot of visitors in this damn prison. I can't believe we haven't banned them yet!"

Neal grunts his assent, "Dan is opposed to this. Something about respecting their rights."

"What about *our* rights? He's quick to forget. I didn't think Dan could be so spineless. Deep down, I should've known when he wouldn't share a bed. He was afraid of antagonizing Dez. That's bullshit! Dez hasn't bothered to show up in so long he must've forgotten he's got two daughters."

"He wanted to blend in with the Archeans. It's his choice."

Sofia scoffs. "A treacherous choice, yes. He'd better stay out of my way in the Refuge."

"What will you do if you see him? Have you thought about Mara in all this?"

"She's old enough to understand. She loved her father, the poor thing. If only she knew what a fool he is!"

"Did it ever occur to you that she might've been seeing him

on the sly? Apparently, your ex found a way to work with the Deltas. They saw him when Nora's team was resupplying the Refuge for the transfer. Mara was around, too."

Her features harden and Neal can feel her anger burning on his skin. Fiona knows whom to take after.

"Eating his fill while his family struggles to survive, huh? Men like him don't deserve to live."

Sofia's voice swells in the small space of the hallway. Neal can understand her anger; If he knew one of his parents weren't doing anything to help, he would blame them for it. Neal and Sofia have that in common. But now that he's leading the Ark, he has to be better. Dan's voice echoes in his head. What would he say to her?

"Killing him won't do any good."

"Some things are worse than death," she hisses. "You should know that."

Neal instinctively looks at the door of the antechamber where the corpses are sleeping. He feels the throbbing lick of fire down his spine.

"Don't do anything stupid," he says. "I'm counting on you. On everyone."

"I'll see what I can do, Master Neal," she says mockingly with a wink.

Dan. Did he really need to spread this bad joke? He sure isn't wasting any time.

"See you in the Refuge, Master." Sofia has a mischievous smile and tilts her head theatrically before walking away with her nonchalant gait.

Neal crosses the rest of the corridor in a flash and reaches his former cabin, where his old belongings lie. A bunch of blankets are stacked in a corner covered with doodles supposed to break the monotony of the place, and empty liquor bottles are lined up. There's whiskey, cognac, rum, and even absinthe. He smiles at the memory of their nights of debauchery. Every time

Anika brought over a bottle from a recent hunt in the ocean depths, he had a good reason to celebrate. Nothing can compete with these spirits.

Many of the Mavericks shared their cabins with others for fear of being left alone, but Neal preferred to keep his privacy. He didn't want to wake the others with his relentless nightmares.

Neal steps onto an object and catches himself just in time not to fall face down. He bends down to grab the culprit and his eyes widen in surprise: another journal. The very first he used before the old lady Farrell gave him the one that he's using now. To think he was going to leave it here. He grabs a bag and stuffs the journal inside, along with some trinkets that will have a second life in the former commander's cabin. He chooses the best bottles and leaves the duplicates behind. Before leaving, he shifts the doodle-covered tile to get the unopened bottles he stored. His bag is already full, and the bottles clink hard when he shoves in an old whiskey. The space beyond the wall calls him, but he puts the tile back. This is not the time.

He leaves his cabin and stops short before climbing back to the upper levels. He decides to branch off and enter the warehouses. It's completely dark, except for a single shaft of light. This light screen was their version of the Moon, more than a hundred meters underwater in their drifting piece of junk.

They call it the Porthole. It's quite bright today, a sign that the sunrays are strong, and the sky is clear. They can't bank on the Ark's lights used during the hunts to light up the sea floor. They've been doing everything to save what little energy they have left.

In the light screen, some parts are darker, dirt that quickly builds up on the outer glass. Anika's team of hunters is always busy cleaning it so that they can continue to look out at the sea floor. One quickly tires of seeing schools of fish, ruins, or hunters at work, but in the lower levels, this is the closest thing to the outside world. They would come here to tell each other stories about the hunters and their discoveries, and about what lies beyond. Sometimes they even dared to look up and imagine the sky and its stars. It might seem like a waste of time for some, but for them it was hope.

Something shifts in the darkness. The strong briny smell that usually comes off the hunting warehouses hangs in the air.

"You!"

The outline of a female figure appears; it's the girl! Isn't she supposed to be in Skyler's care? What the hell is she doing here?

The strange ocean's radiance tints her face with a ghostly teal-blue veil. She alternately touches different spots on her body, as if immersed in a deep meditation. Her pupils are milky and dilated as she stares at something out the window. Her fleshy lips are barely moving, and Neal has to strain his ear to catch her quavering voice.

"They're coming."

She touches her lips with her fingertips and closes her eyes. Her eyelids are smooth, her skin perfectly smooth. If she didn't talk nonsense, she would be breathtakingly beautiful.

"What are you talking about?" Neal lets out, embarrassed by her presence. "How did you even find this place?

"You don't understand. They're coming back," she says, her dark eyes flicking open.

"What the hell are you talking about? Last I heard, you were in a coma." He moves closer and grabs her frigid hand. "Come on. I'll take you back to Skyler."

Dan owes him some explanation. He was supposed to be guarding the clinic with the new Paragon defectors. If this is what their security is like, Duke could strike them any time.

"I'm not crazy," the girl says, stone-faced. She yanks out her hand and heads out.

"What now?" he sighs, rubbing his forehead with a hand resting on his hip.

He would give anything to be back in the combat simulator, so he doesn't have to deal with this nonsense.

"I'm not deaf either," she shouts as she walks away, obviously upset.

Neal swears under his breath and goes after her.

7

SKYLER

The Archives are emptier than ever. People are not that interested in the past, preferring their mechanical and reassuring daily routine. The future is much more attractive with its bold promises. Sound familiar? Of course, his brother speaks of the Promised Land at every opportunity.

The strange girl named Uki confirmed what Skyler suspected: The journal does contain the names of other arks. Not only did Uki react when he mentioned the Sedna, but he finally remembered hearing it when he entered the auditorium of the abandoned vessel. This cannot be a coincidence. Since Uki won't reveal anything else, reading Amaranth's journal is essential. But before taking on such a challenge, he will need to find some peace and quiet.

The usual formalities of the Archives have been relaxed; Skyler is not intercepted when he enters the recessed corridor. He blends in and follows the dim light that pulses at the far end.

The memory spheres collected since the beginning of the project lie in this specially designed room. A large pedestal with a built-in computer lies in the center with an adjoining Nave. They've fallen way behind in encoding the spheres. Unless

Dr. Nazar decides to support the project, Skyler will have to write it off. Dr. Siria, his only patron, died during the Ark's takeover. Neal might be able to help, but if he's anything like Skyler thinks he is, it'll take some convincing.

With a heavy heart, Skyler retrieves his father's sphere and places it in a cushioned case. How would their father have reacted when he saw Neal alive?

The Nave is tempting. He could view their father's memories or at least what little he had been able to save. The sphere would need to be encoded first, but the system is currently down and won't allow it. However, Emily's former boss Yasmina had employed Dr. Siria to develop a more sophisticated technology capable of reading the spheres. What if he checked it out, just in case?

At the Archives' reception desk, a hooded man emerges from a door that shuts behind him and blend seamlessly into the wall. The Sigma Foundation's symbol glows in its place moments after. Before he knows it, Skyler loses track of the stranger. What was this cloaked man doing here?

The clock is ticking, so Skyler must push the thought away for now. His father's sphere is more important than his nagging curiosity.

***

NOT SO LONG AGO, he was here with Emily when the Brotherhood was trying to get their hands on the code that died with Commander Hawk. They combed through his memories using the sphere Yasmina kept safe, and they retrieved the code which gives access to the Ark's central system.

Amaranth. The name of their Ark. Today, Skyler is here for a completely different reason.

He doesn't recognize any of the people who question him at the door but being the sibling of the Brotherhood's leader has its advantages. They don't insist on identification and point to the stairwell since the elevator is out of order. His legs are sore and burning when he reaches the entrance. The Mavericks on duty put him through the metal detectors, check the contents of the box, and ask him some routine questions. Fortunately, they return the sphere to him, satisfied with his responses. It's amazing how his brother managed to unite the Mavericks under his command despite his unfounded promises. Emily might have been the only one who saw through Neal's game after all.

Skyler goes through Yasmina's old office and enters a secret room where she used to conduct her special interrogations. He can't help but think back to Emily's cheerful voice and must stop for a moment, his chest tightening.

Dinah's words come to mind, *"You should visit her too, you know."*

He sighs.

The instruments of torture are displayed without modesty. On the platform, the interface glows dimly. The electrical system of this office must be off grid.

Skyler hesitates. Should he really view the sphere? Having come all this way and not being able to decide seems silly, but something is bothering him. His heart is pounding against his eardrums.

When he places the sphere on the pedestal, fear grips his throat. What if he can't stop watching?

At the sound of his voice, Dylan's memories materialize on the platform as a hologram. As the scenes flash disjointedly into view, Skyler drinks in every detail. For a second, he feels like a patient addicted to drugs, every memory a drop to ease his racking pain.

Childhood memories he believed buried forever assail him violently. With a shaking hand, he reaches out to touch a blurry hologram of his grandparents.

They passed away shortly after he was born, but Skyler recognizes their faces from family photos. He gets chills at their echoing voices. They wear proud smiles as they celebrate his father's decision to pursue oceanography. Of course, Skyler's grandfather was a scientist, too. Dylan would follow in his footsteps and carry on the Goldbergs's legacy.

Skyler now sees himself through Dylan's eyes and realizes that the scene has shifted to a different memory. A five-year-old Skyler accompanies him to the Gardens of Humankind. Dylan turns his back and counts to ten, and somehow his younger voice sounds wrong. In a rustling of footsteps, little Skyler has run to hide. Dylan takes his time looking for him through every bush and branch in his path. Little Skyler giggles. He seems so happy.

The park's lush vegetation suddenly gives way to the restaurant *La Orilla* where their whole family is sitting around a table. It's Skyler's birthday. There are eight candles on the gigantic chocolate cake they are sharing. His father is about to give him a neatly wrapped present that he hid under the table, but Murielle glares at him and whispers, "Have you thought about Allen?"

Skyler is even younger in the subsequent flash of memory. He's about four, his brother Allen seven. They are in their bunk beds, the lit mobile casting multicolored stars on the walls and ceiling. Their mother is reading them a bedtime story that takes place on the Surface. Their father has come to wish them good night and kisses them on the forehead in turn.

In the next flash, Allen tears open a plain brown paper wrapped gift. His eyes light up at the remote-controlled toy plane. Cut. The plane's wing is broken. Their mother, Murielle, pulls Skyler aside and blames him for the accident. Allen says it was Chris's fault, but Murielle is furious. Chris is Skyler's friend, so he should've stopped him. Skyler is grounded indefinitely for being so shameless and jealous of his brother Allen. Their father, who has remained silent so far, stands up for

Skyler who is shaking like a leaf, teary-eyed. Seething, their mother frowns upon the way their father always protects him.

Next, Dylan and Murielle are having a heated discussion in the Goldbergs's cabin, while Skyler and his brother are most likely at the Academy. His father wants Skyler to do his oceanography internship with him at the Deltas, but his mother doggedly insists that his brother Allen have this privilege since he will be the most successful in the family. Why waste this chance on Skyler?

Skyler remembers hating oceanography after that; he believed his father had rejected him by choosing his brother. Had he been wrong to think that?

In the following flash of memory, his mother has aged several years, at the worst of her depression. She has just swallowed pills to calm her attack and shouts at Skyler for being responsible for all the misfortune that has hit their family. His father tries to calm her down to no avail. She wants Skyler to move out and disappear.

Skyler and his brother must be around ten or twelve years old now, and the two of them are at the Observatory with their father. They are looking at the ocean floor, and Dylan says, "This is the world you'll have to grow up in. You'll feel that it is hostile to you, that it rejects you. If you look closely, you will understand: This world listens to us, but we do not listen to it. Learn to listen and maybe we will have a chance to reach the Promised Land."

Subsequently, his parents are at the park with Allen's death looming over them. His mother wants another child to ensure the succession of the Goldbergs. Annoyed, his father objects that they already have a promising son and that she must recognize him as such. She replies that she cannot cherish the source of her pain.

The hologram blurs with an ear-splitting error message, *"The data is corrupted. Please remove the sphere."*

Skyler crouches, still in shock. His body trembling, he holds himself against the platform. His father's sphere is fragmented. There's nothing he can do to fix it. Dylan had already been dead for too long when Skyler transferred the memories.

He wants to shatter the sphere to bits, but this is the closest thing to his father he has now. He was so wrong about him. His father had loved him, had always worried about him, protected him even.

His mother's unconditional love was a lie. How could Skyler have been so blind?

An icy calm settles over him as he lets his legs carry him to the back room, where Emily found Commander Hawk's sphere.

There are so many spheres that he thinks he is dreaming. They are each nestled in their own labeled open box with their owner's name, neatly ordered on rows upon rows of shelves. The hearts of the spheres glow in overlapping greens, blues, purples, and oranges, each with their own electrical signature.

Emily had vaguely told him about Yasmina's macabre fascination with torturing their former prisoners. Though the spectacle of these spheres should delight him, he can only feel disgust at the sight of them. To use people's most intimate memories against them borders on abomination. If he had known his project would serve some evil deed, Skyler would have refrained from developing this technology. Could he be responsible for the pain those prisoners went through? He shudders at the thought of being complicit in this horror, and the familiar feeling of guilt nags at him.

Skyler walks past chilling instruments and stops in front of some particularly terrifying glass helmets Yasmina must have used. Goggles, too? He takes them, with no idea as to what they could be used for. He could ask Nathan, the engineer who worked on the memory spheres, to improvise something.

Skyler stops dead in his tracks.

On the workstation are documents bearing the Sigma seal.

There is an authorization form for borrowing parts from the Deltas and a request signed by Nathan himself. Did he work for Yasmina without Skyler's knowledge? Dr. Siria should have been the one acting under Yasmina's orders. Nathan has been a friend of the family for as long as he can remember, along with his wife Jacinta who even used to knit socks for Skyler when he was a kid. Nathan would have never betrayed his trust.

Skyler bolts out of the secret room with disgust at the gory display, but more importantly, at Yasmina's twisted mind and those who perpetuate the lie and deception.

He hates this place.

8

SKYLER

Box in hand, Skyler is standing in front of the sealed gate of the prison cells.

"Is everything okay?"

He must look pretty bad for a Maverick to notice. It's the same guy who questioned him when he first got here.

"Are visits this way?"

"You'll have to wait for the new warden to come back."

The warden in question, a Maverick in her late forties, finally shows up a good while later. Her hair is fit tightly into a large bun. Her back is bent sideways, probably because of the oversized bag slung over her shoulder. She stares at him suspiciously and asks, "What do you want?"

"To see an inmate." He deduced from her laconic way of speaking that the less she knows, the better.

"It's a little late for that, don't you think? Why aren't you at the Refuge with the others?"

The warden does not wait for an answer and surprises him by grabbing his hand to scan his wristband. She has an amused smile.

"Nervous? I would be too if I were to plot a rebellion against the Brotherhood."

Skyler feels the pent-up tension from earlier stir his insides and gives her a dazed look.

"Don't be a fool," she adds, with palpable arrogance. "We all know you guys are up to no good with your endless visits. But it won't matter in the Refuge. Generations of bullshit, family, and prestige will be worthless. We'll see who comes out as a winner this time."

She peers at her scanner screen, and her voice softens. "Skyler, right?"

He nods without a word, for fear of making her angry. Her face is expressionless.

"If you weren't under Neal's protection, I wouldn't be doing you this favor. Follow my lead."

He mumbles a hurried thank you through the noise of her bag rubbing against her uniform.

"Those madmen from the Atrium have been causing quite the ruckus in the prison."

Once they arrive in front of a cell, her sympathetic manner quickly fades, and she spits out, "Other visitors are waiting, so make it quick."

Skyler hesitates, and the warden doesn't miss a beat. She speaks to him in a falsely reassuring voice, as if she were talking to a child.

"Do you want me to hold your hand?"

"No need. I know him well." She lets out a dry laugh and pulls one of her streaming black locks out from under her bag sling.

"He could surprise you. Those lunatics show their true colors when you least expect it."

"You seem to be quite the expert on the subject."

"Ten minutes, no more," she snaps. "I'll be around."

Knowing that he will only get one chance, Skyler enters

without a word. The stench of dirt and sweat immediately washes over him.

The prisoner is in a better state than he imagined. His resilience is admirable, just like the pesky weeds that infest the gardens; they just keep coming back, don't they?

"I knew you'd miss me," his former best friend greets him as he gets up from the unmade bed.

"You wish."

Chris has a stubble, a little darker than his ashen hair. The ordeals of the last few days must be wearing on him. Watching your father kill people is not something you can push out of your mind easily.

Lost in his thoughts, Chris twitches the hairs of his beard and scratches it nervously where red spots appear. Perhaps his lack of hygiene is making his skin itchy. At this rate, he could easily get a skin infection.

Chris registers Skyler's presence and, despite the despicable conditions of his custody, he flashes a radiant smile, the only thing that is bright in this dank cell. How can light radiate from a person with such dark intentions? It makes for a strange paradox.

"How can you smile knowing what you've done?" hisses Skyler.

"You're mistaken. What your brother has become created this mess."

"You and your father killed trusting Archeans rather than protect them."

Chris doesn't take offense to his accusations whether they are false or not. Still, Skyler wants to be wrong, perhaps more than he'd hoped. Weren't they once best friends? How did they get to this point?

If only Chris could stick up for himself to prove Skyler is wrong about him, just as he was wrong about his own father, Dylan. But Chris stays silent while raking his nails noisily over his beard.

"I know what I did," Chris says after a moment. "Trust me."

He keeps his head down like an unruly child caught in the act. If Chris truly was an accomplice to his father's mass murder, he will be irredeemable.

"And the Sacred Fire, was that also planned by you and your ruthless father?"

Chris looks up at him with innocent eyes, the same ones he had when they were younger. Don't they know each other better than anyone else? Should they even doubt each other? Skyler doesn't know anymore.

"The Sacred Fire was put out by someone else," Chris replies.

"By whom?"

"I don't know. If I or my father had known, we would've done everything to avoid it."

"I wish I could believe you. Really."

"But?"

Skyler takes a deep breath. "You always find yourself in an awkward situation, Chris. It's not easy to trust you."

"Why not enjoy this moment together? That's what I've been hoping for since the moment they threw me in this cell."

Chris remains poised and beckons him to sit on his bed beside him. Skyler does not budge.

"Do you know what it's like to not talk to anyone for days? To be accused of something you didn't do? So, please, come on. I'd like to talk."

"Isn't that what we're doing already?" says Skyler defensively. "What else do you want?"

"To be honest with each other."

Still Skyler stands there, watching Chris with his cheekbones showing at the slightest quirk of his smiles. What could his handsome face possibly be hiding?

The way Skyler treats him is pathetic. What if Chris really has nothing to do with this whole killing spree? There should be a trial before the Ark's Council with evidence to back it up, but the system fell apart when his brother took over. What kind of justice is this then?

Skyler sits beside Chris. The paper-thin mattress crinkles under their weight and seems about to break.

"Remember the last simulation? The one the Brotherhood hacked into?"

Fragments come back to him in flashes: He was finally on dry land with his family and Emily, but the celebrations were short-lived; nature unleashed its wrath on them with a deathly tidal wave that swept up almost all the survivors in its wake. Skyler's family managed to escape, but the destruction had shaken them. The face of the young boy who Dylan rescued is still haunting him because he looked like Allen.

"Yes, why?"

"I've always done everything I could to avoid these simulations, but my father never allowed me to. I mean it's his own invention. Imagine if Duke Kay's own son refused to submit. What would the infernal trio of Harris, White, and Garcia say if they knew? They would have a field day and spread false rumors among all the other bigwigs vying for the Commander's favor. I've seen them court my father, who made sure to keep me out of the picture when I made it clear that I would never join the Paragon. Not that I mind, quite the opposite. I'm not good at pretending, anyway."

Chris pushes to his feet and stares blankly as if he is watching some invisible hologram.

"The first time I spent in the simulator, I experienced a fear I never thought possible. My vitals went haywire, and they had to pull me out. Then they sent me to Med Bay to recover. According to the doctors, it was a post-traumatic shock. My father didn't believe them and blamed it on my weakness. Isn't that what the simulation was created for? To make us stronger and prepare us for the harsh conditions on the Surface? In my father's eyes, I was just an aberration that proved he had been right about me."

Skyler's first simulation had also been a shock. The torrent of memories and emotions had given him terrible nausea. When he emerged, he felt out of touch with reality for weeks, believing he was still stuck inside the simulation. His father had tried to reassure him, but nothing could ever erase the impression that everything could be a lie.

"I couldn't believe that this technology was my father's idea. I felt like he was trying to find a way to get inside my head, but then I remembered that he couldn't even if he wanted to. That was, until the last simulation."

Chris chokes on his words.

"I've seen some scary stuff, Sky. They're in my mind, and I can't get them out. It's no coincidence that I wanted to join the Command under Laurene's tutelage."

"To stop your father?" asks Skyler with a glimmer of hope.

Chris takes a deep breath. "Can I trust you?"

His eyes shine with a sincerity that takes Skyler back to their childhood, when they had vowed to remain best friends. So many unexpected things had happened after that, and Skyler had broken that promise. Yet Chris never gave up on him.

Skyler stares at his feet, unable to find the right words.

"Why did you come to see me?" Chris asks in earnest, with his usual composure.

Fiddling with the box, Skyler's determination that drove him into this cell is waning, and he sighs. "To see through your game."

"Let me guess. The Promised Land is harder to find than expected and you were looking for someone to blame?"

"I'm not my brother."

Chris grabs his shoulder to look deeply into his eyes, and his voice is burning with bitter hatred. "And I am not my father."

He adds softly, "Open your eyes, Sky. Something bigger than

us is at play here. All we've managed to do so far is to survive, but not unscathed."

As much as Skyler hates to admit it, Chris has a point.

"You know, you and I aren't that different," says Chris with a smile. "We're just the game masters' shadows, but it doesn't have to stay that way."

The shadow of his brother. Despite the years, there are things that do not change.

"The Brotherhood is doomed to fail. As for my father, he's too unpredictable."

Chris pauses, his eyes shining with fervor.

"But remember our promise, Skyler. Together, we're a team. Together, we can save the rest of humanity."

The door latch rattles, quickly followed by a shuddering squeak.

"Time's up," the warden scolds as she steps in, peering warily at them.

Skyler springs up, then steals a glance at Chris, who gives him an honest smile. The Maverick warden grows impatient, and Skyler lets out, "We'll see each other again. I promise."

9

NEAL

Neal wakes with a start, disoriented. Dan's steady snoring echoes in the inky blackness of the cabin they share, a luxury compared to the other Archeans crammed in by the dozens. Normally, he would not allow himself such excess, but he wouldn't want to be murdered in his sleep.

He pulls on his thin, sweat-soaked blanket and crouches down next to his bed where he pulls his notebook and pen out from under the mattress. There's a thump on the floor. Neal scrambles to pick up what fell. Without bothering to change, he feels his way against the cold metal of the beds' framing and heads for the green-glowing exit. The corridor outside is narrow, much narrower than any other place on the Ark, because space in the Refuge is limited and overwhelmingly suffocating. A circular room leads to the main entrance with its large, tightly shut door glowing faintly.

He takes a seat on one of the raised grooves leading to the door and lays his belongings beside him. He takes out a pipe, draws a whitish puff that fades into the air, and leans back, eyes closed, letting the substance flow through his body. Gradually, the tendrils of the sedative lull him into their comforting warmth.

Now that he is coming around, he approaches the large bright door, crosses his legs, opens his notebook to a new page and presses the binding to make sure the journal stays open. His pen leaves a smudge of black ink as soon as he begins to write:

Death. Its smell permeates my skin so much that I feel like I am one with it.

Out of habit, he takes another puff of his pipe to clear his thoughts with the tranquilizer. With the pipe wedged between his teeth, he writes furiously:

I gasp in the darkness. My consciousness flutters between the real and the unreal while my body fails me. A door in the distance groans.

The pipe flies out of his mouth and he raises his head to meet Fiona's insolent stare as she puffs on it.

"This stuff's strong," she says, coughing, with tears in her eyes.

"A cocktail specially made by Sofia Reyes."

"Let's not talk about my mother, will you?"

Fiona plumps down next to him with one leg dangling and the other bent, knee against her chest. She gives up smoking after another coughing fit and gives him back the pipe, which he sets aside. Slowly, his thoughts thicken and his vision blurs.

"It makes me sick to think she made my sister in her image," she says. "That's the last thing I needed."

"That's not so bad, is it?"

"Speak for yourself."

She sighs, her cheek against her knee. A contemplative silence settles during which Neal imagines Fiona becoming the exact copy of her mother Sofia. She would be a hell of a sassy heartbreaker. He stifles a mocking laugh.

"We're screwed," says Fiona with a touch of cynicism.

"Your optimism stinks," breathes Neal slowly. His face is so numb he can barely feel himself frowning.

"Aren't you working on a way to avoid people trying to kill each other off? Must be hard. You haven't written much."

Neal forgot he's still holding his journal open in one hand. The feel of the paper against his skin suddenly returns, and he shrugs. "That doesn't mean nothing can be done about it."

"Your optimism will kill you one of these days," she says, her eyes glazed over. "But hey, we all have our weaknesses. Milo…"

Fiona's words buzz in his head, but he can't seem to grasp their meaning. Is it something about their relationship?

"Is he avoiding me? I haven't seen him in a while," says Neal.

"Milo has been avoiding everyone ever since *she* came into the picture." Fiona jumps on her feet. "What jerk would feel sorry for his abuser unless he has a death wish? He avoids me like the plague when he should be spending his time with me."

"A death wish," Neal repeats in amazement.

"You know what I mean."

He looks at her even more confused.

"Milo's too good for her," Fiona adds wearily. "His soft heart blinds him. He thinks he can help."

"Are you talking about your relationship or—"

"Thanks for your moral support. Not."

"My brother avoids me too, if that makes you feel any better," he says, collecting his thoughts. "And I have no idea why."

"What's wrong with him?"

"I seriously don't know."

Skyler should've been happy and eager to be part of the Brotherhood, but a wall has mysteriously gone up between them. Neal bites his lip worryingly. God, is he going to turn out like Fiona?

"Then you should talk to him," she says confidently.

"Why don't you talk to Milo then?"

She glares at him, then snaps back, "You know why."

He knows there is some truth to what she says, but

approaching Skyler is like walking on eggshells. Their last conversation was when Tessa dragged him to the clinic to meet with Skyler, who wasn't in the mood to talk.

In a completely different tone, Fiona exclaims, "We've got to meet tomorrow! The whole Brotherhood. I'll bring Milo."

"Are you serious?"

"As serious as a Reyes can be. And you'll go to your brother."

Tired, Neal closes his notebook. Tomorrow will be a long day.

"Why can't we just get our old base back?" groans Fiona, squirming in her metal chair. "The cushions were classy, but this…"

Gone are the days when they could pretend to be the Commander and his crew in their cozy lair. Now they must make do with a much smaller version of the Ark's Command Center nestled in the heart of the Refuge. Aside from being convenient with direct access to the central system and safe from troublemakers, this place is uniquely boring with its table, a handful of chairs, a few screens, and dull lights. Their predecessors had horrible design taste.

Around the half-moon table, Walker is nodding off at his tablet while Dan is deep in thought, his eyes half-closed. Tessa seems even more distracted since she returned from her mission, so talking about her recent attitude toward him will have to wait.

Fiona managed to drag Milo along despite his obvious objection. That means Neal will have to hold up his end of the bargain and talk to Skyler.

Neal places a bottle of alcohol on the table which startles Walker, who hurriedly pushes up his glasses.

"I brought us a little something to celebrate."

"Now that speaks to me," Fiona says, handing out the shot glasses from the bag Neal brought.

The original label is too worn, but the letters carved into the bottle are still readable. Walker gapes at the amber liquid that takes on a golden glow when placed in the right angle.

"A Zappaka 24. Dark rum," Neal explains. "Apparently, it was a specialty of our ancestors."

He opens it unceremoniously, and a spicy mouth-watering aroma wafts through the air. The shot glasses are passed around almost instantly.

"You're never short of resources," Dan says while sipping his drink.

"Wasting's never been my thing. You should know that."

That's how they learned to survive together among the Mavericks. The Ark only uses a fraction of the treasures the hunters bring back, but it doesn't mean the Mavericks have to do the same. With a little research in the Archives, Neal targeted some basic tools and appliances to improve their daily lives. Once, they tinkered with a kettle they retrieved from the heaps of unused relics. It made a world of difference as it became their only source of hot water. Fiona's mother had taken this process to a whole new level by creating a very lucrative black market. Its network benefited the Brotherhood in more ways than they can count while she turned a sizable profit made of rare collectibles.

"The Archeans are obsessed with keeping everything to a minimum," Neal adds, letting the spice of the alcohol prickle his taste buds. "They were going to get rid of these invaluable bottles."

"Money hasn't been worth anything in a long time," Walker says, tasting the rum with his lips.

Walker grimaces, but that doesn't stop him from downing his drink right away. He's never looked more alert.

"Value is more than just old-fashioned paper bills," Neal says with a wink as he pours himself another drink.

Fiona taps her empty glass on the table, and he slides the bottle toward her. Then, he stands up to address the group.

"I've called this meeting so we can come up with a plan. The Refuge is only temporary. We need to use this valuable time to tackle the problem at its source."

"Find a new place to live," Dan adds, leaning his elbows on the table.

"I propose working on two fronts to ensure our victory. This is our first mission as the commanding crew of this Ark."

His responsibility.

"Any good news from the mission?" asks Fiona, looking at Tessa who hesitates for a moment.

"Not exactly."

Neal hasn't divulged anything, preferring to wait until he knows more, but, of course, Fiona had to screw it up with her usual tact. Dan gives her a confused look, while the others stare at Tessa.

"The Promised Land will have to wait," Neal cuts in. "But according to Skyler, they found an ancient Ark. If it's still functional as your report seemed to imply, Tessa, we might just move over there."

"How are we going to move everyone?" retorts Walker. "The power of the Strahls is running low."

"What if we charged them there?"

"Do you have any idea how long it would take? Our Ark will be a shipwreck long before."

Although he feels the pressure building, Neal keeps his cool and ignores the impatience in Walker's voice.

"We still have to try. We can get the parts we need to repair the Sacred Fire while we wait."

Neal glances at Milo, expecting his advice, but he remains silent, his arms crossed.

"What if there aren't any usable parts?" asks Fiona, whose features have become tense.

He thought about it, but he doesn't want to have to explain Uki's presence on board right now. At least not until she's back in her right mind.

"Take apart the core and bring it back? I'm on it." Everyone turns to Milo, surprised that he's finally speaking. He doesn't seem to mind the risk, intent on unraveling the engineering problem that stands before him.

"We don't even know if—" begins Fiona.

"It's an Ark, right? There's no reason why it shouldn't work. Can I see the report?"

"This job requires more than a century of expertise," Walker says. "Are you sure you can handle it?"

"Someone had to build this darn Sacred Fire in the first place. Which means it can be pulled apart, piece by piece."

Neal hands over his tablet to Milo and asks Tessa to report on her visit. She doesn't go into the minute details, keeping it to the essentials, as she and Neal agreed before their meeting, to keep Uki's presence and identity a secret. When she's done, Milo is still busy reading carefully, and Fiona hangs tough. "This is suicide."

"Their welcome wasn't very charming." Tessa says to lend support to Fiona. That comes as a surprise! "We don't know how many active drones there are. One of them almost cost us our lives."

"Our lives won't be decided by some rogue drones," Neal says. "They must have a weakness. Walker?"

"Find the source that controls them. If there is one."

Neal looks at him quizzically.

"Well, they could be autonomous—some kind of looped programming that's been going on since they were first switched on."

"What if we had them here?" says Fiona with a look of horror.

"Last I heard, the technology was lost in the Flood," Walker says reassuringly. "Our drones are unarmed, as a precaution."

"That doesn't explain their presence on the Sedna," says Dan.

Milo lets out a laugh that shuts them all up. He runs a hand through his hair, an old habit of his.

"Tessa and Skyler made it out alive. I'm going to be all right."

"Are you listening or what?" shouts Fiona, furious. "They only went in and out. You're going to rip apart that Ark's core. If more of these machines exist, that's where they'll be!"

"Stay out of this."

Neal takes a deep breath. For once, he wants to prove Fiona right, but their options are limited. His plan hinges on getting back out there.

"I won't force you."

"You worry too much about me, Neal. Drones aren't going to take away my long-standing title of champion in the combat simulator."

"All right."

Milo has shown more than once what he can do, so why wouldn't he let him? Each member of the Brotherhood has led their own impossible mission to take over the Ark. Since they succeeded once, they can do it again.

"That's nonsense," Fiona protests vehemently. "Are you actually letting him drown in his madness?"

"We're going to need a working Ark to search for the Promised Land," Milo retorts. "Plus, there could be some clues hidden on the Sedna, right, Neal?"

"What happened at the Sacred Fire didn't teach you anything," Fiona says, glaring at Milo who is pale with rage.

"How dare you?"

He opens his mouth but changes his mind and stands up.

Before Neal can intervene, Milo storms out, slamming the door behind him.

Tessa looks uneasy and says, "I know the place well. It'll be easier if I go with him."

"So, we have a plan," says Neal, raising his drink.

They each down their glass while Fiona gulps Milo's untouched rum.

"Where's the damn bottle?" she growls.

10

NEAL

Despite the predictable argument between Fiona and Milo, their meeting went better than he had hoped. They all have something to keep them busy now. Milo and Tessa are working out the details of the upcoming mission. Meanwhile, Fiona is gathering the equipment to extract the parts they'll need, and Walker is making sure they have reliable transportation. The mission will begin as soon as they set foot outside the Refuge. They will have to navigate an Ark devoid of oxygen and borrow a still-functioning Strahl. According to some defectors, the Paragon headquarters should have what they need to survive in those conditions. Of course, the Paragon would.

Now that their plan is in motion, Neal could use a breather, but they must take the Archeans out of the old system first. What could persuade them to recognize him as their rightful leader?

Neal locks the door behind him, and Dan stops playing with his unkempt beard.

"You know you can tell me everything," Dan says, uncharacteristically serious.

"There isn't much to say." They walk together, and while

Neal appreciates Dan's attention, he would rather be alone. Morning spirits don't agree with his stomach.

"The girl," presses Dan.

"Uki. She has a name, you know," Neal replies, more abruptly than he intended. "If you're thinking of adding her to your list of pickups, be warned. Some people might get jealous."

Although there are hundreds of people confined in the Refuge, it still looks and feels like living in a tomb. They only come across a handful of Archeans, probably on their way to lunch.

Soon, the Mavericks will head to their station to coordinate the distribution of the day's rations. Neal will have to hurry to get something to eat. The Brotherhood is no exception to rationing. Privileges have always repelled him, and besides, it would give Leander and the others another reason to goad him. Whatever Neal says or does, the Brotherhood will be under fire anyway.

"I'm not sure Tessa would like your flirting around either," Dan replies defensively.

"There's nothing going on between us," Neal says dryly.

Dan doesn't let it throw him off and continues once they turn the corner. "Maybe there isn't for her, but it's a different story for you."

"Dan, I'm not in the mood."

His best friend raises his arms in resignation. "Whatever you say. And for your information, Sofia is history."

"Speak for yourself. I'd sleep with my one eye open if I were you."

Dan shoves him before finally leaving him alone. Neal looks at his wristband to check the location of each of the Brotherhood members, but only one grabs his attention, really. After he made sure Dan is out of sight, he heads to the dorms in the opposite direction.

The morning stench of bad breath is heavy in the room lit by thin strips of halogen bulbs along the floor and ceiling. Whispers echo like whistles and grow louder as Neal paces the aisles of the Omega dormitory—keeping divisions seemed simpler, logistically speaking. How many of them are part of Leander's insurgent group? Would they go after Skyler and use him as leverage if they knew his brother was here?

It is still early, and he expects to find his brother asleep. However, when his wristband indicates he has arrived at the location, Skyler is engrossed in reading a notebook. If it were not for its worn appearance, Neal could have confused it with his own journal the old lady Farrell gave him, brimming with the secrets of his haunted nights.

The bile rises to his throat, and with it, a persistent nausea. The rum had seemed like a good idea. When did he get such a weak stomach?

"I don't know why you insist on staying here," Neal greets him, leaning against the opposite bedpost. "You clearly can't sleep."

Skyler doesn't look up from the pages immediately. "Did you come to talk about my condition or yours?"

Groans of protest urge them to get out and let the others sleep, so Neal motions for the exit. Skyler complies reluctantly with a look of annoyance. Once they reach the main hallway, Neal wastes no time and says, "I need you to take me to her."

"Now?" Skyler has an incredulous look. "It must be serious."

"How do you do it?"

"Your lack of interest in her was obvious at the clinic," Skyler says bitterly.

Fiona's words from the night before ring in his ears. Neal leads Skyler into an alcove with a fire extinguisher and a fire axe. A small-scale model of the Refuge is printed on a laminated plate, a material more reliable than any screen or hologram that might fail in an emergency.

"You can't keep playing that game," Neal says, feeling the bile burning the back of his throat.

"Let me remind you that the master of this game is you. These are not my rules."

"You do everything to avoid me, and you don't take part in the Brotherhood's operations. I invited you to the meeting this morning, remember?"

"I just don't see the point. I belong with my patients. You should know that. If you remember, while you were off adventuring in the in betweens, I was helping Mom at Med Bay."

"Think of it this way," Neal says, stressing each word. "All the Archeans are sick patients right now. They're all in grave danger if we don't do something. This Refuge is only temporary."

Skyler lets out a sigh.

"I need to learn more about the Sedna," Neal adds in a whisper. "This mission will be critical to our survival, and I don't want to take any unnecessary risks."

"What mission? The massacre wasn't enough to dissuade you from going back?"

"Sky! What do you think? We'll be next if we do nothing!" From the crease in his forehead, his brother seems to be weighing his words. Neal continues, "Did you manage to learn anything from Uki?"

"She doesn't talk much, as you may have noticed," Skyler replies in his usual calm voice. "What I know, you already know, and that's only because I got lucky. It's all in the journal."

"The one you were reading earlier?"

Skyler nods and pulls the worn notebook from the inside pocket of his uniform. "Did you know the first Commander of the Ark was Amaranth Bellerose?"

The name sounds vaguely familiar. Did it have something to do with the stories the old lady Farrell told them in the chapel when they were younger?

"Maybe. What does she have to do with all this?"

"Nothing directly, but it confirms the existence of other Arks."

"And?"

"The rest is mostly about her life on the Ark in its very beginning. I've only managed to understand bits and pieces here and there. I'm still trying to spell out her writing. Let's just say her penmanship is not the most reader friendly."

Skyler pauses, staring at the notebook with its curled pages. Neal wonders if someone will read his own journals in the future and walk through his nightmares. No! He will burn them before anyone can put their hands on them. There is something horribly wrong with pulling apart a dead person's soul without their consent. Is this really what this Amaranth Bellerose would have wanted?

"But it doesn't matter," Skyler continues, carefully putting the notebook back in his pocket as a group of Archeans pass by. "If people on the other arks are still alive, they can help us understand."

"You want us to go look for them? Look, we don't have the resources for that. The arks could be anywhere."

"We do it the same way we did last time."

"We intercepted a distress signal. Even if we were able to locate the other arks, why would they take us in, much less trust us? If their situation is as dire as ours, I doubt it."

"I don't see why the last humans on Earth shouldn't help each other."

Neal rubs his eyes. "You are so naive, Skyler."

His remark seems to hurt him because Sky's burst of enthusiasm dies out just as quickly. He goes back to his stoicism that leaves no room for affection, even for his brother who has returned from the dead.

"The Sedna is our only chance to get through this alive," Neal insists, looking for support in his eyes. "I need to talk to Uki about it. Where is she?"

Skyler remains silent at his question, and Neal refrains from shaking him by the shoulders as Dan does to right his mind. Their relationship has a long way to go before it gets back to what it once was.

Neal follows Sky out of the alcove without making a case for his mood swings. He doesn't have time to deal with his little tantrum. If Skyler were in his situation, he'd understand why he must act this way.

They arrive in front of a door guarded by Nora, who straightens her posture at their approach. She rubs her hands on her uniform and greets them, worn out by her night shift. A furtive glance through the small, recessed window tells Neal that they are in the right place; Uki is sitting in a corner, her eyes half-open.

"Anything to report?" asks Neal, turning his attention back to Nora.

"Nothing except for her strange prayers," she replies while repressing a yawn. "It's … fascinating. I wonder what she's mumbling about."

"Did you ask her?"

"Not really. I only offered to let her take a shower and she refused. I didn't insist."

"You can go rest. Derek will take over." Neal pats her shoulder sympathetically.

"Let me know if you find out what her prayers are all about. I'm going crazy wrapping my mind around this one."

Skyler chuckles, and Neal gives him a sideways glance as he enters.

"What are you doing standing there?"

"She's your prisoner, not mine," Skyler retorts, failing miserably at hiding his amusement.

"Is that how you see yourself too?"

"It depends."

Nora looks at them intently like she is afraid to miss something important. Neal controls his urge to confront his brother and says, "Well, you're not alone. We all are. Prisoners of the Ark and prisoners of this life. We just have to learn to live with it. Are you coming?"

His explanation seems to satisfy Skyler who decides to follow him under Nora's curious stare.

Since the Refuge doesn't offer much privacy, the Mavericks in charge of Uki picked a small storage area—maybe more like a closet—with crates stuffed with spare sheets, blankets, and pillows. Neal recoils at the musty, spicy smell. Judging by the spilled-open crates, Uki quickly got tired of exploring the cramped room. She wrapped a blanket around herself and built a pillow fort that almost looks like some altar.

Neal narrowly avoids stepping on Uki's plate of half-nibbled dinner rotting on the floor next to a nearly empty water jug. Skyler is right: She's being kept in squalid conditions.

"The fish is not to your liking?" asks Neal in a friendly, almost apologetic tone. "It doesn't taste very good anyway."

"Why do you eat them?" she retorts with a hint of anger. Her eyes are wide open, furious at odds with the poise that usually follows a meditation session.

"What kind of question is that?"

Neal casts a distraught look to Skyler who shrugs, "What my brother is trying to say is: What do you normally eat on the Sedna?"

"To begin with, we don't eat conscious beings," she explains a little more calmly, clutching the edges of the pillow on her thighs. "Plus, we don't ask derogatory questions."

And they don't shower either, Neal muses, keeping the remark for himself. Dan would be thrilled to see how well he is able to control himself for once.

"Until recently, we didn't know there were other arks," Skyler adds, taking over the situation to Neal's relief. "I apologize if our ways seem awkward."

"You did not know?" Astonished, she hugs the pillow force-fully. "Perhaps it was better that way."

Questions burn on Neal's lips, but he lets his brother continue. If only she were less ... standoffish, it would make things easier. "What happened on the Sedna?"

Uki seems to think for a moment, but the long-awaited explanations do not come.

"Isn't it obvious?" she sighs. "Everyone's dead."

"How did it happen?"

She touches one of her tattoos, as if by reflex, before letting out in a small voice, "I don't remember anything."

"This is not helpful," Neal says, feeling his brother glare at him.

Neal thinks back to their last impromptu meeting on the lower floors, then adds, nonchalantly, "You were damn sure of what you were saying when I saw you at the Porthole. *They're coming.*"

He displays a mysterious air to add effect. She crosses her arms.

"You think I'm crazy!"

"Take it easy! I never said that."

Uki looks away, as if embarrassed by her outburst.

"No, but you thought about it hard. What exactly is going on here? I'd like some explanations."

"It's ... complicated," Neal and Skyler say together.

They exchange a surprised look, then a shy smile.

"We're not getting anywhere," she says, mockingly. "You brought me here without any explanation. How do I know you're not the ones who killed my family?"

"Do you really think we could do such a thing?" says Neal in disbelief. "I mean, look at us!"

"Yeah," decides Uki who sorts the pillows into two separate piles. "I don't think such a stupid leader is capable of that."

"What if we used a sphere to encode her memories?" chimes

in Skyler, raising his voice at just the right moment. "I just need to grab some equipment. If you *let* me."

"Like what you did with the late Commander? Would you be able to pull the same trick?"

Neal doesn't take his eyes off Uki, curious to know what she's thinking. Why is she refusing to cooperate willingly? They rescued her. She owes them at least that much, right?

"I don't see any other solution," Sky continues, nodding. "With a little time…"

Uki moves closer to Neal to examine his wristband. She brushes it with her fingertips and recoils at the holographic display that materializes, panic-stricken.

"I don't think it's a good idea after all," sighs Neal, who feels his plan is about to fall apart. He swipes the screen into nothingness and says, "See how she reacts to my wristband?"

"Then, I don't know what to tell you!" Skyler says.

"Chill out, little brother." Skyler gives him an interested look as Neal pulls himself together. "We will find a solution."

However, he is seriously starting to have doubts. He must rely on Milo and Tessa to return to the Sedna and bring back the spare parts to fix the Sacred Fire. It will take longer, but hopefully they won't run into any of those darn drones.

"What about Mom? Were you planning to visit her soon?" Skyler's tone has changed, Neal feels his stomach tighten.

"This is really not a good time. Everyone's safety is my priority. She … can wait."

Their mother. It's been so long. The glimpse he got of her last time didn't make him want to find her so soon. The strange feeling, he had in the days that followed overwhelmed him. Is five years enough time to forget one's own mother so much that she is unrecognizable?

Skyler insists, "Neal—"

In a rustle of fabric, Uki stands next to Skyler and stares

back at Neal. She seeks his gaze like someone seeing the sunlight for the first time.

"*Nakka*. You have the name of a ghost."

"What the hell?"

What's wrong with everyone?

Neal moves away to get a breath of air, but at the same time Dan storms in. Breathless, he says, "Neal. We have a problem."

What now?

Uki's face changes from stupor to panic. She slips between them before they can stop her. That girl is definitely not right in her mind. Skyler goes after her, while Neal follows Dan.

The rest will have to wait.

11

NEAL

"WHAT IS IT NOW?"

Neal is tense. He narrowly avoids a carefree couple walking side by side through the tight passageway leading to the communal area near the entrance to the Refuge.

"What's up with the girl, you mean?" corrects Dan, walking briskly ahead of him. "Did you scare her?"

Beneath Dan's deceptively relaxed demeanor lies a real concern. Neal can't shake off the bad feeling he has about Leander. Are they holding the Mavericks hostage? Will they claim control of the Refuge? The threat is growing by the minute, and neither scenario is comforting. Even if the Brotherhood pulled off an extraordinary feat, they are far from being invincible.

"I think she was scared of you, Dan."

"Well, it wouldn't be the first time," his right-hand replies with a nervous laugh. "Isn't your brother coming?"

"I don't think he wants to be involved in our problems. That shouldn't come as a surprise."

They pass the circular room with the tightly shut round door leading to the airlock, then they arrive where they gathered just an hour or two ago. Dan lets out a grunt to scare off some stragglers blocking their path.

"This place is going to drive me crazy," mumbles Dan as he unlocks the door with his wristband.

When they enter the Refuge's Command Center, discussions are already underway between Fiona, Tessa, and Walker.

"Whatever was on the Sedna is coming for us," says Fiona with a sneer. "Just what we needed."

"What?" growls Neal as he walks over to the screen hung on the back wall.

"See this message?" Walker replies, pointing to the screen. "It means there's an unidentified ship and a breach in the loading bay."

Walker takes off his glasses to rub his eyes. Fiona says, "It's as bad as it sounds."

"Maybe not," says Tessa.

"It can't be a coincidence. Do we have flamethrowers?" asks Fiona, sarcastically.

"Flamethrowers?" asks Neal.

"Maybe in the Paragon's arsenal, but you'd have to have access," Walker replies, dispirited.

Fiona turns to Neal and takes on a dramatic air that borders on cynicism. "Because an army of zombies is coming to our Ark."

"What army?!"

"I was on the Sedna," Tessa interrupts them, annoyed. "There was no one else alive."

"No one else but who?" asks Fiona. "I thought they were all dead."

"There was only one survivor, and she was brought back for her own safety. She could've died otherwise."

"Well, that explains it. She sent them our location. Just great."

"She's lost her memory, so I'd be surprised," says Neal.

"Even better," retorts Fiona, sweeping the air with a wave of her hand. "Everyone has their little secrets. Milo, you, Tessa. That's what I call team spirit."

"Fiona," Neal begins, "I didn't want the information to get out until I was sure she was okay. She almost died."

"There are a bunch of zombies after us ready to rescue our princess in distress. Say your prayers." Is she losing confidence in him?

"Can we get a live feed of what's going on?"

"The surveillance system was damaged during the Ark's takeover," Walker says impassively, replacing his glasses. "I'm sorry."

Neal sweeps the room with his eyes, "Where is Milo?"

"He has his little secret projects, too," Fiona answers with a stubborn look. If she reacts this way about Uki, what would the Archeans do if they knew the truth?

"Dan and Fiona, gather the Mavericks to protect the Refuge. Tessa, you're coming with me."

"What are you going to do?" growls Dan.

"Walker will help us meet whatever's infiltrating our home."

"I'll come with you."

"Who will defend the Refuge?"

"I'll handle it," says Fiona. Sofia Reyes's daughter really has inherited her mother's fearlessness and her … unpredictability.

"Fiona—"

"I'll fetch Milo to lend a hand," she says confidently, all animosity gone. "Once he knows everyone's life is in danger, he'll fly to the rescue. Besides, I know our recruits well. A familiar face will make it easier to gain their trust."

Neal gives Dan a knowing look to plead with him to stay.

"Don't even try. It's too dangerous," says Dan.

"I'm not a child anymore," says Fiona.

"Sometimes I wonder."

Before Neal can respond, Walker launches into an explanation, "Our visitors, living or not, are near the Observatory.

They're trying to force open one of the bays that we sealed before the transfer to save the Sacred Fire's energy. I don't see how they could succeed unless they hack directly into the Ark's central system."

"What do you think they are?" asks Neal, clenching his jaws.

"According to the sensors, they're moving. They could be underwater drones—"

"Humans," Dan continues, crossing his arms.

"Or maybe something else entirely," Fiona adds, looking at them in turn. They stare at her.

"What? Those relic hunters' stories are real!" Their lack of response pushes her to continue with a hint of annoyance. "They've found mutant fish before. God knows what lives in that ocean."

"We'll find out soon enough," Walker replies, suddenly livid. "They've made it in."

Everyone holds their breath, as if waiting for a beep, a tremor, or even an explosion following Walker's announcement, but nothing happens.

"Let's go now!" exclaims Neal.

"Keep me posted through your suit's receiver," Walker reminds him as he sits by the control screen. "I'll log in from here."

Neal nods and exits, followed by Tessa and Dan.

"Happy hunting," Fiona tells them in a falsely cheerful voice.

Neal forces his breathing to keep pace with his steps. He glances briefly at Tessa, who has remained silent so far, unflappable. Everyone is preparing in their own way for a decisive mission, deep in their thoughts and dreading what they will find.

They attract the attention of some curious bystanders but do nothing to suggest that the Ark has just been infiltrated. Somehow, whenever Neal crosses their stare, he's reminded that the Brotherhood took their Commander away from them. Should he be ashamed and apologize for the mess they're in because of it?

On their way to the airlock, they pass Derek and Nora who are eating casually.

"I'd give anything just to have a change of air," says Derek, stretching his neck.

"What did you expect? You've been watching too many old Earth movies. I knew it would go to your head."

"What else is there to do but enjoy a few old flicks?"

"There's so much *better* to do. By the way, I've been doing night shifts for a while. Sharing the burden wouldn't hurt, you know?"

"Should I really feel guilty about making up for twenty-five years of boredom? I'm finally getting a proper education about what our world looked like!"

Neal motions for Dan and Tessa to continue without him. He runs up to Derek and Nora, and asks them half-heartedly, "Want some action? It's now or never."

Derek and his sister exchange a surprised look.

"Now you're talking," says Nora enthusiastically.

"Why not?" says Derek, swallowing the rest of his lunch in one bite.

The three of them join Dan and Tessa who are already suiting up. Tessa prepares the airlock, while Neal, Derek, and Nora put on their suits in turn. As soon as he has put on his helmet, Neal lets the oxygen flow.

"It smells musty in here," says Dan with a muffled voice.

Tessa's dull laughter buzzes in his ears, "It's a good thing they work."

"If they *truly* work."

The Ark's disused equipment has never seemed more of a glaring problem. Neal thought it was a problem pertaining only to the lower levels, but it is much more widespread. The Sacred

Fire's malfunction is a prime example of that. At this rate, the ship could sink at any time.

Neal enables the built-in receiver, and it crackles with interference.

"I'll guide you as best I can," Walker says, his voice becoming clearer. "They're still in the bay."

At Tessa's signal, they enter the airlock and are immediately sprayed with hissing gas.

Neal swallows hard. This could be their last mission.

It's hard to believe that thousands of Archeans have walked these now lifeless corridors for over a century. Fortunately, a trickle of light from the helmet pushes back the darkness just enough to guide them. Even the emergency lights are out.

Oxygen hisses inside Neal's suit. As he inhales, his visor momentarily fogs up. If it weren't for the bulky suit, it would be just like their combat simulations armed with their Paragon guns.

There are five of them: Tessa, Dan, Nora, Derek, and him. Whoever gets in their way had better be prepared. The Amaranth is not open to visitors.

"Of all the scenarios we've planned, this is the only one we didn't see coming," says Dan in a dull voice. "Will we ever get to the Promised Land?"

"No one said it was going to be easy," Neal replies, scanning his surroundings.

A week ago, they met here to rescue hostages from Duke Kay's clutches—another moment that could've gotten out of hand, but together they bested the Paragon leader. If that doesn't prove their ability to deal with any contingency, then nothing will.

Tessa lets out a gasp, her face unnaturally pale in the bright beam of his gun. Beads of sweat crown her upper cheeks and her amber eyes are frantically darting to and fro. Neal whispers her name and places a hand on her shoulder which makes her recoil in terror.

"What is it?" shouts Nora, waving her gun in their direction. "Where are they?"

"It's nothing," Neal says, raising a hand. "Keep going. We'll catch up with you."

"Don't mind me," Tessa utters, breathing hard.

"Not happening."

It's been a long time, but the memory of Tessa cuddled up to him when she had night terrors stirs his insides. She never told him about it, but he understands too well the weight of it all.

"You're stronger than you think, Tessa."

"I'm sick of it," she says through gritted teeth. "Will it ever stop?"

Tessa's words ring too true, and the words of comfort die on his lips. If only there was an easy solution.

"Want to go back to the Refuge?"

"No," she answers with a little more confidence. "I need to know who they are."

Neal nods with a knowing look, then holds out his hand covered with an oversized glove toward her.

"Take it." She stares at him as if what he just said was ridiculous. "We are a team, aren't we?"

After a moment's hesitation, Tessa grabs Neal's hand and let him lead her into the darkness.

"You must think I'm stupid," she huffs.

"Why would I?"

"After all we've been through."

"Precisely." Tessa isn't the only one on the verge of a meltdown. Fiona is at the end of her rope, Walker is exhausted, and even Dan is showing signs of anxiety. Wanting to change the course of history is starting to weigh heavily on all of them.

"When I took the Brotherhood on this impossible mission, I

knew it would be difficult. But you can only realize how hard it can get once you're up to your neck in it. No one can be fully prepared for that."

Dan calls them out, a hint of annoyance in his voice. "We didn't want to go on without you."

"You think I'm doing this on purpose?" shouts Nora to Derek. "If you hadn't scared me to death as a hobby when we were young, I wouldn't be so sensitive."

"I have no idea what you're talking about," he defends himself with an even voice.

"Yeah, right," grumbles Nora.

Tessa lets go of Neal's hand and offers him a weak smile, making Neal's heart feel lighter.

"They're about two hundred yards away on your left," Walker's voice informs them, cutting their moment short.

A ringing in Neal's ears quickly becomes overwhelming, to the point where he can no longer hear his own footsteps. A quick check on his receiver tells him it's turned off. Weird.

"Last time on the Sedna," Neal says loudly, turning to Tessa, "you said the drones were making a kind of buzzing sound, right?"

Everything happens so fast that Neal barely has time to register that someone is charging at them. Derek screams in rage and his gun jumps out of his hand like it's burning hot. Dan pushes back his attacker who retaliates almost instantly by sending him staggering backwards with a sharp blow to his head. Before he knows it, his weapon has flown out of his grasp. Tessa and Nora stand back-to-back, ready to fire, but their guns are unresponsive. Confusion washes over them.

The next moment, a dozen ghostly figures surround them, and fighting doesn't seem like a viable option anymore. The strange figures take on an eerie silver glow under Neal's headlight, and he can only think of one thing: Fiona's wild imagination might have been spot on.

"How we meet again."

It's a deep voice, most likely a man's. A figure breaks away from their circle, while the others point eccentric pistols in the strange play of light created by the beams reflecting off their silver suits. The air is supercharged, and traces of ultrasound ring in Neal's ears.

The commanding man towers over Neal and his companions.

"Where are the others?" he continues, agitated. "It's no use resisting."

"Who are you? What are you doing here?" Neal asks, electrified.

"To stop you before you go on destroying another civilization, of course."

The man skillfully throws and catches a metal ball with one hand, and the buzzing sound fluctuates along with it, becoming no more than a whisper when covered by the glove. Is this why Tessa and Nora's weapons don't work?

"*Bror.*" A willowy figure steps out from the darkness. "We should get moving," she adds. "Reinforcements may be on their way."

"Let's go back to the Njord," spits the commanding man. "I don't know what's keeping me from killing you."

"Be careful what you say," growls Dan, still kneeling. "You're standing on *our* Ark."

Without warning, *Bror* hits Dan who immediately counters with an uppercut. The man raises a hand to prevent his lackeys from shooting Dan.

"*Bror*! Enough is enough!" The woman slips between them and brushes past Neal to stand next to *Bror*.

"How dare you call this place your Ark!"

"We have every right, *Bror*," Neal says, taunting. The man has a bitter laugh.

"Who do you think you are?"

"They don't know, Oslo," the woman cuts in before adding something incomprehensible.

"He'll have to learn quickly, because I don't have time to waste with our father's murderers."

The woman utters more unintelligible words, then the man takes a few steps back and hisses, "My name is Oslo. Don't you dare call me *Bror* again."

The buzzing finally fades, but Neal's eardrums are hurting. No one dares challenge Oslo as they are led into the bay. Nora and Derek exchange annoyed looks while Dan wobbles behind Neal, next to Tessa. He must be in more pain than he'll ever admit.

Through the bay window, the sun's rays are dying at this depth which gives a spectral glow to the ocean. The light source here is enough to get a better look at the intruders. They are tall and wear skin-tight bodysuits that are more suitable than Neal's. Their weapons pulse with a strange bluish glow, nothing like the Paragon's pistols. They don't wear lighted helmets but still can get around easily. Are they wearing night vision goggles?

"Are you guys alive? What's going on?" Walker's bewildered voice asks, but Neal doesn't answer so as not to betray the existence of the Refuge.

If the intruders were to learn their existence, they would be in a tough spot. Their only advantage is to know things Oslo and his crewmates don't. If Neal can get them to believe that there is nothing else of interest on the Ark, they might leave. If not, he'll need another plan, and fast.

They are brought onto a ship that is much larger than the Strahls, where several hundred people can be crammed. The dark blue metal glimmers.

The interior of the ship hums, and they take off their helmets in turn. They are put in line and led to a room, without Neal getting a better look at the place.

"What is Thalassa up to?" asks Oslo, his long blond hair shining and his pale skin glowing.

"Thala what?" asks Nora, disconcerted.

"You killed our father," Oslo says, his face tense. "Feigning ignorance will only make your fate worse."

"So, it's all about revenge," says Tessa, holding her oversized helmet against her chest. "What exactly do you know about Thalassa?"

Her question remains unanswered. The girl who jumped in earlier turns to Oslo, "She was on the Sedna, but I don't see the other one."

"This'll make things easy." Oslo pushes Tessa against the wall at gunpoint. Tessa winces, the gun pressed against her jaw. Her hair is spread against the wall, as if repelled by a magnetic field.

"*Bror!*"

"They're about to destroy this Ark too, don't you see, Liz?"

"Where are the drones, then?"

Tense, Neal watches the scene with interest. Who the hell are these people? The only possibility that makes sense is that they come from another Ark, perhaps even from the Sedna. Without Uki to confirm his suspicions, though, he can't be certain.

Dan glares at him so he won't interfere. Tessa knows what she's doing.

"Drones or not, they've broken into two Arks," Oslo says. "It's never happened before."

Now that his hearing is restored, Neal notices that they are speaking with an unfamiliar, rather guttural accent. He lets out an annoyed sigh and interrupts them, "We don't know what you're talking about. Until recently, we thought we were the only ones left on this planet. Tell us what you're doing here or get the hell out!"

Oslo turns his full attention to him and a heavy silence

hovers. The radio crackles, *"Neal,"* Walker's voice rings out noisily. *"I'm sending Fiona and the recruits to get you."*

Just what they needed. Neal squeezes his eyes shut with a sinking feeling.

"How many are there?" asks Oslo, who thunders when no one answers. "I said, 'How many of you are there?'"

The colossus's face reddens dangerously and Neal wonders what he'll do if he loses it.

"Tell them that everything is fine and not to come," orders Liz in a much more controlled voice, but one that betrays concern.

Neal is crippled by hesitation.

The look on his teammates' faces sends a different message: Nora and Derek beg him not to say anything, Dan is resigned, and Tessa … doesn't look at him at all. She's strangely absorbed in her thoughts. Does she have a plan? If only she could tell him what she has in mind.

Neal activates the receiver, and he says, "Hold on. We're on our way back."

"Why did it take you so long to answer?"

"I'll explain later. In the meantime, keep Fiona and the others with you."

"Be quick." The communication ends in a crackle. Neal knows that he's just lost Derek and Nora's trust. At least Dan seems relieved.

"You're not as stupid as you look," Oslo says, finally freeing Tessa who staggers toward Neal. He catches her, but something's off. It must be that strange weapon.

"Are you their leader?" Oslo asks Dan.

"I am," Neal says, feeling the vein in his neck throb.

"Even better." Oslo exchanges a few more words with Liz.

"What does that mean?"

Oslo tilts his head to focus his icy gaze on Neal's.

"My sister believes that you have nothing to do with

Thalassa. I'm willing to give you the benefit of the doubt only if you let us search *your* Ark."

"What if I refuse?"

"We have a guarantee." Some golden-haired guards swarm in and grab Dan, Tessa, Nora, and Derek who are struggling hard. Liz's features tense up.

"I'll go alone with your sister," Neal replies without breaking eye contact. "I wouldn't want to scare our refugees."

"My sister and two guards," corrects Oslo.

"Fine."

"One hour. If I don't hear from my sister, your friends will pay, along with the rest of your lot. I won't hesitate." Oslo's guards escort Nora, Derek, and Dan toward the heart of the ship.

On their way out, Nora says to Neal, "I hope you have a plan."

"Of course, he does!" chides Derek, who brings up the rear.

Alone with Oslo's sister, he grabs the silver suit she pulled out of a large metal cabinet.

"Put this on instead of walking around in your get-up straight out of the sixties."

"For a while there, I thought you were nice, Liz." She looks out the door where the others left a moment ago and briskly rids Neal of his vintage jumpsuit, as she kindly calls it.

"It'll be Eliza for you. And just so you know, my brother has a short fuse."

"Thanks, but I already had that one figured out."

He puts on the suit, an improved version of the ones they have on the Ark. The elastic fabric hugs perfectly onto his body damp with sweat and gives off a cool breath on contact.

"My brother won't be swayed so easily. You'll need solid proof that you're not in league with Thalassa."

Neal has a bitter laugh. "Is this a joke or what? I don't even know what Thalassa is! Why don't *you* talk him out of killing my crew?"

"Truth must be experienced. You can't just say it and hope people will believe your words for it."

She shows him how to control the retractable helmet, which is simple enough, then drags him out of the room where two guards join them. She rushes down the platform to land on the dock.

"For your information, my brother isn't the type to kid around," she says. "He will kill every last one of you."

12

EMILY

It is hot. A blazing furnace.

She will melt if she stays here. In fact, she has already melted, and her limbs are welded to the floor. She is a shapeless mass diluted by moisture.

They pick her up, they put her down. Sometimes she's a flower, sometimes a piece of trash.

Unrecognizable voices mix in a discordant symphony orchestrated by clumsy words. Whistling, mumbling, clattering.

Breathing. Gasps.

Awakening. Emily is lying in the soft bed of Violet's large cabin, with the porthole framing the abyss of the ocean. Some sun rays have managed to break through the water wall and caress her face with their natural warmth. She catches them and bring them to her face, but they slip through her fingers, immaterial, and the room darkens. New energies swarm in, auras that Emily would recognize anywhere even with her eyes shut. Their tendrils galvanize her toes and fingers with a gentle electric current sparkling with static.

Sitting very close to her on the bed is her sister giving her a deep smile, her cheeks unusually hollow. Her face is more haggard than in Emily's memories. Gabrielle strokes Emily's arm, then her hair before resting her head on Emily's chest. She falls in a deep sleep, something her sister would only do as a child. The next moment, she has disappeared, replaced by the timeless face of their mother.

Mom raises her head and gazes lovingly at Emily with a power that rivals the Flood itself; one that could freeze its tides, evaporate its waters, and protect them all from nature's wrath. Mom is the Creator's invisibility cloak. But before Emily can react, her golden light fades, one speck at a time, in a chain reaction that sucks her into nothingness.

No. She went back into the sun to continue to shine.

Dad. Where's Dad?

He is not far from her, sitting at the table overlooking one of the portholes, watching over Emily. The new badge on his impeccable pearly uniform reserved for the highest-ranking officers of the organization tells her he's saved the ship once again. How proud she is! Dad is absorbed in his reading of the Paragon manual, memorizing every commandment of the good vigilante. He knows them all since he updated it himself.

Dad's energy mixes with Gabrielle's and Mom's whose traces are still visible.

Emily is safe. She can return to sleep.

EMILY IS NOT ALONE in this blinding darkness.

Rattles of pain, muffled moans. The desperate wailings make her queasy. Who are they?

"Are you awake?"

A soft, masculine voice, gasping in surprise. Dad?

"Don't do this to me ever again."

Anger mixed with sorrow. A burning aura. It's not Dad.

"I didn't do anything," she utters with difficulty, her mouth pasty.

He brings his face close enough to hers that she can see every freckle on his cheeks and nose in the reddish glow of his fiery aura. His eyes are strangely bright, like great lakes of fire. It is raining with fat sizzling drops of rubies.

"I didn't do anything," she repeats with a little more strength and conviction.

"Of course not."

Milo embraces her, but she's unable to reciprocate. Fatigue numbs her too much. She can feel his feverish body trembling and his rainy cheek brushing against her skin. He sobs in the hollow of her neck.

"I swear I did everything to save you, but I was too late."

The musky smell of anguish is overwhelming which makes Emily unable to sort her thoughts. To save her, but from what? She was with Dad, Mom, and Gabrielle.

"What are you talking about?" she asks, unsure.

"Don't you remember?" he replies, taking a step back. He wipes his face with the back of his hand. The lingering heat of Milo leaves Emily shivering with cold, just like when she exceeds the Ark's mandatory three-minute showers.

"Who are those people?" Emily asks faintly, her mind muddled but clear.

The wails blend into the background in a shapeless mosaic with an overbearing presence. A sea of blurred faces is staring at her in the thick darkness of the room. Through their haunting litany, they draw her into their hellish world. Her heart sinks when the bed dematerializes under her, and she expects to fall at any moment.

"Emily?"

The noise of leather pounding against metal reverberates in the corridor putting an end to their incantation. He has heeded their hungry calls.

Duke Kay steps into the room.

He is holding her mother and sister by the throat, like rag dolls choking on a rope around their necks. With scorn glinting in his eyes, he tosses them at the foot of the bed. He sniffs disdainfully and leisurely straightens the collar of his uniform, where the veins in his neck swell.

Duke kicks at Mom and Gabrielle's lifeless bodies to make his way to Emily, who is gritting her teeth. She lets out a howl of rage that makes the amber lights twinkle brighter, but Duke's demonic aura siphons it all until he glows in an inky blue.

"Who's next?" he says with a toothy grin as he unbuttons his sleeves and carefully folds them over.

Emily is bedridden no matter how hard she tries to get up.

"You killed them," she says in a raspy, almost feral voice.

"This is just the beginning. There are so many worse things than death, my dear." He comes closer and spits, "Bates."

Milo walks out of the room in a rush, leaving a trail of flames in his wake before Emily can say anything to him. Almost immediately, shapeless masses of people stream in around her bedside.

Emily is drawn against her will into a deep and dreamless sleep under Duke Kay's watchful eye.

SHE LETS out a grunt of resignation. The overwhelming fatigue has subsided, but a lethargy tinged with a deep sense of unease … a sense of forgetting something important lingers.

Milo is sitting uncomfortably on a stool by her bed, his head hanging limply to one side. His aura is nothing but glowing coals.

Slowly, fragments of memories float back into Emily's mind, like splinters flaying her skin ruthlessly.

Milo, her prisoner, a Maverick. Freed. She took him out of

his cell, then he saved her from Yasmina's clutches, her former boss with cruel and sadistic impulses.

Emily is bedridden with other patients with varying conditions. Every inch of space is filled with multiple nondescript machines that clutter even the passageway. The patients are crammed into a room no larger than the prison's communal area, where officers like Emily spend as little time as possible, preferring the dining hall. The Ark's endemic neglect has taken hold even in their makeshift ward: splashes of rust gnaw at the walls and dust particles float away like the occasional pollen storm in the Gardens of Humankind. Some patients exchange knowing glances and carry on silent conversations in a mix of inaudible rumblings. Others stare into the void, speaking with invisible beings.

This heat spreads through Emily's every limb as she removes the rough sheet to cool off. An oversized immaculate bandage wraps her left side near the hip. She feels it with her fingertips, for fear of a sharp pain, but feels nothing. She sits up and is out of breath for a few seconds. It must be the medication they are giving her through her IV drip.

Flashes.

She and Milo walking down a stifling corridor. Milo's mocking smile. His enveloping aura. A furnace.

She groans as a sharp headache blooms.

"Are you feeling better?" Milo looks like he woke up too fast. Although his hair is short, a tuft sticks out like an unruly stalk. His features are tired, hollowed out by anxiety.

"I've had better days," she says, two fingers massaging her right temple.

"Dr. Nazar says the next few days will be crucial in your recovery. Don't worry."

Nazar … isn't that Sky's mentor?

Flash. Skyler tells her to be careful. They part ways. They don't know if they'll ever see each other again.

"Where's Skyler?" How would Milo know? They don't even know each other.

"Safe. The doctor said you would feel disoriented. Give yourself some time." Milo acts like the big brother she never had. She lets out a small laugh.

"I must be going crazy."

Something under the stool catches her attention and her momentary joy gives way to renewed anxiety. She remembers her father reading the Paragon's manual.

"My family?" she asks with a lump in her throat.

"They came while you were sleeping. Your sister left this for you."

He bends down to pick up a book from the floor. Emily notices a nasty bump on Milo's head, but he gets up too quickly for her to see whether it's serious. The book is larger than she thought. Her heart leaps when she recognizes the familiar binding. She asks, slightly distraught, "Did you open it?"

Elbows resting on his knees, Milo stands up to stretch before answering, "I haven't had the time yet."

Emily feels herself blushing and holds onto her sketchbook, as she did when she was younger. Embarrassed, she immediately relaxes, aware of her irrational behavior.

"You could've told me before," she says dryly by putting it away on the pillow.

"Don't worry. I haven't looked at it yet."

"You were lucky," announces the doctor with his white coat open, a hand running through his newly gray hair.

Milo gets up and shoves his hands in his pockets nervously, his aura tightening. Emily contains the wave of anguish that threatens to overwhelm her and fidgets with a corner of the sheet.

Dr. Nazar has a dark complexion, and his furrowed brows give him the look of a scholar trying to solve an impossible equation.

"What do you mean?" she asks.

He scratches his forehead with a thumb and crosses his arms.

"Miss Bates. You were in a coma for ten days."

EMILY UNDERGOES a battery of tests that take forever, and then Milo has to leave her alone. He assures her he will return as soon as his important meeting ends.

The initial shock of her coma has passed, and now all Emily wants is to get out of this damn bed. Her notebook winks at her and she grabs it. She looks for the pencil Milo brought her. Where the hell is it?

Freed of her IV, she gets up more easily than she'd hoped. Her neighbor with the graying aura peers at her while she searches around her bed and finally spots it next to the chair. Using her foot, she catches it awkwardly and a derogatory comment makes her stop for a second. She glares at her neighbor and snaps her sketchbook shut near his face.

She may be recovering, but she's not going to let a pervert get the better of her.

Armed with her sketchbook and pen, she shuffles down the hallway, her free hand pressed against her still sore, but sufferable side. The medical staff is so overworked that they don't even notice her walking out of the ward. Not that she will complain, that's for sure.

She leaves the wailing patients behind as she emerges from her fishbowl. Looking at the Refuge's premises, one can tell that the Ark was definitely not designed to cope with so much commotion. The place is sparsely equipped for their urgent needs.

Emily finds a dusty alcove near the makeshift clinic and settles in at an angle, careful not to stretch the sutured skin that could tear easily. How many times has Skyler told her about these unfortunate incidents? She leans one leg against the opposite wall to keep a bearable position.

As usual, Emily silences the passing auras that might distract her, but she fails to do the same with the faint whispers floating in the background. She sighs with annoyance and begins to leaf through her sketchbook.

Each time her eyes meet the faces she has drawn, she feels something familiar, but nothing more. She doesn't have amnesia —tests have confirmed it—but it'll take her days, even weeks, to recover completely. She can't shake the feeling that she came back to a strange world. Milo says it's because they're in the Refuge, but her discomfort goes deeper than that. Something has changed, but what exactly?

She skims over the portraits of her father, mother, sister, Skyler, Chris, a few prisoners, and Milo. Once her brief foray into her past is over, she opens a blank page. Normally, she likes to choose her subject first by visualizing it before even starting to sketch. This time, her brain is mush. No matter how much she wills it, she can't see anything, her mind blind.

The tip of her pen digs into the paper and the bluish ink flows gently, like a leak under control. She stares at the page hoping that her imagination will cooperate this time, but her hand is shaking as she tries to bend the pen to her will.

"Going out and about, are you?"

Her pencil tinkles against the floor. Dr. Nazar stands before her, six feet tall, one hand in the pocket of his lab coat open in an almost delinquent manner.

"I don't know how you do it," Emily comments with a glance toward the clinic. "It's suffocating in there."

"It's not so different from the Ark. A box within a box."

"Do I have to go back now?"

"In fact," he begins, looking around, then giving her a contrite smile. "Maybe it's better to talk about this here."

He leans against the wall. His aura vibrates down Emily's throat and she swallows hard. A feeling of regret washes over her, and the sensation is so strong that it takes her breath away, as if she were in tune with Dr. Nazar's aura.

"I have good news and bad news," he continues, his smile fading. "The good news is that your wound is healing well, and you'll be able to resume your normal activities very soon."

Emily half-hears what he says as she tries to deal with the influx of foreign emotions that overwhelm her. She blocks them as best she can, as she does when she is in a crowd, but the results are not great. She is choking.

"Have you noticed anything strange lately?"

"Like what?"

"Pronounced fatigue, headaches, hallucinations?"

The doctor is trying to analyze her. He must know that something is wrong. Is he judging her? Will she be convicted on the grounds that she is a threat to be eliminated?

"Nothing unusual," she says as she straightens up. The pain is a welcome distraction from the rush of emotions. "Stop beating around the bush. I can take the hit."

Dr. Nazar's emotions jiggle, like a jolting elevator that gives heart palpitations. He is … surprised by her answer?

"Very well," he says, looking at Emily's sketchbook.

It is stained with dark blue ink right down the center, and multiple smudges have spread from the rubbing of Emily's hand.

The doctor continues, "The bad news is that traces of the Syndrome have been detected. An advanced stage." He thinks she is crazy.

"What does that mean exactly?" roars Emily despite herself, her anger enough to ward off the feeling of regret that was about to rain down on her.

"We're not sure yet."

Unsolicited images of Alexander Griffin caught in hysteria flash painfully through her mind.

"What about the treatment?" she hears herself say.

She's crazy. You can see it in Dr. Nazar's eyes. He pities her, and anything she says is worthless to him.

"There is no such thing. We can keep you here for observation—"

"No, no, no. I'd rather not."

She'll never get out of that fishbowl again.

Milo approaches them. Dr. Nazar seems to understand Emily's concern.

"I'll come see you later," the doctor says, getting up. "At the clinic."

He excuses himself, then walks away. Frowning, Milo comes to sit so close that it should be forbidden.

"What is it?" he asks, gesturing to where the doctor was standing.

"Nothing."

If Milo knew she is going crazy, he would never want to talk to her again.

"I didn't know the doctor had discharged you," he comments with a glint of hope in his eye. "That's good news."

"Can you leave me alone?"

Milo's aura connects with hers, and a shudder ripples through her.

"I'm sorry. I didn't mean to … disturb you." Before she has time to take back her words, Milo slips away.

Emily sighs, exasperated. She hits her forehead with her sketchbook twice, then rests her head on it, still reeling from the intrusion of the auras. From the shocking news and from Milo. Damn it!

"Will you tell him?"

Emily's blood runs cold when she recognizes the voice of the man standing near her alcove, which should have been her haven of peace. Philip Farrell. Violet's brother.

"Why should it concern you? What the hell are you doing here anyway?"

"I thought you'd be happy to know I'm still alive," Philip replies, wearing his favorite cardigan over his Academy polo shirt and sporting his pretentious glasses. "Last time we met, we went to hell and back in that forsaken barn."

"Look who's talking! You were in cahoots with those guards."

"If that's what you want to believe," he says, slightly offended.

"Don't tell me I'm wrong."

The barn was only the beginning. Then there was Yasmina's torture, the empty feeling left by her coma, and now … the Syndrome.

Strangely, the corridor has almost emptied, and Philip's energy escapes her. Not that she is complaining. He pulls up the bottom of his cardigan and polo shirt before Emily tells him to stop. Horrific marks streak his skin: They look like the bites of the Paragon's electric prods. The pattern of his scars is not random. Any specific points of contact? Skyler would know.

"What are these … things?"

She cannot imagine what tool or person is capable of such horror, Yasmina's torture room and its sordid display still fresh in her mind.

"I was the object of their experiments."

"You ran away?"

"Long story," he says, pulling his cardigan back on, looking uncomfortable. "Hopefully, you believe me now."

These marks are definitely convincing. He's probably not crazy enough to invent his martyrdom. He may be annoying, but he is Violet's brother, after all.

"You must hide from them," presses Philip by pulling her by an arm despite her protests.

"What for? To go where?"

He lets go at her anger and raises his voice, "Anywhere! Away from the Paragon! Now that they know you have the Syndrome, they will do anything to get their hands on you. To experiment on you."

Emily's brain, still foggy from her coma, is racing to the point where the day's meager meal threatens to kiss the ground. She clings to the edge of the alcove to keep from falling.

"I can't just disappear," she stammers. "My family, Milo—"

"No one will come to save you this time."

A primal fear grips her chest. Who would want to save someone who will die of the Syndrome anyway? She remembers similar cases among the prisoners: Griffin, Reed, and the rest. They were a bunch of weirdos to avoid, the weakest links in the Ark, a danger to everyone's safety. Her former coworker Iris nearly died at Griffin's hands. Will Emily become that kind of monster?

If she walks away from the people she loves, they will be safe from her. Her loved ones would only suffer knowing the truth about her.

"It's just the two of us, then," she sighs, stunned by the sudden turn of events.

Philip watches her with a worried look. He's just as in a bad shape as she is with his gaunt face, his shaking hands, and his hunched back. But it's more than that. It's as if he had become an empty shell robbed of his presence.

Emily gasps at the sudden realization.

Philip Farrell no longer has an aura.

13

SKYLER

SKYLER LOST TRACK OF UKI THANKS TO NEAL'S CARELESSNESS. HE kept her prisoner all this time! What was his brother thinking?

As he chased after her, Skyler found himself in the section of the Refuge dedicated to the Ark's prisoners. Short of breath, he slows down the pace, defeated. Uki went into hiding to avoid returning to her closet. It's not like he can blame her. Neal's incompetence is ludicrous! She could teach them so much about what's going on, about life elsewhere, and maybe even give them a glimpse of the Promised Land.

Chris's words come back to him: The Brotherhood is doomed to fail.

Their quagmire is but a telltale sign. Not only are they trapped in the Refuge, but the Archeans can barely tolerate the Mavericks. There could be an outbreak of the Syndrome at any moment as it did decades ago during Ivanka Torres's time, and to top it all off, their Ark is damaged beyond repair! Without a miracle, they won't come through this one.

Skyler wouldn't know they are keeping the prisoners here temporarily if it weren't for the Maverick warden he saw last time he visited Chris. The cabin doors in this corridor are rusted with mold producing spores traveling through the air, and the fact that the other Mavericks standing guard are coughing noisily is worrying, to say the least. The Syndrome will pale in comparison if lung disease starts to spread. Since they cannot afford to have any Maverick assigned to cleaning, it is only a question of time before a wave of pneumonia affects them.

The warden's sharp look is unmistakable and pierces through Skyler.

"Looks like you can't get enough of these dregs. Being loyal to the old system will only get you so far."

"Say what you like, though I doubt my brother would approve of your false accusations."

"Aren't you the smart ass! Your little visits are a little shady if you ask me."

She's speaking nonsense. What exactly does she know about him? What her brother wanted to tell her? That's the problem with the Mavericks: You're either with or against them.

"You've got guts; it's a fact," she says with a sly smile. "Not what you'd expect from Neal's cozy little brother. He was so insistent on finding you, but I knew he was worried about nothing."

"He sent me to get a prisoner," Skyler says through gritted teeth. "Chris Kay."

The warden gives him a skeptical look and sniffs loudly. "Neal would have told us if—"

"Something happened. Dan came to get him in a hurry."

A coughing Maverick with his hand on an invisible earpiece approaches to confirm the situation. "Fiona is asking for backup."

"That one doesn't waste time," hisses the warden whose expression changes to surprise. She glances at her bag a few steps away.

"Make sure the door is locked on your way out," she says,

tugging the door open. "Who knows? Maybe you'll take over my shift next time." She grabs her bag and runs off with the other Mavericks, leaving him alone. Without a second thought, Skyler goes in.

None of the prisoners are handcuffed and Skyler recoils. Do the guards know?

An unpleasant shiver runs down his spine when he sees Laurene who pointed a gun at him not so long ago. The scenarios he played in his mind over and over to explain Yasmina's death at the Second Officer's hands bubble up. Laurene looks different this time: weary and barely surprised to see him here. She is wearing a strange-looking wristband and reading quietly.

"These good-for-nothings are sending children to entertain us now?" says Duke, leaning against the opposite wall. "Pathetic."

The air is hot and heavy. Duke Kay is still dressed in his almost impeccable uniform, with the collar and cuffs unbuttoned. He rolls the tips of his mustache between his fingers, staring at the ceiling.

"Sky," Chris shouts. His face is tired but relaxes as he approaches.

"I came to get you out of here."

Laurene seems like she couldn't care less, but Duke perks up. "Under whose orders?" asks Chris's father.

"My own."

Duke raises an eyebrow with an amused expression stamped on his face. "As I said, children. Only a true commander can make sensible decisions. To think that the Goldbergs would work with the enemy! I should've eliminated your bunch while I could. Son, your tastes are lacking in the company you keep."

"Better than a father who is a murderer."

Duke slowly stands up and says, "That's not how I raised

you. Even if your poor mother gave you crazy ideas, you would be nothing without me. You owe me that at least."

"Nice try," Chris says with a wry smile. "See you on the other side. On the Promised Land, if there is one."

"I'll remember that," Duke croons.

They are about to leave, but Chris freezes, fighting an invisible pain. "The wristband."

"Let me see."

Remembering the modifications Neal made to his wristband, Skyler gently bumps it against Chris's and, after a few taps, manages to disable it. His brother really does trust him blindly.

They shut the door behind them as Duke Kay watches them leave with a menacing look, even through the window. Moments after, the door rattles furiously with silent screaming.

Skyler presses on as if the cell were going to blow up, Chris on his heels.

"Doesn't it bother you to have a father like that?" asks Skyler when the noise finally subsides.

"Every day, believe me."

Stunned by Duke's demonstration, they walk along the empty corridors without a word. They turn a corner and come across Leander striding along.

"Chris!" he exclaims in disbelief. "They finally let you out?" They exchange a friendly hug, and Chris glances at Skyler.

"Things need to change," Skyler replies, his heart pounding against his chest.

"You're not the only one to think that way. Trust me," says Leander, then hurriedly adds, "You guys should find the others in our group. It's happening now."

"What exactly?"

"I'll see you guys later." Leander smiles at them and rushes over to where Skyler and Chris came from.

"Do you know what he was talking about?" inquires Skyler, suddenly concerned.

"How would I know?" laughs Chris, hands in his pockets.

"I don't know. He's your best friend."

"You can't imagine how much I missed the good old Skyler! Come on! I don't want to miss all the fun."

Chris's familiarity is baffling. For a second, Skyler wishes they could rekindle their old friendship. Not only because they share a common goal, but because they support each other.

They pass a half-open door where his brother and a woman with a strange accent are talking.

"Is this enough to convince you now?" Neal asks in an upset manner.

"My opinion doesn't matter. But my brother will want to see for himself."

"There was never any question of you guys coming here. I thought we had an agreement."

"I told you that truth is a lived experience."

"It's all crap! Just get to the point and stop playing with me!"

"You have a lot to learn."

"But neither the time nor the desire."

A sigh. The woman continues, "You are in no position to bargain. We can accommodate a hundred of yours on our ship. No more."

"So, now you're willing to help?"

Silence.

"I won't choose!" Neal roars.

"Then you all die," she replies. "This has happened too many times in the past. And please, stop pretending. We all know you're screwed."

"These people are counting on me! To abandon them is to deny the very mission of the Brotherhood."

Neal's voice breaks, but the woman continues, unshaken. "If you are a true leader, you will do the right thing."

"They're here!" shout voices near the airlock.

Skyler casts a bewildered look over his shoulder, and Chris urges him to follow. What is that woman doing with his brother?

They join the huddled mass of people welcoming a group of strange-looking guards that do not bear the Paragon's insignia. A tall blond-maned man stands on the landing and only then does Skyler realize that they are pointing sophisticated weapons at the crowd. Chris's face drains, and he casts a worried look at Skyler.

Curled up in a corner, Uki is watching the scene with horror.

14

NEAL

"Henry Wilkins."

Eliza and Oslo watch as Neal stands on the raised platform leading to the airlock, reading each of the two hundred and two names on the makeshift list. In just a few hours—Neal didn't keep count under Eliza's insistent gaze—he had to choose who would go, prioritizing the engineers and medical staff. He allowed himself a few bends so that those who remain in the Refuge would have a better chance at survival, at least until he found a better solution. He settled on choosing one person per family, even if it means splitting them up. This is the only way each family's legacy will be able to carry on.

The thunder of protests and tears that follow each name is unbearable. Neal can almost smell the pungent odor of burning flesh, and his body stiffens. They are no more than corpses enjoying a last breath of life before the Incinerator reduces them to ash. He stares at the names unable to meet their accusing eyes. They were right to doubt his rise to power from the start. What leader would let strangers control their Ark?

Neal could resist, but the truth is, he is afraid. Until today, his nightmares had been confined to his mind; now they have become reality. His night terror is beyond understanding, but the destructive power it holds every time he speaks a new name is real. No one should have this kind of power. It is a sin too hard to atone for.

Oslo's guards must often resort to brute force to bring over the chosen ones. The glint of their technologically advanced weapons is enough to deter the rebellious. At first, some Archeans resisted—Neal himself considered it—but the magnetic field coming off the weapons can paralyze even the most foolish.

Neal too is paralyzed, but not for the same reasons. The Archeans believe that the chosen ones will be mistreated. They don't understand that those who stay will be going through hell. He is breaking his promise to save all of them, and even worse is the silence that binds him from telling the truth.

"Anna Zamora."

The last name on the list. Yet, the room is just as crowded. All this time, he nurtured the hope that Fiona, the Mavericks, and the defectors would come and save them. This small, well-trained army would know how to get them out of this predicament, but they have shown no sign of life. Neal has doomed them all to misery.

"That is all," Neal lets out, swallowing hard. "I'm sorry, but you don't have time to get your belongings. There's not a second to lose."

A familiar figure meanders her way through the crowd still under the influence of the magnetic field. What the hell is Uki doing? Eliza sees the surprise on Neal's face and follows his gaze. She says something to Oslo in their language, then a couple of guards break away to grab Uki effortlessly. She doesn't struggle as they take her away.

When she walks past Neal, Uki whispers, "You are not alone."

Compassion? After he gave the order to take away her freedom? She had her reasons to run away. She even called him a ghost. Perhaps that is what he is: the pale reflection of a man who claims an Ark that wants to have nothing to do with him. He offered them no more than an unattainable ideal, a comforting illusion: the Promised Land. Promised for whom? Not for sinners anyway.

The insults come from all sides, but neither Oslo nor Eliza seem to care.

"We're done here," exclaims Eliza. "Let's hurry before things get ugly."

"What exactly?" asks Neal with an edge.

"You don't want to find out," answers Eliza with a worried look.

They drag him into the airlock thundering with the Archeans' protests. Oslo's guards bring up the rear, making sure no one follows them.

"How can you leave knowing they're doomed?" hisses Neal, who feels rage mixed with disgust plowing through his stomach.

"People will live because you made a choice. There was no other way."

"This is inhumane."

Skyler will remind him of his mistake for years to come. But the worse is the way his brother looked at him… Burning alive like in his worst childhood nightmares wouldn't be nearly as bad. His notebooks are filled with musings about where he saw that steely, disgusted look before it started haunting him in his sleep. But those notebooks will sink along with the rest of the Ark.

At least Skyler will be safe. It could be years before his brother forgives him, but at least those years will be spent together. Neal acted out of self-interest, but his family is all he can hold on to for now.

"And yet, there is nothing more human than to survive, *ung leder.*"

Neal puts on his helmet to cast out Eliza's mirthless smile.

15

EMILY

"If it was your intention all along, you should've told me."

Philip brought her to a buzzing electrical room riddled with circuit breakers giving her a severe headache. Really? To think she believed his preposterous story about the Paragon's experiments!

"My sister was supposed to wait for us here," Philip argues.

"Violet? What would the high priestess do in a place like this?" Emily retorts, her nerves about to jump.

Philip rolls his eyes, but she doesn't care. A sweet aroma of food is coming through an air vent, flooding her mind with syrupy waffles. What she would give to eat a proper meal! She's been feeding on ration food for far too long. Now that her initial nausea has dissipated, she could swallow anything.

"Where are you going like that?" Philip intercepts her with a touch of irritation as Emily steps into the hallway.

"I don't know about you, but I'm starving."

"She said she would be here," he insists, following her.

"It's obvious she's not coming. Besides, the canteen is just next door," she adds, pointing a finger straight ahead.

He nods, and she slips into the squalid canteen where long benches are crammed together, and fishy smells of food curiously blend. Emily can't shake the strange feeling that the layout has been copied from the Sanctuary. Thank goodness this canteen doesn't contain any of those horrible vending machines! Some people would find that annoying, but Emily is salivating at the thought of choosing any food she likes. The selection at the counter looks poor, but she checks it out anyway, hoping to find something nutritious. Her gaze falls on a loaf of bread and without a second thought, she grabs it and starts nibbling. Since no one is here to ration the servings, she helps herself to some soup which tastes not bad considering all those years of gobbling up modern-day oatmeal.

She eats too fast. Her too-full stomach pulls at the tender skin of her wound, so she slows down. There may be no waffles, but there is pudding, which is just as good. She indulges before getting back to her companion whose motives still elude her. The Syndrome must already be running deep in his mind to give him this wacky idea of getting her involved in his madness! Hopefully, she won't end up like him just yet.

The rest of her pudding is tantalizing, but she refrains from taking another bite. Why is it that every time Philip is around, the worst always happens to her? He showed up when she was incarcerated in the park, when she learned about the Syndrome taking root inside her, now with the Paragon conducting their sordid experiments!

Philip is busy inspecting some dishes that have hardly been touched: frozen soups, hardened pieces of bread, half-full glasses. Only then does Emily realize that there isn't a single aura around here.

"Where is everyone?" she thinks aloud as she joins him.

"That's what I'm wondering," he says with a blank stare, worry in his voice.

Screams. A lot of screaming.

Philip hurries out of the canteen, and it takes Emily a beat later to follow him out, dreading what they will find.

"Slow down," Emily says as she struggles to catch up with him, her side aching. "We don't know what's going on."

Philip stops dead in his tracks at the fork when the voices become more insistent, the crowd in a frenzy. It's a rally, and not just any.

"The Brotherhood has abandoned you," rants a voice that freezes Emily in place.

Duke Kay, leader of the Paragon, who dragged Emily's mother and sister to the foot of her bed. No, that can't be true. Didn't Milo tell her during her lucid moments that the Brotherhood had arrested him? What is he doing here then?

There are so many people that Emily can't make out the faces as they merge into a tide of auras.

"Now that those madmen from the Brotherhood are gone, the Ark is ours!"

A roar ripples among the restless crowd. It's hard to tell if they're rejoicing or raging. Emily uses every bit of energy to block out the maelstrom of sensations threatening to pull her into their madness.

"You saw with your own eyes that these rebels contaminated your families. And then, they broke their empty promises to join the enemy. They disgraced every generation that preceded them. Shouldn't they pay with their lives to atone for their sins?"

Emily leans against the wall to avoid directly facing the dizzying crowd. Beside her, Philip's face is unrecognizable.

"My bastard son, Chris Kay," Duke continues with a blood-curdling laugh of contempt. "He disgraced me too."

Sweat pours down Emily's face, and she moves away a little to recover her spirits, but Duke's voice follows her like a parasite.

"He is weak. Our family is the Ark and no one else. I am

your father, and you are my children. All those who oppose the true Commander are threatening to kill our family."

Emily can't take it anymore. She wants to leave now, but she catches a familiar face that leaves her breathless.

"It's time to purge the Refuge," Duke says, squeezing Leander's shoulder.

What the hell is Leander doing there?

Philip shoves her away from the chanting crowd ready to take arms. As they turn a corner, Philip props her up so she doesn't collapse. They pick up the pace, and as the distance grows between them and the crowd, Emily feels like she is emerging from underwater.

"How do you … do it? I mean, all these feelings?"

"You never get used to it," he says flatly.

In the harsh light of the Refuge, Philip is wincing with pain as well. She had been too focused on her own condition and didn't even notice that he's struggling just as much. They can't wander around the Refuge, while Duke and his followers are prowling … not without getting help.

"They're going to kill us," says Philip harshly. "Or worse. They may even have already gotten their hands on my sister. We're done for."

"There is only one person who can help us," Emily says, recalling the distinct warmth of his aura. "This is our only chance."

"What if they have my sister! They have no right! They can't—"

"Violet is stronger than you think," she says with unexpected force. "What would she say to you?"

Philip's face looks like a water-sodden painting heavy with worry. Blotches drip down the canvas under the pull of gravity, mixing into a kaleidoscope of colors.

"What would she say to you, Philip?" she insists, just as

distraught as he is. Talking stabilizes her, prevents her from getting lost in the pandemonium of her mind.

"May the Creator guide us," he stammers. "The Creator knows what's best and we must believe in Him."

"Then, you have to believe it yourself," Emily says with a growing conviction that resonates in the very marrow of her bones.

Emily is not sure if it is her speaking. The Syndrome could be speaking through her or perhaps Violet's wisdom has crept into her mind.

Philip inhales deeply as they sink in the winding corridors of the Refuge in a drum-like beating of metal.

16

EMILY

MILO WILL KNOW WHAT TO DO. IT'S THE ONLY THOUGHT THAT anchors Emily to the path of reason.

The hallways all look the same, just like on the lower levels, when Milo left her, and she woke up alone in the middle of nowhere. Philip is no help, probably imagining the worst scenarios about his sister Violet. Emily, herself, is struggling with her own demons that are taking root inside her. Since her awakening, her body is no longer hers, with this persistent fog clouding her brain and making her feel weak and impotent. Thinking too much about these strange sensations and thoughts will have the better of her.

Milo. Where the hell are you?

The echo of their breath is symphonic. As she crosses a corridor, a magnetic aura bolts, and a new silence sets in. She shouts, her voice breaking. "Daddy!"

Despite the age draining him little by little, she could recognize his ever-perfect poise in a thronging crowd. No one would know at first glance that her father is a man who lost his dreams when he lost his wife.

A gasp of surprise.

The familiar embrace makes her feel dizzy with joy, as if they hadn't seen each other in months. His grip is more solid than she remembers, his smell more pungent.

"Why are you wandering around, Emily? You should be in bed, resting."

"Don't worry," she lies, wanting to make this moment of normalcy last longer. "Dad, where is Gabrielle?"

His face hardens, "We can't stay here."

"We must find Gabrielle and meet up with Milo." She swallows her fear of having to face Duke's army. She doesn't intend to be part of his purge.

"I know where your friend is," he says, massaging Emily's neck, as he did when she was younger.

Emily is no longer a child, but her father's aura is still soothing in a special way, giving her the calm and reassurance, she needs right now. Philip's features also seem to relax, looking almost serene, like one of those marble statues the Sigma Foundation sometimes retrieve from the seabed.

Her father, Jeremy, leads them down the opposite hallway to a slightly recessed room. He unlocks the door, revealing a group of armed people ready to burst out were it not for his raised hand.

Milo makes his way over to Emily and pulls her into a warm embrace in front of everyone. Caught off guard, she doesn't even resist. Milo's amber aura is too intoxicating.

"So that's it," snarks Fiona Reyes from right behind. Her face has changed so much since her time in prison. She's gained weight and is in much better shape, judging by her wiry muscles. She didn't waste any time.

"Emily could've died," Milo says, finally releasing Emily from his embrace. "Everyone on this Ark matters whether you like it or not."

Before Fiona can counter, Emily's father comes to her rescue, "We don't stand a chance against Duke," he says earnestly. "He has the Paragon and a host of Archeans to back him up."

"Not all of them," Fiona says with a smug look, surrounded by a small army gathered in this enclave, pistols at their sides. "I won't surrender without putting up a good fight."

"For now, we stay put," Jeremy commands. "As long as we hold this place, we have an advantage, but we need to get organized, and fast."

"With a high-ranking member of the Paragon by our side, how could we fail?" gloats Fiona, anticipating the fight to come, clearly visible by the tremors of her florid aura.

"Things could get ugly fast."

When Dad goes into strategy mode, he needs space. Emily decides to leave them to their arguing while she explores the premises they're using for the time being. Milo and Philip cast her curious glances but don't follow her.

Their resistance group occupies a repurposed dormitory. The bunk beds have been pushed against the walls to make more space, weapons are stacked in every nook and cranny, and mattresses and pillows have been arranged to create a mat where Mavericks train. The horrors of the last few days have taken their toll, and their numbers are too few.

Emily shudders at the thought of what awaits them. Duke and his mob won't stop until they have eliminated every person who opposes them. Had they all been living under the illusion that the Ark had been somewhat peaceful over the years despite their being trapped? Emily might have believed it for a while, but not anymore. She knows all too well that their differences will get the better of them sooner or later.

Emily sits on an empty mattress stacked with pillows and leans against the wall. Instinctively, she touches her healing wound and winces in pain. Drowsiness gets her at the same time she feels an arm embrace her. Even with her eyes shut, she recognizes the energy that tingles her arm.

"You're going to provoke Fiona's wrath if you keep playing with fire like that," she mumbles sleepily.

"I know how to tame fire. Dan taught me."

"If we get out of this shelter alive, I'd like to see that," she says, happy to put their problems aside for a moment.

"You'll have to work hard for it." In the half-light, the auras have been lulled into slumber to Emily's delight. She looks at Milo and relishes his loving gaze.

"Look who's talking," she teases, pulling Milo's arm away from her. He looks strangely disappointed. "For now, I'd rather avoid another firestorm coming my way if you don't mind."

"I've got to go back. Try to get some rest." He squeezes her forearm tenderly and walks away.

Fiona's little army organizes itself in the second section of the refurbished dormitory, under Jeremy's orders. Emily recognizes many of the former Paragon members as they walk past one of the few lights still on at this late hour. When Dad was nominated to take over the title of Paragon leader, they had supported him, but did nothing when he was ousted. Today, they seem to have regained confidence in him. Will that be enough to fight off Duke?

With her weakened body and mind, Emily is deadweight, just another Archean who needs constant protection. She hates it.

Most are sleeping, but sleep evades Emily. All kinds of worst-case scenarios for what might happen to them swarm her mind, feeding her fear. No matter the outcome of this revolt, her fate won't change: The Syndrome will claim her.

Frustration bubbles inside her. She has gone through Yasmina's wicked torture play and narrowly avoided death. Why hasn't the Creator had enough? Is this the price to pay for interrogating prisoners?

She can't hold back the tears from scraping her cheeks with

shame and desperation. No way in hell is she going to let the Syndrome spoil her mind without a fight.

A familiar presence grazes her aura. Milo? No, this energy is far too cold and distant. Could it be coming from the other side of the wall? In the corridor? It's just a feeling, but if it's who she thinks it is, it could change everything.

In the darkness, Emily slinks to the door, careful not to trip over the bodies and legs splayed near the exit. Someone grunts, and she holds her breath.

"What are you doing?" whispers Milo, who has snuck up beside her.

"It's too hot in here."

He brings his face closer to hers and asks, clearly annoyed. "Why do you always do this to me?"

"What?"

"This! Your attitude. I know you were about to sneak out. I hate it that you never tell me what's on your mind. I spent days and nights at your bedside thinking you were gonna die. Ever since the Sacred Fire—"

"If you want to feel guilty for what happened, that's not my problem."

"That's not what I mean, and you know it." Although she owes him her life, she can't owe him forever. Milo grabs her hand swiftly and opens the door for her.

With a sigh, she pulls out her hand, and he blushes.

"Why do you always have to complicate things?" asks Milo with an annoyed sigh.

"I don't need a chaperone," she says in her defense as she walks down the hallway.

"You could at least thank me. Without your chaperone, you wouldn't have made it out."

She grumbles, knowing full well that he's right, then strides away, Milo on her heels.

"You certainly didn't open the door for me because I asked," she sighs.

"I wanted to go out too, you know."

"Or follow me," she mumbles, secretly happy he followed her.

Traces of the familiar cold aura she detected earlier linger, but its owner is long gone. Venturing here alone is not the smartest thing to do. But wasn't it exactly what she had intended to do two minutes ago?

Milo is watching her with a rueful smile.

"You can't imagine how much I wish I knew what's going on in this head of yours."

"You would probably break into a run," she retorts.

"Is that what you want?"

"Maybe not," she admits, distracted by the etheric fumes that come to her in waves. "Who will open the door for me next time?"

The owner of the aura is nearby, and Emily stops. It's a man.

"Wait for me here," she mumbles hastily to Milo, who decides to listen to her for once.

She rushes toward the magnetic pull guiding her steps and before she knows it, she faces Leander. He has changed much since they parted ways over Mira's dead body at Delta Labs; he looks sickly and bony with bulging eyes. Before she reaches him, he turns around feigning surprise, although he deliberately lured her here. Auras don't lie.

"What's happened to you, Leander?"

"I could ask you the same thing, Emily," he says, his look is serious and determined.

The soft-hearted Leander stumped by his lack of confidence is no more. And to think that he couldn't confess his love a few weeks ago. His pain feels oddly familiar. She felt it too when Mom died. It is one of those fateful encounters with oneself that can go horribly wrong if left unchecked. A spiral of despair that seems insurmountable that pushes us ever closer to the abyss whenever we let our guard down.

"Wake up!" she bellows, unable to forget Leander standing by one of the worst persecutors in the Ark's history. "I was with you when we found Mira. Nothing suggests the Brotherhood is responsible for her death. It could just as easily be the Paragon!"

At the Academy, they were told about a worldwide war where bombs dug craters that swallowed whole cities. Some of the recruits were teenagers when they left. When they came back two or three years later, their faces told a different story. Something irreplaceable had been stolen from them: their innocence. They were broken. That's exactly what Leander looks like—a little boy who was forced to witness the true face of humankind.

"I'm sorry," he croaks, looking torn.

"I am too," she adds more gently.

The Refuge's glowing lights seem frozen in time as if the Ark were slowly choking to death.

"Why do you want to join the Brotherhood? Don't you see that they are the source of all our problems on the Ark?"

"If only it were that simple," she says with a bitter laugh. "But things need to change."

"Did you know that Neal and his gang left us to rot? So much for wanting to save us! That's not what I call change."

"Working with Duke Kay is not the way."

"The Brotherhood killed Mira," he continues, stubbornly. "They destroyed this Ark, tried to kill us all, and tore our families apart. Isn't that enough to convince you?"

"I know you're upset, but—"

"Don't pretend to understand what I'm feeling because this," he says, pounding his chest hard, "is only a fraction of what's going on here."

Conflicting emotions warp his face. Despite her years of experience reading people's auras, even she cannot understand how deep his grief runs. Leander's aura sends a shockwave that makes her recoil.

"I was wrong about you," she says, frightened. "You've always been on their side."

Leander pushes his oppressive aura against her, drawing closer, and Emily steps back under the pressure of his overwhelming energy.

"What are you doing?"

"You think you can convince me that the Brotherhood is what we need. The reality is that you are dangerous, Emily. To all of us."

He pulls out a gun. Fully loaded.

"You will submit to Commander Kay's will," he barks.

"You can't be serious. You're out of your mind!"

A shot rings out. Behind her, Milo came out of hiding and is now charging at Leander like a rabid animal. The gunfire multiplies. Milo manages to disarm Leander by throwing himself at him, and their gunfight turns into a brawl.

Emily panics with the auras crashing around her in a shower of sparks. Dizzy, she runs back to their base to warn her father and the others. No one else can die before her eyes. She suppresses her tears as she hurries down the hallway, shaking like the surprise box she had prepared for Gabrielle's birthday. It was a rare book that Emily had procured by unconventional means. To make the surprise last, she had asked her sister to shake the box to guess what was hidden inside. The excitement in Gabrielle's eyes was worth its weight in gold. She was so happy. She was…

Her sister is standing straight ahead.

In this empty corridor of the Refuge, her sister, her sweet little sister, is also running, to escape an evil that knows no limits.

"Gabrielle!? Wait!"

Emily goes after her despite the pain lancing through her

body. Around the corner, she steps into a corridor that seems out of this world. Vines are coiling on the walls, muffling the echo of her voice shouting her sister's name. Where is she? Her sister can't possibly have vanished into thin air!

Emily freezes. She is not alone. A stealthy presence crawls across the metal, the walls, and the ceiling through the multiplying vines winding around her feet, up to her legs, until it wraps her entirely. Her labored breathing shallows.

Don't be afraid.

"Show yourself," she winces.

I am here.

"I don't play this game!"

You want to play? You should've told me sooner.

The lights go out.

17

SKYLER

Skyler lost Chris in the crowd.

The airlock's antechamber bristles with frightened sobs and loud protests. Those who try to return to the Refuge are called back to order by the armed group blocking their passage. There are about a hundred Archeans—one per family to be precise—chosen by his brother Neal. They will be taken to a safe haven, or at least that is what they are told.

Skyler grunts silently as he struggles vehemently with the bulky astronaut suit that he has to put on. The archaic suit is nothing like the simple, elegant uniform worn by their pale-skinned and golden-haired captors glowing with mystery. Who are they?

They must be connected to the Sedna somehow. Maybe he would find something about them if he had more time to decipher Amaranth's journal. But the most surprising thing in all of this is that his brother has remained silent, obeying their orders willingly. Skyler swears to himself he will get to the bottom of this as soon as he can talk to him privately.

Once he finally slips on the puffy pants, Skyler hastens to pull up the zipper while the others have already started to evacuate. He just needs to pull on the sleeves equipped with over-sized gloves which he must then use to attach his helmet to the metal ring of his collar.

"Need help?"

"Where have you been?" asks Skyler, relieved. Chris gives him an amused smile.

"I'm here. That's what matters, right? Turn around."

Chris handles the suit with ease and in no time, Skyler is suited up to his neck, with the cumbersome tank weighing painfully on his back. Hopefully, he won't have to wear that awful thing for too long or he might run out of air.

Speaking of which… The air is running thin, so much so that he starts to gasp. Already suited up, Chris points to some sort of dial on his wrist. Skyler adjusts it as best he can and gasps in relief when a fresh breath of air starts blowing nicely. He breathes greedily with an awful taste of chemicals in the back of his mouth. How can relic hunters put up with this kind of equipment daily?

Chris asks him if everything is all right and then shows him how to communicate by way of a small built-in radio. The airtight glass helmet wouldn't allow sound to come in other-wise. Skyler gives him a thumbs-up when he hears his voice crackling.

They are pushed along the antechamber with a small group going through the airlock leading to the Atrium. Their leader holds a stick that gives off sparks before turning into a glowing torch that pierces through the pitch blackness. Skyler, Chris, and the rest of the group follow their only hope for survival quietly.

Their miniature sun tears through the darkness until they reach the bay skirting the Observatory. A gigantic vessel, big enough to block out the entire glass screen, is moored outside the Ark. Skyler doesn't know much about ships, but this one looks much newer than the Ark. There are glowing symbols adorning its hull which look oddly like something he has seen in Amaranth's journal, now pressed against his chest in the inside pocket of his uniform. If only he could have a minute to himself, he could start unraveling this mystery.

They board medium-sized ships, like smaller versions of Strahls, with limited capacity, which means Chris and Skyler must wait their turn. Skyler remains on the platform of the Observatory to imprint the strange symbols in his mind while Chris leans against the wall with his arms crossed.

"What?" asks Chris.

"Who could've thought there were other people like us out there?" says Skyler. "They came out of hiding from the far reaches of the Great Ocean to become our trigger-happy saviors. It's quite the tale. No one could believe that."

"Didn't your oceanographer dad used to tell you that life always thrives, even in the most remote places?"

"I'm sorry about your father," Skyler says, thinking about what happened when he rescued Chris.

"You know, he didn't become the leader of the Paragon overnight. He fought his own battle against the very people he should protect. Maybe he got what he deserved."

Skyler watches Chris's silence with respect. He can't imagine how painful carrying the burden of a murderous father could be.

"Maybe I should have stayed too," Chris says in a low voice.

"You're not like him. You could've run away with the Commander, but you didn't. You came to save us. We were able to stop your father because of you."

"Sometimes I wonder if a part of himself lives inside me and that scares me. What could I become?"

Chris's face darkens as they are ordered to board. His expression unreadable, he disappears into the waiting vessel before Skyler can add anything.

THE STATE-OF-THE-ART SHIP HAS A NAME: the Njord. Although its size is only a fraction of the Ark, its facilities are remarkable. There is no mold or repelling odor, and its furnishings look newer and stylish: browns, grays, and whites overlap in the clean fabrics that cover some tables, most of the seating, and even some of the walls. In the quarters the Archeans will share during their journey—no one seems bothered that they have no idea how long this will take—Skyler feels his mattress, covered in a warm, silky pile of carpet-like blankets that have nothing to do with the brutally coarse blankets he's always slept in.

Chris's attitude is worrying. Since their talk at the Observatory, Chris has not spoken to him, not even looked at him, and when they arrived in their quarters, he chose a bunk away from the others. So now Skyler is wedged between Edelsa Harris, the Harris's heiress he used to date back when they were students at the Academy—not because he wanted to, but because their families were trying to match them—and Kahlo White, her new conquest. They are discussing how horrible the smell of musk is and the suspicious exotic material of their bedspread. Between each of her sentences, Edelsa sneaks glances at Skyler who is trying in every way possible to hide from her view and to avoid garnering her undue attention. She belongs to a past sealed shut in his mind, and he intends to leave it to rot.

Skyler walks across the rows of bunk beds, not so different from the Refuge, and stops in front of some glaring paint-brushed symbols on the only clear portion of the wall. Their meaning eludes him, and he releases a sigh of frustration at the growing feeling of being a stranger in unknown territory.

"Feeling out of place?" asks a woman.

She is the same woman he surprised conversing with Neal, her flowing golden hair shimmering like their long-maned leader.

"It's a rune of protection for sea travel," she continues. "You can never be too careful."

"Where is my brother?"

"How should I know?"

"That would be just like him to send someone to run errands for him. Why else would you talk to me? There's not a single Archean who's had this honor so far."

He thinks he sees the ghost of a smile just before she turns away. Skyler follows her out of the quarters into the main corridor which makes a soft hydraulic humming noise.

"You don't look alike," she says in her thick accent.

"Time can do many things."

"It amplifies the essence of who we are but does not contradict it, despite our circumstances."

Skyler frowns, unsure of what she means. She notices his hesitation and explains, "It's not easy to leave the ark you've lived on all your life."

"It depends. The last few weeks have been tough."

"It could've been worse. Much worse, trust me."

Skyler shudders, but before he can question her further, they stop in front of a door that looks like a private cabin.

"In the meantime, just try to move on. The transition will be easier that way."

The door opens to Neal, and the mysterious woman walks away without another word.

"Eliza may seem surly at first, but she's reasonable," says Neal, leaning against the frame, his hands in his pockets. "She's the reason why we didn't get wiped out by her brother Oslo."

Skyler walks stiffly into the well-stocked private cabin equipped with runes, cushions, a thick mattress, canned food, and even a bottle of alcohol. While the Archeans are squeezed into a cramped dormitory and agonize over their families left behind on the Ark, their supposed commander isolates himself in more-than-better conditions. He even brought a bag full of his belongings. It's a shame knowing the Archeans were rushed out of the Refuge with nothing but their clothes on. How is Neal different from the previous commander?

"Is there something wrong, little brother?" asks Neal as he shuts the door.

"You chose them," Skyler says, clearly remembering the discussion he overheard between Eliza and his brother. "What about the others? Where's Mom?"

Neal takes a deep breath before answering, "What else could I do? I didn't invite those people on the Ark. Those were their terms, or we'd all be dead meat."

"The Brotherhood must be here, I suppose?"

"Dan and Tessa only. Fiona, Milo, and Walker stayed in the Refuge. Do you really think I'm that selfish?"

"I wonder."

"Why don't you listen to me for once!"

Skyler swallows his pride, his jaws clenched.

"They suspect us of murdering the people on the Sedna. I did everything I could to prove our innocence," says Neal. "Anyone could be a commander if it was that easy, you know."

"And you trust them although they were intent on killing us off?"

"Why weren't you by my side when I needed you?"

Skyler had gone to find Chris in hopes of changing things their way. Have they already missed their chance?

"Sky, you belong by my side."

"Sorry, but I'm not interested."

"For someone who isn't, I find you very critical of my decisions."

Skyler lets out a mock laugh. "We seek very different things."

"We're a family, Skyler. The Goldbergs. If that's not worth anything to you, then nothing will be."

With their father's death and their mother still in the Refuge, they might as well say their family is a thing of the past.

"Times are changing. So should you," adds Neal.

"You mean you had every right to kill Dad and leave Mom behind?"

Neal becomes livid, but his rage is cooled off by a blaring alarm. Harnessed benches fly out of the cabin walls. Great! Exactly what they needed.

Skyler is still struggling with the straps when the turbulence kicks in.

"We'll go back for the others," Neal says as the vessel shudders. "I give you, my word."

18

SKYLER

His first rays of sunshine...

It took three days of uncomfortable travel to finally get answers to his questions.

The artificial sun of the Gardens of Humankind is no match for this light ball that floats in the middle of the sky and pierces through the glass barrier between them and the outside world. He feels like his chrysanthemums basking under the sun lamps. The skin of his face tingles, and at this very moment, he can imagine what a flower feels like in photosynthesis.

He would like to stay longer, but Oslo and his sister Eliza's guards urge them to hurry down a passage skirting a snowy mountainside. A cloud of condensation forms with each exhale when the sun sinks behind the rocky wall towering over them. Skyler can feel the skin of his face tightening in this cave-like den as a hush of gasps slowly takes over the throng of Archeans. Skyler cannot tell whether they feel joy, sorrow, or relief at the sight, but he knows he has waited for this moment all his life and hoped for this chance with all his soul. Then why can't he feel anything but an eerie calm?

One side of the passageway opens onto a snowy plain that

sparkles for miles. A domed structure is nestled in the mountain range that extends into the horizon. From this angle, the sun is partially covered by the snowy peaks, and the earlier heat is fading into memory.

Tessa is shuffling along, gazing at the sky, and Skyler slows to a crawl. They haven't spoken to each other since their mission on the Sedna and blaming it on the lack of time would be a lame excuse.

"Where are you?" she mumbles, her breath fogging up the glass. "For years, I knew what to do, but now… I just don't know anymore. I need you."

"You mean Zack?"

Tessa catches his arm with surprising strength. "How do you know this name?"

"You mentioned it before. I mean, I think so."

It was during their foray into the in betweens when they fell into the ventilation system of the Gardens and inadvertently inhaled toxic fumes. That name … had he just imagined it?

A group of Mavericks casts them curious glances. Neal breaks away from the pack to join them. "Let's stick together. We have enough problems as it is."

Tessa avoids Skyler's gaze, then her trembling hand finally relaxes. She walks along with the Mavericks without another word, but Neal stays behind.

"So long as we don't know if these people are friends or foes, I feel more secure knowing you stick by my side, little brother."

"I do very well on my own. Isn't that what I've been doing for the last five years?" Skyler stares at the dome looming over them. Neal finally lets out a sigh before leaving him alone.

As they reach the main dome, the glass wall gives off enough heat to warm up the air of the man-made tunnel. Dylan, their father, would have understood this marvel of technology. But Skyler's mind drifts away as he ponders about the Njord that carried them across an ocean. How did these people survive the Flood?

"This is North Star, our base. The glass creates a greenhouse effect that serves not only as a heating system but also as a source of renewable energy to power the entire base," Eliza explains to Skyler, who stopped briefly to touch the glass.

As he passes by, Oslo casts a disapproving glance at his sister and moves along toward the dome.

"It's so cold in here," says Edelsa, the Harris's heiress.

"Believe me, it's much colder outside. In the winter months, however, we must rely on geothermal energy, the natural heat coming off the ground. The daylight hours in the northern hemisphere are extremely short and otherwise insufficient to power the base. These months are the most difficult, but there is no need to worry. There are still several months of fall to enjoy."

"I can warm you up," whispers Kahlo White, and Edelsa blushes when she casually meets Skyler's eyes.

The dome is abuzz with life like a beating heart, as vendors haggle over the day's finds displayed in rows of open crates. The market could pass for the Ark's relic hunts were it not for the exotic goods: branches, thorns, oils, fish, clothing made of the same material as the Njord's bedspreads, metal pieces of every shape, carved wooden objects, crushed blocks of a gritty whitish stone, and countless other knickknacks. Skyler's ignorance pains him as he realizes he has no idea how most of those objects can be used.

As they make their way through the hagglers, the hubbub dies down to hushed whispers. The onlookers peer at them, their features so varied that Skyler has trouble noting their differences. The entire world seems to be gathered under the cover of this dome, a world no bigger than their Ark.

He would like to stay longer, but their escort tightens up and takes them out of the dome into a room inside the mountain on the edge of the Star's center.

The echoes of their footsteps and the dull hissing of their breath contrast with the hum of the dome. Here, everything is narrower. Some passages are reminders of some remote in between Skyler and his brother never ventured in, for fear of not being able to get out.

A choking feeling just like in the Refuge grips his chest as they file through a tunnel that looks every bit like a quarantine area they used once during a pneumonia outbreak on the Ark. Skyler couldn't have been more than seven years old at the time, and they'd been pulled out of the Academy temporarily while recovering to limit the spread. His classmates had panicked at being separated from their parents, but Skyler had enjoyed his stay and had helped the medical staff, eager to learn their secrets.

Now, their hosts explain that their isolation is only a temporary measure imposed on every new refugee on the base. They make sure to leave out any technical detail, much to Skyler's dismay. A towel is stuffed into his hands, and he is shown to a side room where white steam rolls along the rocky ceiling.

Skyler locates Chris and decides to follow him. They are forced to wear small goggles that obscure their vision, then must bathe in ultraviolet light, presumably to eliminate any harmful microorganisms.

What kind of crises have these people faced in the past? Could there be any other rampant disease around here besides the Syndrome? The old Earth was infested with deadly bacteria and viruses, seen by some Believers as a blatant manifestation of evil. They resorted to unsavory methods to exorcise this evil, which gave Med Bay a lot of headaches, according to Dr. Nazar.

As the ultraviolet light dims, they creep through a new darkness to a door that opens to the outside followed with gasps of surprise. From the cliff where they stand, the mountains embrace the snowy plain that stretches to the horizon and beyond. A steaming hot spring lines the mountainside at their feet, and there are natural rocky pools that the cool wind whips up in waves. The chill doesn't reach them, though, the vapor being hot enough to repel it.

"Not quite the welcome I was expecting," says Chris with a smile. "But definitely the lavish lifestyle I didn't know I needed!"

"No more three-minute showers," Skyler agrees, eagerly taking off his clothes to wade into the pool first.

A pleasant shiver runs through his body, the heat relaxing his muscles instantly like a long-needed balm. Skyler shuts his eyes and the myalgia crippling his limbs slowly drains out as if by magic. Time stops and, for the first time, he feels like he can finally breathe.

As he explores the misty waters of this corner of paradise, soft gravel rolls under his feet and wisps of smoke blur his vision as if he were wrapped up in some sort of giant silky quilt. Near the edge, the blanket of snow covers the rest of the mountain and is peppered with heaps of dark rocks, with the constant bubbling breaking the surface of the hot spring humming in the background. The host of details to take in makes him dizzy, and he must grab the rocky edge so as not to fall. Nothing on the Ark prepared him for this.

Someone is wading sneakily behind him, and Skyler has just enough time to turn around and catch him in his fall.

"Didn't think I would miss the Ark's dirty metal floors," Chris says, leaning on Skyler's shoulder to keep his precarious balance.

"You know I hate that," Skyler says, jaded.

"What?"

"You were trying to catch me by surprise. You used to do that all the time."

"All the more reason," Chris adds, sliding his hand down the back of Skyler's neck, with a smirk. "There's nothing bad about wrinkling your face a little or else you're going to turn to dust at the slightest laugh."

Skyler pushes Chris away, who can stand very well on his own, and sits in an alcove that gives an unobstructed view of the hot spring. Chris is slow to join him with a wobbly foothold, feigning some mysterious injury.

The steaming heat in this winter wonderland is unsettling. Is the hot spring being fed by the belly of the mountain? Dylan used to talk about the ocean floor being pocked by underwater volcanoes ready to burst and eject millennia-old lava to the surface. Their safety depended on the likelihood of a lethal jet splitting through the ocean and melting the Ark in its wake, and his father made sure this never happened.

"Look up," says Chris, pointing at the skyline.

The sky is streaked with subtle hues of orange and purple, the sun hidden by the surrounding mountain ridge. Elaine Farrell kept a painting of that sort in the Sanctuary, but Skyler never actually believed this landscape could be real.

His first sunset.

Perhaps he was destined to go to the Surface. His parents' desire materialized in giving him his name. *Skyler*, which refers to the sky. He always wondered if it was his mother's fantasy or a jolt of his father's scientific mind. Destiny or not, here he is, closer to the stars, about to rebuild a new world.

The celestial hues carry him into the encroaching darkness of the night sky. Snow-capped lanterns warm to life and, from the bottom of the pools, shimmering beams filter through the aquamarine water.

Skyler grazes the surface of the water with his palm and dips his hand in, watching it grow to illogical proportions, but then someone abruptly pulls him out of the thermal bath and shoves him into the snow. The icy cold bites his flesh and takes his breath away with it.

"What the hell is wrong with you?" gasps Skyler, blanketed in snow.

"Can't you feel the cleansing power of the eternal snows?"

chuckles Chris, who adds to Skyler's glare, "Seems like this is a tradition here. Look around you."

A peal of laughter spreads among the Archeans as they roll around in the snow, something Skyler can't remember hearing since childhood.

"You haven't lost your talent for making up stories," says Skyler with a hint of annoyance.

"I hate it when you scowl at me like that. Considering I've saved your life more times than anyone else alive, you should trust me completely."

Smirking, Skyler pushes Chris in turn, and they mingle with the others in a wave of euphoria. Snow flutters in the wind and joyful shouts ring out in the night air.

When their skin is reddened by the bitter cold and their breath runs short, they sink into the comfort of the thermal baths. Skyler relishes in the combined effect of the cold and heat that swiftly induces a sense of deep calm. He dips his head into the water to rinse off, then wipes his face. From the entrance of the mountain, Eliza is waving at him before walking over the snowy path.

"Your new girlfriend is on her way," Chris notes mockingly under Skyler's glare.

"I don't want to hear any more of your drivel."

"Is everything okay?" puffs Eliza in a clear voice.

"Living a dream," says Chris. "That is, if you can read between Skyler's frowns."

Eliza lets out a frank laugh.

"No one can resist the baths, not even my brother Oslo," she says, glancing toward a misty section. "Cleansing off our past is a must to live under the stars. Life on the arks is anything but merry."

"Under the stars?" asks Skyler.

"They watch over us," she answers, pointing up, "but we must be able to receive their light. They've witnessed *Ulykke* and know better. This new life we have here feels like a kind of test. You'll learn soon enough that this world is not ready to receive us."

Even though Eliza speaks an arcane language imbued with heathen mythology, Skyler can grasp in a way he cannot explain.

"A wound that can't seem to heal," he says.

She nods, then hastily adds, "Are you a doctor?"

"In the flesh," Chris replies, taking Skyler by the shoulders.

"The last I heard, you are a doctor as well," says Skyler.

"Have you already forgotten my tutelage with the Second Officer?"

"You won't get away with it this time," retorts Skyler, who stresses to Eliza, "He's a doctor."

"Even better," she exclaims, clapping her hands. "I have a favor to ask of you. Don't worry! You'll be rewarded for your effort."

Eliza rushes toward the mountain's gaping entrance, urging them to hurry. Chris says in a falsely cheerful tone, "So much for my vacation."

Skyler looks on enviously as a group of Archeans are having fun swimming over a gushing stream of water that sprays on and off.

"I wonder what our reward will be," says Chris as they wade out of the hot tub. "If this spa seems mundane to them, I can't imagine what else they have here."

"Don't get too many ideas."

"You don't even know what I'm thinking!"

"Well, then, enlighten me."

Chris stares at him with a half-smile, like it is the most absurd thing. "You're not ready for this."

Archeans are sipping their drinks out of large mugs, sitting in a steaming antechamber filled with a strong aroma that reminds Skyler of Elaine Farrell's ingrained habit of smoking the Ark's Sanctuary with sage. The smell is less enticing here, woodsier, perhaps a blend of essential oils extracted from the local flora. Some unique species might freeze under the snow cover, but when spring comes, they will surely bloom once more. Owning a decent natural garden would be such a relief after having to put up with the Ark's inhospitable environment for all these years.

"After a thermal bath, *akav* clears the mind," Eliza explains as she watches them dress in simple cream-colored clothes. "There would be too much interference otherwise."

Chris grabs a cup, but Eliza takes it back swiftly.

"It would be better to wait a little, *after* you help me. If our resources weren't so limited since our last operation, I wouldn't rush you, but—"

"What operation exactly?" asks Chris, who is in no hurry to leave.

"*Alt til sin tid i rett tid,*" Eliza dodges while fidgeting nervously with something in her pocket. Her face bathes in a warm light as she says, "The translation escapes me, but here we believe that everything happens at the right time."

Some mysterious wisdom permeates Eliza's soft and gentle words. Isn't this exactly what happened? Their timely arrival on the Amaranth couldn't have been a coincidence.

"Anyway, we'll get a chance to talk more," she adds, setting the cup where Chris took it. "The clinic is this way."

Chris gives him an unreadable sideways look. Does it have something to do with Eliza? Before he can say anything, Chris follows her. They retrace their steps in the passage carved in the mountain's underbelly and emerge in the hushed dome washed with moonlight.

"Where is everyone?" asks Skyler.

"The curfew." Eliza strides across the empty stalls with a skyward glance. "The sun is timid around these parts."

The wing that houses the clinic is partially glassed, mostly sheltered by the hillside, and withdrawn from the main center of activity. The starry sky twinkles as they arrive, and Skyler cranes his neck to marvel at the splash of colors. Eliza's frantic voice brings his stargazing to a swift end.

"*Er de fremdeles våken?*"

"*Noen av dem.*"

Eliza's features deepen when she turns to Chris and Skyler, "Rolf will explain. My brother is waiting for me, but I'll check on you later. *Tusen takk!*"

Eliza slips away, leaving an underage boy, who should be studying at the Academy, with them.

"They've been on oxygen for several days, but without a doctor to treat them, we're just putting off the inevitable."

"Where are they?" asks Skyler, surprised by his keen observation.

"This way."

Rolf's blond curls bounce as he leads them into a room where makeshift beds line up, a sharp contrast with the newer facilities the rest of the base enjoys.

"Can you save them?" asks Rolf.

"We'll let you know once we know more. Has anyone examined them?"

"Me, but I…"

Rolf fixes his gaze on one of the victims. Skyler doesn't miss a beat and says, "We'll do everything we can to save her. I promise."

"I want to see," says Rolf. "I want to learn."

Skyler sees himself in Rolf, when he was only seven years old and insisted to accompany his mother to work whenever he was off from the Academy. Dylan had tried to talk her into bringing Skyler along despite his young age, arguing that nothing could stop a child's curiosity. His father had been right. Skyler had found a way to sneak into Med Bay and watch the nurses and doctors stitch and administer injections, until the day he did his first surgery. He would always remember it. When the excitement and fear set in in the weeks that followed, he knew he would never tire of it.

"Get some gloves and syringes ready," Skyler replies with a smile.

"Are you sure?" asks Chris hesitantly.

"We'll need his help."

Rolf mutters profusely *takk, takk*—which Skyler imagines is their way of saying thank you—and hurries to gather the medical equipment.

"Ready to work together?" says Chris, his voice subdued by the hissing of oxygen tents in the background.

This place, with Chris by his side… It all feels so natural. Skyler finally realizes how precious their old friendship had been.

"More than ever."

19

NEAL

Neal is hot. Dan is steeping beside him, his arms spread wide and purring with contentment, looking snug on the rocky outcrop they share. How can he relax while sweating it all out in these baths? The other members of the Brotherhood lay it on thick, even calling it a *paradise*. If boiling alive is their idea of heaven, Neal wouldn't have bothered to chase the real Promised Land in the first place.

He doesn't pay much attention to what Dan, Derek, and his sister Nora say anymore. Nor Tessa, who couldn't talk more than a corpse. They haven't shared a bed in so long that he wonders if it ever happened. Seems like times truly have changed.

Just like his brother. Skyler has been putting the most distance between them since their wholly unsuccessful attempt at burying the hatchet on the Njord. Neal's reunion plans didn't account for Skyler's change of heart about their ideals. He can't help but wonder when their relationship became so complicated. Could the problem have something to do with the Brotherhood? It's a possibility, but any bid to make up is doomed unless Skyler opens up to him.

He hits the water which splashes on Nora's face.

"What's gotten into you?" she snaps. A spray of water hits Neal, and his hair drips onto his glistening tattoos.

"Are you guys done vacationing?" says Derek, who is not the type to meddle. "Doesn't anyone feel ashamed about taking it easy while our people are dying?"

The unease spreads. Neal blames himself even more, even though he knows he had no other choice. Walker, Milo, Fiona, and her mother Sofia will find a way to keep them alive long enough for him to come up with a new plan. But for that, he'll need everyone.

"It's not an ideal situation, I know, but we'll have to make do for now," Neal says despite the look of disagreement on their faces. How he wishes he could hide in that goddamn steam!

"Can't say it's our best shot," says Dan, smoothing his splash-wet beard. "But for now, it'll have to do."

Nora responds testily, "I thought the Brotherhood was more than that. More than all of us. You speak like the other Archeans have no say in the matter. How is that different from that good old Commander?"

Neal steals a glance at Tessa who stays silent, brooding over some impenetrable thoughts. "Tessa, it'd be nice to have your opinion for once."

She raises her head to look at them in turn, immersed up to her shoulders.

"I don't think my opinion is worth much at this point. The die is cast. We need time to come up with a new plan."

"Wait!" shouts Nora. "We wouldn't even be here if I had waited for my brother to come out of his shell and do something with his life."

"Nora! Why do you always have to bring it up? What if I told everyone that Mom had to wean you off when you were seven?" Nora's face flushes.

"I've heard enough anyway," she retorts dismissively and

walks away.

"Where are you going?" asks Neal.

"I need time," says Derek, leaving as well.

Tessa swims away without any explanation, but Neal grabs her arm, the contact tingling against his skin.

"Bad timing," she says, breaking free of his embrace. Speechless, Neal slams his fist so hard that an arc of water flies over the flawless blanket of snow and digs a grotesque gash of meltwater.

"You can't expect us to be cool about the way things are now," says Dan calmly, even in their desperate situation.

"Easy to say when that's all we have left. The Brotherhood's no more."

Neal trudges away with his words hanging heavily in the steamy air, heading for the exit. Oblivious to those staring at him, he picks up his clothes and dives into the dark passageway. He glowers at someone about to stop him and pushes his way ahead, happy to get away from all this crap.

Homey smells soothe his restless mind and guide him through a series of interlocking smoky rooms strewn with cushions. Neal chooses the furthest spot and dries himself with a towel from a pile provided for them. His skin chafes at his rubbing too hard, but the pain is a thousand times better than the pang of shame ripping his guts.

Once dressed, he plumps down on a cushion, crosses his legs, and shuts his eyes like the others around him. Whenever he would get too excited after a fight in the simulator, Dan would have him go through breathing exercises, which is exactly what Neal does now.

The last weeks go through his mind in a flurry of vivid impressions, and he lets the memories wash over him without trying to tease out their meaning. He screwed up in every way.

"Your body is too tense," Dan tells him as he sits on the opposite cushion in a swoosh of air.

He keeps his eyes closed so he doesn't have to start all over again, relaxing every muscle from his shoulders and neck, the tensest spots on his body, down to his fingertips. The aromatic smells overwhelm him to a point he can almost taste them.

"It's not easy for anyone, Neal," Dan says meditatively. "You're not alone."

"I don't think that's going to solve the problem."

"You're too hard on yourself."

"Why do you still believe in me when my own brother can't?"

"Because I watched you grow, and I know what you're capable of when you put your mind to it."

Neal breaks his concentration and moves to stand up. At the same time Dan opens his eyes and says, "Your obsession with your brother could kill you, you know."

"And your honesty will," Neal says with a half-smile. "I'll see you later."

Neal blends in with the small groups of Archeans moving in the opposite direction. They might only be a few who made it here, but it's still a step in the right direction. Unlike in the Refuge where the Mavericks would express their respect, they avoid making eye contact. Neal has the impression they're whispering behind his back and not in a good way.

He should've stayed with Dan. When building the Brotherhood, Dan was the first to join and the most loyal member, even during Neal's search for Skyler.

The Brotherhood will always be his only true family in this strange world. Neal never told anyone, not even Dan, his confidant, but he has no clear memory of the Goldbergs since his fall. Neal's mother was no longer herself when she saw him, but he felt like a stranger returning to a foreign land. Perhaps that explains why he didn't even think of saving her when choosing who would board the Njord. It may seem cruel, but he has only ever cared about Skyler. No one can possibly understand how he feels, much less Dan who grew up exclusively among the Mavericks. Without Skyler by his side, even the Promised Land becomes futile.

They are assigned rooms deep in the mountain which they access with an old-fashioned key card. Neal realizes their wristband doesn't serve much purpose anymore; yet he keeps it as a reminder of a debt to be repaid.

He sneaks away from the pack led by two guards with no desire to fall asleep and wake in his ghastly nightmares. Despite the array of interconnected tunnels, he finds his way back easily using the smallest details to orient himself: the alignment of the walls, the grooves in the floor, even the contrasting smells. Having navigated the in between of the Ark has its benefits.

Neal takes in the dome for the first time since he got here, for he couldn't stop obsessing over his problems. The privacy the dome offers, with the starry sky, the thin shafts of white lights coming from the surrounding structure, and the hush that has settled with the soft rumbling of water cascading down the metal piping, is exactly what he needs.

The gigantic dome is divided into several levels equipped with an intricate hydraulic system and the metalwork is truly impressive.

A whisper that sounds like a whistle catches his attention. A shiver of fear runs through him as he takes notice of Uki sitting a little farther away. She's dressed in her usual outlandish attire, her lips twitching frantically. She is counting her beads, her eyes turned skyward, as if reading the stars. They both freeze when their eyes meet.

She wasn't on the list of people he saved.

THE NIGHTMARES ARE BACK, and this time, his brother is there.

Skyler is bedridden and seriously ill. His sickness is a

mystery, but without Neal's care, his little brother has no chance of healing. He fetches cold compresses and puts them on Skyler's forehead whenever his breathing quickens. He doesn't understand everything Skyler says, but he listens, nonetheless.

Now he knows. Skyler is telling stories from his past when Neal had disappeared; the years of absence left a deep scar. Skyler describes how their parents reacted when they learned Neal was missing: the shock, the tears, and rage. They vented it all at the one person who should never have been blamed for his mistake: Skyler.

Teetering between moments of lucidity and hysteria, his brother tells disjointed stories as an invisible evil eats away at his mind. Neal visits the Chapel to pray, the only cure he knows. When he returns to his bedside, Neal spoon-feeds Skyler, even though he expels most of it.

One day, when Neal returns, a sheet covers Skyler's body. Dan is standing by the bed with a grim look on his face. Neal's rage bursts out as he hits Dan in the chest, his best friend embracing him despite the blows.

His brother is dead, but Neal swears to himself that he will keep him alive forever in his mind and beat death herself if he must.

———

NEAL WAKES up with a bad case of nausea. He gropes around for his notebook, but his fingers close on a piece of wood he found on his way back last night. The panic sweeps him, and he relieves himself in a bucket by the door, the tart taste of last night's dinner burning the back of his throat.

Damn it.

Neal examines the room the members of the Brotherhood all share, his memories coming back in fragments. They were already asleep when he returned late last night.

Derek, Nora, Tessa, and Dan.

It is the wee hours of the morning, and Tessa's bed is empty. Neal decides to go looking for her. He needs to find a way to forget this horrible nightmare, and only she can reassure him when these episodes haunt him.

He meets the darkness of the tunnels and before he can find his bearings, Oslo stops in front of him flanked by a small entourage.

"I was just coming to look for you," he says.

"I need to freshen up." Neal straightens up awkwardly, still restless with nausea.

"We're not savages. My guards will take you to the bathhouse, and you can grab breakfast on the way," Oslo sneers, sizing him up. "You'd better spruce up all right. We've got a lot to talk about."

Oslo leaves him with his two guards who chat him up on the way to the baths. Neal answers curtly, still shaken by the crisp images of his nightmare. What he would give to see Tessa right now.

"I need to see a friend. Could I—"

"It'll have to wait."

Neal bites back a derogatory comment and storms into the baths while the guards wait at the entrance. The water is hot in the large baths carved into the rock of this large man-made cavern, sunlight streaking through the cracks and holes in the ceiling. He splashes his face to pull himself together and puts on clean clothes available in a remote corner offering some privacy. This comes to him as a surprise considering people here don't mind walking around naked.

The guards waiting outside guide him to a modest room that serves as a canteen, but Neal refuses to eat anything. They don't insist and instead take him to see Oslo in the dome, near the place Uki was praying the day before. Oslo cuts his discussions with refugees short to greet him.

"Not too disappointed by our hospitality?"

"If we had met under better circumstances, I might've considered it. I hope our conversation will be fruitful."

"One thing at a time. First, I have something to show you."

To be honest, Neal couldn't care less. The only thing that could change his mind is whether Oslo intends on going after the remaining Archeans stuck on the Ark.

Their group takes a sloping passage, and Oslo is not very talkative, much to Neal's relief. The end of the tunnel leads to the top of the dome, much higher than he had imagined.

A platform with a hole at its center gives an astounding view of the glass sphere and its multi-layered rings that run along the edges of the dome. Thousands of plants of differing sizes crowd each ring with an impressive number of refugees watering, pruning, and picking them.

"It was my father Anzen who came up with the idea to grow our food this way. With so many refugees in a world as cold and inhospitable as this island, we had to find a way to feed all these people. Let's have a walk, will you?"

They descend from the platform to step onto the first ring dedicated to specific varieties of fruit.

"Plants that require more light can be found up here. Each lower tier reuses the nutrients from the previous tier in a complex system engineered over the years."

Normally, Neal would be blown away with this technological feat, but not right now.

Oslo stops in front of a rich apple tree and touches several of its fruits before picking one that he bites noisily.

"When will we return to save those left on my Ark?" asks Neal, on edge.

"My guards told me you didn't eat anything. Weeks of rationing are bad for the body, and every refugee must remain healthy. This is the first principle my father preaches, and I intend to uphold it." Oslo hands him a fresh apple which Neal gladly ignores.

"I don't see how an apple will save thousands of Archeans from certain death."

"I have good reasons for doing what I did."

"If sacrificing so many people is considered noble, people should start calling me the Creator."

"It's not about nobility or any of that crap. You have no idea what lies outside these walls. Or maybe you're dumb."

The guards exchange worried glances, clearly uncomfortable, except for one, who has a beard as thick as Dan's and fixes his stare at Neal.

"Unless I can talk to your father who sent you, I have no interest in arguing with you," Neal says. "And nothing can justify sacrificing my people. My will won't bend even if a monster is threatening to eat us in the ocean, whether it is to save my Ark or to reach the Promised Land."

The many speeches he had to give in the Brotherhood's name come back to him, running off his tongue. If it comes down to fighting their so-called savior, he will do so willingly.

"You've got some nerve, I'll give you that," says Oslo.

"When will I meet your father? Otherwise, this conversation is over."

"In due time. This base will not survive without help. I count on your collaboration and that of your people to help at the base."

"What about the Ark's rescue mission?"

Oslo seems to be considering his request, smoldering. "We'll see if you keep your word. We need each other equally."

"I'll keep that in mind," says Neal, finally lowering his gaze.

"Reidar!"

Oslo leaves him in the lurch with the thick-bearded guard. He looks at Neal with his piercing blue eyes and says, "Can you use an axe?"

20

NEAL

HIS HANDS ARE CRIMSON AND FROZEN. REIDAR HAD HIM CHOPPING wood outside all day, and the fresh air did him some good, even if he couldn't spare a minute to explore the area or marvel at the nature that lies on the Surface. With each swing of the axe, Neal channeled his frustrations of the past few days, a welcome exercise that can replace his sessions in the combat simulator during his time here.

Starving, he gorges himself on an endless variety of food ranging from fruits to vegetables to meat that he suspects comes from small livestock. He would like to see this farm with his own eyes, but for now, he simply wants to enjoy the new flavors. At first, he tasted each food carefully before helping himself, but as the people waiting in line grew more impatient, he picked a little bit of everything, just to see what he likes.

There is too much food for a single person, but he stuffs himself on the potatoes, his favorite—the people around him were kind enough to chat him up and let him know what they were. Despite the substantial number of people at North Star, most of them know each other, except for the refugees who have only been here a few months. Oslo and his gang have taken it upon themselves to rescue the arks drifting in the Great Ocean. This rescue mission would be commendable were it not covering up some other mystery. Some names are whispered like something has happened to them. Since Neal has no choice but to stay here for a while, at least until he can reach the Amaranth with a solid plan and, hopefully, the support of Anzen, Oslo's father, he can only wait. Going against the tide would only drown him.

His meal finished, he leaves the canteen to find Dan, but at the corner of his eye, he sees Tessa going in the opposite direction. He decides to follow her.

He picks up the pace and soon, they walk across the dome to enter the long glass passage they took after getting off the Njord. He catches up with her, but she is so absorbed in her thoughts that she doesn't notice his presence.

"Did I miss anything?" She flinches and slows down only briefly as realization dawns on her face, then resumes more slowly with Neal in tow.

"You could say that," she says.

"A personal mission?"

"I'm not sure. I'm probably wasting my time."

Neal stares at her for a moment. "For someone who isn't sure, you seem pretty determined."

"You would do the same if there was a chance to find our Ark. Unless you've already moved on."

"Is that really what you think?"

"The others have lost faith in you, Neal. You should've consulted us before making such a big decision. This could ruin all our efforts of the past five years."

"Have you lost faith in me?"

Tessa slows to a complete stop. "I … don't know. I don't know anymore."

The early night shrouds them in this uncrowded part of the

base with only the starry sky glowing brighter than the day before to light their way.

Neal takes Tessa by the shoulders and stares into her eyes studded with tiny shimmering stars. She gently pushes him away.

"I hope we can make it through this time."

"What are you so afraid of?" asks Neal. "We're here to support each other."

"You know it's more complicated than that. It's not an easy question to answer when the world is hanging by a thread."

"What are you not telling me?"

She walks on with Neal in her wake. "You wouldn't understand. I don't quite understand it myself."

They finally reach another smaller glass dome housing a lagoon that serves as a docking bay, where the Njord and other ships are moored. The heart of the base is hidden away by the crest of the mountain while the moon casts a silvery glow on the tranquil water.

Tessa seems to be searching for something by the way she is peering through the encroaching darkness, but her words linger in Neal's mind. The Brotherhood has lost faith in him. How could he ever get their trust back? Dan will support him, no matter what he decides, but Derek, Nora, and the other Mavericks who were brought to the base will be harder to convince. He needs to meet with Oslo's father, get his support, come up with a plan, and rally the Brotherhood with the Mavericks, just like he did before. So long as the Ark is not already rotting at the bottom of the ocean, he still has a chance to set things right.

"I knew it," Tessa says as she approaches one of the smaller ships. She checks an illegible inscription on the side of the hull that seems to make perfect sense to her. Her face darkens.

"What did you find?"

"This ship was also on the Sedna during my mission with Skyler."

"Are you sure?"

"They followed us."

"Were the people from North Star on the Sedna?"

"Likely so."

"You said everyone you found on the Sedna was dead. Do you think they had a role to play in this?"

Tessa takes a deep breath before letting out a long sigh. "It's worth looking into. They could pretend to be our saviors to take us out. What exactly do we know about them?"

Oslo didn't give him the impression he expected during their stormy morning encounter. Add to that their breaking into the Amaranth at gunpoint. Without Eliza's help, they would all be dead. Until the true leader of North Star reveals himself, Neal will give them the benefit of the doubt. But something's definitely not right. If they were on the Sedna, why didn't they save them? They seem to make a habit of it according to the other refugees in the canteen.

"This place is crawling with refugees from other arks. What if some of them are from the Sedna?" he muses.

"Discovering their origin would be a good start."

They cast a last glance toward the mysterious ship and retrace their steps in the glowing glass passage. The stars seem to be burning under a green tongue of flame in the most unreal spectacle Neal has ever seen. Tessa also takes notice of this breathtaking view and says, "Will the Promised Land look like this?"

"Do you still believe in it?"

"If this place exists … then anything is possible."

"What if this is the Promised land?"

"We would know, wouldn't we?"

Neal had figured he'd have some sort of epiphany, some deep feeling to be in the right place, but he's not so sure anymore.

"Promise me we'll be together when we find it," Neal breathes.

As they're about to enter the main dome, they come to a stop, and Neal takes advantage of this moment of solitude to get closer to Tessa, yearning for her more than ever, the pain of his last nightmare about to cast its ugly shadow in his mind.

"Why the uncertainty?" she asks, looking inexplicably vulnerable.

"Sometimes I get the feeling that you might disappear without warning. Call it a hunch."

"Does that scare you?"

Neal pretends to be thinking about it, although he already knows the answer.

"Yes."

Tessa smiles shyly, then casts down her look. The seconds stretch as Neal hopes she will reassure him, tell him that he is wrong, that he is imagining things, that fatigue makes him sentimental, and that a leader should not be so weak. But she doesn't.

"You are the heart of the Brotherhood. Never forget that."

She lets her hand slide down his chest with an unreadable expression and leaves.

"YOU LOVE HER."

Uki was watching them from the edge of the dome. Her prayer beads float in front of her with her thumb frozen in motion. She pins him with a stare brimming with curiosity.

Neal lets out a mirthless laugh and glances around to make sure Tessa is gone.

"You're not a prisoner anymore," Neal says, annoyed. "There's nothing keeping you from wandering around the base and forgetting we ever met."

"There's something about you," Uki replies, moving closer to him. "I won't be able to until I find out why."

"Everyone thinks I'm a failure. I built a promising group that could have found heaven on Earth, but now I'm just an opportunistic leader who gave up too soon. Another nightmare to add to my collection, as if my sleepless nights weren't torture enough. That's all there is to know."

"Nightmares? What kind of nightmares?"

"The kind you'd rather not know about. I'm sick and tired of dealing with all this crap."

"I know a way. For your nightmares."

Although he knows it makes no sense, Neal wants to believe Uki might be telling the truth. What if he doesn't return to the Brotherhood's cabin? Tessa won't keep him company tonight, anyway. She's made that clear enough.

"Unless you're a magician, I don't think there's much you can do."

"You just have to believe. Follow me."

Before he can protest, Uki grabs his hand and drags him forcefully into the tunnels. She glides deftly, standing still at times, like she is sniffing the air or listening to some ghostly voices. As they move deeper into the base, Neal loses his bearings and his mind wanders. Wasn't Uki rescued from the Sedna? She might be able to shed some light on what happened! But then reality hits him: She lost her memory. He's back to square one.

"Here," says Uki, kneeling. "Give me your hands."

Neal stares at her, standing awkwardly in the middle of this empty rocky chamber lit by some electric torches ensconced in the walls.

"Why do you have to be so weird?"

"You did follow me here. You're the weird one."

Resigned, he kneels, one knee at a time, against the polished rock with an exasperated sigh. Uki doesn't waste a second and grasps his hands with vigor, her eyes shut. The callouses on her fingers chafe Neal's hands still tender from the cold, and he wonders if she got those from constantly praying with her beads.

"Close your eyes or it won't work," she chides.

How does she know? He closes his eyes. Immediately, a string of images from the last few days populates his mind, with Tessa's voice repeating the same words, "You are the heart of the Brotherhood. Never forget it."

"Your mind is so noisy," complains Uki. "Keep it down, will you?"

Neal lets out a clear laugh. "Don't tell me you can hear my thoughts. Nobody can do that."

She drops her hands abruptly and shifts to get up.

"What are you doing?"

"You're wasting my time."

"Alright, alright! I got it!" Neal closes his eyes again, hoping Uki will resume her… What would he call it? Treatment? He makes a superhuman effort to silence all those voices that urge him to save them. When he manages to enter the same meditative state Dan taught him, Uki takes his hands once more.

"That's much better. Now think about what you see in your nightmares."

The riot of sensations plows through his gut as he conjures up the image of Skyler's dead body, the strange chapel, and his unanswered prayers. His legs are prickling with pins and needles.

"You believe these things exist," she says.

"What? Can you really tell what I see right now?"

"Do you think I can?"

"*You* brought me here."

"Do you think I can?" Her tone is insistent, with a hint of anger and irritation.

"Could you explain yourself clearly like everyone else?"

"You still haven't answered my question. Do you think I can see what's in your mind or not?"

"Yes, yes!"

She pauses for a moment before adding in a much calmer and serene voice, "Then I can."

It's probably his imagination, but needles are tingling every inch of his head.

"What do you see?" he mutters, his face numb, and feeling like his brain is being dissected. A strange impression envelops him and Uki's hands melt into his, becoming his only anchor.

"Fire. A lot of fire burning in your heart. For lost things. It's hot. Scorching."

His never-ending fall keeps coming back to him, with new variations, new details. Sometimes he just falls for hours. As the years go by, the nightmares multiply, the scenes become more complex. The sense of reality is too great for him to believe it's just his imagination. The only constant is those flames. They haunt the corners of his mind, ready to consume him, dead or alive.

Building his new life with the Brotherhood was not enough to free himself. Even being in a completely different place, here at North Star, where nothing around could trigger his memories, his nightmares persist.

"How will this help me get rid of my nightmares?"

"It's a matter of belief. If you believe it exists, then it exists. If not, then it doesn't."

Could his brain have created his nightmares from scratch? When he ended up in the lower levels, a place isolated from everything he had ever known, fear nagged at him for years, not knowing if he would be able to adapt. At some point, he thought he wouldn't ever come out of this mess. All he could think of was finding his purpose. It was his way to stop believing in the lies he had grown up with.

The lower levels also had its fair share of scary stories, like this hungry creature living in a furnace. Of course, it was implausible, too simplistic. As a young man, he believed it was a woman pretending to be a loving mother—the Mavericks were mostly orphans—a kind of enchantress. She would catch any stray orphan and cage them in her eternal flames with her domesticated creatures to keep watch. Some speak of the Sacred Fire, others of the infamous Incinerator where fire fed her to keep her alive. After six o'clock at night, they had to stay in groups taking refuge in heaps of blankets they used as makeshift beds in the recesses of the abandoned cabins. But of course, Neal soon realized that this was just a ruse to have the Maverick children stay in bed and keep them within sight. As he grew older, however, he discovered that routine visits from the Paragon to service the Incinerator almost always happened after six. The unfortunate who had ventured out around these parts, out of stupidity or audacity, never returned. Were they really just stories? Neal had always avoided these places afterwards, not for fear of encountering these fabled creatures but having to deal with something much worse: the Paragon.

Could he have been repressing some rooted fear because of some children's stories? What if his haunted nights were just that, scenes fabricated from distorted memories, a product of living through years built on absurd stories?

"My nightmares aren't real, are they?"

His voice sounds funny, like the one he had when he was younger and all alone in the lower levels. He is swimming in an ocean of darkness where space no longer exists. His mind straddles Uki's like two air currents going in opposite directions.

"It's up to you," says Uki when they open their eyes at the same time without consulting each other. "Do you think I'm real?"

"I can touch you, so yes," he says, the answer being more than obvious.

"Really?"

They no longer touch and when he tries to grab Uki's hand, he grasps at the empty space, as if she had deviated from her trajectory. Is this an illusion?

"I can see you," he adds, standing up at the same time as her, confused.

"Like this?"

She disappears instantly, and Neal feels panic crawling over him, just like when he loses control in his nightmares.

"So, I don't exist," says Uki somewhere around him.

"I can hear you." He spins around, dizzy from the movement. "Shit! You're not real?"

The strange breeze from earlier is coming from somewhere behind him where Uki is standing. How the hell did she get there?

"Tell me how real your nightmares are."

Then she disappears.

21

EMILY

M ILO KNOWS SHE HAS THE S YNDROME. H E SAW HER. H E SAVED her from herself. She can't imagine what would have happened without him.

Her hallucinations are already taking on a life of their own. She expected to see so-called Fairies, not this.

"I'm going crazy."

"Why didn't you tell me?" raves Milo. A gash runs across his cheek, courtesy of Leander's gun.

Milo led her to an abandoned cabin to take cover. At least, Leander's poor marksmanship worked in their favor. She would mourn Milo's death if Leander had had any training. He must have returned to his master like the good lapdog that he is, looking for reinforcements now that he knows their location.

In short, they're stuck in this cramped place.

"How was I supposed to tell you? You think it's easy for me?"

"I thought we were past hiding things from each other. I thought you trusted me!"

"I never said I didn't trust you!"

Why do their conversations always lead to nowhere? The calm collected Milo is what she needs right now so she doesn't fall into the madness gripping her by the throat. Who knows when that thing, that presence, will come after her?

"Is there anything else you're not telling me?"

Emily carefully omitted the strange ubiquitous voice. That would be too much. But under Milo's insistent gaze, who risked his life to save hers, she could bend any second.

He grabs his face with both hands when she finally explains everything.

In the darkness, Milo's flaming aura glows like a burning torch. Time drags on, and then he whispers, "Evelyn."

He lets out a long sigh that expands in the cabin before dissolving into a haze.

"She also had the gift of God. Quite the opposite of what the Archeans believe. They would rather call it a disease. A Syndrome."

"The gift of God?" asks Emily.

"I didn't realize it until it was too late. Maybe I was the only one who suspected it. But one day I knew. It's all in the eyes. I was stupid enough to think she only had eyes for me, but that's because she had the gift."

Melancholy reduces his aura to the flickering flame of a candlelight, the same Emily used to light once a year as a vigil for Mom. Emily and her sister would pray not only to remember Mom, but also to protect their family from the Ark's injustices and its cruel need to rob them of a normal life in every conceivable way. Mom is a martyr who suffered so they could have a place among the last survivors and their treacherous Ark.

Whenever Dad could, he would accompany them in their prayers with warm hugs and a few tears shed. Sometimes Gabrielle would fall asleep before the candle went out, but Emily would always stay awake hoping that Mom would show up. Ever since the auras appeared to her during that first vigil as the flame faded, Emily knew this moment would always be when their connection is strongest. By giving her this gift, Mom made her stronger.

Yet tonight, she cowers. Milo's energy feels different, like a cool breeze that fails to warm her.

"Evelyn could do extraordinary things. She always managed to improve the lot of the Mavericks, to get her hands on food-stuffs in the Ark's restaurant, to steal tech reassembled by the Deltas, and even snatch Paragon uniforms. She would not divulge any details about her so-called personal business, but she was always one step ahead like she could read our minds. I couldn't understand how she could do it. At the time, she seemed nearly invincible. At least that's what I thought."

His voice falters. He looks like he is pondering a perfect painting whose deeper meaning escapes him.

"It wasn't until she opened up to me that I finally realized there are things beyond our understanding. But that doesn't mean those things are bad. Evelyn was a blessing and her gift had something to do with it."

His gaze falls on Emily, but he doesn't see her. He is looking at the ghost of his past.

"I should've known about you too."

"I'm not Evelyn," replies Emily. "My hallucinations will drive me crazy, Milo. That haunted voice is anything but a blessing. It wants to hurt me."

"If Evelyn succeeded, you can too."

"You were simply in love with this girl."

"Are you jealous?"

"That's not the point. She seemed special because you had feelings for her. Not because she had the Syndrome or that goddamn heavenly gift."

Milo doesn't know what it's like to live with this thing inside. It has lodged itself in her head and is taking deeper roots every passing second, until she has no choice but to surrender.

And Milo thinks his heartfelt stories will save her! What other nonsense can he come up with, seriously?

"We should meet up with the others to plan our next move," he says half-heartedly.

His energy is low, like someone who's just been hurt, and Emily's heart sinks. Does he really believe she has a gift, or is it his way to lift her spirits?

"Thanks," she says. "For trying to cheer me up."

Milo hesitates for a split second before heading out of the cabin first.

What an idiot she is!

She follows him out and at every turn, Emily expects Leander to pounce on them. Milo gave him a good enough scare to get him out of the way and think twice about coming after them.

It makes no sense to Emily how Leander found the courage to come to blows. In fact, there are many things about the past few weeks that she never thought possible, starting with her long descent into madness. The question now is not if it will happen, but when.

The Syndrome is a vice pounding at her skull. When Emily has her eyes closed, the presence is heavy and menacing. She can't let her guard down even for the briefest instant. The Ark's carcass hums a funeral song that Emily dreads. Danger hides everywhere, and she honestly doesn't know how much longer she can hold out.

Since their run-in, Milo has turned his back on her, and she wonders if things between them will ever get back to the way they were. Things haven't been easy since Mom's death. Emily's shattered mind has been growing into a wash of sand slipping through her fingers, as she struggles to piece together what once was. Maybe there isn't any way to fix this.

Overwhelmed, Emily swallows hard, her breathing shallow.

"How are you holding up?" Milo asks her, patting her on the shoulder with his warm hand.

"Please be honest with me," she lets out, stopping a few steps away from their destination.

"I always am, you know that."

"Do you really think we'll make it?"

"Fiona and your father have a small army at their disposal. That's a trump card we can't dismiss."

"Can we beat the Paragon? Or even Duke Kay?"

Duke's menacing figure hovering like a vulture around her bed in the infirmary still makes her want to scream. Chris would know how to beat his father at his own game. He's challenged him more than once. No one knows his weaknesses better than him. But where is he now?

"What can you do against the most powerful man on this ship?"

"Have you forgotten who's in control of the Refuge?" Milo replies vehemently. "The Brotherhood will not kneel before the man who slaughtered generations of Mavericks and led campaigns to purge us from the Ark. I won't let him play the same card again, Emily. Do you hear me?"

"But he is the next in line for becoming Commander. You know how the Archeans like their traditions."

"Pick your side. And fast." The metal of the walls is nearly melting under Milo's scorching aura. Emily thought she was the chink in his armor, but oh was she wrong. It was Evelyn all along.

"I'm sorry."

"You're not yourself," he says more gently. "Pull yourself together."

Emily stiffens when he presses a kiss against her lips, a bead of sweat rolling down from his upper lip to meet hers. The salty taste of fatigue and stress sobers her up. Their lives are at stake and at the end of the day, there can only be one winner. One of

Violet's divine proverbs would be welcome just about now. Her friend would surely remind her how mysterious the Creator's ways are sometimes. At this thought, a faint smile stretches Emily's lips as Milo takes her hand.

"You see? All you needed was a little help."

Milo opens the door, looking smug, but then Emily feels the blood drain from her face.

An eerie silence chills the hideout of their little resistance that was teeming with life a couple of hours ago. Bodies are spread here and there, their faces pale as ashes. Milo is already kneeling to check if they're still breathing. Emily doesn't need to ask: his horrified expression speaks for itself.

"I knew them all," he mumbles, choking. "All of them."

There can only be one winner. Emily freezes in place, unwilling to see if her father is among the victims. Stunned, she holds herself against the wall, her breath quickening. Milo crouches, a hand against his chest, his eyes wide. Then Emily realizes what's happening and shifts around.

She struggles with all her strength against the door that shut behind them. Milo tosses his wristband, but she misses the catch. Her knees give out, and her vision blurs. Almost blind, she gropes for the wristband. When her fingers close on a metal object, she gathers what little energy she has left to drag herself close to the reader and stretch out her hand clutching the wristband to open the door.

A cool breeze full of oxygen blows into the room. Emily pulls herself out and takes a deep, rasping breath. She coughs and gasps, and once she comes to her senses, goes back inside to find Milo mumbling incoherently, gasping for air as if he'd nearly drowned. She slumps down next to him, barely realizing what might have happened.

Why did the ventilation system in the warehouse fail?

No one should have been in a warehouse in the first place.

The emergency system would've cut off to preserve habitable areas in case it would run out of energy.

"At this rate, we won't survive much longer," Emily says when Milo has recovered enough to speak.

"They're all … dead," Milo repeats in shock.

"Milo…" begins Emily, but words fail her.

A stormy aura is approaching, but Milo is still in shock. Emily stands up defensively.

"What do you mean, *your sister is gone?*" shouts Fiona in the hallway.

"She was with that damned priestess and the girl," replies a woman whose aura eerily mimics Fiona's.

"And where were you? Still fiddling? Or doping?"

"Is this truly what you think?"

"I'd have to be blind not to see through you."

Fiona points to the duffel bag the woman slung over her shoulder, her hand clenched on the shoulder strap. The woman's aura takes on a scarlet hue.

"Don't forget who gave birth to you, Fiona Reyes," she says threateningly.

Emily's suspicions are confirmed: She is Fiona's mother. They don't share the same features—Fiona's face is more delicate, less ravaged by drugs—but they have the same fiery blood.

"As if that made any difference!"

"You're just like your father!"

"Milo?" croaks Fiona, who has reached the entrance, putting an end to their argument.

Fiona's mother arches an eyebrow at Milo, who's still blue-lipped. Her waxy face melts with scorn when she sees Emily cuddled against him.

"Persistent, aren't you?" says the mother.

"What did you do to him?" Fiona presses, with a steely glare at Emily.

"She might be tough on the outside, but I don't think she's capable of that."

"It's *her*."

Fiona's mother gives a puzzled look at Emily, then bursts in laughter. Why doesn't Milo say anything?

"When you snuck off to the labs with your boyfriend, I wanted to shoot, but my other daughter Mara stopped me. If only you knew how much her tender heart makes me sick. Her father's trait heritage in her is hard to suppress, even for me. But what can we do? We all pay for our past mistakes sooner or later. That's what life teaches me day after day."

"Sofia," Milo murmurs. "Emily has already redeemed herself more than once."

"Don't be too forgiving. Her boyfriend is fawning all over Duke Kay as we speak while plotting how to kill us softly. As for her…"

The mother approaches with nonchalance and an expression of amusement that disgusts Emily. This isn't a game! Milo squirms, but Emily pins him down, keeping her chin up. The auras feel each other's edges, like water and oil stuck in the same pot.

Sofia looks at them in turn and lets out an almost delirious laugh that reverberates against the screeching metal walls.

"You are pathetic."

Emily presses Milo's wristband against the reader. The giggles die down as Fiona and her mother move closer to get a better look.

"Who's laughing now?" Emily says.

"They sure didn't waste any time," mutters the mother, scratching her glowing wrist under the neon lights.

"Who?" asks Milo, and as soon as he gets up Fiona throws herself into his arms and smacks her lips on his. The mother watches Emily's reaction with interest.

"He's too good for you," Sofia says smugly. "Why don't you

scamper off and seek out your boyfriend, huh? You wouldn't want to make him jealous. Men can be unpredictable when pushed to the edge."

Emily rushes down the hallway to forget what just happened. Even the Reyeses, who are Mavericks, think she's just a monster. Nothing will ever be possible between her and Milo. What was she thinking? She was their persecutor at the prison, an agent gleaning information no matter the cost. No one will ever replace her real family, the only people she can trust on this wretched Ark.

The rustling of fabric has Emily stop dead in her tracks. The Paragon.

"Don't kill them right away. The Commander will want to make sure no one else is hiding in the blind spots of the Refuge."

His face is swollen from his fight with Milo, but he is unmistakable. Leander is leading a squad of Paragon soldiers in her direction. Emily is about to turn around, but a bludgeon strikes her hard, and she lets out a scream of burning pain.

"Who else is here?" asks Leander, stepping next to her.

"I don't receive orders from virgins," Sofia says, spitting on the floor.

She rummages through her bag as the Paragon agents look on nervously, pointing their fully loaded pistols in their direction despite Leander's raised hand. With frightening speed, Sofia tosses weapons at Fiona and Milo, who glances with dread at Emily. His aura unfolds at the same time his gun loads.

"Don't kill them! He'll want them alive for the show," snarls Leander. "But no one said we can't hurt them."

22

SKYLER

Little Lola doesn't like her name.

She prefers to be called Rose, which is much more *charming* and *appropriate*. Rose was the first to wake up after Skyler gave her oxygen treatment and a detoxifying cocktail. Benefiting from his experience at the Command Center—sometimes engineers who dealt with the Sacred Fire had similar symptoms—Chris figured out the victims had inhaled a toxic gas. Although he could not pinpoint the source of the toxin, Chris made the connection.

Lola—sorry, Rose—is such a ball of energy with her eccentricities and exactly what Skyler appreciates most about his job. He doesn't merely save lives; he can work miracles. The little girl's story could have ended prematurely, but now that she's out of harm's way, she can move on to the next chapter of her story and perhaps play an important role in other people's lives. The ripple effect this creates is immeasurable. No one can imagine what impact one life can really make.

She was the victim Rolf was staring at with concern earlier.

Rose loves to talk about her family, especially her brother

Leo. She has a family that Skyler envies, the kind he thinks about when he wakes up after a night of challenging work.

Skyler stretches, still wrapped in blankets, while Chris is snoring at the other end of the couch.

Eliza drove them to her house so they could get a decent night's sleep, away from the noisy, uncomfortable dorms they would have to share with the rest of the refugees. A little privacy doesn't hurt. And what better way to learn about their customs than to spend time in their home?

A window covers part of the back wall, and the soft amber-pink glow of dawn colors the horizon. Skyler sits on a cushion to gaze at the silent spectacle. Wisps of powdery snow dance and curl around stunted trees weathering the cold in a barren field. Skyler had always imagined a living world, nature in full bloom, but there is nothing like this here. The birds that should be chirping have flown away, and the greenery that would fortify this place is choking under the thick layer of snow. The mighty mountains of dark rock deter anyone who could entertain the crazy idea to scale them. Skyler and the others are at the edge of a world holding its breath for fear that the Flood will return.

Yet he realizes at that very moment that he could never return to live on the Ark. He would find a way to stay on the Surface, even if it meant losing everything. It is both terrifying and comforting.

The monitor at the entrance beeps, then a hulking figure stands in the doorway. The ambient lighting turns on, dissolving the morning quiet. Long blond hair, free of the uniform, spreads down his back in a torrent of gold, like the honeyed rays of the evening washing over snow. Eliza's brother is much more muscular than any man on the Ark which could only be attributed to sustained physical activity and a healthy diet: two things that were beyond their reach on the Ark.

"What does this mean?" exclaims Oslo angrily as he runs a

hand through his hair.

Chris grumbles in his sleep while Eliza comes down from the upper floor wearing woolen slippers that look like the hand-made socks Jacinta used to knit for Skyler.

"They should be sleeping with the others. I thought I had made it clear about not giving any special treatment to strangers."

"*Bror*, calm down," she says boldly, standing on the last step with her hand resting on the banister. "They saved Marko's daughter and the others who were put into induced comas. The least we can do is give them a warm welcome."

"*Hva i helvete!* Are they doctors? You should've told me earlier, Liz."

"I was going to, but you didn't give me the chance." With all traces of anger gone, Oslo looks significantly younger, almost Neal's age.

"They must train apprentices now." Oslo crosses the room, his mane glistening in the timid morning rays. "If we can't keep our refugees alive, the Star will die. Everything *far* has built could fall apart."

"I know, *Bror*. I'm well aware of that."

Eliza's voice is low and sad. Skyler has been watching their exchange from the dark corner of the room and decides to chime in. "The North Star will not fade." He steps out of the darkness, and the sun's warmth caresses his back. "So long as we're here, we will do everything we can to keep the Star glowing with life."

"This is a commitment not to be taken lightly," Oslo warns him softly. "A generation was sacrificed for the North Star to thrive. There was no battlefield, or shots fired. The challenge was the unforgiving cold and the people gathered under this dome: They are as diverse as the fish that swim in the Great Sea, eating each other. What our colony needs most is people willing to unite despite our differences."

"Skyler's right," says Chris. "Isn't that why you brought the refugees in the first place?"

"Building a colony after the calamity is the greatest challenge humanity has ever faced. Many people are not willing to invest. Life on the arks was just a taste."

Oslo looks at each of them with a brilliant gaze. The badge painted on his long coat gleams in the increasing daylight.

"It's a good thing we know about challenges," says Chris. "Who wouldn't want to see humanity get its due?"

"You should sleep a little more," insists Eliza, looking at them in turn. "*Walhella* wasn't built overnight."

"That's okay. We're used to it," Skyler says, giving Chris a knowing look.

"*Dugnadsand*," answers Oslo with the shadow of a smile.

"Community first," translates Eliza. "But first, lunch."

Her wool slippers rub noisily against the stone floor as she busies herself in the kitchen.

"You're not skipping lunch again, *Bror*. And I could use a hand."

Oslo joins his sister at the pans. Meanwhile, Skyler and Chris head for the bathhouse to wash. Although everyone goes about flaunting their naked bodies, Skyler has a moment of hesitation.

"Don't tell me you're self-conscious," Chris teases him, shamelessly stripping away his clothes. "With everything we've seen in Med Bay, that should be the least of your worries. Better get used to their ways."

"I should've insisted that my brother leave you on the Ark."

"Knowing I was falsely accused, he would've let me come anyway."

"That's what you think. You can thank me later." Skyler gives him a smug smile and slips out of his underwear before dipping into the baths in front of Chris's bewildered look.

After the longest bath they have ever taken, they return to

Eliza and Oslo's apartments amidst the din of kitchen utensils. Lunch is served: an open-faced sandwich with butter, cucumber, apples, cheese, green bell pepper, and an egg. As a bonus, they are even served oatmeal. Skyler can't help but think of Emily, who hates it. But the tea, though, is a real delight!

"You have dairy?" inquires Skyler, who tastes the milk in his tea. "And fruit?"

"It's a good thing we escaped the Ark of Satis in time," says Eliza as her brother eats the first of three plates, a long strand of his hair sticking out of his bun. "The journey was hard on the livestock. Some of them didn't survive. It's a miracle they can reproduce here. Only the refugees knew how to take care of them."

"Why don't you hunt for game outside?" Skyler asks candidly.

"The winter is so harsh that nothing grows out there. Few, if any, animals venture around the base. Plus, the mountain range makes it impossible for our scouts to explore the land beyond," she explains matter-of-factly. "Tell us what it was like on your ark. What did you have to eat?"

"Fish, fish, oh, and … fish," Chris says with a wince, the way he holds his fork strikingly different from Oslo's. He has this peculiar way of sitting upright and using his fingertips to hold his utensil as if attending a royal feast. This is what growing up in the Kay's family has made him, it seems.

"A fruit or two with luck," says Chris. "One time the crops rotted because of some contamination in the water system. It was a terrible mess. Feeding almost two thousand passengers is no small task."

"Two thousand?" chokes Oslo. "The other arks didn't even house half that number. Well, the ones that haven't been destroyed so far."

Skyler swallows hard and Eliza segues, "I'm going to take them on a tour of the base so they can get their bearings."

Oslo is getting ready to start his third and last plate. How can anyone eat so much? All this food is a week's worth of rations in the Refuge.

"Alright. Can I count on you to take care of the trainees?"

"Sure!"

"I'm going to negotiate with this Neal. Though he's got ice in his belly, it's a shame he doesn't know how to use it right."

"My brother?" can't help but ask Skyler.

"Are you related? If so, I'd appreciate it if you could talk some sense into him. He's a stubborn one."

"My brother and I … it's complicated."

"It's not about to change, isn't that right Liz?"

"It's a *daily* struggle," she says, tossing a wool slipper at his head.

THE NETWORK of tunnels fashioned over the years leads them near one of the peaks. Volcanic rock and the occasional iridescent chips shine through like precious gems.

Their climb is slow and painstaking with Chris lagging.

"It's crazy how life on these arks can be harsh on your body," he says, panting.

Without so much as a bead of sweat, Eliza slows down so they can catch up with her. As they finally reach the top, a cold and gusty wind lashes at their faces. A thick cloud of vapor that must come from the hot springs drifts away as a jet that reaches a dizzying height roars through the air like the breath of a dragon.

"My father used to tell me about these underwater gas jets, but this is the first time I've seen something like this. What is it exactly?"

"Skyler is fascinated by just about everything," Chris

comments with a wink to Eliza. "Just let me know if he gets too annoying."

"Oh! This is the geyser of Sindre. I'd suggest you stay away from it. Its waters can burn through flesh in a matter of seconds."

"I know where to take you next," Skyler says to Chris, who looks shocked.

"You wouldn't dare."

"Don't give me a good reason to consider it."

They are standing on a platform with an unnatural symmetrical shape, wide enough for two people to walk side by side, but Skyler would rather file through. With the gusty winds and the lack of railing, the risk of breaking his neck against the cliffside makes him uneasy.

Traces of ancient lava flows ripple across the rocky face of the surrounding mountains that almost look like the carvings of a mad sculptor obsessed with rendering his vision close to perfection. Skyler has never quite understood the subtle beauty of art, and what little he knows he owes to Emily. She used to constantly scribble in her notebooks at the Academy despite her teachers' disapproval. If she saw this scenery, what would she draw?

"It's beautiful," says Skyler.

"Beautiful and treacherous," replies Eliza. "Not only does the mountain range enclose us, but the winters are long and harsh. Though the Star was built many years ago, the warrior's ordeal has only just begun. Without an army and a community that can support itself, we are simply waiting for the sword of Damocles to fall upon us.

"Our refugees will lend you a hand," says Chris.

"It would've been easier if everyone had joined us," says Skyler, thinking about his mother and Emily, and all the others they left behind.

Since coming here, he has pushed his guilt aside to keep

himself sane. If his brother refuses to go back and save them, Skyler will.

"Imagine if no one had been rescued," says Chris. "We wouldn't even be here to talk about it."

"When are we going to save the others?" asks Skyler with an edge.

Eliza hesitates for a moment before answering. "Though my brother is in charge, I might be able to convince him."

"Chris knows who the other Archeans are and their expertise. Having spent time at the Command Center will be useful after all."

"I'm curious how your group managed to settle in the middle of nowhere," Chris says, changing the subject. "How long has it been?"

"The Nords were the first to discover this land by chance. They led an expedition in the middle of the night when *Ulykke* started. That night, a star shone brightly, illuminating this piece of land not found on any map, so they moored their ship to take refuge here and the Star was born. At least that is the legend we are told."

"All this time, really?" wonders Chris, stealing the words from Skyler. "To think that our good old Commander had us believe we couldn't return to the Surface until a century later. It's shocking."

"The arks' true purpose is something we don't quite understand yet. But that could change if my brother stops following in our father's footsteps." Eliza gestures beyond the pathway. "There's a little more to see around here. Follow me."

They walk across the rocking platform buffeted by the wind, its metal structure squeaking and its tiles suddenly slipping beneath their feet whenever the gust intensifies. Chris loses his footing once and barely has time to get ahold of Skyler's shoulder.

"Be careful," Eliza yells across the howling wind. "This platform hasn't been checked for a long time."

The sky is low and enveloping, but Skyler resists the temptation to gaze at its vastness. He watches his step, aware of the long fall that would ensue if he were not careful enough.

The sweeping panorama stretches to a plain boiling with steaming vats of water that form an enormous, half-frozen lake. Unless there are valuable resources hidden, it is a less-than-ideal place to settle a colony. The Deltas' expertise on the Amaranth could help them exploit the land to their advantage and perhaps make their life easier. Isn't it what his father had devoted his life to while studying the ocean floor's topography?

The Star needs the survivors of the Amaranth.

They continue their climb, threading their way between two peaks and stopping several times to catch their breath. The wind gives them a welcome respite on this side with a view of the towering dome, crowned with reflecting sunlight, and the rolling sea of gray that stretches to the horizon, heavy with brooding clouds.

"An antenna?" asks Chris, pointing toward another peak obscured by their side of the mountain.

"*Eyr* has kept the North Star safe since its inception. Its barrier cloaks the base from detection that neither a radar nor satellite can breach."

"Perfect to get away from the arks," Chris says, as he leans against the fence, arms crossed.

"Aren't you supposed to locate them?" asks Skyler, puzzled.

Eliza bites her lower lip as she stares at the sea taking on a darker hue.

"No one knows exactly what caused Ulykke. When our ancestors built the Star, they gifted us Eyr, for when they would no longer be here to watch over us. I have faith they're still watching us even now."

"Ulykke?" asks Chris. "Is that someone's name?"

"Isn't it the Flood?" says Skyler on a hunch. "When the world was submerged?"

"A legend, but it would be too hard to grasp for a foreigner. However, there is mention of the Great Wave. I guess that might be your flood."

Why is the Flood so mysterious here?

"We were taught that the Flood was a divine punishment," protests Skyler. "I'm not versed in the Creator's Sacred Messages, but..."

"You should know by now that it's a load of crap," says Chris. "During my training with Laurene Milcah, some high-ranking officer talked about a rare weather phenomenon. I guess that was just the tip of the iceberg. We'd need access to the founders' records. But who knows where they are?"

"We've come across ten different arks over the years," adds Eliza. "Most of which have been destroyed."

This is not a mere coincidence. Somehow, the founders had enough time to build these incredibly advanced arks before the cataclysm. Their knowledge may have been lost over time, but with any luck, bits and pieces may point them in the right direction. Although Chris dismisses the role of the Creator, Skyler isn't ready to go that far.

"And Thalassa?" asks Chris.

"My brother spoke to you about it?" asks Eliza, her features tense.

Skyler stares at Chris, who never ceases to surprise since their arrival. Could Laurene have let him on to some secret information that he is only willing to reveal little by little?

"I've ... heard stories about it," Chris replies, sounding angry at himself for saying too much.

"Oslo jumps to conclusions to justify his actions." Eliza exhales a cloud of condensation, the sun concealed in the snow-laden sky. "He must have had a field day crossing the Njord with the *akav* flowing. As far as we know, Thalassa is just that, a name."

Thalassa. Skyler gets closer to the edge of the platform and looks at the snow plain that looks duller than this morning. A kind of gray veil muffles the howling of the wind into a whisper and freezes the sea in time. How many other places like this exist beyond the Great Ocean?

Something cold tingles his nose and makes him flinch. Tiny flakes whirl around and crash into his face. Snow unlike he's seen before. This one is more compact, the telltale sign of an oncoming blizzard they used to have on the Surface.

"What if Thalassa is a place?" suggests Skyler, who can almost hear Neal's voice.

"They are only stories our father used to tell us about a mythical place my brother takes a little too seriously."

Eliza's voice dies in the eerie stillness. She looks at the sky and says, "It's time to climb back down. There's still one place I'd like to show you."

"Where it's not as cold, I hope?" Chris blows into his hands as he rubs them together.

"Depends for whom."

They return to the comfort and warmth of the mountain at a brisk pace despite the thin layer of snow that makes the metal platform slippery. Skyler stays close to the rocky wall with Eliza in sight, who looks like she's hopping with perfect balance. Chris follows close behind, his hand resting on Skyler's shoulder. As they finally make it back into the tunnel, the storm rages behind them and seals the entry with a wall of snow. They made it back just in time.

EVEN AT THE heart of the mountain, the wails of the storm reach them, mixing with the smells of wet earth and formaldehyde.

Eliza guides them through a section of the base protected by a security system that combines various sophisticated biometric tests that Skyler has never seen before. Chris voices Skyler's silent questions as to the origin of these facilities.

"The North Star was a military base at the time of the great wars that predate the arks," Eliza explains as she places a hand on a glass reader pulsing with a greenish light. "It is believed that its network of tunnels occupies the entire island, but its security system prevents us from exploring its inner depths. The discovery of this section was a stroke of luck. Marko, one of our refugees, recognized the mechanism of this door and was able to reprogram it. However, most of the tunnels are inaccessible, sealed with an obsolete technology that even Marko cannot understand."

"So, Marko is an engineer?" asks Chris.

"He is Lola's father, the very same little girl you saved. He insisted on meeting you, but I refused."

"Why?" asks Skyler, surprised.

"You'll see."

A mist reminiscent of the Gardens of Humankind rolls at their feet as soon as Eliza unlocks the door. She motions for them to enter first and shuts the door behind via a hidden console.

The facilities are … unconventional. Dozens upon dozens of compartments are built into the walls, each identified by a number and a series of symbols. This place feels like a sinister replica of Delta labs.

"What's the point of this place?" says Chris with a frown as Skyler tries to ignore the strong smell of pickle stinging his throat.

"Our forefathers threw our dead into the sea despite our beliefs that their bodies should be preserved under the frozen ground. But with all this snow and ice, it is almost impossible to do so here."

"You mean all these boxes have people in them?" coughs Skyler.

"Rotting dead bodies, you mean?" says Chris.

"Why not simply burn them in this case? At least they would have some semblance of dignity," says Skyler staring back at Eliza.

On the Amaranth, deadly illnesses can spread rapidly throughout the ship if bodies are not cremated. The principles of the Creator are clear: The soul can only be freed and return to His kingdom in this way or else it remains trapped in a never-ending hell.

The memory spheres do not violate this sacred right, as they keep only a superficial copy. Dr. Nazar and Skyler often argued about this, but Mrs. Farrell's approval finally settled the debate.

But freezing the dead like they do at the Star goes against their principles. Skyler understands Chris's rage. All these souls are unable to move on.

"Wouldn't they have to be dead in the first place?" whispers Eliza flatly.

Skyler freezes and casts a worried look at Chris. That smell…

"For what purpose?" asks Skyler, trying to figure out what this facility truly is. "Their bodies must decompose somehow. You sentence them to a half-life on the Surface!"

"They will find rest one day," insists Eliza, staring right back at him with resolve. "But they have a far more important task which is to protect us all. By keeping them here, their souls merge to create an invisible barrier stronger than anything we can imagine. They inspire, they give us the energy to keep going. This is a place of honor for those who raised us, protected us, and gave their lives so that we could rebuild a new world."

"*Eyr*," Skyler murmurs, speechless, remembering the antenna on top of the mountain.

Eliza strides toward a newer compartment with a built-in stone cast into the metal. A handle reveals itself as she hovers her hand, and then she pulls. Skyler recoils at the same time and runs into Chris whose jaw twitches.

The compartment rolls open to reveal a body bathing in a reeking fluid. A jet of air hisses angrily as the wiring is exposed to the light of the lab.

"Anzen Nord."

With a gasp, Eliza regains her composure as she wipes the thick, viscous liquid from the face of a bearded man in his early fifties who looks every bit like Oslo. He has the same golden hair, even longer than Oslo's like he never cut it. Scars adorn his face, some fresher than others and glossy.

Skyler can't take his eyes off the sapphire-colored eyes that gaze ahead. Is he even conscious?

"Is this your dad?" Chris asks casually, his teeth clenched. Skyler shudders at that, but Eliza keeps a placid face.

"He was half-conscious when Oslo brought him back from his last mission. My brother would give anything to grow old with our father by his side. But his childhood dream ended abruptly when we least expected it. We can only find solace in that Anzen Nord is still protecting us even as his spirit lies between worlds."

Eliza smiles knowingly at her father one last time before shutting the coffin back in a rattling noise that startles Skyler.

Skyler cannot shake off Anzen Nord's face, his eyes open, not quite dead yet as if life were holding on to him. Chris looks troubled and Skyler wonders if he felt it too.

When Skyler turns his attention to Eliza, she melts into the darkness of the room until she disappears.

"It's no coincidence that we've managed to survive this long," she says, her voice echoing. The lights turn on, row after row, to reveal hundreds and hundreds of identical compartments except for their gold plates. "But it comes at a price."

23

EMILY

"I'VE NEVER LIKED YOU."

Leander's harsh words hurt more than she wants to admit. The barrel of his gun pushes against the hollow of her shoulder blades and gives her the distraction she needs to dispel the embarrassment of being his prisoner.

Their little group didn't stand a chance against the Paragon even with the Reyeses on their side. Sofia was the last standing, and she certainly gave those agents a hell of a time. But even the strongest submit when it comes to choosing between life or death. Fear always wins over audacity. Emily has seen the lot of them come and go at the prison. Those stupid enough to ignore their fear … well, they're not here to testify to that anymore.

"Aren't you shocked?"

"What do I care? The last thing I want to do is listen to your moaning."

"If my life was at stake, I would pay more attention."

Emily rolls her eyes to herself because Leander can't see her face from where he stands.

"If I were you," she replies, "I'd just suck up to Duke and shut my mouth. You're not helping your cause."

By way of reply, they hit her from the back, and she lets out a painful groan.

Emily is not sure where they are being taken, her sense of direction unreliable since her mind is clouded by that strange haze that set in after she woke from her coma. The Refuge isn't that big anyway. She'll know soon enough.

The magnetic cuffs against her wrists bitterly remind her of when she was held in the Gardens' barn. The memories flood her in flashes. What fate could be in store for them this time?

Milo and the Reyeses remain silent during the long walk to their fateful death. After the slaughter in the Atrium, Duke Kay knows no limits. He will want to get rid of them, no questions asked.

Emily tries her best to catch Milo, but all she can make out is his unnaturally pale aura. Fiona stares at the ground, her pink aura darker than ever. Reyes's mother, however, boasts this nonchalant and deceptively relaxed expression as her aura shivers with fear for her daughter's safety. She tries to get closer to Fiona by pushing her captor a little more.

The hallways all look the same, but the smells don't lie. These Paragon agents haven't washed their uniforms in a long time. The rich aroma of stew reaches them at last, though it isn't strong enough to overpower the musky smell.

Of course! They're taking them to the Refuge's canteen.

"I hope you like it," Leander whispers cheekily.

Emily is tempted to warn him but thinks better of it. She will need all the energy she can muster in case an opportunity presents itself. Milo and the others might have given up hope, but they haven't heard the last of her yet.

A welcoming committee awaits them: Duke Kay, of course, but Emily's attention is focused on her father Jeremy, tied to a metal pole in the center of the room. It's an instant relief to know he's alive, but they're separated immediately: Milo is on one side, Fiona on the other, and her mother, Sofia, near the entrance. Emily is brought in front of her father, the place of honor. His head is lolling, unaware of her. They probably drugged him with tranquilizers.

"Kneel before your Commander," Duke Kay thunders, threateningly. "Now."

Leander kneels first, then everyone else in the canteen follows in sync without blinking. Have they been practicing? Emily has no recollection of ever seeing the Paragon engage in such practices. Well, the Academy never really explained in great detail how the Paragon works, but for their humble goals of serving and protecting the Ark at all costs. This demonstration of Duke's power must be part of that, but something feels wrong. She tries to read him, but she can't see anything. And then it hits her.

Duke Kay's real intentions escape her because he has no aura.

Nearby, Milo is brooding as he finally kneels, followed by Fiona, while Sofia is wrestling furiously with the guards.

Emily's thoughts are racing. Her extrasensory abilities have become much more sensitive lately. Everyone in the canteen is glowing in ribbons of colors, the same she got for Gabrielle's birthday party. She should have no trouble perceiving Duke's aura then. Something's not right.

"Yes, even you, Emily Bates," barks Duke, his polished leather boots gleaming in the neon lights. He moves toward her like a disembodied spirit that has shed its aura. He presses forcefully on her shoulders, and her knees buckle against the cold tiles. At the same time, Dad glances her way, squirming in a coughing fit that drowns out the words meant for her.

Panic knots her throat as the horrifying images she dreamed while in coma suck in her will to resist. Duke Kay is towering over her in the flesh, willing to do anything to make her bend.

"You were more talkative last time," he remarks with a hint of interest. "I see you've let go of your annoying barnyard princess arrogance now that my son isn't here to chaperone you."

"What's there to say anyway?" she answers flatly.

Duke stares at her with a suspicious look on his face, his salt-and-pepper beard perfectly combed and oiled, glistening under the baking neon lights. He rolls the point of his mustache between his thumb and index finger as he sizes her up. His mouth is half-open like he can't decide which word to fall back on. Finally, the shadow of a smile veils his lips.

"A lot. There's a lot to say, Miss Bates."

Duke steps back to watch Dad squirm against the pole. Emily looks away for fear of losing control.

"The Paragon is more than a division," Duke continues, pulling a metal box from his crisp jacket. "It is a unique organism that lives and breathes on its own."

He carefully opens the shining box and contemplates its contents before taking out a long cigar the color of ground coffee. He sticks the cigar in his still half-open mouth. A long dancing flame spouts out of a metal lighter and burns the end of his cigar. He squints at the thick puff of white smoke he inhales. "And I control it."

The lighter snaps shut like the blade of a knife being sharpened.

"Don't worry," he says, pointing to the cameras. "Everyone still alive in the Refuge can see you. I made sure of that."

The feeling of déjà vu won't leave Emily as Duke elaborates. She knows how it all ends. It's an endless movie that keeps replaying.

"Don't you have something better to do?" she replies, the spicy smoke prickling her nose. "Let's get it over with."

"I wouldn't want to spoil the show. The simulations with your mother have given you too many fanciful ideas to my liking."

"Why are you interested in my simulations? I'm just one of many Archeans."

"That would suit you."

"Leave my daughter alone!" Dad shouts hoarsely.

Duke's cigar turns crimson, and Emily can almost feel her heart being singed to a crisp. When the smoke clears enough for her to see Duke's face, he looks surprised. Then he laughs, blowing a stream of smoke directly into Dad's face who starts coughing again.

"Your daughter hasn't been yours for a long time. From the moment she was born, she was already mine."

"You're rambling," says Emily. She could swear Yasmina is speaking through him.

"Oh! and she doesn't believe me!"

Duke's smile multiplies on each of the agents' faces present in the canteen. The result is horrifying and unnerving, to say the least.

"You know, everyone you see here wouldn't hesitate to give their lives to me."

"Then they're just as twisted as you are."

An agent gets up and comes over without a sound. He undoes his uniform, one button at a time, as everyone stares, mesmerized. Duke watches the process intently. The layers of Kevlar drop to the floor and reveal a fit, swarthy man. The sides of his head are shaved, but his black hair is longer on top and tied into a short ponytail. His face remains expressionless as he stares at Duke, waiting for a command.

A foul-smelling liquid is sprayed at him just before Duke's cigar hits the ground. He grabs his agent's chin with one hand and admires him like a work of art, a smirk on his face. It is too late when Emily realizes what is going on as Duke steps back. Unflinching, she watches as the flames lick the agent's legs, and in less time than she can fathom, he is burning alive like a sun.

"Agent Miles served me well, but his heart was too soft,"

Duke raves. "Letting a member of the Brotherhood infiltrate our ranks is unforgivable."

As terrifying as it sounds, the agent makes no sound, as though he is bathing in water instead of roasting like a skewer. Emily starts to gag at the burned flesh reeking of the canteen's daily menu. Shortly after, the agent's green aura explodes in a dazzling glow as life leaves his body, and she winces in pain.

He drops on the floor like a doll, and a couple of stony-eyed agents throw buckets of ice water at him, splashing Emily in the process. Once the flames are out, they grab the charred body and drag it out of the deadly silent canteen.

"Commander," Leander calls out impatiently. What does that jerk have to do with all this?

"Yes, yes, I know," Duke replies, annoyed. "Go on."

"All of this is his fault!" Leander says, pointing to Dad, who simply frowns. The frequency of Dad's dark blue aura is so low that Emily wonders if he is even conscious.

"My father always did what he was asked to do," she interjects, recalling all the times she couldn't see her father because he was too busy working overtime with the Paragon.

She also remembers his honorable mentions, the leadership position that slipped through his fingers despite all his hard work, and all the agents who have faith in him.

"If this Ark were not so corrupt, he would be our Commander," she adds, the words flogging her heart.

Milo flinches and gives her a sideways glance. Despite the hurt, Milo must know deep down what their Ark really needs: a good and just man. No one else but Dad is better suited for the task—not even the Brotherhood with their fancy ideals. She doubts the Mavericks can truly save them all regardless of what Milo has shown her. If they could, Duke Kay wouldn't be a self-appointed commander today.

"Agent Miles was just a pawn under your father." Leander says scornfully as he steps toward her. "He helped the Brotherhood take over the Ark and infiltrate Delta Labs. He is the reason Mira is dead. *He* killed Mira."

"I was with you, Leander," Emily snaps, feeling her world fall apart. "My father wasn't even there! You know that."

"We have the footage. Sorry to break it to you, but... Actually, no. No one should feel sorry for vermin. Your father is just a dirty traitor."

"Dad, tell me it's not true," Emily blurts out, trying to make eye contact with her father. "Tell me it's all a lie!"

"Tell them!" roars Leander with Duke looking on with satisfaction as he lights himself a new cigar. "Tell them what you did, you bastard!"

Leander spits in Dad's face, and Emily springs to her feet. Two agents force her to the ground, and she groans with pain.

"I had no choice," croaks Jeremy, struggling to stay conscious.

"No choice?" shouts Emily, disbelieving.

"Emily. Please, please, please! Just listen to me! Everything I did, I did it for you and Gabrielle. You will never be safe here until—"

Leander punches Dad in the cheek, probably his first time punching someone judging by the pain contorting his face. Immediately, Duke pushes Leander aside and whispers to Dad, "Our traditions are not foreign to you. Water washes away our sins, and fire sanctifies. Mere mortals cannot live in this new world without a sacrifice. The only way to survive is to rise from our ashes, stronger than ever."

Damn these psychos and their delusions! And to think that a complete lunatic leads the Paragon! Now, how is she supposed to get out of this madhouse?

"I should've known that putting your wife to death wouldn't be enough," Duke spits.

Thinking about her mother conjures up the pain and nightmarish images that have haunted Emily since childhood. She bends over, ready to scream at the world. It has to stop once and for all! This madness, this madness!

"My son should've stayed away from you." Duke hisses, kicking at Emily's knees like she is some vile scum. "But now that he's no longer here to defend you, I can finally take care of you. Call it poetic justice."

Ash from his cigar crumbles onto her sore thighs. She opens her eyes, almost certain she's going to burst into flames, but she doesn't. Instead, Duke takes one last puff of his cigar, before he clicks open his lighter, then points it at Dad's clothes.

Emily looks at Leander with pleading eyes. "How can you follow this monster?"

"I want to see justice be done," Leander replies, confidently. He adds contemptuously, "And may it never happen again as long as I am alive."

"Watch your father burn," Duke laughs maniacally.

She shuts her eyes with a groan, her breath taken away.

"I said, look!"

An agent holds Emily's head firmly in place while another forces her eyes open by tugging at her eyelids. Her father is sprayed with the same foul liquid, and her heart struggles as she dreads what will happen next.

Her father's aura retracts when the flames meet his tender skin. Unlike Agent Miles, Dad screams. He screams, shattering the world in his wake.

The flames grow and extend like a creature feeding on oil. Emily curls up in the fetal position, drowning in her pain. The inevitable happens: Dad's aura explodes in a shower of bluish sparks that cascade through the fire with purple hues that consumes him. She tries to stifle her screams of pain with her fist, biting until she tastes blood. When her voice fails, the agents release her.

They don't dispose of her father's corpse like they did with Agent Miles. No, they leave it there in front of her like a trophy.

Someone is stroking her sodden hair. Milo. Did they release him too?

"They will pay for what they've done. I swear to you," he whispers, his voice trembling.

In the chaos of footsteps splashing around them, the sprinklers stop. A few steps away, Duke finishes giving orders. Milo stiffens.

"Why don't you get my father out of here?" croaks Emily, shuddering. "He's dead. Why keep him here?"

A smile lights up Duke's face as he smooths his dripping beard. Milo holds Emily close against his chest.

"You didn't think there was enough food for everyone on the Ark, did you? Spending over a century on a planet that gives nothing in return is an exceedingly long time."

Emily's stomach churns.

"You heard that right," says Dad's assassin. "Our modern-day oatmeal is reserved for our best passengers, after all."

Oh, my God. This is a nightmare. This life is a nightmare!

She clutches Milo's arm who won't let go. Her insides burn, the images of her damned meals making her retch uncontrollably. This ark is worse than hell!

"There's something I don't understand," Milo says in a strained voice blurred by her gagging. "Why pretend you were a prisoner when you could've walked out at any time? You're controlling them with your thoughts, aren't you?" Duke's face softens, as if indulging in Milo's words.

"Who would be stupid enough to play all their cards at once?"

"Why jeopardize the Ark to achieve your ends? The Sacred Fire is dead!"

After recovering from her shock, Emily tries to follow Milo's train of thought, but she can't quite follow it.

"Not when you know how to fix it," Duke replies mischievously.

"That's what I thought. You're the one who took it out."

So, Duke was the one who attacked her at the Sacred Fire? It was a man, yes. Of that she is certain. Light-skinned. Everything was so light and bright.

"Not exactly," says Duke. "It was someone else who was willing to help. He even came up with the idea. Too bad he's not here anymore."

"Who?" rasps Emily.

"All in due time, Miss Bates. Now that my stupid son is gone, it's high time I cleaned this mess of a place first."

Milo helps Emily to her feet. Duke does nothing to stop them, nor do his automaton agents.

"I can break you," Duke bellows with satisfaction.

"You can always try," says Emily, surprised at her own boldness. "It didn't work last time."

"Because the Syndrome hadn't weakened you enough."

"You're nothing but a pale imitation of Yasmina," she answers with a fervor that feeds on Milo's energy.

"Agent Mirza had her own plans, and they failed or else you wouldn't be standing in front of me," says Duke, joined by Leander and his other agents. "*My* plans have anything but failed simply because you will help me of your own free will."

Duke's inky gaze pierces her, unreadable. She clings to Milo as the voice that had been silent until now rises at that very moment.

It's only a matter of time, Miss Bates.

24

SKYLER

THE BLAZING TORCH PUSHES BACK THE POCKETS OF DARKNESS that cluster in the shaft deep in the heart of the mountain. Skyler ensconces himself in its fiery light, trying to find his bearings. Just how many of these passages does the Star contain?

When Skyler isn't busy tending to minor ailments at the clinic, he spends his free time exploring the base, his favorite pastime that reminds him of the time he used to foray into the in between with his brother. It keeps his mind busy and his curiosity at bay until he is allowed to go outside. Eliza assures him that they will once they have acclimated themselves.

Having Chris around during those long strolls wouldn't hurt. It would be … fun, just like the old days. But Chris has been isolating himself ever since they got here and speaks little. During his dark moments, as Skyler calls them, he can disappear for days with no telling where he might hunker down.

It happened once at the clinic when Skyler needed his help with this little girl called Rose. He wanted to run some more tests on her to make sure the ill effects of the poison gas hadn't left any permanent damage. When Chris was supposed to be testing the samples and it took longer than usual, Skyler found him spacing out. He flinched at Skyler's voice and spilled their samples, contaminating them along the way. He mumbled an apology and stormed out of the clinic.

They haven't talked about it since. It will take time before their friendship goes back to the way it was when they were kids. In the meantime, the moments they spend together are a reminder of how delicate things are between them. Still, Skyler believes he can trust Chris in this new world. Together they can build something better than the Brotherhood. It's their promise and Skyler intends to uphold his end of the bargain.

The secluded section Skyler is exploring today is situated in a large cavern glowing under the torches lining the walls. He slowly descends the stairs carved into the rock and drinks in the warm, mysterious air, his idea of a safe haven where anything is possible. There is no metal here. Those who came before chiseled right into the mountain's belly to locate its heart.

Halfway down, drawings on the lit walls depict scenes akin to the paintings in the Sanctuary of Humankind on the Amaranth. A mix of colors blends nicely, and though their majesty escapes him he gazes at them from the corner of his eye as he climbs down the shaft.

A large five-pointed star is painted on the bottom, with each of its branches connected to a passageway. Larger torches are set up circled by four large statues: two men and two women in warrior guise. Skyler picks a passage at random. A long-haired warrior clad in armor and wielding a two-handed sword pointed at the sky beckons him.

The murmuring echoes accompany him as he walks down the passageway leading to a circular room. Sticks and bowls of food lie at the foot of another faithful representation of that same valiant warrior. Are those offerings?

There are some flowers, fresh and wilting, but none that he can identify. Where could they have come from? Such wildflowers cannot bloom in the ice, let alone in this harsh climate. Perhaps they grow them in the greenhouses?

Skyler leaves the room and slips into another passage, this one guarded by a statue of a woman who looks like Emily, with her short hair and her mischievous, piercing eyes. Although it is only a piece of rock, he brushes it with his fingertips and a current flows through him, as if Emily were here to guide him.

This time, luck is on his side. The passageway leads to a larger room lined with stalactites and a floor riddled with puddles of water slowly filling with droplets raining from the deep roof of the shaft. He climbs down a few steps where people are gathered around a series of altars flanked with austere statues. Most are wearing white tunics and Skyler feels as if he is intruding on a secret assembly. Nobody pays real attention to him, too busy chatting or whispering prayers. Skyler walks silently around them, gazing at the immortalized heroes, when a voice calls out to him, "Sky! Sky!"

Emily's sister hugs him hard, sobbing. Her tunic is oddly soft. Her hair is just as silky, and he strokes her instinctively, the same way he did whenever his mother would have an attack.

"Have you seen my sister?" Gabrielle asks once she has finally calmed down. "I've been looking for her everywhere. Dinah refuses to tell me where she is."

"I don't know. I'm sorry," he says, the ache still unbearable. "Is Dinah with you?"

She nods and points to the familiar figure of the priestess, the legitimate granddaughter of Mrs. Farrell, leaning over one of the offerings at the foot of the statue that looks like Emily.

"You should go and see her," says Gabrielle with a twinkle in her eye, then she turns on her heels to join a circle of young people wearing the same tunic.

Skyler walks briskly in the priestess's direction, his heart beating a thousand miles an hour.

When they first met, Emily's grim prognosis had Skyler go

through his brother's senseless death all over again. The priestess had been there for him, to listen and provide what little comfort she could. They haven't seen each other much since, other than during her occasional visits to his mother seeking clarity. He still hasn't thanked her for that day, nor for her priceless gift: Amaranth's journal bequeathed to her by her grandmother Farrell.

Dinah Farrell snaps out of her prayer when he calls her name. Her surprise turns into a gentle smile when she catches sight of him.

"Praise the Creator! How glad I am that you have survived His trials!"

"Thank you for everything. For the journal. For my mother." *For me*, he wants to add, but the embarrassment cuts him short.

"My grandmother would've done the same, I'm sure. It is the mission of the Ark's priestess after all."

Skyler echoes her smile, scrambling for the right words befitting a person of her status. Nothing seems good enough to express his gratitude.

"Does Emily…" she asks, but her words die at Skyler's confusion. "I'm sorry, I shouldn't have."

"I will convince my brother to go back to the Amaranth and retrieve them."

"Emily woke up."

Skyler freezes, breathless. "She is … awake?"

"Yes. She came around after being transferred to the Refuge. I tried to reach you as soon as my brother told me, but you know the rest. It's my fault… I should've found another way to tell you. But I find comfort in that there must be some untold reason why the Creator saw fit to save her at that particular time."

Hope and a resolute determination permeate Dinah's voice. She genuinely cares about Emily, as a true friend. Their friendship is even more amazing knowing how resistant Emily is to anything related to the Sanctuary and the Creator. Mrs. Farrell's granddaughter must really be special.

"My brother Philip is also on the Ark. Both are in my prayers." She glances nervously at the statue where she was praying, looking more human than her position allows.

"Aren't you worried you will be disappointed?" asks Skyler with utmost care.

"Faith. The people here come from different arks, but they are all guided by the same invisible force that transcends anything we can imagine. I'm sorry. I shouldn't bother you with my beliefs."

"I'm not like Emily. The Goldbergs were never devout believers, but they did give to the community whenever they had the opportunity. And as for me, I..." Skyler catches his breath and gives an embarrassed smile. "I've always wanted to believe. But sometimes I wonder whether what I do is worth it."

"You are where you are supposed to be, Skyler. The Creator gives us opportunities. We just have to find meaning in them to guide us. Everything that unites people here, for example, is a common force that goes by different names, different faces, but that force remains. It transpires even in this place. Can't you feel it?"

Something different beats and lives within these walls. The coolness of the passageway has become an enveloping, almost transcendental warmth. Being with all these people, but especially those from his own ark, makes Skyler confident that if they could make it this far, they still have the power to do something.

Emily is alive.

The priestess puts her hand on Skyler's arm, and an electric current goes through him.

"It's not a coincidence," she says with a smile. "The energy is strong here. And the people who built this base knew that. It's only a matter of time before we get back on our feet and welcome a new destiny."

"We can support each other." Not only Emily or his mother, but all the Archeans, wherever they are. The thing they need is an anchor to steady them.

"I'll do my best," she says, her expression changing as she spots someone behind him.

"Are you meeting without me now?" says Chris, looking falsely offended. "I've been looking for you everywhere, Sky. I was dying of boredom and here you are having a fun time with the high priestess."

"There's no need to be so formal," Dinah replies, looking embarrassed. "I should be the one to show more respect, Officer Kay."

"It's a worthless title here. Anyway, I'm much more useful with Skyler to keep me in check. Why shouldn't I use my medical training to help?"

"Are you being selfless now? It doesn't suit you," asks Skyler, with a hint of sarcasm.

"My heart has a place for those who deserve it. Take the high priestess, for example. And don't you worry! You have a special place too, Skyler."

"Is that supposed to be a compliment?"

Chris looks at him condescendingly, like a father catching his son lying to his face. "Anyone would want to be Chris Kay's best friend. Stop pretending you have no clue."

"If it makes you feel better," Skyler concedes, looking away.

Dinah awkwardly holds back a laugh, though she ends up laughing heartily, tears welling up in her eyes.

"What?" ask Skyler and Chris in the same voice.

"It's nothing. Nothing bad anyway."

Emily's sister takes Chris by surprise by giving him a hard hug. "My goodness! My queen has survived the tribulations that have shaken our kingdom since our last conquest." Her sobs muffle his voice, and he kneels, speaking softly to her. She ends up half-crying half-laughing. Chris has a hidden talent with children. Where did he learn this?

"If you don't mind, I have a queen to take care of," Chris says, taking her hand gallantly. "I'll see you for dinner, Skyler. I've knocked together something with Eliza's help. I'm sure you'll like it."

He moves away with a delighted Gabrielle, all traces of sadness evaporated.

"We will rescue those who were left behind," the priestess says with conviction.

"Doesn't this go against the Creator's wishes?" asks Skyler, doubtful.

She has a mischievous smile on her face, one she obviously borrowed from Emily herself. "He can sometimes be cooperative if you know how to ask."

"How do you do it?"

"Let me show you," she says, motioning to the altar. And as she leads him away from the crowd, the warm light of the torches stokes the charred embers of hope in his heart.

CHRIS SURPRISED HIM AGAIN. The night before, he and Eliza prepared a real feast, with Skyler's favorite meal from when they were kids. Chris replicated the dish to perfection: exquisite grilled freshwater salmon dipped in a lemony cream sauce served on a bed of wild lettuce leaves with crushed walnuts—the exotic dish names of *La Orilla* have always been popular. Eliza was just as delighted by the meal and added the recipe to her thick cookbook. Her father was a gourmet, and she and Oslo learned they could win him over for just about anything if they could fill his belly.

Skyler wishes a good day to Rose, the little girl who chose a name for herself, and sits to fill out some paperwork. He sees her every day at the request of her father Marko, a refugee from the Navigator's Ark. Her tests are clear, but according to Eliza, he insists.

Chris sneaks into the office and closes the door behind him. "You are definitely her hero."

"You think so?" asks Skyler, raising an eyebrow.

"The poor girl has gone through a traumatic event, and you saved her life. So yes, you are."

"How can you be so sure?"

"Do you remember? I used to work in the birthing department while you took care of some old bag."

"Well," says Skyler, wincing at the jab meant for Mrs. Farrell, "this old bag, as you say, was once our age."

"Yes, doctor," he replies in a mocking tone, but not in the least offensive. Chris seems to have recovered since their visit to the temple where they met the priestess and Gabrielle.

However, Skyler is still worried despite the apparent lull that has set in. The Amaranth is fast approaching a point of no return that even the Creator might not be able to stop. A meeting with his brother Neal is inevitable, but for now, Skyler smiles at Chris despite his snarky humor.

"Have you uncovered anything about the poisoning yet? No one can tell me where and why the leak occurred."

"These people have no resources. Haven't you noticed?" replies Chris as he plops himself down in a chair.

Their means are indeed limited. Rolf and the other apprentices are complete beginners. It will take years before they can run the clinic by themselves. Skyler has already taught them disinfection and other related tasks that won't endanger any patients' lives. Since the enormous responsibility of running the clinic rests on Chris and Skyler's shoulders, any help is welcome. But the situation is critical. They're not doing too badly despite the challenges, and they have earned people's trust along the way, but this trust comes at a price.

"We can't afford another tragedy of this kind," Skyler says. "Imagine the havoc it would cause. This clinic was run properly before … something happened. Something Eliza and Oslo won't tell us. The circumstances of their father Anzen's death are murky."

"What do you suggest?"

"What if we conducted our own investigation?" Skyler knows he has just opened Pandora's box, but neither the trainees nor Eliza are going to help them.

After a while, Chris says, "We'll have to be extremely careful." Skyler is organizing his files to keep his mind from reeling. "Who knows what these people are capable of if they can sacrifice their own under the guise of heroism. They can't even face the fact that what they do is worse than murder."

"At least the kids don't know about it." As if on cue, a group of children is eavesdropping through the window.

"Of course!" shouts Chris, jumping to his feet. "Rose is the key."

"What do you mean?"

"I'm sure she wouldn't mind a surprise visit from her new best friend." Skyler processes what he says with a frown.

"Do you really think her family will just let us waltz into their house to interrogate them? The Paragon could, but the North Star is not the Amaranth."

"Marko trusts you. You saved his daughter's life. Besides, didn't he ask Eliza to meet you?"

And she hasn't let him for some unknown reason. Eliza has been acting as the middleman ever since they got here.

"It might work," Skyler concedes. "It's worth a try, anyway."

"Exactly." Chris opens the office door just as the giggling children scurry away and gives him an inquisitive look.

"Where are you going?" asks Skyler, confused, as he reaches

for him.

"You need a sidekick. Don't all heroes have one?"

Chris gives him a pat on the shoulder before going out first.

ROSE'S FAMILY cabin stands out from the others which are plastered with drawings and symbols specific to their culture. Theirs is strewn with all kinds of objects making it look like a toy store.

"This toy plane is awesome," notes Chris, who grabs a contraption pieced together from recycled metal parts that shouldn't fit so neatly together, but somehow do. "Remember our remote-control planes? They were so rare and fun, especially since I was always the winner."

"My brother did beat you."

"Only once. And then they were banned for some bogus reason."

"It wasn't safe, especially where the seniors lived."

"I'll get a rematch one day, I promise. Even if I must terrify some old bag on their way to lunch." Despite all these years, Chris will be Chris.

"Has something happened?" asks a middle-aged man as he emerges from the cabin under the flashing multicolored lights.

"Not at all. Chris and I came to make sure your family is all right. You must be Marko, Lola's father, I presume?"

"We're meeting the victims of the incident to find out what happened," Chris cuts in authoritatively with a sideways glance at Skyler.

Marko looks a little taken aback, but eventually says, "Of course, of course. Come on in. Had I known you were coming, I would have tidied up a bit."

This visit had better be worth it, Skyler muses as he follows him inside.

This home is quite different from Eliza and Oslo's. Parts and scraps are strewn across the floor in a dizzying chaos. Several baskets contain rotors, small engines, propellers, wheels, wiring, lights, and other contraptions that have been sorted methodically, like those stalls in the dome when the market is open. The rest of the booth consist of mounted shelves that display Marko's creations, which range from vehicles to metal animals.

"Children of the new refugees have a tough time adjusting to the life here. Most have experienced trauma that keeps them awake at night. I figured they needed a distraction, so I decided to do what I do best."

"It's amazing," says Chris, excited about the models. "Do they work?"

"Of course!" Marko says enthusiastically, pleased that an adult is interested in his handiwork. "They're all equipped with an engine of their own. Wouldn't that be a waste, leaving this junk lifeless without a bit of tinkering?"

A plane whizzes past them in the apartment and Skyler is sent back to his childhood with his brother Allen. These little contraptions may seem harmless or even silly, but they create unforgettable memories. For Skyler and Chris, they were pilots of their own, darting through the passageways, and the skies were at their fingertips. It was the perfect escape from the Ark.

"Are there several models?" asks Chris as Skyler leaves them to their frantic discussion, more intrigued by the rest of the curios in the next room.

"My husband won't let your friend out of his sight now," a female voice calls out to Skyler. "His passion is out of this world. I hope your friend doesn't mind."

A tan-skinned woman with slender limbs and long dark hair stands in the doorway, the only space available amidst heaps of miscellaneous parts.

"Isabela," she says, giving out a hand Skyler shakes. "And I would bet my life that you are the doctor who saved our daughter. She won't stop talking about you! I couldn't mistake you for someone else even if I wanted to."

"She's adorable, isn't she?" says Skyler, who is not used to receiving this kind of welcome. "Is she doing all right?"

"Yes, and not just her body. She had been feeling rather lonely lately, but ever since she met you, I can tell she's happy."

So, Chris was right all along. He does have a gift with kids.

"How are you?" asks Skyler, sounding as professional as possible.

"Me? If you mean my health, everything seems fine," she says. "The routine has set in."

"Sorry we didn't tell you before coming by for a visit. To be honest, it was kind of a last-minute decision."

"It's nice to see that people of your expertise are here to look after us. With everything that's happened, it's hard to feel safe from danger."

Isabela coughs lightly, and Skyler gives her a worried look.

"The heating is not very good in many parts of this old base," she says dismissively. "Anyone who ventures too far from the dome will inevitably catch a cold."

"Was your daughter in one of those parts when her symptoms began?"

"She prefers cooler places. In fact, she always hangs out in the same spot with her friends."

"Can you take me there?"

"Marko, I'm going to work with the doctor."

"Please call me Skyler."

"And you, Isabela," she adds with a wink.

Marko and Isabela whisper something to each other, and Marko falls back into his conversation with Chris, who gives Skyler a knowing look.

Isabela leads him to a section of the base that Skyler has not yet visited. After all this time exploring, how can there still be some tunnels that escape him?

Isabela looks amused.

"Although I've lived here for years, I sometimes end up at the little temple while I mean to go to the mines. My team leader makes fun of me every time, but I know that every minute counts. Our manpower isn't enough… Careful! This fork can be treacherous if you don't pay attention."

Skyler finds his bearings now. His jaunt from the other day is still fresh in his memory. A motley of stars and other odd designs form a fresco on the bare face of the rocky wall. It is filed in places where some jutting pink rocks have been left intact as ornamentation.

"The Star has a wealth of valuable resources, but you have to know where to look for them," says Isabela, brushing crystals that range from a milky hue to some deep blues and greens with her thumb. "The mountains are full of them, especially as you go deeper into the ground. These gems were brought here by whoever inhabited those caves a long time ago and then embedded into the rock as a special artform. They were worth a fortune before the Flood, but they have no other use now. There is no point in extracting them."

"Isn't that what you're mining here?" asks Skyler, mesmerized by their mysterious quality, distinctly different from the pink nuggets.

"Money is worth nothing here, even if this system has found a way to survive on the arks. Well, on ours at least. We only mine what is useful for the base."

"Did you used to live on an Ark?"

"Yes, until seven years ago. It's a long story, but Thalassa had other plans for us, and our death was the answer they sought."

That name again. Thalassa.

"Is that how your Ark was destroyed?" she asks.

"Not exactly. It was a mere coincidence; a little longer and we would have been out of oxygen."

"Thalassa," hisses Isabela. "They are everywhere. Failures of that kind are never a coincidence."

They approach a space wider than the poorly laid-out narrow passageways, as if the base had been built in a frenzy for lack of time. Some large white crystals with matte and light pink reflections emerge in the middle of a large pond. Small groups of people equipped with pickaxes mine the ore they toss in old wheelbarrows. The walls are inlaid with bright piercing lights where coils of wires hang. It almost looks like this place was not part of the original base.

"It's a salt mine. It's a lot less exciting than these gems, isn't it? But this salt has interesting properties that allow us to store the energy necessary for the proper functioning of the base. The technology of the Sacred Fire is impossible to reproduce with our limited means, so we had to be creative. It's all thanks to Anzen Nord that we were able to achieve this feat."

"Wasn't there a power source built into this base?" wonders Skyler, who can't believe they have to do such demanding work when ships like the Njord are moored near the coast.

"The reactor has long been decommissioned. Since no one is qualified to maintain it, let alone understand how it works, an alternative energy source had to be found. I spend most of my time here, and the children often accompany us so we can keep an eye on them."

They cross the large puddle that dampens their shoes, and Isabela exchanges many heartfelt greetings with the miners, young and old, men and women—basically, anyone willing to join in and give back to those who brought them safely to the Surface. Skyler smiles and introduces himself as a refugee of the Amaranth. He realizes that this base may be the place where he will spend the rest of his life. His throat tightens at the thought.

At the end of a long passage, they emerge into an antechamber where large stalagmites almost block the entire way.

"This is the perfect place for any child," says Isabela, whose voice echoes. "They can play for hours on end and never get bored with all those nooks to hide in. Over there is my daughter's Bellerose Castle. Don't be surprised if she takes you there for tea one of these days. It's only a matter of time."

Isabela smiles for the first time since they met. She even lets out a little laugh as she watches children playing.

"It's good to see them enjoying their childhood. The Surface should be their playground, but since winter is unforgiving and we don't know the area well, we prefer to keep them safe here."

Skyler examines the surroundings to locate the source of their poisoning. He strolls along the famous Bellerose Castle where toys, gems, and other finds are stashed. Nothing seems wrong. At least, nothing that can explain how children and adults alike were poisoned. There is no smell or anything to suggest that the source of the toxin is here.

"It's a beautiful place," Skyler admits, nostalgic for his own childhood that seems to have flown by at the speed of light. *Without his brother.* "Pretty impressive how much effort they've put into it."

"Yes. They don't do anything halfway." Skyler glimpses a downhill passage a little further on and walks over to look. "At the far end of this corridor is a door that no one has been able to open."

"Are there many of these doors?"

"Several, yes. Hardly anyone knows what's in there, especially since no one takes the trouble to examine those doors. It's probably for the best. Relics are not the solution to survive in this miserable cold. It's probably best to forget about them."

Isabela has another coughing fit that has her shed a bead of sweat.

"Are you sure you're all right? I can examine you at the clinic."

"It's nothing, I assure you," she says at Skyler's insistent look.

"I've been working here for so long. The others would be sick if there was something bad here."

"Does Rose like to go to other places?"

"You're calling her Rose," she says, rolling her name. "You are definitely part of her fan club."

"Sorry, I should've said Lola."

"I know she doesn't want to take my mother's name. No one can blame her since she has no clear memory of her grandmother."

Isabela has a look that Skyler has seen too often on the Ark: that of a grieving woman with vague memories that will fade over time. The Creator never tires of making victims with his Plan.

"My mother perished with the others on our ark. Naming her was a way for me to keep her alive through my daughter. Selfish of me, I know. But we do what we can to keep those we love a little longer."

The memory spheres come back clearer than ever in Skyler's mind, and his heart sinks knowing that they may already be sleeping at the bottom of the ocean.

"I think you should ask my daughter your questions yourself. She will gladly take you to wherever they like to play, I'm sure. Now that I think about it, why don't you stay for dinner after my shift? That would certainly please her. Will you be able to find your way home by yourself? I can ask Krystal to walk with you."

Skyler accepts the offer for dinner but insists on returning on his own. He needs time to think.

He goes back the way they came, but it is not the mysterious poisoning that occupies his mind. The memory spheres cannot simply disappear with the Amaranth. Every human being should have a right to use them in this new world. But how can he achieve the impossible? He should have apprenticed in engineering, even if it meant spending the rest of his life rotting in Delta laboratories or baking in the Sacred Fire.

He looks up just in time to avoid running into another locked door that Eliza and Isabela mentioned. As he is about to turn back, his curiosity has the better of him, and he grabs the handle with a sigh of annoyance. What if a security system woke up and machine-gunned him like that killer drone on the Sedna?

He pushes as he closes his eyes like it could protect him from his misdeed somehow.

The door opens.

The interior is pitch-black, and Skyler gropes his way to a dim light source. He recognizes some writing in a language he finally understands. This place is probably the remains of the old military base. Has the Creator finally decided to show him the way? Dinah would smile at that.

Reactor ... close ... equipment...

This is the reactor that Isabela told him about earlier. Why is it so easy to access?

Something shifts behind and he jerks around. What could be living here, so far from the rest of the base?

The thing lurks in the shadows. For the first time in his life, Skyler feels a visceral fear in the pit of his stomach. What if it's an animal? Don't they need to find some shelter to safeguard against the cold? This network of tunnels seems like the perfect hiding place for creatures like this one.

For fear of attracting the thing's attention, Skyler backs away toward the exit without a sound. A movement to his right brushes at him, and he scans the darkness, his muscles tense. So much for being a small animal in distress. That thing is big.

His survival instinct is battling against his nagging curiosity, but then reason kicks in. Sometimes curiosity can be a killer.

Skyler counts his steps toward the exit and pulls the reactor door shut.

25

SKYLER

Marko used to be an engineer on his Ark. He lets Skyler use his old workshop, a converted cabin where a workbench takes up most of the space. Piles of nameless junk were cluttering the room up to the ceiling, but with a few baskets and a lot of patience, Skyler has brought back its luster. The workshop is serviceable enough now for magic to happen.

This time, he wants to experiment on his own, something he should have done a long time ago. Being on the Surface where everyone must adapt, Skyler has no reason not to try. This is his project, after all.

Engineering is not what he had imagined. He painstakingly follows the instructions Marko has scribbled down for him in a document he's compiled with schematics of the memory spheres' inner workings. There will be a lot of trial and error to make an actual sphere.

Skyler sighs as he tries to connect part of the sphere's integrated circuit for the umpteenth time. Weeks of work were necessary to finally get to the part where he needs to jam on a silly solder joint. If Jacinth's husband could do it, why couldn't he? In his small, dark cabin on the Ark, he had successfully grown flowers of his own.

"Skyler getting his hands dirty is a sight to behold." Chris has come to tease him the way only he can. Some people have a particularly odd way of showing their friendship.

"How nice would it be if you could make yourself useful instead of bothering me?" Skyler replies, dropping the circuit and tweezers on the work desk. He takes off the monocle that gives him augmented vision to peer at the intricate design of the circuit board.

"Go on. Don't mind me."

Chris is acting a little strange today like he's hiding something. He intently watches Skyler stare blankly at the unyielding circuit board.

"You should take a break," Chris says.

Skyler was about to try again to connect one of the hard-to-reach branches, but his lack of dexterity with the tweezers is exasperating. He would know what he was doing with a scalpel.

"I would love to, but I don't think I can reproduce the memory spheres. Unless you can give me some bionic hands instead of this pair of useless hands? If so, I would be grateful. By the way, could you stop staring at me with that goofy look? And stop smiling while you're at it, will you?"

Chris is one distraction too many. Skyler squints at the thin line that needs welding.

"I can't help it, sorry. I prefer to smile instead of keeping my serious looks like a certain doctor in this room. Just stop for today."

"Give me one good reason."

"Only one? So, let's see … because I have a surprise for you!"

All right. Skyler puts down his instrument when he sees that he screwed up the wafer by soldering the wrong circuit. He'll have to find Marko to fix his mess.

"You win," Skyler admits, arms raised. "I'm not getting anywhere with this anyway."

"Give yourself some time. Engineers are not made overnight. It would be way too easy, and the Creator knows this life is anything but simple."

"If I had the assurance we could live another day, I might consider taking my time."

"You sound like Emily. Come on! I've got just the right thing for you, Sky. Close your eyes."

"What now?" grumbles Skyler as he complies. What is it with Chris today?

"Hold out your hands." Skyler feels silly, and Chris scolds him, "Not like that! Cusp them like you're about to receive the blessing. Better."

Something soft brushes against his palms, and a floral scent tickles his nose. He opens his eyes and Chris is all smiles.

"Flowers?"

"Do you like them?" asks Chris, hands behind his back.

They are beautiful with their large red petals bordering on crimson. Those flowers must be native, and unlike anything he has seen on the Ark. Skyler inhales to soak up their distinctive aroma.

"They smell good. Where did you find them?"

"That's part two of my surprise."

"What? Are there several parts? You know I must work on this project."

"There's no rush. It'll be nice to spend some time together, away from all these obligations you keep imposing on yourself. You act like nothing has changed and yet here we are on the Surface."

Between the clinic, his visits to Rose's family, his long strolls in the tunnels, and the occasional errand he runs for Eliza, he didn't have a minute to himself. Or did he? Maybe keeping the memory of the Ark at bay was a way to keep him safe.

"I don't have any pots," Skyler says awkwardly. It would be a shame not to treasure these flowers. Not only are they beautiful —and perfect for his little garden—but this is the first time Chris has gifted him anything. Keeping these flowers alive for as long as he can is a promise Skyler can make.

"That's okay. I can get you some more of them later," says Chris with a strange smile. "Hurry before I change my mind."

"Why don't you tell me where to find them?"

"You really don't know what the word surprise means, do you?" Chris takes Skyler's hand by force, leaving the small bouquet on the worktable. They will wilt without water by the time they come back!

The contact of their hands breaks when they are far enough away from the workshop.

"I really wonder what bug has bitten you to make you change so much."

"A bug? What bug?" wonders Chris.

"The one crawling on you when you found those flowers."

Chris leads him into the main dome of the Star, but they don't linger. A patient from the clinic could recognize them and strike up a conversation at any minute. Instead, they go through a glass corridor that runs along on the opposite side of the mountain, like the one they came through when they disembarked from the Njord. With the approaching sunset, the glass gives off a pleasant warmth.

They emerge into a bend nestled strategically so that the sun doesn't bathe the place all day. The bay glows brightly in the background, and when they are close enough, the corridor branches off into a medium-sized dome that Skyler has never seen before.

"You'll love this," Chris says with a hint of excitement in his voice. "I'm sure of it."

"How did you find this place?"

"It's top secret!"

A massive rock filled with lush vegetation sits in the center and extends to a series of smaller, interconnected domes. An intricate network of branches, roots, and foliage intertwine, and Skyler is amazed by so much beauty. Might the pre-Flood Earth have looked like this? He heaves a sigh of relief. "It's amazing."

"Come on."

This section of the Star is serene and uncrowded. They skirt around the knoll that teems with invisible life among the trees and vines hanging down on either side. A chilly breeze kisses their skin where a gigantic waterfall crashes into a large basin. Its water flows to the other domes built around their own rocks of varying sizes featuring unique vegetation. Skyler takes a moment to enjoy the refreshing waterfall. After walking such a long distance in the glass passage that has become a furnace, standing here is the closest thing to paradise.

"We can go up this way," Chris shouts over the din of the water. "This is the best view."

They climb a flurry of stone-etched stairs fraught with branches, and they must duck most of the way to avoid getting their faces lashed to shreds.

"The Gardens of Humankind pale in comparison," muses Skyler, who can't hold back his excitement.

"So, do you like it?" asks Chris, grabbing him by the shoulder.

"I love it."

"Wait until you see the rest."

They continue to explore this surreal garden with its heady floral and woody scents. Arches ring the walkway as they proceed, gradually rising above the thick vegetation with a clear view on a mightier waterfall that connects to a dome-covered bay. Fish laze about and feed on algae and other marine plants at their feet, and Skyler cannot help but smile. The beauty of this odd place is fascinating.

"We're almost there," announces Chris at the waterfall's foot.

Meanwhile, the sun is sinking toward the ocean in a torrent of light. Their path forks inside the rock, and the lush foliage shuts them off from the rest of the garden. They walk for a while, the vines cracking under the soles of their boots and the thick leaves of trees brushing their faces. When Skyler pushes aside a leaf bigger than the others, he gasps at the sight: a secret garden.

It spans several floors, with clusters of flowers of every imaginable species and color. The same red flowers Chris gave him are clustered in a hard-to-reach corner on the edge of a rock beyond the bush. He must have had a tough time gathering those.

"I can't believe you found this place," Skyler says, crouching next to a bed of rare lilies he's never seen before.

These lilies are quite different from their usual pearly white. They are a mottled pink, and the outline of their star-shaped petals is traced with white. Skyler brings the long orange stamens close to his nose and inhales their spicy scent.

"How did you know I like flowers in the first place?"

"You brought them almost every day to your patients in Med Bay. Then I saw you flower-picking at the park once. When I stumbled upon this secret garden, I knew I had to bring you here."

"Chris, I never thought I'd say this to you, but..."

Skyler gets to his feet, and Chris looks at him like he's holding his breath.

"I don't think I could survive without you here. They may be just flowers to you, but to me..."

Emotion suddenly grips his throat and sting his eyes.

"Skyler ... are you okay?"

"Sorry, I shouldn't have smelled those lilies," he replies, sniffing. "I'm probably the only one finding an interest in them, and I'm allergic. Talk about bad luck."

Chris's gaze falters for a moment, then he says more lightly, "You can invite me if you feel like it. I like this kind of place, too.

You don't find this peace and quiet anywhere else on the base and its harrowing tunnels. No wonder they use this garden as a monument."

"A monument?"

"See the statues over there?" Chris points to a space at the foot of the rock where a bunch of plaques are engraved with inscriptions and drawings. "I did a little research and discovered they inscribe an epitaph here before they freeze their dead in the ground. This place is a kind of Garden of Eden, where the dead are laid to rest."

"A cemetery." The word itself has the power to suck the life out of this paradise, and Skyler blames himself for saying it. This fragile haven must be protected.

Those epitaphs eat the flowerbed like a growing cancer.

"That doesn't change the fact that they don't release them from their physical bodies," Skyler adds, thinking back to Anzen Nord hanging between life and death to hold the barrier around the base. What sort of Machiavellian technology can require the human body to be used as a power source?

"What if we're wrong?" says Chris. "About death. About life."

Why would Chris question everything they learned on the Ark? The Command had its flaws and kept many things from them, but their education was fair.

"What comes from the earth must go back to the earth," Skyler argues. "Using their bodies to power a machine goes against that cycle."

Who could have designed such a tool without any ethical concern for the dignity of those people sacrificed? Even if they consented, they had no idea what they were getting into. Who can imagine what it is like to float between life and death?

"I've been thinking about why they keep them alive, and the conclusion scares me, Chris. I don't want others to suffer the same way because these people have lost their minds."

"So that's why you want to recreate the memory spheres

here. Do you think they will accept them?"

Skyler considers his point before responding. "I don't see why they would refuse. The spheres are a way to honor their dead which is one of their principles."

"How is this different? They will be forever imprisoned in glass."

"It's not the same," Skyler defends himself. "It's a copy of their memory, not exactly a replica or the essence of who they are."

"And you think those who will see holograms of their families, friends and loved ones will be swayed by your explanation?"

Chris stresses every word, but Skyler insists. "Eliza will help me. I don't know what happened on their arks, but it's bad enough that no one dares to talk about it. This Thalassa has broken these people from the inside. If they are repaired, they can find their way back to reason."

His mother was in limbo for years, then finally got out. The potential of the spheres is too great to simply ignore. It is an opportunity.

"Shouldn't we enjoy the fact that *we* are not broken?" asks Chris, fiddling with a twig.

Skyler gets closer to the flowers that shiver in the fresh breeze brought by the waterfall. Aren't they broken in their own way, too? They have lost the Amaranth, their friends, their family, and their innocence. Only a thread of hope that erodes a little more each day holds them together.

"We spend most of our time in the clinic helping those in need. Isn't that the best thing we can do?"

"Don't you ever think about anything other than work?" asks Chris with a shade in his voice that Skyler can't quite identify.

"What else is there to think about? We don't live in a fairy tale, let alone a paradise, even if this is the closest thing to it."

"Did you not think for a moment that this paradise might

not be a physical place?"

This Promised Land may just be a garden contained in an artificial dome. Skyler laughs hollowly. Why does this thought irritate him so much? The truth is no one told them what this land would be like.

"If this paradise doesn't exist, then what's the point?"

Chris places his hand on Skyler's chest who tenses by instinct. The warmth that spreads across his body and the familiarity of Chris's touch calm him down.

"It's so simple, Sky. All along, our paradise was here. Don't tell me you forgot."

"Being happy," Skyler whispers. "Is that it?"

"It's a good start," says Chris, letting his hand fall limply.

So simple and yet so painful to think. Why isn't there more to it than that?

"There's one last thing I want to show you," Chris says as he slips into the foliage leading to the flower garden.

The branches whip Skyler's uniform as he sets off after him. Chris's head comes in and out of view as the dirt road descends into the garden. He can almost hear him laughing, just like when they were kids and used to stroll in the in between. The memory comes back to Skyler in flashes: the laughter, the fun, the world frozen in time. Is this what Chris meant when he said that heaven lies in their hearts? Through their memories and feelings? But what is the point of chasing happiness if it is so fleeting?

Flowers flit like shadows from one color blob to another until Skyler reaches a mass of polished stones with cryptic messages, set about large rocks cleared of vegetation and washed by the half-light of sunset. This place looks like the North Star's own version of the Sanctuary of Humankind.

Skyler has lost sight of Chris and looks around to get his bearings. He takes the steep path that skirts the rock's dark side, straddling the roots of shrubs while feeling the wet rocky surface as a guide. He heaves a sigh of exhaustion once he reaches a makeshift footbridge.

He keeps his gaze forward for fear of losing his footing at this height. The glowing torrent of water sends an icy spray of water as Skyler walks along the wall behind the roaring waterfall where Chris waits for him, leaning against the rock.

"What took you so long?" Chris says, unmoving. "I almost thought I'd have to go get you myself."

"I'm here. That's what matters, right?"

As they look ahead side by side, the curtain of water seems to be opening onto a world full of secrets washed by a sea of gold.

"Sky," Chris whispers, his voice weak. "I know our relationship hasn't always been easy, but—"

"I couldn't see my own mistakes."

Chris doesn't say anything. He looks deep in his thoughts, his brows furrowed just like in his dark moments. "Thank you for giving me a second chance. I feel like…"

Skyler gives him space to think, pushing away his fears of having Chris reject their newfound friendship. There is no way Skyler can accept going back to the way it was between them for the last five years.

"When we were chosen to leave the Ark, I went back inside and couldn't find the courage to leave everything behind," Chris continues. "Something was holding me back. My father. What son would abandon his father when he has the power to set him free? Yet my father hates me, even though he tried to convince me otherwise. When I saw him prowling with his Paragon agents in the crowd near the airlock, I just knew. He made it clear that I wouldn't be welcome aboard if he lived."

The hurt in his eyes wrenches Skyler's heart. There is nothing worse than being rejected by one's own family. He can attest to that after watching his father's memory sphere. His mother had never liked him either.

"I gave a thought about what could keep me on the Ark if not for my parents. Emily and I had always been nothing else but good friends. But then I thought about my friend Leander who was madly in love with Mira. He had found his own piece of heaven in her. I was left wondering: Where can I find my own paradise where I can lose myself, hope, and dream? My father had denied me that right, but somehow, I knew I had already found it elsewhere. That is, until my stupidity ruined everything."

"I didn't know."

"Each of us undergoes these experiences of questioning and awareness. It's like a rite of passage. But in these moments, I need…"

Despite the growing darkness that swallows the garden, Chris's eyes are glimmering in gold.

"You're the only one I trust, Skyler. With you, I feel like the paradise I dream of is within reach. Nothing that can happen here can scare me because I've found you."

Between two breaths, Chris's lips meet Skyler's. A tender, trembling kiss meant for the dearest person of all. The promise of a future in a world wounded by their sins.

Their lips part. Chris retreats with a troubled look, and the taste of salt lingers. A tear.

Holding their breath, they stare at each other longer than their kiss lasted. Meanwhile, the moon has robbed the sun of its throne to expose the dark side of the world.

"Chris." Skyler means to grab him by the shoulder, but Chris recoils like a frightened animal.

"I shouldn't have. I shouldn't have done that. Skyler, I … forgive me."

Before Skyler can say anything, Chris disappears in the creeping shadows. Only the loud din of the waterfall remains in the depths of the night, unanswered.

26

EMILY

How can someone control the mind?

Emily has been brooding ever since she became the special prisoner of Duke Kay, the leader of the Paragon, the Ark's special forces. He controls the mind of his agents without the Archeans' knowledge.

The Creator may be quiet, but he is listening. Violet would be proud of her finding refuge in the Creator's light. But what Emily really needs is her unwaveringly resilient friend: Violet's light.

After years of interrogating inmates as part of her job as an agent, here she is now: a prisoner. How pathetic! If what Duke says is true—he likes to talk during his nightly visits—the rest of the Brotherhood and the Mavericks, including Skyler and Chris, have left the Ark for God knows where. Without divine intervention, no one will come to her rescue. Though she hates to admit it, obeying Duke's will is her only way out.

This is all part of some mind-control program, a power that shouldn't even exist. Emily curses herself for not being science savvy like the Deltas. The only one who could figure out this riddle is Milo, but of course, Duke painstakingly keeps him away from her. He forces her to watch videos of his forced training in the Paragon's army. In them, he's being brainwashed in drills that border on torture, worse than any simulation they've ever been put through—electrical impulses, hypnosis, mutilation. The list is long.

All she can hope for now is that her sister, Gabrielle, is far from that madhouse and that Duke never finds her. With her at least, the Bates will not die out.

Her cell at the Refuge must be the one Duke was rotting in before he found a way to break out with his automaton agents' help. What if it was Leander who betrayed them all? To think they grew up together ... yet he didn't bat an eye when sentencing Dad and handing him over to the greatest murderer of the century. Controlling the minds of an army *is* like murder. No one can willingly accept being someone else's puppet. No one.

The screen lights up which means it's time for a broadcast. She never knows if she's being forced to watch on replay or live, but what difference does it make? The image isn't as sharp as it usually is. Ripples are running across the screen as if the camera were underwater. Strange.

Emily sits in an utterly uncomfortable corner, the only place she can get a clear view of the recording and brings her legs against her chest to chase away the chill from the metal flooring. As soon as she lays her eyes on the screen, it draws her into this illusion of another world projected to her.

Milo. Always Milo. If Duke is trying to play with her feelings, he's wasting his time. She won't give in that easily. When her father died, she zoned out to protect herself. It's the only reason why she's still alive.

A squad dressed in Paragon training uniforms accompanies Milo as they walk through a strangely familiar place like their Ark.

"Why are you filming us?" Milo growls at the agent following him with the camera.

In response, the cameraman takes a close-up of Milo who looks naked without his flamboyant aura. His bulk has shrunk like he is not getting enough to eat, and his uniform wrinkles where muscles should bulge. In the blue darkness of the water tubes lining the corridor, his face is so pale that his freckles look out of place.

"Cat got your tongue, huh?" Milo lets out a heavy sigh, frowning. "He couldn't care less about us."

"As long as the dirty work gets done," Sofia replies, looking like she's in her natural element. "Duke won't trust a group of Mavericks who stole the Ark's command right under his nose."

"A security, huh?" snorts Milo, looking away from the camera bouncing at their every step. "No one would want to risk their lives on a mission like this."

"I say there's a much more interesting reason than that," Fiona says with a satisfied look. "They do it for *her*." This might be what the agent had hoped for from the moment he turned his camera on because he zooms in on Milo whose eyes light up.

"What better than to watch us die during our mission?" adds Fiona bitterly.

Emily swallows hard at that. What the hell did Duke ask them to do? Wasn't using Dad as a scapegoat enough?

"Would he really go to that much trouble?" asks Milo.

"This man burned his agent alive for all to see," Sofia adds, nonchalantly walking past the camera, which looks like interference for a second.

Once the image returns, Milo's face is in close-up. A flash of understanding passes through the irises of his eyes as they contract, his breathing deepening. He stares at Emily through the camera's eye. She swears she can feel him by her side.

"Emily. I wish I could've stopped all this," he says with a hint of regret, like when he rescued her from Yasmina's clutches.

She rages at her helplessness, unable to answer him. Her body goes numb as she squeezes her legs as hard as she can.

"If you can hear me, you're still alive," he says. "Don't forget that."

He knows. Milo is about to add something, but his attention turns to something to his left. His face immediately loses its bluish tones, blown away by an imaginary strong gust of wind. He squints at something off camera. She shouts at the cameraman to give a clear shot of the source, but the only thing she can see is Fiona's carved back.

"Ever dealt with a colossus before?" her mother Sofia asks with a hint of sarcasm.

"We should simply move everyone here," Fiona says, tying her hair into a tight bun. "It'd be a lot less hassle than *this*."

"It's one thing to save everyone's lives, but another to convince hundreds of people to leave the ship they grew up on," Milo says solemnly. "Nothing can ever replace the Amaranth."

The screen finally shows something Emily never thought possible: The Sacred Fire, its flame roaring with life. The light source is so powerful that it radiates, the pixels of the camera not doing justice to the beauty of this technology. Did they find a way to fix it?

They talk about the Amaranth like they are somewhere else … on another ark? This realization stuns Emily, who moves closer to the screen, wishing more than anything that she could go through it.

"Are you a poet now?" Fiona taunts him. She takes a harness out of her bag and puts it on swiftly, tightening the straps with deft hands.

"I know you were never fond of poetry. But you've got to admit that there is some truth in it."

"I have no affection for the Ark. All I want is to live long enough to tread on land."

"Then it starts here," Milo says, walking toward the Sacred

Fire, his harness in place. Fiona gets closer to him, then kisses him passionately without warning.

Emily looks away, her heart skipping a beat. Of course, Reyes must be doing this on purpose. She'll take any shot she can at Emily. It's so childish. Like Emily is going to fall for it.

"For luck," Fiona whispers, their silhouettes darkened by the Sacred Fire's glow against the light. "You'll need it if you plan to climb this."

"It's not like it's never been done before. This wonder of technology was assembled, which means it—"

"Can be taken apart. I know."

"Keep talking and we'll be cooked alive before even starting," Sofia scolds them. "There will be plenty of time to celebrate if we pull this off." They are putting on their helmets when the broadcast ends. Emily sighs with rage.

This mission is suicide! Only qualified engineers can hope to dismantle the Sacred Fire. Why is Milo so stubborn? Even under Duke's orders, he could at least try to resist!

The walls of her cell have never seemed so constricting as they do right now. She paces back and forth, then goes to the window of the door, raging. Another inmate gives her a curious, pleading look through the glass, but her aura is out of whack, so Emily can't read her. Emily loses patience and moves away from the door, holding her head with both hands. She curls up to silence her growing anguish. Her control is slipping. She knows it. She can feel it.

How is she supposed to calm herself, knowing Milo could die at any moment?

That night, she can only fall asleep by replaying Milo's words over and over in her head, like the favorite lullaby her mother used to hum to her before Gabrielle was born. So long as Emily is alive, there is a glimmer of hope that she can see Milo again. Someday.

THEY BRING HER FOOD. Duke takes a wicked pleasure in feeding her modern-day oatmeal. Tears spill on her face as she forces the gunk down her throat. She moans with pain, fear, and humiliation. The onslaught of horrifying images is slowly gnawing at her soul, as if watching her father burn was not enough. It'll take time to break her, and much more than that.

When the door to her cell is open for service, she catches the sideways glance of the disheveled inmate again. Days and days of neglect have smeared her face—Emily has seen her fair share of broken inmates at the prison—making her almost unrecognizable, but not quite.

Her golden aura is ebbing dangerously—a little more and gold leaves would rain down around her. Laurene Milcah, Second Officer of the Command, was Chris's mentor. They met not so long ago, but this feels like it happened in a past life. Before Emily woke up from her coma in the Creator's hell. She was judged, oh yes, she was! The purgatory in all its colors, its righteous injustices, its abysmal pits. The missteps she's racked up bury her under a mountain of treachery and defilement. *This* is the divine retribution meant for her.

Like the other night, Laurene means to talk to her, but Emily has no energy to spare. She slides the trap door shut at the shadow of a once-respected member of the Command. How easy it is for someone so influential to be reduced to this: flesh, fear, and death in waiting.

Emily would give anything to draw, to kill time, and let her muscle memory take over her restless mind. She fears the jaws of hurt and desperation could crush her like a bag of bones at any time.

That's it! She grabs the spoon she's stuck into the leftovers of her modern-day oatmeal. She has no recollection of eating any of it, but the half-filled bowl of gunk convinces her otherwise.

Do they usually put the spoon directly into the bowl or beside it?

Emily gives up on wondering, already busy with spoon-carving the outlines of something—she couldn't tell what—into the wall. The metal spoon quickly warms under her cool, numb fingers. Her memories of Alexander Griffin, her former inmate, brush her mind and an uncontrollable hysteria seizes her. Why are those walls so hard to carve! Even after rubbing, scratching, pressing ferociously, only a thin silver line shines on the matte surface. It's exhausting and clearly not worth it, but the path to reason can take some surprising turns.

What portrait was she working on after her coma, just before Philip plucked her from her little haven in a corner of the Refuge's infirmary? For her sketch to look like anything, it would take her days. And who will be there to see it besides Duke?

Speaking of the wolf.

Duke walks into the cell and scans every inch of it, taking in every detail he's memorized over time. He may not have an aura, but his body speaks for itself.

He comes to sound out her condition, or rather to make sure the modern-day oatmeal is working its way into her mind. His visit comes shortly after watching Milo and the Reyes family's suicide mission. Emily refuses to talk and realizes by the same token that ignoring Duke Kay's presence is a big mistake. He's not used to being disobeyed and things can go down the wrong way quickly.

As much as he'd like to convince her otherwise, Emily has more than one option to change her fate. The spoon is tempting, but from experience, she knows it'll only provide her some temporary comfort. Even if Duke were blind by her doing, he would retain his omnipotence. He has an army ready to back him up and a lapdog to do the dirty work. She needs to use something else against him.

"You're eating. That's good," he says with a mischievous smile. The hand he used to hit her is still bruised.

Damn! They serve the spoon next to the bowl! No gagging this time. Duke would be thrilled if he knew she's getting used to the food.

"I'm glad the oatmeal is to the lady's liking. From what I hear, she is known to have special cravings in *La Orilla*."

"How long have you been watching me?" she replies, surly. "If indulging in a decent meal on this Ark once in a while is sacrilege, well, you should've stopped me when you had the chance."

"Everything in its own time. We can't change the fate of the human race in a few days, can we?"

"Such a noble goal! If that's what you tell your agents to earn their trust, no wonder they're at your beck and call. It's not so different from the Brotherhood, after all. You're selling a dream."

He smooths his well-oiled beard with the shadow of a smile. He's in a good mood today.

"If only it were that simple," he replies in his deep, authoritative voice. "People are easier to break than you think. Most do it with gusto because they don't know how to run their lives anyway. They all want the same thing: to serve a cause bigger than themselves."

"The Creator's wish," Emily repeats from memory, thinking of Violet who would make a better conversation partner.

Duke gives her an interested look. "But some of them resist and pose a real problem."

"I guess I'm one of them," Emily scoffs, feeling the muscles in her face tense.

"Why state the obvious?"

"To feel important. Different. Something other than a wretched Bates. I like to assert my individuality. It allows me to live. To survive."

"Miss Bates," he says, crouching beside her, not bothered in the least by Emily's white-knuckling her spoon.

For a moment, she has second thoughts about not giving into her dark desire for revenge.

"I'll get you something to draw with," he says, his breath reeking of stale cigar smoke. "You look like a whore, scribbling on my walls. A woman of your standing should not indulge in such unworthy activities."

The stench lingers, even after he leaves. Emily's own sketchbook comes an hour later with her usual pencils.

———

DUKE VISITS her more often and stays longer each time. The smell of cigars permeates every inch of Emily's cell, a sore reminder of Dad's sacrifice. Duke treats her like his confidant with his insistent monologues, chaining cigar after cigar. He doesn't care about her answering or not. In fact, he is more receptive when she remains quiet. He needs to be listened to, obeyed, the very traits of psychopaths. Again, it might seem obvious, but being unable to read his aura is frightening. She's learning to read him more and more easily, a result of the considerable time they spend together. Funny when you think he should be busy with his duties as a so-called commander. But the advantage of having an army that caters to his every whim must be to be able to waste his time on something trivial, while his puppets mindlessly go about doing his job. Do what I say, not what I do—the dream of every commander harboring sordid fantasies.

Eventually, he saw his portrait in Emily's sketchbook. He seemed pleased enough to allow her to doodle in his presence. She makes no secret of the fact that he is her model of choice now. With each stroke of her pencil, she strips away the layers of his armor, slowly teasing out the truth about him.

Other people are apparently allowed to visit her. Philip Farrell is hanging around the door, looking at her. He seems to have gotten off lightly once again. He looks well fed and free to move about, always in the right place at the right time. She puts aside her sketchbook, out of politeness.

He moves closer to her, nose wrinkled, bothered by the stale smell of Duke's cigars, which lingers for hours after his visits. The Ark's defective ventilation needs some serious patching up. Her makeshift cell was not meant to keep someone in for days on end.

"All I care about is your sister, Violet," Emily says flatly. Philip is wide-eyed, seemingly surprised by her animosity.

"I may not be my sister, but I can help you," he insists, almost begging her. "You can defeat him."

How can he be so sure? Where was he when Duke sacrificed Dad in the public eye? When everyone else was out of oxygen and choking to death?

Her rising anger subsides when she sets her eyes on an object in Philip's hands.

"What is that?" she asks abruptly, frowning. Despite her behaving distant around him, he takes a chance at drawing closer.

"You know how my sister is. She wanted something to help her commune with the Creator. So, I thought a deck of cards could serve as her medium. It was supposed to be her birthday gift."

Philip can't possibly be conniving with Duke, though he always manages to miraculously avoid the worst. He is a Farrell, the most respectable family in the Ark's history. Emily simply cannot treat him as an enemy. Hasn't he tried to help her in his own way?

He reads her aura like an open book and sits beside her with renewed confidence. Emily picks up one of the hard glossy cards, smooth under her fingers. Every card has an ichthys on the back, the same symbol of three fish caught in the wheel of life from the Sanctuary. The other face features an elderly woman finely hand-painted, probably in oil, a medium that has never sat well with Emily. The brushstrokes are delicate with careful attention to detail. Her eyes drift up at Philip like he is a completely different person. His talent is raw and real. She shouldn't have misjudged him on his paintings. And here she thought he was an amateur only capable of painting lousy biblical scenes.

"Who is it?" she asks shyly.

"Our grandmother, Elaine Farrell."

So, *she* was their grandmother. She looks rather serious on this portrait, but her many lines of expression tell she has an easy smile. When Violet invited her and Gabrielle to bake cupcakes in her cabin, she mentioned the matriarch for the first time. Violet had just moved into their late grandmother's cabin and seemed to have inherited quite a legacy.

Emily scans the deck, one card after another: a tilted vase of water, a crashing wave, a glowing light, the tip of the Ark, the faces of former commanders, a sea dragon straight out of a children's story about the Great Ocean, a hunter in a wetsuit, a treasure trove filled with coins of various metals—the same they used to play with at the Academy—, a mythical fairy with a mischievous look—Emily stops a little longer on this card, her stomach lurching—, a basket overflowing with fruits, a large flame wrapped in a cocoon strangely similar to the Sacred Fire, a wide-trunked tree with drooping branches, a cluster of crimson flowers, a mirror with a blurred reflection, and a child with a cross-shaped scar. She stops when she realizes that her grimy fingerprints dull the surface of the cards. Embarrassment grips her for ruining such fine artwork. She hands over the now-sullied deck of cards.

Philip shuffles the cards deftly, cascading them to a respectable height as Emily looks on in amazement. Seeing such a deck on the Ark, let alone someone who knows what to do with it, doesn't happen every day.

"Draw one," he offers pleasantly, which brings her out of her reverie.

"Why?" she asks stupidly, suspicion nagging at her.

"You'll see. The Creator's Ways are not so easy to make out, you know."

Emily can't help but roll her eyes at Philip's mocking tone. He unfolds the cards face down and presents them to her. She draws one with a moment of hesitation, guided by the impulse.

"The North Star, the one that guides when one has lost his way," he says, turning over the card Emily picked, painted with an illustration she hasn't seen before. It is a five-pointed star in purplish blue glowing in the clear night sky. "It comes up a lot in the Creator's writings." Philip places the card back on top of the pile to get a better look. "It will always be there with you, wherever you are."

A surge of emotions overwhelms Emily, who doesn't know if it's Mom, Dad, her sister, or even Milo, but pieces of them are in this card. She can almost feel it.

"A hunch," adds Philip in front of Emily's contemplative silence. "Believe it or not, Violet always says to trust our intuition."

Intuition. It's kind of like auras, right? She reads them and they respond to her.

"You call her Violet now?" Emily teases.

"I kind of like it. It's more colorful than Dinah."

"I have a copyright on that name, you know? It'll cost you." She manages to let out a short laugh and her cell dissolves, her mind finally free. The feeling is fleeting, but the relief lingers a while longer.

"Consider it payment for the time you spent gazing at my artwork for free," Philip points out, dropping his serious air. Emily sees a whole new side of Philip.

"That's not even true! Your paintings are on public display in a busy corridor."

"You did take the liberty of snooping around the Sanctuary," he says, surprising Emily. "Nothing escapes me, especially when a trace of sugar is stuck on one of my splendid paintings. It's all right, I forgive you. See how benevolent I am?"

"I can't believe that Duke or anyone else from the Paragon would allow you to keep me company. Especially not someone of your ilk. Kindness is not part of the mind-control program or anything that has to do with the Paragon."

"You know they can hear everything we say, right?" Philip warns with a sideways glance.

"They already know everything about me, things I don't even know myself. I can see it in Duke's eyes when he talks to me. And as creepy as it seems, the same goes for his agents when they look at me."

As if on cue, the Paragon guards on duty open the door to signal the end of the visit. Philip slips a card under her pillow and as he leans forward, a scar in the hollow of his neck jumps out at her, the same as the child's card. "I'm counting on you to stay alive long enough to give it to Violet," he says with a faint smile.

Emily is torn between asking him what he knows about Gabrielle and where his mark comes from. By the time she makes up her mind, Philip has already left.

HER HEART-TO-HEART TALK with Philip leaves her happier than she has been since waking up from her coma. She spends the whole following day feverishly drawing in her sketchbook.

She draws the cards from memory as they scroll in her head so she can remember them, starting with the North Star card Philip left for her. When her memory fails her, she creates her own cards, though the exercise is much more complex than she thought. Which symbol or element should she choose? She tries and gives up after several unsuccessful attempts. Nothing inspires her within the four walls of her cell.

That evening, the Creator might have been conspiring to grant her wishes. They finally transfer her out of the Refuge. The Sacred Fire seems to have been restored, or else they would've suffocated as soon as they emerged from under the Atrium. It can only mean that Milo's impossible mission was a success.

Each of the Paragon agents salutes them as they walk past, just like any good mind-controlled automaton would. How can Duke have a constant hold on so many people at once? It makes no sense at all, and yet … isn't thought-controlling people far-fetched anyway?

Her conversation with Philip adds to her fading memories when she dozes off in her new cell in the Paragon headquarters teeming with automatons.

In the morning, they don't allow her to wake up leisurely as in her old prison. Blinding lights on the glass walls burn her retinas.

"We can finally get started," Duke Kay's raspy voice whispers.

27

NEAL

"Do you think it'll work?"

"I hope so, anyway," says Skyler, who doesn't look as confident as he did an hour ago when he was doing the final checks.

"She really wasn't easy to convince, you know," Neal adds in a muffled voice. Uki is chatting animatedly with Tessa who glances his way. Ever since Uki made a comment about his relationship with Tessa, Neal always feels like they are talking about him.

Skyler scowls like he does every time someone doubts him, but Neal will need to see those memory spheres in action himself to believe they work.

Their little group enters a room in the base's clinic. Skyler has everything ready: a reclining chair with a glass globe—surely a memory sphere—set in some sort of pedestal. Everything seems tidy and well organized. Uki tenses up when she steps into the room, and her smile dies, but Tessa brings her back into the conversation to keep her mind busy. If this is what it takes to get Uki's memories back, it's worth it. So far, Tessa and Neal haven't found any other survivors of the Sedna. Their only way to learn more is to unravel the mystery shrouding her and her strange power. Neal never slept so well in the years before his strange experience with her. However crazy this might sound; she found a way to dispel the darkness that had been creeping on him.

"You just need to settle here," Skyler instructs.

Tessa holds her hand firmly and gives Uki a tender smile. "I'll be right here."

What Neal would give to have Tessa smile at him that way. They would need to be honest with each other about their feelings, though, and that would mean sharing their deepest fears. He cannot blame her for avoiding it. He has been doing so himself for a long while.

Uki is lying on the reclined bed, half seated with her sphere giving off a strange glow.

"How are you feeling?" asks Skyler calmly.

"Nervous," Uki says, groping for Tessa's hand.

"You won't feel anything. The sphere will simply copy some of your memories."

"Sorry for being late," says Eliza as she shuts the door. "My brother can really be a pain sometimes."

"No worries," Skyler replies, smiling.

She joins their small group clustered around Uki and glances at the sphere. "Glad to see you made it through your project. You're good at this."

"Did you design this thing yourself?" asks Neal, skeptically. "I thought you were a doctor. Not an engineer."

"I tested it on myself, and it worked. There's no need to worry."

"See? Even your brother can surprise you," says Tessa, raising an eyebrow.

"No distractions," Skyler says to them, and their words fade into silence. "Let's start by relaxing. Close your eyes, Uki."

Tessa sits beside Neal who is tempted to put his arm around her waist. The rebuff of the other night rings in his ears, so he crosses his arms. She does nothing to get closer to him either.

Uki is taking deep breaths as Skyler's words carry her through a relaxing scene just like the meditation sessions Dan taught Neal for years. He would fall asleep, and his nightmares would resurface every time. No wonder he hates meditating so much. He feels a pang of jealousy at seeing Uki excel at what Dan has been killing himself to teach him with no results.

Once Uki's breathing has calmed, Skyler says, "You'll hear a beeping sound. It's only the machine synchronizing with you."

A screen that Neal hadn't noticed lights up with some waves forming a graph, and then the beeps come on.

"Think about when you were on the Sedna. Imagine what it looked like. Focus on something familiar like your cabin."

Everyone is holding their breath as Uki remains still. Neal can't help but move a little closer to the edge of his seat.

"Go back to the last moment you remember."

"I think... I'm there."

"Focus on the feeling of emptiness or confusion you are experiencing."

The waves almost immediately take on a strange shape. Skyler taps something, and a fan whirrs to life. Beads of light flick on in the center of the sphere, floating back and forth for a while before multiplying. From this distance, it's hard to see exactly what's going on, but Skyler's satisfied expression says it all. After a few minutes, Skyler removes the electrodes he placed on Uki's head, and then Tessa checks on Uki as she helps her stand. Uki nods sleepily, and Skyler directs them to an adjoining room where a second screen has been set up. The place looks like a sparsely furnished consulting room, with cabinets and a sink, much like the Refuge's infirmary. There are only two chairs, but no one makes a move to sit.

"Do you mind if we look at your memories?" asks Skyler with a serious look on his face. "It's your decision."

Uki looks at them in turn.

"Do we really have to go through this? It's too late to back out now," Neal says, annoyed.

"These are her memories, not ours. I don't think you'd want us to play in your head without your permission." Neal bites back a comment when he catches Tessa's disapproving look, then looks away.

"I don't mind." Everyone's eyes shoot at Uki. "I can't remember by myself. It's the least I can do to help you in return."

Eliza doesn't take her eyes off Skyler while he taps away at the screen. Isn't Oslo's sister a mystery? The way she looks at Skyler like he's about to perform some grand magic trick doesn't sit well with Neal. She did show them the underbelly of the base when she likely had nothing to gain except drawing her brother's ire if he found out. Is it even a good idea to have her here with Uki's sphere laid bare?

The screen turns on before Neal can decide to act on it. A blurry image is taking shape, and it takes a moment for Neal to realize that they are seeing a scene through Uki's eyes.

Uki is surrounded by a line of people in a room littered with cushions. A woman is kneeling before her.

"Is it true what they say? Do you really have the power to cure us of the disease?"

"You could say that," replies Uki in a voice that is different from today's, more confident and worthy of respect.

"Please, I beg you!" The woman raises her head, her eyes filled with the kind of adoration only reserved for a goddess.

"It's painful," says Uki in that same regal voice. "You have to want it from the bottom of your being."

"Yes."

"Do you fully trust me?"

"I do."

"Your hands."

Neal remembers asking Uki to rid him of his nightmares in the temple, and a chill of familiarity runs down his spine. Uki's eyes are riveted on the screen, her hand tightly gripping Tessa's.

Images scroll by at lightning speed, and the woman's screams louder and louder. For a second, Neal can imagine that every fiber of her muscles is being ripped out.

Are these images inside the woman's head? This is insane!

Uki's eyes widen as a hellish noise reverberates through the room where other men and women are kneeling on cushions, panic-stricken. The woman Uki was treating topples onto her back in shock, unconscious or dead from stopping the procedure midway. People in the line squeal in surprise and jostle to let a familiar man walk up to Uki. He is mighty with a manic smile hanging from his lips, his hair surprisingly white for his age.

It's the warden from the Amaranth's prison. The very same who helped the Brotherhood break Fiona and Milo free. But what the hell is he doing on the Sedna?

"I heard that you can cure people of a mysterious disease? I'd like to know if I have it."

He kicks aside the unconscious woman in his way dismissively and brings one knee down, an awkward position for a man of his caliber.

Uki's hands are trembling, and the warden ends up taking her hands by force.

"Don't be afraid," he cajoles.

A flurry of visions assault Uki. Flesh, blood, death. There are so many that Neal can't register it all. Uki manages to break the contact in a gasp. The warden's face is disappointed, almost innocent. He asks, "Is there a cure for this?"

Gunshots. People in the room crumple on their cushions with blank stares. Uki retreats, then collapses while treading over the piling bodies. They were people who came to ask for Uki's help. All around her, they fall, one after another in a storm of blood and screams.

There are no survivors.

Neal struggles to watch it all the way through. The others cry out in amazement, all of them except Eliza.

"Don't you worry," says the warden. "You won't remember a thing."

He buries something in Uki's head, surely some kind of injection, and then a loud noise drowns her breathing. Her eyes snap shut and the screen goes dark.

"You don't have to watch," Tessa says to Uki, then turns to Skyler. "That's enough!"

"Wait!" says Neal before Skyler disables the sphere. "It's not over!"

Uki opens her eyes. She is in an odd room, with strange veils floating around. The guard doesn't seem to be around.

"It's him!" shouts someone. Then the words blend into something that sounds like Oslo and Eliza's language when they speak to their guards.

"I didn't think there would be any survivors," says the warden.

Uki frantically looks around for a way to escape.

"After all the trouble I went through to rake out this dirt-filled ark. You should've stayed holed up deeper in the ocean."

Moving over to the other side to hide, Uki watches what is happening in the nearby hallway: Men wearing the same uniforms worn by Oslo and his gang when they landed on the Amaranth are pointing their weapons at the warden. He seems annoyed, but afraid of the mob who could butcher him on the spot. One of them calls out, "By the Star, if someone had told me that a man of your kind existed, I would've never believed it. Straight out from hell."

"Far!" shouts Eliza, moving closer to the screen.

The burly man has a thick blond beard and long hair, the exact replica of Oslo. He charges toward the warden who curses at him before letting out a chilling laugh. Uki is heaving from panic as she tries to find a better hiding place before the war cries come.

She throws herself into the corridor and runs at full speed until the screams die behind. Neal has the feeling that the squad is being massacred. Uki dares to look over her shoulder: the burly man is being ripped apart by something bright with the warden towering over him, bathed in a shower of blood.

The interference becomes too great to distinguish anything else. The sphere burns out, and Skyler pulls it out of its pedestal. He lets out a cry of pain and the sphere rolls onto the ground under the furniture. Neal brings his brother over to the sink and runs cold water over his burned hand.

"What should I do?" shouts Neal, distraught.

"The cupboard on the left," indicates his brother, his teeth clenched. Neal grabs a compress and dips it under water, then offers it to Skyler.

"Do you need anything else?" asks Neal, feeling helpless and stupid.

"I'll be fine."

Neal sighs as he runs his hand through his hair. Uki is shaking like a leaf in Tessa's arms, who is equally pale like she woke up from a nightmare.

"No one is to tell my brother Oslo about this," Eliza says firmly, staring into space. "You hear me?" She looks at them in turn, and Neal knows he has been lied to all along.

"Was that your father in Uki's memories? What was he doing there?"

"I don't know what Oslo told you, but—"

"He's dead! Was someone going to tell me or were you going to use this against me?"

"Listen—"

"You're just like your brother! So much for negotiating with your father. All that time wasted while the Amaranth might be that maniac's next target. I will hold you accountable for this, Eliza Nord."

Eliza's face flushes, but she manages to keep her composure. "Our father's squad perished while trying to save the people of the Sedna. We will *not* send anyone to be slaughtered on your Ark if that's what you think."

"And yet you came once," Neal continues, glancing at Tessa stroking Uki's head resting on her chest. The girl from the Sedna seems on the verge of a breakdown, an all-too-familiar feeling growing in his throat.

Skyler stares at him intently. What is going on in his head? Is he judging him? Is he waiting to see his reaction? Now would be a good time to get his support.

"This carnage…" Neal says with a confidence that surprises him, "won't go unanswered. I'm going to talk with your brother, whether you like it or not. It's time to get things moving."

Neal walks out of the room while Skyler stays behind. And that's what hurts him the most.

28

SKYLER

Rolf has been staring at him for a while, like a statue that could adorn the little temple. This miniature version of the Sacred Fire blazing in his eyes is a power to be reckoned with. He has Neal's passion which drove Skyler to push through with his ideas. This drive is pure energy that asks to be heeded, to be shaped into a desire, a vision. It could burn everything in its path if not tamed properly.

"I'm ready," Rolf finally says as Skyler checks the oxygen levels of some patients suffering from pneumonia.

"You are *not* ready."

Oxygen hisses through the tubes. It was the same sound when they emerged from the Refuge, suited up and unaware of what lay ahead. This nagging uncertainty that anything can happen at every breath is a weight that Skyler has been burdened with for years. Deciding a patient's fate cannot be taken lightly. Emotions are sneaky and always find a way to wreak havoc in the moments of quiet and doubt following such a decision.

The same happened with his mother. By wanting to keep her close, by telling himself that he was the one who needed to take care of her, he gave in to his emotions and his desire to see her snap out of her depression. His internal struggle finally came to an end when he admitted defeat. But then, something unexpected came along and changed everything: His brother, the antidote to his mother's mysterious illness. This is his sin to atone for.

Skyler wasn't ready for this.

"You said you would teach me," Rolf insists, looking at Skyler at eye level despite their age difference.

"Why don't you prepare some hot water and clean towels? We're running low on sterilizing soap, so you'll have to make your own solution. Just follow the instructions I've written on the board. Make a copy for the next time."

"I want to care for them, not wash them."

"Every action counts. The treatment itself is just one step in the process. Care involves keeping them clean and sterilizing everything. They are vulnerable to other infections that could put them in grave danger."

Rolf inhales deeply, his inner fire burning brightly. "When, then?" Skyler sorts through the files he will need to update, Rolf following at his heels. "You think I'm too young. Too immature. That I don't take it seriously. I know every person at the Star by their first name. Bjarne, Dag, Jord, Kjersti, Trine…"

This is what scares Skyler the most. "These people's lives depend on us. We can't afford to make mistakes," Skyler replies, more abruptly than he intended. "Sterilize the instruments, and then make sure they all stay hydrated, especially the father. His condition could become critical if we are careless."

Rolf contains his disagreement this time and goes to fill a basin, while Skyler stares at his files absentmindedly. He doesn't know most of these names. What happened to them?

· · ·

FOR THE REST of the morning, Rolf performed the tasks given by Skyler, who studied Marko's notes while keeping an eye on his apprentice.

After the successful experiment with Uki's memory sphere, Skyler decided to get into the rudiments of engineering to bury Chris's kiss in his memories. A tangle of feelings weighs heavily on his chest, especially since Chris has been avoiding him like the plague. Hopefully, time will sort things out.

For the time being, he is absorbing Marko's notes that will help him develop his sphere project. Marko is patient, for which Skyler is grateful. Every moment they spend together, Marko could be putting up some toy to make another child smile again. Skyler vows to use his knowledge to return the favor as soon as he can. As he discovers new concepts, he imagines how the clinic could use a makeover. The Creator knows just how much they need it.

"Am I intruding?" asks Eliza, shyly, which doesn't sound like her.

"A break won't hurt," he replies, setting aside the documents and casting a glance over Rolf emptying a used basin.

"Engineering?" she says, tilting her head to read the schematics he's working on. "There's definitely not enough work for you at the clinic. Or maybe you're just crazy."

Skyler lets out a hearty laugh. Sometimes he wonders if he's bordering on madness with his new idea for the spheres. It is not like he has anything concrete now, but with better knowledge, he senses there could be another use for them.

"What I have in mind has nothing to do with engineering, though," she continues, pretending to think. "Just a little exercising."

"Why not?" he says, happy to be able to leave his hideout. "That way we can catch up on things."

"Don't forget to bring your coat."

Skyler raises an eyebrow, then grabs the soft coat Isabela

gave him as a token of her gratitude for saving her daughter Rose. The coat was tailored by a fellow worker, who spends all her spare time doing wool work, and is most useful when the cold drafts sneak into the tunnels on cloudy days.

"I'm counting on you to make sure their oxygen levels stay up," Skyler says to Rolf, whose eyes light up in disbelief. "They stabilized this morning, so they should be fine. If anything unusual happens—"

"I'll go get Chris," he replies, discarding the bowl with a little too much enthusiasm. "I'll take care of it." Eliza says something in their language, and Rolf nods promptly as the students at the Academy did whenever they were told to behave.

With a wry smile, Skyler follows Eliza as she leads him out of the clinic into the comforting warmth of the main dome.

"Rolf is a quick learner," she says. "Only if you give him the chance."

"I'm not the best teacher. I leave that to Chris."

"Always Chris." She holds back a laugh, and Skyler doesn't dare ask why. Chris might have talked to her. "You have a good heart, you know. You even helped that girl get her memories back. I've never seen anything like it before."

All traces of the anger Eliza showed that day are gone.

"Without Marko's help, I wouldn't have gotten anywhere."

"Marko?" she repeats, as they pass the corridor leading to the secluded garden. "When my brother learns that—"

"Skyler?" Tessa is standing in front of him, dressed in a strange midnight blue Kevlar armor, something Oslo's guards would wear, but not quite. She looks worried.

"We're taking a walk," says Skyler. "Is something wrong? You look pale."

"It's great," she says awkwardly. "It's a beautiful day, perfect for a walk. I should do the same."

"Care to join?" asks Eliza, glimpses Tessa's gun at her hip. "Sorry, you must be busy helping my brother."

"I need to find Neal first. We were supposed to meet here, but... I should probably get going." Tessa leaves suddenly without another word. What is Neal up to?

"Too bad she doesn't like me," Eliza says, looking hurt and staring at the spot where Tessa vanished. "I'd like to get to know her."

"Don't take it personally. Tessa can be a little weird sometimes." The many times they've crossed paths, she always has this air of mystery. "She's not the talkative type."

Eliza's gaze lingers on the dome, her eyebrows furrowed. When Skyler asks if everything is all right, she says, "Just a feeling of déjà vu. I'm sorry."

She gives him a smile, before walking into a tunnel dug into a small mountain. They quickly emerge on the other side which opens onto a snowy plain, and Eliza motions for his wool coat. "It'll be a little cooler than usual."

Eliza hands him what she calls snowshoes. They are over-sized shoes that look like the giant slippers his mother's best friend used to knit for them when she wanted to get rid of her old skeins of yarn.

"We won't need them for the whole trip. I'll tell you when."

They strap their snowshoes on their backs and step out into the cold north. Skyler's cheeks tighten and his mouth freezes, a totally different experience from their hike to the summit. The strong wind blows unobstructed here.

"It's a good thing the weather is nice today," says Eliza with a smile. "If not, the skin on my face would literally fall off."

"I didn't think it could get this cold," Skyler says, shivering.

"You haven't seen anything yet. When the Long Night sets in, no one will be allowed outside. Temperatures drop so low that a single minute outside can freeze anyone. The Star has everything we need to keep us warm, but it needs rigorous preparations before winter. We use salt crystals to store solar energy during the summer so that when winter comes, the living quarters, the greenhouses, and the garden remain heated. At least, the cover of the mountains helps to keep the heat in."

It is hard to imagine what his first winter will look like, but one thing is for certain, the dome and the heart of the mountain will become their only home. This harsh world will force them into isolation no matter what.

"The Academy should have prepared us better."

"The Academy?"

"On the Ark. Our children are taught how to survive on the Surface, but *this* is a completely different world than what we were ever taught."

"The arks were... How should I put it? Incomplete. The whole rescue plan had glaring flaws that we keep uncovering. And then..."

They come across a few scattered trees that offer them some temporary cover, and Eliza heaves a sigh. "There is always this kind of curse every time we visit an Ark."

"A curse? Isn't that a bit far-fetched?"

"This is what we say when something bad keeps happening and is linked to someone or someplace. It's like some sort of plague."

Their boots kick pebbles as they cross a beach strikingly different from the Paragon simulation. This one is cold, gray, and inhospitable. The smell the gently lapping waves bring is soothing, yet the stiff breeze urges them to seek cover.

"This is where our ship ran aground. We didn't know the surrounding waters well at first, but luckily, we discovered the base or else we would've frozen to death."

"Haven't you been here for generations?"

"Our legend says so, but for some unknown reason, our ancestors left long ago. It was our father Anzen Nord who brought us back, following the footsteps of our predecessors. The North Star we know is no more than a dozen years old. My brother and I first grew up on the Nord Ark, before moving here. I know how unnerving it can be to start over, but it is a necessary sacrifice."

As they walk along the beach, the smell of decay wafts over, and, as if on cue, Eliza points at a grounded ship in the distance.

"Your Ark?" asks Skyler. The nose of the bulky vessel is turned over in the sand, and its body, eaten away by the elements, extends into the water.

"No. It sank somewhere in the ocean. This is one of our ships that managed to escape from Thalassa's attack."

She pulls her scarf to show a scar in her neck brushing against her spinal cord.

"A drone almost decapitated me when severing the frame of the ship. I am still alive today thanks to my brother's foresight."

"What exactly is Thalassa?"

"This conversation is getting too serious. Should we go for a walk in the forest? Dusk has a way to fall unexpectedly."

Skyler does not press on for fear of reviving painful memories. The cover of the forest will be more inviting than this death-bearing beach anyway.

They go up the gentle slope that leads to a deep-green forest, much darker than the trees of the Gardens of Humankind.

"Pine trees?" hazards Skyler.

"Have you seen any before?" she wonders, picking up a thorny twig. "Our ark didn't have any trees so you can imagine the surprise the first time we saw these. We decided to call them *Gran*."

Skyler grabs a twig to examine. The thorns are soft and tough, but pleasant to the touch because of their rounded tips. He brings the twig to his nose and inhales its familiar aromatic scent.

"I'm probably the only one on my Ark fascinated by plants, though it was easy enough to find information about them in the Archives if you knew where to look. It's a shame the Academy didn't bother to teach us."

"The ark hives? What is it?"

"It's a database full of images and videos of everything that existed on Earth. Didn't you have one?"

"I don't think so. Hopefully, your ark isn't cursed like the others." Her face momentarily clouds, then she points to a clearing in the forest. "This is where we're going. The snow is too deep here, and there are rocks that will get in the way. We should still be able to travel through that path since there hasn't been a storm in a while."

"Didn't we have a storm last time?" says Skyler, recalling their walk over the mountain range where they glimpsed the *Eyr* barrier.

"No. The storms here are … quite an event. Isn't there any mention of this in your big library?"

"Reading and watching is one thing but experiencing is quite another." Skyler feels like he's back in the timeless maze of the Archives, where he could dream freely of the new world. "For a long time, I wanted to experience everything possible, everything that wasn't on the Ark. Anyone would have dissuaded me, starting with my parents, by saying it would pass, that the walls of the Ark are the limits of this world. They would say: *Reality always catches up with us in the end.* But still, I didn't want this dream to end."

Skyler takes in the gray-blue sea of water to his left, the snow-white sea beneath his feet, and the thorny emerald sea of trees to his right, and he has no words to express how he feels. He resists the urge to close his eyes and simply be, lest he wakes up in the Atrium with the genderless electronic voice telling him that the Paragon simulation has just ended.

The boundaries of his world did fall. He was right to keep hoping.

Chris is right. Skyler can't simply continue to pretend he's on the Ark. Reality must not catch up with him.

"Being here … is a miracle," Skyler muses. "Whether it's the Creator's work or not, I don't intend to waste this chance."

Eliza says nothing, her gaze directed toward the mountains. After a while, she looks at him with a glint of silent understanding.

"I'll make sure of it," she says with the shadow of a promise. "It's time to put on our snowshoes. Do you know how?"

"Kind of." It turns out putting snowshoes on is not as cumbersome as suiting up in the Refuge.

"If I go too fast, just tell me," Eliza says, eager to get onto the trail. "I lose myself when I walk through this forest. It's like meditating." Skyler knows exactly how she feels—it's how he felt whenever he walked in the Gardens of Humankind.

The snow squishes under their footsteps with the fresh fragrance of pine hanging in the air, and a glance at Eliza tells him that she is also breathing in the beauty of nature. The cold subsides and the beating heart of life keeps them warm in a way that no Ark ever could.

Walking with snowshoes is not easy, and his lacking physical condition soon reminds him of that. He should get serious about this *do what you preach* mentality.

"After a dozen times, you'll see, you won't feel it anymore," says Eliza, who notices the growing distance between them.

"Is this an invitation?"

"If you will," she says with a knowing smile.

They slow their pace, and Skyler takes advantage of this to better appreciate the local flora. Even if all the pines look alike, they differ in a multitude of ways. Not only do their trunks come in different shapes and sizes, but also the arrangement of their branches forms incongruous patterns like characters frozen in arabesques. And their thorns have varying hues, ranging from a sunburnt green to a deeper shade in the half-light.

A howling sound like no other freezes him in place, putting

his senses on high alert. Eliza stops dead in her tracks at the same time and scans their surroundings. The howling repeats, then stretches into an echoing sound. Aren't they alone in these woods? Immediately, Skyler thinks back to the three-dimensional model from the Academy showing them a bear that had terrified the poor student in their class.

Can bears howl like that?

"It must be …," Eliza doesn't have time to finish her sentence, because something leaps at Skyler who loses his footing while trying to avoid it. He struggles, snow flying in all directions, as a rush of panic numbs his body. A wet, raspy tongue licks his face, choking him, but then he hears Eliza's loud laugh.

"Koda likes to meet the new refugees before the rest of the pack," she explains, petting the massive, furry beast that finally leaves him alone. "She's a northern dog. She wouldn't hurt a fly, even frozen."

"A … dog?"

Koda wags her tail in a funny way, boasting her snow-white coat patterned in black, looking at him curiously with a sky-blue eye and a hazel-brown eye. The beast is massive, and Skyler can't believe creatures like this actually exist.

"Let her smell you," Eliza says as she continues to pet Koda. "Show her your hand gently."

Skyler extends a trembling hand, and Koda comes over to sniff it thoroughly. Once her inspection is complete, she licks it profusely, tickling Skyler until he laughs uncontrollably. Satisfied, Koda jumps to the trail and watches them expectantly.

"Does she want us to follow her?" asks Skyler hesitantly.

"Perceptive, aren't you? Just because these beasts don't talk doesn't mean they aren't smart. Come on."

Eliza and Skyler follow Koda who bounces happily through the snow heaps. She barks impatiently every time they stop for Skyler who can't keep up. Fortunately, she can't talk. Along the way, Skyler wipes off the cold, thick saliva drying on his face with the breeze creeping through the pines.

In a large clearing, other dogs like Koda run after each other yelping excitedly. Logs of wood are strung against the frame of a hut made of the same material. Several thatched cottages with smoking chimneys form a camp where people are working on some new construction near the edge of the forest.

"*Skogenslofte* is our plan to establish a permanent colony outside the base," explains Eliza. A bunch of children are playing with the dogs, and, a little further, little Rose rolls around in the snow with one of the dogs tickling her with its muzzle.

Eliza gives him a tour of the small rustic colony made of thatched cottages boasting a shiny coating. Their roofs cascade on each side, almost touching the ground, and the entrance sits in the center of a triangle-shaped frontage.

"Some of the refugees say that technology has ruled us for long enough, and that it brought upon *Ulykke*. This pace of life isn't suitable for everyone. It's labor-intensive, and no one is prepared to face the harsh elements of nature. Many who move here end up returning to the base, but those who stay are doing well enough."

"Have you thought about moving here?" asks Skyler, curious.

"My place is by my brother's side. Since our father died, he needs me more than ever. Who else is going to keep an eye on him?"

"I can take care of myself very well, Liz." Oslo emerges from the largest of the thatched cottages with Neal and a handful of guards. Skyler tenses at the sight of his brother, who looks unhappy to see him here.

"If only that were true," says Eliza. "How are the preparations going?"

"Well, given the timeframe. But still, I'll ask them to move back to the base."

"Why is that? *Skogenslofte* is what *far* has always wanted."

"With our recent losses, we barely have enough people to maintain the base. Without the Star, no one can survive. *Skogenslofte* can wait."

"You can't!"

"Times are changing, Liz."

"We'll leave you two alone," Neal interjects, pulling Skyler aside who takes one last look at Eliza before she switches to her native tongue to argue with Oslo.

When the cover of the pine trees is thick enough to muffle the noise coming from the colony, Skyler halts. Neal turns around, looking exasperated.

"What the hell! Where have you been all this time?"

"I knew you were going to say that," Skyler replies flatly, with a strong desire to return to camp instead of playing this senseless game. "The answer seems obvious to me."

"We are family. We can no longer ignore each other."

"When are we going back to the Ark to save the others? Our mother? Our future sister?"

Skyler said too much.

"What?" exclaims Neal, looking darker than Skyler remembers. "How long have you known about this?"

"Forget I said anything," Skyler says weakly, his confidence melting like snow in the sun. "You never cared about our mother, anyway."

Of course, Skyler did his research in his spare time as they prepared to move to the Refuge, more out of curiosity than anything else. It doesn't matter what gender the child is but being able to give her a face and maybe even a name makes it more real, maybe even a reason to forgive his mother for never believing in him.

"Maybe you're right," Neal concedes, his eyes shining with hurt. "I wasn't there for her, or for Dad. The worst part is that my memories of them are so distant I feel like I never loved or even knew them. Sometimes I think I should've died the day I fell."

"Don't act like you're the victim!" shouts Skyler, outraged. "You have a responsibility toward all of us."

"Consider other people's feelings before blaming them for your problems. You could've saved Mom, Dad, and your best friend Emily, but you didn't. Whose fault was that?"

"Certainly not his," Chris interjects, emerging from a shrub.

"This is our family matter, so get lost!" Neal clenches his fists with a steely look for Chris.

"Instead of blaming Skyler, who never stopped caring for his family when you mysteriously disappeared, why don't you go find Oslo?"

"Whatever," Neal spits before striding back to the colony.

Once his brother is far enough away, Chris turns to Skyler. "Sorry, I heard everything. How are you holding up?" It's the first time they've spoken since their kiss at the garden, and his stomach tightens.

"My brother can be a real jerk. I should be the one apologizing for him."

"Just because you're his brother doesn't mean you should take the blame for his selfish behavior. For someone who claims the title of Commander of the Amaranth, he should know better. All I see is a coward."

"You're probably right," Skyler adds with a bitter taste, and they go deeper into the quiet of the woods.

"What do you think of this place?" asks Chris who seems tense. "It's better than I ever imagined."

"I like it too, but it's very snowful. Is snowful a word?" Skyler manages to wring a smile out of Chris, whose face is painfully red from the temperature dropping by the minute. Nightfall is already approaching.

"Did you see those big dogs? They're adorable!" says Chris

with a childlike excitement that brings back memories. "I've always wanted to see them."

"You? Really?"

"Don't you think so?"

"They have their charms," says Skyler, who can't shake the feeling of dread ever since his close encounter with that creature in the abandoned reactor at the base.

"Koda can be quite intense at first, but she is the leader of the pack and watches for intruders. She cares for her people like her own family, keeping a close eye on them. I think your brother could use some time with her."

The dogs start barking insistently, and it doesn't sound anything like earlier. Though Skyler knows almost nothing about these beasts, he can still sense that something is wrong. They exchange a worried look and hurry back to the colony.

As they step over snowdrifts, a powerful arc of electricity rips through the sky, followed by an ear-splitting shockwave. Silence sets in while fear pulses in the crackling air.

Oslo is shouting orders in the camp which has been plunged in total chaos. Koda and her pack form a protective circle around crying children while the guards rescue men and women trapped under a thatched cottage that collapsed under the impact.

"What's going on?" asks Skyler as he helps Eliza remove a wooden beam with a moaning woman trapped under it.

"*Eyr*. Nothing else has the power to create such a shockwave." The barrier that feeds on Anzen Nord and hundreds of human beings held between life and death. What happened to them?

"Nothing more stands between us and Thalassa," cries Eliza, blanching. She helps the victim freed from the rubble sit, and Neal joins them, facing Oslo with a grim expression.

"Everyone must evacuate."

"Not so fast," cuts in Oslo, hand raised. He speaks with Eliza in their language, and Skyler sorely envies their partnership. Meanwhile, Neal rushes off toward the forest.

Skyler chases him and comes close to falling headfirst into a snowdrift. He picks himself up at the last moment but struggles to keep his pace and breathing at an acceptable level. His footwork is unstable, but his brother won't slow down.

"Neal!" He keeps moving forward, and way too fast. "Allen!" shouts Skyler more forcefully before he runs out of breath. The echo of his voice gets lost in a new shockwave. The shrubs shudder, sending a shower of ice falling onto Skyler who drops to his knees. The sky takes on a strange purplish veil that comes and goes. Is it the *Eyr* barrier acting up?

He stays still, catching his breath, sweat freezing over his face. His brother is out of sight.

"Why didn't you wait for me and Oslo?" Eliza runs over to him with deep furrows on her brow. Skyler bites his lip in frustration.

"My brother," he says, grabbing Eliza's hand to get up. "I know him. He's going to do something reckless again."

"We can stop him together," she says, keeping Skyler's hand in hers. "The Star isn't that far."

"Careful, Liz," says Oslo as he passes them with his guards. "We do as we say."

"We mustn't lose a second," says Eliza to Skyler.

While they are about to join Oslo, Skyler sees Chris by a nearby pine tree, his glance fixed on Skyler's hand in Eliza's. Skyler retracts his hand, but it is too late.

"Are you coming?" asks Skyler, uncomfortably.

"I think… I'll stay with the kids," he says, his face flush with cold. "Someone must take care of them. They're our future."

Before Skyler can add anything, Chris turns away and walks back to the colony.

29

EMILY

EMILY OPENS HER EYES WITH A START.

The last person she expected to see was Sofia, Fiona's mother. She stares at her in the strange gloom created by the dormant purplish-blue neon lights, never quite turned off, even after the conditioning sessions. Emily prefers to keep her eyes closed most of the time. The burning sensation is omnipresent and unbearable, thanks to the daily onslaught of bright lights directed at her.

"Don't look so surprised," Sofia tells her, framing the glass doorway. She looks like she is in an undercover mission somehow. "I may not be Milo, but I've got experience."

"No kidding."

Her bag is slung over her shoulder and her training uniform is the same she wore during her mission with Milo. The fabric is burned in places that it wasn't in the video. Her being here is way too suspicious. Emily bluntly says, "It doesn't make sense. Why do you care what happens to me?"

"That's my business."

"I kept your daughter under lock and key," insists Emily, puzzled. Then she adds coldly, "She was my prisoner."

"Maybe she needed it." Sofia's answer stuns her. What mother would say that about her own child? "How much longer were you planning to rot in that cell? We must get moving before Duke's lackeys wake up. The tranquilizers were from an old batch."

"I won't ask you how you got them."

"Better not to."

Emily is about to follow her, but then motions for Sofia to wait. Her heart races at the thought of leaving her sketchbook behind, so she grabs it quickly along with the card of the North Star that Philip gave her, carefully tucked under her pillow. She slips the card into her worn pocket and joins Sofia who rummages in her bag as they walk away.

"I thought the Paragon had confiscated them all on Crystal Night." Emily pries when Sofia pulls a weird-looking tube out of her bag.

"The Raven has a reputation to uphold," she says simply. "It's the product I first became known for. The very thing that earned me the trust of my customers."

The Raven. Understanding finally dawns on Emily.

"What?" asks Sofia, frowning as if Emily was a creep.

"The black market," Emily continues slowly. "It was you."

"That would be me. What was once a part-time gig quickly became a necessity. I get asked for all sorts of things, drugs mostly. It's not the easiest thing to find with those Paragon dogs lurking around every corner and the Deltas fiercely protecting their beloved labs. These drugs should be available to everyone, but hey, business wouldn't be as good if they were."

The Mavericks really snuck into every part of the ship. To think that Emily once made a deal with one of them, and not just anyone: Reyes's mother herself.

"Which do you prefer?" Sofia asks with interest. "Crystal, moss, or Arahmis seeds? If you want to forget about this shithole, I have just the thing. I can give you a good deal."

"Actually, it was for a book at the time," Emily replies stupidly, remembering Gabrielle's birthday. "A gift."

"Books are not so popular since they wear so quickly. I thought you'd be a little bolder, but then again, first impressions aren't always right."

Says who, wants to answer Emily, but she wouldn't want to rub her rescuer the wrong way. Reyes's mother could just as easily turn her in to Duke.

"I don't see why we should make these drugs available. Those drug-addicted inmates I've interrogated are beyond repair."

"People on this ship are broken. Even more than you might think," Sofia explains with a forced laugh. "Who could blame them? A life locked away in some tin can at the bottom of the ocean is no fun." Her words resonate with Emily in a strange way that reminds her of her mom.

They walk along a trail of snoring guards lying on the ground. There are so many of them, yet Sofia took them all out by herself. But then, they come across shards of glass and half-eaten sandwiches. Lunch time was a tad too filling today.

"How's Milo?" Emily asks casually, praying she didn't let on the nerve-wracked mess she is ever since they took her away.

"He's alive if that's what you mean. I wouldn't be here if it were not for him."

Her aura rustles, and her face darkens.

"That one doesn't eat, it seems," Sofia grumbles, grabbing her bag. "I hope you can fight."

"I can defend myself."

Leander is waiting for them under the emergency exit sign that casts a greenish glow on his already sickly complexion. His hands twitch impatiently, ready for some action.

"Why?" asks Leander. "Why would you break out of the Paragon HQ and risk your life in the process?"

"Like you care," Emily replies. "You're probably secretly hoping I would burn alive on the stake."

"The lapdog is doing his rounds?" taunts Sofia cutting Leander, his mouth half-opened. "You shouldn't make your master wait too long. Or maybe he can already see through your eyes with his mind."

"He doesn't control me," Leander replies through gritted teeth. "I follow him willingly. And so should you."

"Sacrificing my humanity to serve a psychopath?" Emily snorts, feeling a bit weak. "Is that really what you expect me to do? And here I thought he was speaking through you. I was wrong. You're no better than he is, rotten to the core."

"Emily. Don't make the same mistake your father did."

"My father was the scapegoat of your sick desire for revenge. You should be mourning Mira rather than lashing out at innocent people." Her voice is quivering, but she presses on, giving in to the grief that feeds her rage. "I won't ever answer to your kind, so get out of our way."

Her assurance earns her a nod of approval from Sofia while Leander's face flushes with annoyance. A mob of agents rushes to his side as he regains his composure.

"If you don't care about my kind, know that the feeling is mutual," he says, incisive. "Recognize Duke as the rightful Commander of this Ark now, and he may spare you."

"He's not my commander," Emily says slowly, taking a few menacing steps forward to give her words more weight. "He may be yours, but he's definitely not mine."

Sofia draws a long dagger out of her bag, and Emily can't help but think about the plastic replica her sister made from those medieval stories she loves reading. The dagger sings as it swiftly disables the agents flanking Leander who is too slow to react. Sofia dives forward and drives her blade into an agent's neck unprotected by the Kevlar.

Emily feels a rush of adrenaline giving her hope she can get out of here alive. She was never keen on using weapons for self-defense, but her father taught her martial arts that are just as effective. She can almost feel him coming back to life thanks to her muscle memory. It's a good thing Duke has fed her enough. She isn't in top shape, but it'll do.

They exchange punches, kicks, and dagger strikes with their assailants. The smell of victory grows stronger until Duke suddenly appears, sizzling with fury as his inky gaze pierces Emily. A searing headache beats against her temples, but she doesn't relent. She is too close to freedom.

In the chaos of battle, Emily can't hear Duke, but then Leander abruptly retreats, and the mob becomes more coordinated. Duke inhales, like he's in deep meditation, his fists clenched on either side of his body.

The guards bludgeon them relentlessly, and their hits become increasingly difficult to parry. Sofia is sweating profusely by her side as she knocks out two more agents, freeing Emily from a chokehold. Emily steps back to assess the situation and catch her breath. Her thoughts freeze when her sister's voice calls out to her from the hallway leading to her cell. It's a Fairy.

"Why do you fight? Can't you see it's useless?"

The Fairy masks Gabrielle's face like a second skin. No! It's an illusion! She must resist! But Emily feels her strength leaving her and a veil shrouding her brain in confusion.

"I have to try," Emily replies, faltering.

"Even if you take them out, where will you go? The Ark is under his control. The Brotherhood is no more. The surviving Mavericks are poorly organized."

Emily's headache spikes with the crystalline voice of the Fairy, and she lets out a moan of pain. Her legs give when she receives a blow on her shoulder. She remains conscious through it all even as her vision blurs.

The Fairy's presence is fading when Emily becomes aware of

her surroundings again. The deathly silence that fell in the room is broken only by her labored breathing following Duke's.

"I almost forgot you knew each other," Duke says to Leander, as he abruptly replaces his uniform. "You should have warned me."

Duke walks over to Sofia who is held down on her knees by four agents.

"An artifact," he says disdainfully, picking up the dagger and looking at its reflection under the neon lights. "I'd be curious to know how you got your hands on this."

"The same way you go about screwing up people's minds on this ark."

Duke snorts, unimpressed. "Having a Maverick in my ranks will be a nice addition. Take her to the transition lab."

Emily shakes uncontrollably as she anticipates what is to come. They were doomed from the start. The glimmer of hope Milo sent her is gone and Emily's soul with it. Duke Kay will show no mercy.

"I must say your mother was much more docile," Duke says, planting his boot beside her. "She knew there was nowhere to hide. She learned to enjoy her privilege of spending time with me, willingly! I expect no less from you, Miss Bates."

30

EMILY

"I can't believe Duke is letting us roam freely," Fiona's voice whispers, waking Emily who had been tossing and turning between sleep and wakefulness since her return to her cell in the Paragon. Is this a broadcast? Yet the screen is dark.

Emily blinks and rubs her eyes. Did she dream of Fiona's voice? She shivers at the thought of the Fairy wearing Gabrielle's face who showed herself just before her capture. Another hallucination. She clutches her head with both hands, eyes screwed shut, her bare feet against the cold metal of her cell. How long does she have before she sinks for good?

"We still have some time," Milo's warm voice replies, freezing Emily's heart. "And to answer your question, his eyes follow us everywhere. Look at them."

Emily opens her eyes with the feeling she's being watched without her knowledge. The screen is still dark. But then, how can she hear Milo and Fiona's voices? Through the walls? Or maybe it's Duke's new tactic.

She expected him to come to her, more furious than ever, to put her through more of his nerve-wracking sessions with the flashing neon lights, or better yet, yammering on his endless monologues, but he didn't. The horrible impression that Duke could be controlling the Fairy in her head, that he found a way to break into her mind, deeply angers her. She scratches her arms, the warming of her skin reminding her that she is flesh and blood, neither trapped in her head nor dead. She is Emily. She is real.

An unusual rubbing and snapping sound she only heard in coma startles her. Duke is coming! She leaps on her feet with overwhelming dread. To think that the prisoners once feared her, but that is ancient history from a past life. Her karma will take care of her or what's left of her anyway.

She stands up. When did she sit again? Or maybe she never got up. No, no, no. This visceral panic clotting her blood, stealing her breath, arching her body in anticipation of Duke's arrival. She is not crazy.

Emily stares at the entrance, unchanged.

"What are you doing?" hisses Fiona's annoyed voice.

"Trust me," says Milo.

Then an electronic voice chimes:

Welcome to the Atrium, where the dream of a better future unites us.

The artificial voice echoes powerfully in the cell and makes Emily shiver. Can Duke's Fairy imitate different voices? All the voices Emily has heard in her life? Why drag her into this when it could all be over quickly?

The screen lights up.

Emily holds her breath.

Did the screen really turn on?

The image buzzes into view, though not as sharp as the usual broadcast. The camera is lying on the floor, staring back at Milo's scrunched up face with Fiona in the background.

"We should've killed that bastard when we had the chance," roars Fiona, pacing back and forth. "That same bastard who slaughtered everyone who didn't pass his test like it was a show!

And he would waste any Maverick without even a test! We can't let him become the commander of the Ark, you hear me? Neal may have gone dark, but it is our duty to stop Duke before he gets too powerful!"

"Not so loud! Someone could hear us," Milo rebukes her, adjusting the camera so that the image is sharper. "Killing some Paragon agents is not the answer. We must gain people's trust first. And wait." Fiona lets out a sigh and sits in one of the simulation terminals, legs crossed.

"Why do you insist on carrying this thing around?" Fiona whines, throwing a contemptuous glance at the camera.

"It's not just any camera. It's a replica of the camera we were filmed with."

"It doesn't look like it anyway. It's way too small."

"It's an enhanced, miniaturized, and much more practical version. Walker showed me how to connect to different frequencies, the same way he synchronized the Ark's takeover."

"Any word from Walker?"

"Duke uses him to locate the Mavericks who got away."

Fiona's face changes dramatically, a glimmer of understanding in her eyes. "Always working for *her*, huh? While I'm trying to get us out of this mess, you're risking your life and Walker's to patch this shit up!"

Milo doesn't answer, but his blank face says a lot about his state of mind. Fiona crosses her arms.

"I know what happened to Mom. She didn't get caught stealing from the warehouse. You asked her to go rescue that bitch!"

"Stop calling her that! Her name is Emily," Milo replies forcefully. "And by the way, she's changed for the better."

"Risking your life is your business, but my mother's?"

"I didn't force her."

"I'm sick of your lies! My mother would never agree to that. Even when she was just a junkie hellbent on hooking up with the unfortunate handsome guys who crossed her path. Even when she didn't care about us starving in a moldy corner on the lower levels. It was always her welfare before anyone else's. She would never take part in your messed-up rescue plan."

"Your mother had her reasons to step in," Milo replies with his usual composure.

"What exactly did you tell her? Did you even consider *me* in all of this?"

Milo stands up. "Can you stop thinking about yourself for once?"

"Like mother, like daughter? Is that what you want to say?" retorts Fiona on her feet. Her stubborn attitude hides something else, but without her aura, Emily can't put her finger on it.

"I'm sorry. I didn't mean to," Milo says, running a hand through his hair. "She's your mother. Just because I never knew my parents doesn't mean I have to act like a jerk."

Silence sets in until Fiona breaks it. "I can't believe this damned Duke is sending us back to the Sacred Fire after what happened last time."

"He needed someone to get the capacitor out of the other Ark. And now, who is in a better position to install it? It's also a way to keep us busy. We need to come up with a plan while we still can." Fiona moves closer to him with embarrassment for venting on him. She tilts her head to meet Milo's downcast gaze.

"Are you sure you can handle it?"

"It's not so bad, trust me. I'm more concerned about what's going to happen to all of us. The Sacred Fire will be back online once the capacitor is calibrated. Restoring the Ark will give Duke the power to carry out whatever he has in mind." Milo winces in pain as he pivots to pick up the camera.

"Let me see for myself if you're okay."

"Doesn't it bother you that a psycho could run the Ark?"

"I don't care about Duke so long as he leaves us alone. Come on, show me."

"Not here."

"What? It's not like your body is a secret to me."

Milo resists by pulling the top of his uniform down, but Fiona manages to reveal his torso. Emily holds her breath, covering her mouth. Burns blacken the crusted skin in multiple places. And his hands are redder than normal.

"We don't have the same definition of nothing," Reyes says quietly despite Milo's horrific injuries. She grabs the camera, and the view changes to the gaping hole leading to the Refuge with the simulation terminals on either side of the stairs.

"Be careful," Milo whispers with a touch of panic.

"Why?" she says, shifting the camera so much that Emily must look away, feeling queasy. "Because your obsession with her will drive you crazy?"

A man emerges from the Refuge, and Milo's voice strains again. "What are you talking about?"

"Don't play dumb."

"Shit!" The nondescript man is walking toward them, his eyes fixed on his wristband. He shouldn't be a threat to anyone but his silly expression hiding a vile egomania and a sickly servitude does not lie: It's Leander.

Milo snatches the camera from Fiona's hands and slips into a simulation terminal. Fiona gives him the stink eye as she crouches.

"I didn't like what I heard last night," Duke's deep voice thunders.

Milo steadies the camera at an angle to watch the exchange between them. Leander turns sharply toward Duke coming opposite from a perpendicular gate flanked by his procession of zombie agents.

"I wanted them to recognize your power on the Ark," stammers Leander, looking perplexed. "I don't see how—"

"You're missing my point. I'm talking about the way you … act without my consent. It bothers me. A lot."

Leander shifts embarrassedly.

"You were Chris's best friend. I suppose that should entitle you to some special treatment from my part, but your unpredictability is a problem, Leander Berger."

"Our families have known each other for generations. Our loyalty to the Kays has never wavered."

"It's true. Maybe I'm being too harsh on you," Duke says, lighting a cigar with his metal lighter. He lets the open flame burn for a long time before snapping it shut with a metallic clink as sharp as a blade. "When I was your age, passion drove me too. But the only thing that interests you is revenge for the girl you loved who was killed in such a horrible way, and blah blah blah."

Leander blanches.

"I know what love is. It gives us incredible strength, but it also makes us very unpredictable. Now that you've got what you want, what will you do? Be careful how you answer."

Duke takes a puff that envelops him in thick smoke. The Paragon agents beside him are not bothered, their posture petrified. Emily knows what's coming, but this time she feels no sympathy for Leander. Maybe Dad would still be alive if not for him. Dad would have been able to stop Duke before he could commandeer the Ark. Dad would have become the rightful commander.

Leander drops to his knees, and Duke remains unflinching. He takes a good look at the end of his cigar burning slowly.

"What should I do?" pleads Leander in a quavering voice.

"That doesn't answer my question," Duke utters, tossing ash inches away from his face. "You have one last chance."

"I … I want to serve you."

Duke's laughter seems real. Even Emily believes it.

"It's a very coveted position indeed. For now, Miss Bates has that special privilege. It will take a lot of work to replace her."

"Tell me what I should do."

Duke circles around Leander who looks miserable and almost pitiable.

"Submit," Duke concludes. "Submit yourself completely to me. It is the only way. Until I know every inch of your mind, I can't give you the right to serve me."

Terror fills Leander's eyes, his will faltering.

"How?" he finally asks in a small voice.

"The conventional method won't work with you," Duke replies, giving the false impression that he's studying him, but Emily knows it's all an act. "You have the Bergers's legacy to thank for protecting you from the greatest evil of our time. Do you see where this is going?"

In a perfectly synchronized movement, the Paragon agents encircle Leander who is on the verge of panic. Two of them grab him by the arms, while another stands behind. Leander swallows hard when the tip of a sleeping taser brushes the back of his skull before bursting into a purplish glow.

"The principle remains the same. I need to breach your mind," says Duke walking through a hanging cloud of smoke. "Sometimes more … radical methods are required."

"I don't understand," Leander stutters. "I am ready to do anything to serve you."

"This shouldn't scare you then. To serve is also to trust your commander blindly."

"I trust you, sir," Leander utters painfully, struggling to stay conscious.

"Unfortunately, this show of trust is unrequited." Duke stamps his cigar with his boot and steps away from him.

Leander begs for mercy, but Duke closes his eyes with a hand raised. Another agent stands at an angle and presses his taser onto Leander's temple. As Duke closes his hand, the unmistakable sound of the discharge burrowing into his skull is horrifying. And his screams…

The Ark shakes so hard that the screen wobbles precariously.

"Shit!" shouts Milo when the camera crashes to the ground, and the image cuts off abruptly.

Emily has just enough time to grab onto the frame of her bed bolted to the floor. She levitates for a second, her heart afloat, then hits the floor hard. The jolt has passed.

Once the ship's tilt has returned to normal, Emily sits back on the end of her mattress, still in shock. The screen is off. There is no evidence that it was ever turned on.

Was everything she saw and heard real?

"The next phase of the program can begin," Duke announces, dressed in a new royal blue ensemble. He seems just about to attend an exclusive party for the Ark's prestigious families.

Emily sits in a chair that would be comfortable if she wasn't a prisoner. An identical chair sits on the opposite side, empty. The circular room is just as distressingly gray as Emily's cell except for two rings of purplish neon marking the perimeter. The false leather of the armchair gives off a strong synthetic smell and creaks under her fingers clenched on the armrests.

Duke approaches holding a familiar-looking box. "Yasmina was a little crazy, but she had some darn good ideas, wouldn't you say?"

Between them stands a strange machine, and in its center, he places a spherical glassy object that will expose Emily in an unparalleled way.

Her memory sphere! The very same one that Yasmina recorded when she peered into her mind to learn everything about her. Emily had completely forgotten about it.

She lets out a moan of embarrassment that pleases Duke. His half-smile says it all.

"To great evils, great remedies," he says with false sympathy. "I expected more satisfactory results from you, but something in your mind is still beyond my absolute control. This new experiment should solve the problem once and for all. Not that I don't enjoy my time with you, Miss Bates, but I am a busy man, you see."

A few hours earlier, he got rid of Leander and now it's Emily's turn?

"Don't worry. Once the program is complete," Duke explains, "you won't be left behind. On the contrary, you'll have a special place at my side."

What Leander wanted.

"To serve me. Any of my agents would kill for this chance. They all dream about it. But dreams can be a dangerous thing for those without a master."

Emily swallows a gag, knowing full well what he is referring to.

"You'll see. I am known for fulfilling my promises."

Emily's sphere projects a constellation of colors in the thick half-light of the room. Duke ensconces himself in the opposite armchair and casts a complicit glance at her. Metallic talons clasp their heads, and Emily stiffens.

Duke lets out a grunt of satisfaction as he closes his eyes. Before Emily can figure out what is happening, she is sucked into nothingness.

31

NEAL

A STRANGE WAVE RIPPLES THROUGH THE BRUISED SKY IN THE SAME shades of purple that covered Neal's body after his endless fall to the lower levels.

He dashes toward the base without hesitation, ignoring Skyler's call.

After confronting Oslo about hiding his father Anzen's death, Neal wants to stay out of the North Star's affairs. Oslo never cared about the Amaranth. He only wished to hunt down his father's killer which led him to their Ark. Nothing more.

Eliza knew that the information in Uki's sphere would rekindle his obsession with revenge, but Neal was hoping deep down that Oslo would rescue those left behind on the Amaranth.

He won't.

The North Star is not the safe haven and semblance of a Promised Land it claims to be. The Nord family has enemies who will stop at nothing to finish what they started on the Sedna.

Uki did warn him that they were coming. This morning, she said she had this … premonition—what else should he call it?—

the same kind of premonition she had at the Porthole. As crazy as it sounds, she knew something was going to happen, and Neal ignored her. People on the Sedna believed in her strange visions, didn't they?

His hellish nightmares. She was right about that too.

He can't pretend he knows how this strange way of seeing things works, but ... sometimes you just need to accept it before it drowns you.

He knows what he must do now: Gather the Brotherhood and leave before it's too late.

A crowd of refugees is gathered in the main dome, pointing to the bruised sky in a thunder of anguished shouts. "They're coming for us."

"When will they finally leave us alone?"

"Dad, I'm so scared."

Families huddle together with their terrified little ones amidst the chaos in the dome. Neal scrambles to locate the Brotherhood as quickly as possible. But he can't simply ignore their distress. He can't run away and abandon them. Not again. Isn't that what he did on the Amaranth by breaking families apart and leaving them for dead in the Refuge?

He goes rigid in the crowd, unable to shake off the shame that chokes him. Is this what the Mavericks always do? Lurk in the shadows and clear off at the first sign of trouble?

Their problems are not our problems.

Who had repeated these words to him? Dan, Sofia ... his mother? Why can't he remember something so simple? They must share this world fairly; he is certain of that. The victims of the Flood have forgotten, and so they have been suffering for over a century for their sin.

Have the years spent away from the life on the Ark turned him into a cowardly, selfish idealist? Not even capable of heeding his own words about the Promised Land? Promised to whom exactly?

For everyone, he said. But it wasn't true. He never believed it, not if one must earn their place in this new world. He never said it explicitly, but his arguments with Milo about it had fueled his conviction. Those who neglected the Mavericks, set up an unjust system, or committed a crime against the Ark would not be allowed to follow them. Their punishment was to perish with their abominations on their conscience. The plan was to convert the Ark into an eternal prison without ever reaching land. These people had all the time in the world to repent, but they preferred to wallow in their power in the microcosm they created. This artificial world they designed to crush the seeds of humanity, to mold them into a new paradigm that would give birth to a new civilization built on the same gruesome values from before the Flood—power, aristocracy, and greed—an infernal triad. The Brotherhood—Neal—couldn't afford to risk these bastards pulling the same trick on his hard-won Promised Land. Even if his idea of justice is real, Neal doesn't belong anywhere else or here, among these people he's about to leave to their predicament.

He has disappointed them, abandoned them, betrayed them. And yet, they all share this imperfect humanity bound by this constant fear of losing everything.

Did he even care about the small colony outside these walls, all that they have achieved? Of course not. He was blinded by his desire—no—his demands that Oslo be held accountable for his lies, while the man was simply trying to protect his people.

This time Neal is not looking for the Brotherhood. These people need help. His help.

Standing by the glass wall where Uki was gazing the other night, Tessa is scanning the crowd, fitted with a strange armor bearing the symbol of the moon embracing the sun.

"How did he do it?" she mumbles furiously.

"What's going on?" asks Neal, frowning. "That shockwave—"

"They destroyed the barrier."

"Who are they?"

"Where are the others?"

"Oslo and his guards are on their way, probably with my brother. Where are Dan, Nora, and Derek?"

An ugly crack runs across the surface of the dome and spreads into several ominous branches. Screams erupt from all sides as a gaping hole forms followed by a dull explosion that sends a million shards of glass in every direction. Tessa presses herself against Neal as the refugees trying to escape are swallowed by the swarm of small blades raining around them. The noise grows even louder after the glass has settled on the floor, but the source remains a mystery.

"The clinic," Tessa says, pulling herself out of his embrace.

Oslo and his guards spread out to create a security perimeter, shouting orders at the top of their lungs for the refugees to find cover, but then a dark swarm swoops through the yawning hole in the dome.

Drones, those filthy pieces of flying metal shooting at anything in their line of sight. The vision of horror in Uki's sphere plays before him. Smaller groups of them break from the swarm of infernal machines, and a hail of bullets comes straight at them. Tessa uses her body as a shield, and before Neal can stop her, the bullets ricochet against a magnetic light barrier that spreads around them. As soon as the danger has passed, the barrier vanishes, and Tessa drags Neal into the passageway leading to the clinic.

They walk against the throng of families and refugees scattering in every direction, machine-gunned by the drones. Blood and flesh pile up at an alarming rate. Soon, Neal and Tessa are no longer dodging people running, but striding across lifeless bodies all around. Oslo's guards struggle to take down the drones who are relentless in their attack even with their propellers severed. Whenever a drone is disabled, more come to replace them. Were it not for the guards' pulse guns sending destructive arcs, everyone would be already dead.

Out of the corner of his eye, Neal spots Skyler and Eliza making their way to them with Oslo's guards, but they are stuck.

"My brother," Neal whispers to Tessa, who shifts back.

"Hide in the clinic," she says, leaving him at the door of the wing that seems unaffected. The drones are focusing their attack where they can do the most damage: the dome. "I'll go get them."

Neal nods and slips in. He shuts the door behind and presses his head against the frame, breathless with exertion. People in the clinic are staring at him with a scared look on their faces.

"No one gets out!" he shouts. "Or you will die." He doesn't need to be so harsh, but terror has no time for long-winded speeches. Children and parents alike are sobbing at the thought of the horrors they experienced on their arks.

Will this cycle of terror ever end?

"What's all the racket?" asks a tall, curly-haired teenager coming out from the back of the clinic.

"You don't want to know."

"I knew it was Neal, dummy," says Nora to her brother Derek walking down the same corridor.

"Tessa told us to stay—" Her brother falls silent when he sees Neal.

"The Brotherhood is reunited." Dan stands between them before Nora can hit Derek on the shoulder.

Neal breathes a sigh of relief as he exchanges a friendly hug with Dan, then gives a nod to Nora and Derek. They explain the recent events under the watchful gaze of that teenager comforting a small girl in tears.

Tessa told them to meet at the clinic, saying she found a way to get back to the Amaranth. Meanwhile, Nora and Derek who joined the Star's armed forces were training in a special section of the mountain when Tessa interrupted their weapon training.

Dan has been gathering information on the refugees since their arrival. This morning was no exception when Tessa found him at a daily refugee gathering where they share what their old lives on their arks was like. He was on his way to the clinic to visit some refugees suffering from a nasty cough that seems to be spreading rapidly.

"Are you finally going to tell us what's going on outside?"

The door slams open and Eliza, Skyler, and Tessa enter as if on cue.

"How are you holding up?" asks Neal, grabbing Skyler's shoulder to make sure he's alive. His brother doesn't say a word, but the look on his face speaks for itself. He's mad at Neal for leaving without them.

"It's hell," says Eliza in a deep voice. "Where did these drones come from?"

"Tessa?" asks Neal.

"We had to get to the clinic another way. Eliza led us through an underground passageway that must have been used before the base was converted."

"Where's Uki?" Neal realizes with fright. "Wasn't she with the other refugees?"

"She could be in another section of the base," Eliza replies, tense. "For now, we need to stay alive and destroy these abominations. My father did not sacrifice himself so the Star would fall. We must go back."

"This is madness," says Tessa. "No one is equipped to deal with them. My armor isn't invincible."

"I've never seen this symbol before, not even among the Paragon of your Ark," Eliza remarks. "Where did you find it?"

They all stare at Tessa who tenses up, and a heavy silence settles.

"What are you hiding?" presses Eliza, with a hand on her pistol.

"Tessa has been with the Brotherhood for a long time," Neal argues. "She is not the enemy, Eliza."

"What a coincidence considering the circumstances, wouldn't you say?"

"Without her, we would all be dead!"

The North Star is supposed to be built on the site of a former military base, with many unexplored tunnels. With what Nora told him about Oslo's armed forces, it shouldn't be too hard to find a high-caliber armor in their armory. The pre-Flood civilization had some advanced technology of their own. The existence of the arks is proof enough of that fact.

"Unless we're all equipped with the same armor, I don't see how we'll be able to fend off this attack," says Nora.

"There are more," Tessa says, hopeful. "But you need to get to the boarding bay without getting shot down."

"Impossible," says Eliza. "The drones have swarmed the dome, and we must go through it. We could venture into the tunnels, but the drones will find them soon enough."

The whirring din outside the walls of the clinic suddenly wanes and a deathly silence sets in. They exchange worried looks.

"Is that it? We've lost?" Derek asks out loud what everyone else is thinking.

"The North Star doesn't fall so easily," Eliza replies confidently. "Our defenses may not be many, but our father trained them well."

"Didn't those drones kill him on the Sedna?" asks Nora bluntly.

Eliza shoots Neal a dark look. "Why did you tell them?"

The Brotherhood is his family. Without their trust and support, they can't give the Star a chance to recover from this assault. He had to be honest with them.

"Do you hear that?" says Skyler.

A whistling sound. And it's getting closer.

They form a semicircle in front of the door, with their guns pointing straight ahead, while Skyler and the teenager instruct the families to take shelter in the clinic.

The door is now their only barrier between their world and the nightmare of Uki's memory sphere. Where is she? She is the only one who survived such an attack. She could help them.

The whistling intensifies, and they tighten their grip on their weapons. Tessa stands in the center to shield them in case… The door blows open with a startling crash, and Tessa's energy shield deploys in a glowing shell that burns the debris on contact. What remains is that same foul smell that kept them from sleeping when the Ark's Incinerator was at full throttle.

Through the smoke of the detonation, the silhouette of the Ark's warden appears, surrounded by drones. At least, the families have had time to take refuge in the inner rooms under Skyler's command. No matter what happens to their line of defense, they will have done everything they can to protect the survivors.

Well done, little brother.

The warden wears a maniacal smile like the attack is something exciting. On the Amaranth, Neal was reluctant to work with him to free Fiona and Milo. There is something about his expressionless face that makes him look like he is part of the prison itself, the perfect monster spoken of in the Incinerator legends. And here he is now storming the North Star with his killing machines following his every move. He strides toward Tessa, who stands between them as their shield, and steps over the molten half-moon-shaped metal.

"Ludo," says Tessa in a strained, almost pleading voice. "You don't have to do this."

"Look who's talking," he replies with a beastly smile. "Imagine if your uncle knew what you did."

"What are you doing here?" Neal will not just watch and let Tessa face this demon alone. "Your name wasn't on the list. How did you leave the Ark?"

"Neal," Tessa gasps, her voice sounding urgent. "Stay out of this. I can handle it myself."

"If he brought about the destruction of the Sedna and now the Star, he is our problem."

"You could've at least waited until your boyfriend is dead and buried before falling in love with another," Ludo says playfully.

Without warning, Tessa shoots at Ludo who doesn't bat an eye. His armor melts the bullets on contact which fall with a thud one by one. A stray bullet hits a wobbling drone, ripping apart a piece of metal, revealing its circuits that flash with a bluish light.

"You can't get rid of me, Tessa. After all these years, you should've realized that."

"She is with him," Eliza shouts, pointing her gun at Tessa. "*Forreder!*"

Ludo raises an eyebrow, and an almost demonic grin appears on his transparent face.

"Tell them what you did," Ludo taunts her, unconcerned about the power he holds over their lives.

"Nice way to overshadow the killer that you are," Tessa replies, taking another step.

A projectile from a drone grazes her cheek, leaving a bead of blood in its wake. The armor didn't activate. They're really screwed.

"Tessa," Skyler gasps. "You owe us an explanation."

She keeps staring at Ludo. "Ludovic is my partner for a mission."

"What mission?"

A silence stretches as Neal tries to figure out what is happening. They are partners on a ... mission? Is that why it was so easy to convince the warden to release Fiona and Milo? Because he was in league with Tessa?

But this mission she's talking about has nothing to do with the Brotherhood. How can she work with this … demon?

"Destroy the Amaranth."

Gasps of surprise come from all sides, and Neal feels an icy stab of betrayal in his gut.

"Tessa!" Neal shouts, breathless. "Tell me it's not true!"

He shakes her by the shoulders. She can be anything but a murderer. What game is she playing?

"Look me in the eye and repeat what you just said," he urges her, trying in vain to make out the lie.

Tessa's eyes are blank, and her mouth hangs half-open. Neal wants to kiss her to drain Ludo's poison coursing through her veins. The Tessa he knows can lie to get her way. When taking over the Ark and supporting the Mavericks, she did so countless times for the Brotherhood. It was a noble cause. But to kill off a civilization?

No, no, no! Tessa must have a plan. She always does—like when she infiltrated the Paragon without telling them. She can see the hits coming before they happen, always in the right place at the right time. Neal thought they were flukes. If the Brotherhood's plans could be carried out, it was because of her.

Neal swallows hard.

Was it all luck? Or did his love for her blind him of her true intentions? Was he stupid to believe that she liked him? Was he part of her murderous plans?

He would have known. Every one of their victories and defeats from securing the passenger log, to the access codes, to the Paragon simulation program, not to mention their kisses, their love, all of it…

"Ludo and I have been tasked with destroying your ark, Neal," Tessa repeats, looking him straight in the eye.

… was a lie.

The distance that has grown between them since Commander Hawk's death. Had this been her objective all this time? To use the Brotherhood to weaken the Ark and destroy it?

There were so many other ways to do it! Why choose the Brotherhood, a group of rebels cloistered in the lower levels, on the fringes of Archean society?

Yes, of course. He understands now. To keep her operation under the cover of anonymity, she used the cover of an operation already set in motion by the Mavericks. This way she could understand the underside of the ship and cripple it. By joining the Brotherhood, she had all the advantages she needed to do so, without even exposing herself.

Was Tessa a Maverick or an Archean? This detail, which had seemed insignificant, had never bothered him. Until today. He remembers what she had told him then. *I'm a bit of both.*

What does this mean?

"By whom?" Eliza rages, her pistol buzzing with energy.

"Thalassa," Tessa breathes weakly. "I'm sorry."

This invisible force attacked the other arks and forced the North Star to rescue thousands of refugees for fear that humanity would die out at the hands of a mysterious evil. How could this happen? They were on the Amaranth, an ark completely cut off from the world. A world with only one ark!

Except that Tessa had never doubted Neal's claims about the existence of twelve arks. She had supported him when others had doubted him, but he believed it was because they were a special pair. After all the time they'd spent together, he would have supported her just as much, no matter what she offered, because he trusted her.

This had been his biggest mistake.

"Why didn't you say anything? Why didn't you tell me?" asks Neal, weighing his words, feeling betrayed as never before.

"Because that's what she does best: lie," Skyler answers for her. "Now you know how it feels."

Neal wants to say it's different. His relationship with Tessa had always been special. But he's not so sure anymore. He needs time to sort out the truth from the lies. Where does Tessa's lie begin and end?

"Skyler is right," says Tessa firmly. "I have been trained, like Ludo, to lie, to infiltrate your ark and destroy you from within. To learn more about you, to find your weaknesses, to exploit them, to gather any intelligence that could be of value before putting an end to your existence. You don't realize you are a danger to us all. A plague that must be eradicated."

Neal's fingers tighten in Tessa's shoulders who swallows with difficulty. He lets go of her by moving back one step, then another, disgusted. She cannot have lied with a straight face during all these years.

She's not only a liar, but an … extremist. A murderer. The words burn his lips, but he refuses to accept it to be true. He may have been fooled, but Tessa can't share Ludo's bloodlust.

"Sacrificing generations of survivors," he mumbles, as the edges of his nightmares merge with reality. "Who could be twisted enough to lead such a mission?"

Neal feels his world turn upside down. At that very moment, Dan joins him, followed by the other members of the Brotherhood who close in around him, putting as much distance as possible between them and Tessa.

"What about that armor? Were you planning to join the warden to destroy the North Star? That must be another danger to eliminate, right?"

"That wasn't part of the plan," she says. "Some things changed along the way."

"Nothing has changed," replies Ludo, irritated. "Disabling the barrier was easy."

"I can see why my uncle kept you around. The North Star and the Sedna … were never part of our mission. For example, the way you enjoy other people's suffering," says Tessa.

"Isn't that what the Gods' Executors do?" Ludo asks.

Tessa blanches.

"Who else? You never told me anything about—"

"Your uncle. If you had listened to him like the good little girl that you are, you would know. But we wouldn't be here to talk about it. You would have learned."

"This mission is over."

Ludo's face loses its glow, and his fingers twitch strangely like those of a demon clad in a human body ill suited for him.

"And how do you plan to do that? You have no allies left. Not me, not your new friends. Look at them pointing guns at you. You're no better than me."

"Don't get them involved in this. Let's settle this in the dome."

Ludo bursts out laughing. "I'd love to. I always told your uncle that you were an impending problem to deal with. But let me warn you, I don't like the simple act of killing. There's a whole new world between life and death."

The words of a demon. What if the old lady Farrell's stories were true?

With her head held high, Tessa replies, "This mission is doomed to fail. Too much blood has already been shed."

"Come, then," Ludo cajoles her. "I'll take care of the others later."

The barrage of drones moves aside to let Tessa pass without a glance for them. Neal's heart sinks. Ludo lingers and says in a honeyed voice, "Don't worry. Your turn will come. There are so many things I've always wanted to try, but no prisoners to experiment on. The Ark's prison was a gold mine for the senses. With a little improvisation, you won't be disappointed. In the meantime, don't make life difficult for me or these drones will take care of keeping you ripe for what comes next."

A swarm of drones blocks the entrance while Ludo walks away whistling happily.

As soon as the door shuts, Eliza shoots an electric arc from her pistol that sends a couple of drones crashing against the wall. After a split second of hesitation, the others join the dance with their new pistols from the Star's arsenal. The drones retaliate haphazardly and soon, the clinic's lobby has become a battlefield. Neal covers for Skyler, who is unarmed.

Faster than Neal would have thought, the dozen or so drones are smoking on the ground. It takes a moment for the others to relax. The electric shock that Eliza shot at the drones seems to be their weakness.

"You should've told us what you were planning to do with those drones," Neal scolds Eliza.

"Wasn't it obvious? There is no time to lose."

"Didn't anyone hear what that lunatic just said?" shrills Derek. "I don't want to find out about his fantasies."

"Oh, Derek, man up, will you!" sighs Nora as she grabs her augmented pistol and hands it to Neal. "Since when does the Brotherhood bow to the demands of a lunatic?"

"We're in the minority here, mind you. There must be thousands of these drones out there! He'll come for us."

"You'll be dead long before," his sister reassures him.

"How can you be so confident?"

"Because I'll be doing you a favor by sparing you this misery," she replies, mimicking a rifle shot. "Stay here with the survivors. They'll need help when that Ludo or his drones come back."

"Should that make me feel better?"

Neal heads for the exit with Nora, but Dan stands between them. "I won't let you make a mistake, Neal. Tessa betrayed us all. The first chance she gets, she'll kill us."

"I'll be the judge of that," says Neal. Then to the rest of the Brotherhood, he adds, "I am not forcing anyone to follow me. This fight is beyond the Brotherhood's plans."

"You haven't learned anything!" shouts Skyler angrily. "You

want to play hero again?"

"I'm coming with you," says Eliza. "Oslo will need help. My father's murderer will have to step over me before he can destroy our home."

Skyler stands on the opposite side with the rest of the Brotherhood. "There are other ways to make a difference. Right now, Tessa is fighting Ludo. It's a perfect distraction to join the survivors and evacuate. They'll need help, and this will be our time to regroup."

"My brother's right," Neal says to the Brotherhood. "Find a way to get the hell out of here with the others on the ships. If the Star falls, we will need survivors to rebuild. Head for the Amaranth if you can."

"The armors…" says Derek. "We could go get them in the bay."

"If you can find them," says Neal. "But it's a long detour. Focus on helping the refugees. We'll hold off Ludo as long as possible."

If his sacrifice can save them, Neal will do it willingly. He no longer wants to shirk his duties. Isn't that what a true commander does, stand until the last moment to protect his crew?

"Don't die a second time," Skyler says with a frown. Neal will never know whether his brother supports his decision, but he knows what's right: saving lives.

"If I die again, I'll come back even stronger," Neal replies, giving Skyler a quick hug. "Be careful."

"Skyler," says Eliza with a hug of her own which makes him blush. Neal looks away with a half-smile. Then Eliza joins Neal and Nora on their way to the dome.

As they get closer to the battlefield, bolts of energy shoot out from all sides and crash against the glass. The hellish din sounds like the skies are being ripped apart in the dawn of a new apocalypse.

32

EMILY

EMILY MOSEYS ON CONFIDENTLY WITH THE PIANO ROLLING ITS gleeful notes. Her evening dress is her favorite color: a purple that changes shade with her mood. From the railing over-looking *La Orilla*, Emily is thrilled to see that the restaurant is teeming with people from all walks of life and families, even the most reputable. They chat with champagne flutes in hand by her paintings on easels set around the restaurant, revamped for the occasion. The usual smells of food are overshadowed by the guests' perfumes mingling in an aromatic floral mist: It is the smell of her next victory, provided this evening bears fruit.

"Miss Bates? It's nice to see you again."

It's Cohen, the waiter who was making eyes at her last time. He hasn't changed one bit, looking neat and warm, his move-ments swift and calculated. After a second look, Emily notices that he looks more mature with a stubble and a mustache which give him a natural charm.

"All these people are here for you tonight," he adds, bathed in a woodsy scent that reminds Emily of her walks in the park with Skyler, when they still had time for a quick jaunt.

Will he come tonight? Emily secretly hopes that her best

friend witnesses this major step in her new life. He would be so proud to see that she has invested in her passion.

"They are very eager to meet you," Cohen adds, giving her his signature smile.

"I still can't believe it," she says, blissful. "I guess dreams can become more than dreams if you put your heart into it."

As if to prove her right, she spots an exclusive group from the Ark: Catalina Garcia, the owner of *La Orilla* with Adeline White who sits on the committee for the Sigma Division, known for her interest in both old and new art. She organizes secret art tours for a handful of people who recognize the beauty and power of art. Tom Harris, on the other hand, is a flower enthusiast, as his flowery shirt attests. He has the final say on the Garden's landscaping. Tonight must be an opportunity to promote his perfume collection. Garcia and White are in the middle of a conversation with Harris, who has them try out his latest products. He carries an elegant leather case with a small set of bottles in the inside pocket of his jacket.

"Come on! Your talent was exposed many months ago," Cohen explains, motioning to another waiter to welcome the newcomers. "It was only a matter of time before you were offered a place of honor. Mrs. Garcia has been talking about your art exhibition for the past few days. She made sure your talent would shine."

"Sometimes I wonder if I deserve all this attention," says Emily, her eyes wet with emotion. "With everything that's happened in the last few years, I..."

Cohen places his index finger on Emily's lips and meets her gaze with that expression Dad used to give her when she was drowning in her memories of Mom.

"This evening is for you, Miss Bates. There will be other times to reminisce. Savor every moment."

He offers his arm, and she accepts with a smile. She wipes away with a quick gesture the tears that threaten to slip from her eyes and, together, they walk down the few steps that lead to the heart of this soiree. If only her parents could attend.

A peal of laughter catches her attention. She glances toward one of the large windows, with its oversized curtains, heavy with a royal red velvet-like fabric. She lets out a gasp of surprise when they reach the bottom.

"Violet!" she can't help but squeal.

At first glance, she thought she was mistaken, but it is indeed Violet. She has shed her priestess garments and opted for a fitted cream tunic adorned with a bizarre silver symbol relief. Her red hair cascades down her back, her small mouth pointed like she has been caught red-handed. Her hands are clasped in front of her, fidgeting with the hem of her tunic.

With an unspoken agreement, they embrace each other tenderly, and Emily can immediately feel a wave of comfort. The man Violet was talking to slips away to talk to the Rosses, an up-and-coming family that promises to offer unparalleled medical technology: a bed that can analyze the human genome and edit it to treat most diseases on record. They certainly didn't come here for the art exhibit, but they deem the event is important enough to attract the leading figures of the Ark. The mere thought makes her squeal inwardly.

"You look great in your tunic," adds Emily, who can't help but brush the tunic's fabric with her fingertips. "I feel like I'm rediscovering my best friend."

"Do you think so?" Her cherubic face still shows that naive uncertainty that Emily makes a point of chasing at all costs.

"There is no doubt about it," Emily assures her, squeezing her hand gently.

"I wouldn't be surprised if my grandmother disapproved. I just hope it doesn't affect my bond with the Creator."

"Who says priestesses can't enjoy themselves a little once in a while? I'm sure He and your grandmother must be toasting without our knowing." They both chuckle softly.

"Actually, I found this tunic in one of Grandma's boxes," Violet explains quietly. "I guess she would have wanted me to wear it for a special occasion like this one. I'm so glad you decided to pursue your dream. My brother Philip told me that it was only a matter of time before your art took off."

"Are you talking about me by any chance?" chimes in Philip, still wearing the same cardigan and that nerdy expression that looks out of place in the crowd.

Emily can't help but roll her eyes. He knows how to ruin a magical moment. "What are you doing here? Always in the wrong place at the wrong time."

"Don't I have the right to attend my greatest rival's soft opening?" he says, not the least bit bothered by Emily's animosity. "If this keeps on, Mrs. Garcia will take down all my paintings in the hall and replace them with yours."

"Don't try to sweet-talk me. I don't think Catalina Garcia would be so easily impressed. She's seen all kinds of artists before me."

"I'm serious. If you don't believe me, go ask her yourself. Although you might interrupt the deal, they're already making on one of your pieces. Mrs. White also wants them for her next private soiree, and Mr. Harris is talking about creating a perfume inspired by your best designs. If that's not fierce competition, I don't know what is."

Violet looks at them, obviously amused by their exchange. When she realizes that Emily and her brother are watching her, she suppresses a quiet laugh and says, "Glad to see you two are getting along. Maybe you should consider a collaboration."

Philip's eyes light up while Emily's festive mood threatens to evaporate.

"No," Emily quickly replies, earning her a surprised look from Violet. "I mean, the timing is bad. I want to give Mrs. Garcia and Mrs. White my full attention for their proposals."

"One success at a time. Well said, Miss Bates," Cohen butts in, for which Emily is grateful.

Violet suddenly becomes aware of Cohen, who had not said a word until then. He had remained just as alert as when he scans the room for plates to serve and glasses to refill. Sensing he's being watched, he straightens, head bowed, and steals a shy glance toward Violet. Emily doesn't miss a beat.

"I already have an inkling of an idea for our future collaboration," says Philip, gently pushing Emily toward the paintings. "How about a tour of your artworks for our brainstorming session?"

Although Emily would rather wander around catching snippets of conversation here and there, with the chance of being invited to discuss her work, she indulges in the game knowing full well that it will please Violet. And in any case, Philip is a renowned artist who could very well propel her career. If he was able to seduce Mrs. Garcia with his reproductions of biblical scenes and myths about the Flood, then he may be able to tip her off if she pays attention.

Philip is a true chatterbox who doesn't mind being answered by nods and monosyllables, Emily's secret weapons to keep herself from drowning into the anarchy of his endless opinions and ideas. After a litany of possible interpretations of the founders' portraits, Emily glances toward Violet, now busy chatting with Cohen standing awfully close to her. He slips a crimson-red flower into her hair, and Violet's face turns the same color.

Philip pulls her forward, and Emily sighs with annoyance. What she would give for him to leave her alone! He gives her a tour of the exhibit, commenting on the portraits and ways to merge his style with hers to create a symbiosis that would charm the entire ship, including the half-wits who know nothing about art and the thousand-year-old legacy left by their ancestors.

At last, a patron recognizes Philip. Emily takes advantage of her newfound freedom to look at the remaining paintings near the stage. She feels strangely exposed each time she caresses her paintings with her eyes. Her life's work is on display for all to see. These are not her original works, of course. She transposed them to a more appealing medium: acrylic on canvas. The originals—if a buyer is interested in purchasing them—are in the Academy's storeroom.

She sits at a table before the stage and scans the restaurant expectantly. Skyler and Chris are still nowhere to be seen. A tad disappointed, she digs into the seafood canapés. The cream and garlic shrimp melt in her mouth in a delight so divine that she closes her eyes to savor it.

"I always knew you had this talent, but you wouldn't listen to me," a woman calls out to her.

Emily's eyes snap open to a middle-aged woman who offers her a glass of champagne which she gladly accepts.

"This grape variety will make the pleasure last, believe me," adds the lady while munching on a canapé with a sip of sparkling.

The woman wears large glasses with spotted frames and has platinum hair tied neatly with a long fringe that falls on her cheek. Her loose blouse shows wrinkles along her neck and her thin penciled lips make her look like a living portrait, herself.

"Professor Paradis?" gapes Emily who puts down her glass.

"I haven't changed my name after all these years, Emily," the Academy art teacher replies in a nasal voice, her head tilted like her thick glasses are too heavy. "But seriously, I'm glad you remember me. I didn't teach the most important subject, but you were my best student. Ah, this wine!"

Mrs. Paradis swirls her wine in a grand masterful gesture that makes her whole body sway. She smells the contents before taking a long sip until the glass fogs up completely, including her glasses.

"Catalina Garcia has always had such impeccable taste." She wipes her glasses with her shirt before putting them back on the tip of her nose. "It's no coincidence she stopped in front of one of your best works."

Garcia and White are raving about her portrait of Mom, inspired by one of her dreams, the year after her death. Emily was so overwhelmed with emotion in the days that followed that she rendered it on paper. It was the first time the auras revealed their vibrant colors, right after the vigil.

And to think that all this time since graduation, Emily could have been indulging in her art. Why had she dismissed all hope of seducing them with her portraits on graduation day? What stupid idea had crossed her mind?

"If you ever feel like it, my dear Emily, I have some projects that might interest you. Projects that could let you discover the hidden dimension of art. You would make all those fools in this room and the Commander himself tremble if you wanted to!"

"And now for the centerpiece of this exhibit," Cohen says as he addresses the guests.

Smiling, Emily thanks Professor Paradis for her interest and assures her that they will stay in touch. Mrs. Paradis looks satisfied, then help herself with some more wine and feeds on every canapé.

Conversations die down and the guests gather near the stage that has been specially set up. Emily looks at them in turn with growing anxiety. What was the centerpiece again? She has no memory of it.

Philip takes a seat next to her, eager to talk about what has just happened. Emily sips the rest of her sparkling as Cohen describes Emily's tumultuous journey from a fearsome prison agent to a mysterious portrait artist redefining the genre with her candid look on human nature and its evanescent beauty.

"Would Miss Bates do us the honor of coming on stage?"

Out of nowhere, a spotlight shines on her, and she can feel people staring.

Philip urges her to go. She stands on her wobbly legs, and everyone applauds energetically. Heart racing, Emily steps onto the small, makeshift stage where the musicians were playing earlier. In the background, the grand piano is holding its breath by the centerpiece: An easel covered by an immaculate canvas cloth. The microphone is passed to her, and she grabs it awkwardly. What is she supposed to say?

Violet is nodding to her to go on, and Emily catches the wisps of her aura pulsating with life. A small detail, but one that speaks to her. Emily knows what to say.

"Art is a way to reveal a part of us that would otherwise be invisible. Our ancestors understood this and that is why I believe in its … transcendental power. A unique language, worth learning and exploring."

Emily meets Professor Paradis's eyes in the crowd, and she is nodding vigorously in agreement. With a deep breath, Emily speaks on a more personal note with a sense that everyone who has come tonight is not here to judge her, but to appreciate her work and her vision. The initial fear that threatened to petrify her on stage dissipates like a bad headache that had compressed her brain for too long.

"The inspiration for this masterpiece comes from a particular encounter I had at the moment I needed it most," she continues, her heart quickening. "A pivotal moment that made this exhibition possible."

Emily slowly walks over to the easel, as if it were the most precious and dangerous thing there is. She inhales, her hand trembling. Her throat knots without her knowing why, and for a split second, the room is empty, the air around her cool and steamy.

She turns toward the audience and with a dramatic flourish of her hand, removes the sheet that rustles onto the ground. The crowd gasps. Emily is shaking so hard that she forgets to look at the masterpiece herself.

"You never told me," Milo whispers in her ear, his arm now around her waist.

A thunderous applause ensues, and Emily can't believe she is being congratulated. They like her art. No, they *love* it! For the first time in her life, she is someone to be respected, admired.

Emily cries. She made it.

She turns to Milo with emotion knotting her throat, her cheeks wet with salty tears. He smiles at her and grabs her chin between his thumb and forefinger. She closes her burning eyes in anticipation of the kiss. But then, she feels Milo's body stiffen. When she opens her eyes again, the glint in Milo's eyes is distant, and a ruby-colored bead slides down his cheek. Emily collects the warm drop on her thumb and forgets to breathe.

Before she knows what's happened, someone yanks her away. Milo reaches for her hand, then collapses amidst cries of fear.

Milo was killed.

During the happiest time of her life.

33

EMILY

Philip's voice is trying to bring her back to reason, while the crowd shoves them around.

"Emily. We must go now!"

"Who did this? Who did this?" she repeats mechanically, without her brain really registering the chaos that makes the curtains of *La Orilla* flutter wildly.

The Paragon agents are swarming the restaurant forcing the panicked guests to rush toward an emergency exit. The agents ransack everything in their path, including her paintings, without even a glance. Emily watches the scene of horror, paralyzed.

"Snap out of it! If we don't get moving, they will kill us all!" Philip says holding her by the shoulders.

"I can't," she hiccups.

Then, she grabs the hand that Philip holds out to her and finally breaks out of her daze.

They break into a run inside the restaurant via a corridor that overlooks the private lounges lined up on either side. Everything seems unreal, like Emily's body no longer belongs to her. Philip guides her through the chaos and for once, she doesn't balk and does what he asks. Left to her own devices, her body would no longer respond.

The distinctive blasts of guns and cracking of electric tasers erupt from the corridor. Philip chooses a remote empty lounge and orders her to stay inside and wait for him. Breathing heavily, she tries to regain her composure. What the hell is happening to her? Her forehead is burning, and she can't explain her overreaction from earlier. It's like something in her head prevents her from thinking clearly.

Milo. Someone killed him from the crowd, probably the Paragon. She doesn't remember seeing anything. Maybe they took a shot from the railing? But why? Were they stalking him? None of this makes sense.

A bad feeling twists her guts, the same she had on the morning they arrested Mom. Emily knew something was wrong. Mom hadn't eaten a thing, though she had a sweet tooth just like Emily. Right before the Paragon agents broke into their cabin, Mom had made her promise to stay strong and never forget her. Dad had locked her up in the bedroom so she wouldn't see Mom be arrested. A week later, she knelt with her family at Mom's public execution.

This time, Emily's intuition is clear. They want her, the last of her name. Milo was just a faster way to get to her.

Violet enters the lounge, looking bewildered, followed by Mrs. Garcia. Philip shuts the door just as a long arc of electricity explodes in the corridor. The smell of burning fabric spills into the lounge with the muffled screams of guests stuck outside. Philip and Emily hurriedly lock the door of their temporary shelter.

"Cohen stayed to help the others," says Violet, shaken. Her beautiful tunic is soiled, and Emily embraces her, trying to calm Violet's trembling. Emily strokes her hair as she used to do with her little sister Gabrielle every time she dreamed of Mom's death.

"I'm so sorry," Violet hiccups, leaning on Emily to stand. "I shouldn't… I shouldn't lose myself. The Creator… The Creator can help us. Praying. We should pray."

"My restaurant is my whole life!" moans Mrs. Garcia, with tears in her eyes. "The *Signor* must save my restaurant. My restaurant, I tell you. Who will properly feed the survivors? Remember the real *comida*?"

The owner of *La Orilla* begs Violet by grabbing both her hands, clinking her wristbands and rings.

"The *Signor* will grant my request, *si?*"

"The Creator responds to the well-being of each person," says Violet, who regains her priestly composure, with a look of serenity and determination.

"This *maldito* Paragon is the source of all our misfortunes. The *Signor* must take care of it."

"Let us pray."

Mrs. Garcia and Violet hold each other by their forearms and close their eyes, mumbling words over and over, the din from outside fading a little more with each verse.

"What are you going to do now?" The question is directed at Emily. Philip doesn't take part in the praying, which Emily finds surprising considering his roots.

"What is there to do?" she asks, helpless, Milo's face imprinted in her mind.

"It's up to you," he says. She sees something strangely familiar in his expression. He adds, "If they find you, everything is over."

A formidable discharge of energy shakes the door on its hinges. Mrs. Garcia utters a cry of surprise, followed by a host of incomprehensible swearwords.

"Emily," prompts Violet, eyes wide open. "You are the only one who can save us."

A ripple on the walls tugs at Emily, and she knows her friend is right. She knows this place better than anyone, although she can't explain it. The fabric-covered wall ripples like a water surface, then she runs her fingers along, and a sudden sensation of emptiness besets her after walking about ten steps.

Emily frowns, takes a step back, and decides to pull the curtains wide. A large window overlooks the Great Ocean glowing under the Ark's spotlights they normally use during their relic hunts. This view is oddly disturbing. This emptiness…

"Philip, can you help me? This window is not supposed to be here."

She grabs a chair and strikes the glass that won't break under the impact. When Philip strikes with her, the result is almost instantaneous. The glass bursts in a torrent of water that the carpet drinks greedily.

Emily expects to run out of breath, but it was just a cold shower. She was right, this was no ordinary window. It was an illusion.

A dimly lit hallway looms before them. Emily glances at Violet and Mrs. Garcia, who are deep in their prayer. Philip gives her a calm smile and says, "Shall we?"

THEY LEAVE the chaos of *La Orilla* behind them, and the quiet of the secret passage is as loud as thunder. As they walk, the darkness swallows the remaining light and soon enough, Emily can only trust her legs for carrying her onward.

"Philip?" she asks but receives no answer. She touches her face at times to make sure she still exists in this world of darkness. Without warning, something slams into her waist repeatedly.

Laughter.

Glowing silhouettes are chasing one another. No, they're frolicking. They're children. She quickens her pace to follow them, and then she is no longer in that strange corridor, but in a room barely larger than the Bates's cabin, with that same contorted light, where the children sit cross-legged on the floor with others. An eclectic collection of junk like in Emily's drawers is piled up in every corner. The children seem to enjoy it, each of them playing with their favorite object that keeps their hands busy.

Who are these children?

Philip is already in the back of the room watching the scene unfold before their eyes. He looks serene, as if planning his next painting by memorizing as many details as possible and taking out the most unusual elements.

There are also two middle-aged women. The older one is clad in the Sanctuary's robes and telling stories, while the younger is hiding behind a lectern, pulling the strings of two puppets acting out the story. The scene unfolds in silence, the laughter and words translated into facial expressions and lip movements that Emily works out easily.

No one pays any attention to her or Philip. She joins him so that she can face the children. To her shock, she knows almost all of them.

Allen. Fiona. Violet. Philip.

Something stirs inside her, buried so deeply that she would have never known it was there in the first place, just like those relics they hunt for under the waters of the Flood. Perhaps the hunters feel the same way when serendipity strikes, and they come across astounding treasures choking under a century-long buildup of debris.

"Mom used to bring me here when I was a kid," says Emily.

"It's unbelievable how fast the years go by," Philip replies, not in the least surprised by what she said. "This was my favorite part. When Grandma told us her stories, they brought me to another world that still inspires me today. My paintings are …

an attempt to reproduce this world that I discovered through her."

"Your paintings in *La Orilla*?" asks Emily, dumbstruck.

"No. These are meant to please the eyes of my patrons. I have a personal collection stored in the Sanctuary. You've already had a glimpse, but I don't think you're interested anyway. We had quite different interpretations of the stories we were taught here at the Chapel. The beginning of our differences, I suppose."

There is a touch of sadness in his voice and suddenly, Emily remembers.

She got along well with Violet at the time. She hated Philip, who grabbed all of Mom's attention by always being smarter than the others. But the thing is, they all knew each other back then, even before Gabrielle was born. This is a memory of Emily's past. Of their past.

"Our grandmother, Elaine Farrell, and your mother, Tina Bates, had a common vision. They wanted to unite all the people of the Ark," Philip clarifies, reaching out to his grandmother as if to touch her, but his hand goes through like a mirage. "Their mission."

Mom puts the puppets away and comes out from her hiding spot under the children's silent clapping. The young Philip dashes to show her a new drawing he made. Mom congratulates him peering at his drawing with interest while he explains the world that he develops day after day through the stories they are told each week in the Chapel. This time, Mom gives him a puppet of her own making. He looks delighted like it is the most beautiful gift in the world.

A pang of jealousy and anger bubbles inside Emily. When she meets the eyes of each of the children with young Philip last, she understands. "I hated them. All of them."

She had been an only child until then, and her mother was her whole world. Her attention was what she cherished most.

Then the other kids caught her whole attention, and Emily was set apart, feeling less important, a shadow that couldn't shine.

Emily adored her father, but the Paragon took up much of his time. It wasn't until after Mom's death that they became so close. Her mother was filled with kindness and goodness in her, guided by a mission that asked for more than just raising a single child from a low-standing family. She wanted to make a difference, and this was the price to pay.

"How could I have forgotten all this?" says Emily, who doesn't understand the mix of emotions that are churning in her stomach.

"Our minds can be very effective in making us forget," answers Philip in a non-judgmental way. "Often it is to help us go on, without the burden of the wounds we carry."

The countless simulations Emily went through to rescue Mom haunted her for so long, not to mention her father's terrible end, but this feeling of losing herself has become more bearable, less unsettling. Sometimes Emily wonders if it's because life has let her down so many times, and now she simply can't muster the energy to fight anymore. But there is something more. Being unable to explain what had happened with Mom's execution nagged at her. Why, why, why?

Emily says hoarsely, "So... I blamed them for Mom's death."

Because she needed it. To make sense of all this horror and injustice. Everyone was guilty of her punishment, directly and indirectly. Time has changed things for the better, though. She has become more mature and understands that the world works like that, that there are people with great goals, ready to sacrifice everything to reach them. Other people are the cogs of a clock ticking toward a brighter future.

"She was my first portrait. Mom." Emily moves closer to the woman who was once her mother. She would like to caress her face with her fingertips to hold her beauty in her hands. "I couldn't bear to see her gone forever, to be unable to see her smile again. I decided to bring her back to life with a pencil. To bring her back to life, if only through an illusion."

The memory continues to play out before her eyes, indifferent to its audience. The motions are set, anyway. There is nothing they can do to change that.

"I thought you used art the same way I do," says Philip with an interested look. "To remember everything that escapes us. To discover a world outside the walls of this Ark."

"Maybe I do, after all. But illusions won't ever replace reality. It's a fact."

She inhales deeply and looks away from her memory, starting to dematerialize in tiny sparks of light, and this lost bond linking her and Philip comes back to her.

"I lost my whole family," she says with emotion, but with a budding resilience. "At the hands of the Paragon. No. At the hands of people seeing a reality distorted by their sordid pleasures."

"I'm so sorry," says Philip. For a moment, Emily feels like she can hear Violet through him.

"Don't be. I'm not the only one who has experienced atrocities. The Mavericks in this Chapel are a good example. My mother wanted to help them for a reason."

Philip nods respectfully, his eyes downcast, then beckons her to follow. The two of them slip to an unexplored part of the Chapel with a recessed corner.

"The Mavericks also have their way of mourning their dead. They do so here."

Bowls and pots of all kinds are arranged on shelves fixed to the walls. Wax candles burn silently in the sparse, smoky space.

"They write the name of the deceased on a piece of paper before burning them with some aromatic flowers of their choosing. Smells, they say, bring us closer to our deepest memories, more so than a photo or everything else."

He halts in front of a transparent bowl that contains blank pieces of paper with a worn pencil right next to it.

"Give it a try," offers Philip.

Emily carefully approaches the space exuding an inexplicable energy. She chooses a piece of paper and etches her mother's name on it. After a moment's hesitation, she grabs another and adds her father's name. Emily sticks her nose in various pots of dried flowers with faint smells, and once she has tried all of them, she picks one for each of her parents: The dried remains of a wildflower for her mother, and a subtle scented one for her father.

Taking a cue from the remains of previous offerings, Emily prepares two small plates and sets them on the floor. She dips the first piece of paper in the flame of a dripping wax candle and places it in the first plate. Then she repeats the process.

Kneeling, she watches the paper burn and takes in the aromas that fill her nose.

A torrent of happy moments with her parents floods her thoughts as she takes one breath. There are memories she had forgotten, and those that keep her company when she feels lonely.

She gets up to her feet to take another piece of paper and decides to write her own name on it. Philip watches her without a word, his face impassive. For a moment, Emily feels like he can read her mind, and she almost expects him to stop her, but he doesn't.

Emily lights her name with a sweet flower. She watches the flame quickly consume the darkening paper and the withering petals. The sugary aromas, however, do not waft through the air. Shouldn't there be a smell?

"What does that mean?" asks Emily, with a touch of panic.

But Philip has disappeared.

34

NEAL

"Tessa may be a traitor, but the girl can fight," Nora says as they enter the electrified dome where Tessa fends off Ludo's blows with finesse.

Neal is drawn back into the battle simulation he spent so much time practicing with the rest of the Brotherhood, when their group was still pursuing lofty ideals to change the course of the Amaranth's history. It is a shame that his best fighter Milo is not with them. But that won't stop Neal from fulfilling the duty he took on himself when he decided to take over the Ark.

If they make it out alive, Neal can handle Tessa's case, he is sure of it. He may be crazy to believe that someone capable of accepting such an aberrant mission could be reasoned with, but he doesn't believe that Tessa could have been lying to him all this time. She said it herself: She doesn't approve of the attack on the North Star. It's an opening that gives him hope. He will reason with her or at least give her a chance to explain herself.

"You're not wearing any armor," Neal points out to Eliza who is about to engage with a drone. "You'd better stay out of the way."

"Neither are you. I may not have an energy shield, but this little wonder has its perks."

Tessa glimpses them out of the corner of her eye and hollers at them to back off.

"You taught him well," says Ludo between two shots with his drones assisting him. "But those who don't heed my warning will pay dearly."

Neal doesn't waste a second to load the augmented gun Nora gave him. Despite training alongside Oslo at their arsenal, the trigger options confuse him. Eliza doesn't miss a beat and reminds him how the controls work.

"If you push this button here, make sure you keep your distance. The recoil is incredibly powerful. It's the same blast I used to zap the drones in the clinic, but there's a significant delay. The best we can do is create a diversion to support Tessa. Follow me."

"Don't use the other options," Nora warns him. "Derek almost got his head blown off trying."

Eliza engages the first group of drones that swoops down on them. Neal's muscle memory from the battle simulator kicks in, and although he's not at his best, he manages to hit several pieces of that flying junk. Tessa is fighting with Ludo in a gust of lightning arcs, while Neal and Eliza are making their way through the ever-growing swarm of drones converging on them. They get into a rhythm that works well: He stuns them with an electric shock, Nora and Eliza finish them off, and soon they are gaining the upper hand. But then a stabbing pain in his shoulder chills his ardor.

"It's suicide without proper protection," curses Neal, upset at being so vulnerable.

As he retreats from the battlefield, he stumbles upon a guard who was shot in the eyes. His brain is pulped, but his armor is intact. Neal quickly undresses him and haphazardly puts the armor on.

Eliza covers him with a battery of energy shots as soon as she spots him. "You don't wear a warrior's face, but sometimes all it takes is a good dose of determination. That's what makes the difference between those who change history and those who become its victims."

His wounds are cooling like the armor is seeping a healing gel onto his skin. It may not be Tessa's armor, but it will keep him going for a little longer. The barrage of shots fly past him as he makes for Tessa, glowing with her shield being bombarded with a hail of bullets and energy pulses.

"Go back to the clinic," she yells at him when he finally reaches her in his new armor.

"I couldn't protect my Ark when I had the chance, but I won't fail them a second time."

He thinks about Tessa, Eliza, Nora, and his brother evacuating the refugees. They didn't hesitate for a second. Neal already lost the Ark; he's not going to lose the base too. Anything he can do to stop Ludo, he will do. He will die trying to be the commander he always wanted to be.

As for Eliza, she is forced to retreat under the threat of a new wave of drones so dense that Neal can barely make out her silhouette. She is too far for him to help her out, but an opportunity presents itself just like the one that always earned Milo the title of champion in the battle simulator: the element of surprise.

Neal pulls the trigger and his gun buzzes to life. To hell with Nora's warnings! The seconds tick away as he struggles to keep his line of sight under the growing pressure, and Ludo's moving ever so slightly, which makes it nearly impossible to get a clean shot of his back. Tessa spots him out of the corner of her eye and understands what he is trying to do. She forces Ludo to back away in his direction, but Neal's heart skips a beat when he realizes that Tessa is also in his line of fire. At the last moment, he wavers.

The shock pops his ears, and he loses his grip. The blast that follows is so powerful that he is thrown off balance and hits the ground hard. Debris crash down on all sides, and Neal's guess is that the top floor of the dome is collapsing. A gust of glass shards whiz over them, the hydraulic system spills along the untouched walls and the many trees and plants are buried under a mountain of rubble. Neal braces for impact, the smell of wet earth clogging his lungs, but by some miracle, the shock passes. Stunned, he tries to get up and, amidst the smoke, realizes that the drones that were there a moment ago were crushed.

Neal falls back to his knees, breathless. He knows he's hurt, but he doesn't want to look for fear he won't be able to focus on what's more important: Tessa needs him now.

It takes a while before a figure emerges from the rubble, and it's not the one Neal was hoping for.

Ludo's armor is smoking, the whole side charred by the blow. It looks completely useless. The electronic circuits are burned out based on the sparks zapping the air around him. He staggers toward the passageway that leads into the mountain without a glance like he is pulled by something. Neal tries to get up again and gives up with a grunt. Even with all the determination in the world, his fight is over. His gut is sticky with a slimy substance he'd rather not look at. In the simulator, he could take off his helmet and forget about his poor performance. This time, his defeat will result in a slow and painful death as his fluids spill everywhere.

Finally, a second figure rises, slender this time. Tessa! He tries to call out to her, but instead ends up moaning in pain which gets her attention anyway. She sails through the rubble to join him, her armor shining in the setting sun. At least, she is in much better condition than Ludo. She drops from the top of a large piece of debris nearby and drags herself toward him to check the wound on his cheek covered with blood.

She helps him into a sitting position, his back against one of the vats that used to hold a fruit tree. The way the Star grew their food here on the many rings stacked on top of each other was such an impressive feat of technology, and Neal ruined all of it.

"Everything I touch, I end up destroying," he utters with a wince. Still, the angle of his body allows him to breathe better and control the pain to an acceptable level.

"Thank you for not listening to me. You found a way to save me."

"You were doing fine without my help. All I did was create a little distraction."

He attempts a smile which Tessa returns, her eyes shining with sadness.

"I don't believe a word you said earlier, Tessa," Neal groans, his position already uncomfortable. "You're—"

"Skyler can fix you. He always does. It's what he does best."

"No," he retorts, not having the strength to clarify his thoughts. "He left with the others. You should do the same. Who knows what Ludo will do to us when he comes back."

"Did you see him?" she wonders, immediately scanning her surroundings hazy with a fine glass dust. "Where did he go?"

"The mountain. Hurry before he finds them."

"Not without you," she says in a strangled voice, a tear spilling on her wounded cheek.

"I can't and you know it. The Brotherhood... Skyler can't die. They need you."

Tessa's breathing is shallow as she searches the pockets of her uniform. She grabs onto a tube and hurriedly applies a cold gel to Neal's naked stomach wound where his new armor used to cover. The sensation is both great and awful at the same time.

"It can't replace a doctor, but it should give you some time."

Worn out, Neal thanks her by blinking. She gets up and wipes her face with the back of her hand.

"Thank you. For risking your life for me."

"I didn't do it for you," he whispers weakly. "But... for our future."

Tessa nods, then leaves in the same direction as Ludo.

Though it's not the end Neal had expected, he knows his brother will do everything so the others can escape before it's too late. At least, Neal did his best to slow Ludo down and give them enough time to find more refugees and reach the boarding bay. He has faith that Tessa is not the heartless agent she claims to be. Why else would she try to help them?

There's still no sign from Eliza and Nora. Maybe they managed to escape too.

Neal lies on his back to rest, while the frost tingles on his wound, as if metal bugs were making their nests there. The ceiling of the main dome is cracked in more places than he can count. Despite the destruction he wreaked, he and Tessa were lucky enough to have been in the center of the dome and were spared from most of the large debris that fell around in a ring. Eliza and Nora were not in that safe zone the last he saw them. Did they die because of him?

His thoughts are racing. Images of his nightmares merge with the fire that burns the twilight sky threatening to suck him through the glass of the dome ... a reminder of where he came from and where he will return.

Snow crashes on his face and his vision blurs.

The Promised Land may not be so far away after all.

35

EMILY

The Paragon is coming.

The Chapel is no more than a derelict place in the depths of the Ark, but nothing can escape them. Their omniscience is both absolute and terrifying. Emily slips quietly into the comfort of the darkness that has brought her here, with the slim hope of evading their vigilance. Thanks to Violet and Philip's warnings, she now knows that if the Paragon gets ahold of her, she will bitterly regret it.

Her instinct guides her in this invisible maze. Her escape seems almost futile, for this ship is an empty cage. Wherever she goes, they will eventually locate her, again and again, until she gives up. Yet she sweeps her eyes across the compact darkness around her, hoping to find a place that is more familiar to her.

The prison's corridors are like a second home. Whenever they lead to a dead end, more cells fill the gap between madness and reason. Emily wanders, confused. Shouldn't she be at the entrance by now? Her panic grows as she fails to understand this twisted place that exists by its own laws. It's as if the architect of the Ark had a sudden change of mind after years of admiring his creation, realizing it was flawed. Its angles, its curves, and everything in between conspire to keep Emily out.

My agent. My daughter.

Yasmina's voice haunts the narrowing corridors. The Fairies must be back to embody her worst terrors like they have done to many others before her. They know about Yasmina and the atrocities she has put her through. They warp reality to drive her crazy, to break her mind into submission.

The entrance to a giant safe—the prison?—looms straight ahead and euphoria fills her. Maybe she still has a chance. Emily starts running as fast as her lungs will allow, each stride longer than the last. Ludo emerges from behind the door with a sickly appearance, but with disturbing finesse. His face is a mask of impassibility hiding a whole other world of unbridled lust.

Ludo waits for her with that timeless expression, his hair and beard washed by time. His sneer hanging on his face could smother any idea of freedom a fugitive on the run could have.

"What are you doing here, Emily?"

"I could ask you the same thing."

"You weren't planning on coming through here, were you?" His distrustful gaze pierces her.

"And why not?" she asks matter-of-factly.

"This door keeps the prisoners and their madness inside, and I make sure it stays like this. Those who pose a threat to the Archeans must be controlled. Those are the rules. You should know them by now."

"Who doesn't know them?"

Ludo has a brief laugh, his arrogance transpiring with each of his breaths.

"You're on the wrong side of the door, Emily," he scolds her, like she has been playing this game for too long. "Hadn't you noticed?"

"This is a mistake. Let me out."

"Female officers can become a threat after spending too

much time with the prisoners. Especially when they fall in love with one of them."

What business does he have with Milo and the rest of the Brotherhood?

"Stop messing around and let me out," Emily replies firmly, her voice echoing against the metal walls. "Now."

"The rules are the rules," he says, walking toward her with a threatening look and the maniacal smile she knows too well.

They cross swords, kicking and punching at a furious pace. Emily chains every hold Dad taught her. The dress she's wearing is awfully embarrassing and inconvenient, and she longs for the training uniform she used then. The transformation of her outfit is instantaneous. Could it be a new simulation of the Paragon?

She doesn't let herself fall for this little trick and keeps fending off Ludo's attacks. She knows he won't waver. Each blow bolsters her confidence, and Dad's teachings guide her as they usually do. Ludo's strength is formidable. He seizes Emily's fist in midair and pushes her back with such power that she slides more than six feet back.

Clearly at a disadvantage, Yasmina's calling in her mind becomes more persistent. Emily wills her to show herself. Armed with an electric prod, Yasmina appears almost immediately at her side, looking as real as she was in the Command Center before Laurene executed her. How is this possible? It has to be a simulation.

Ludo fends off the simultaneous blows of Emily and Yasmina with superhuman dexterity.

His bare hand blocks the electric prod charring his skin to mere flesh. Then, he sends Yasmina to the ground in a sharp thrust. He licks the fat of the muscles running along his arm before obliging Emily and Yasmina to follow his steps so he can anticipate their blows and block them mechanically.

"I should've killed both of you when I had the chance," he

says between gritted teeth. The shock Emily receives takes her breath away, and she drops to her knees. The memory of her side wound sends a distress signal to her brain.

"It was you at the Sacred Fire," Emily says with conviction, looking him straight in the eye.

"Collateral damage. You shouldn't have been there in the first place. You were a hindrance to my mission."

"What mission?"

Was the Sacred Fire's system failure his handiwork? What did he plot during all those years pretending to be a harmless prison warden? He must have had a strong motive to bear such a lousy job.

Because of him, hundreds of Archeans were unable to reach the Refuge or were sacrificed in the chaos that followed. If the Sacred Fire had not been sabotaged, the Brotherhood would still be together, and their plan to reach the Promised Land would be in motion. Dad wouldn't be dead. Duke wouldn't have taken control of the ship. So many missed opportunities! Emily can't change the past, but she can do justice, and to hell with it if it's just a goddamn simulation!

The electric prod sears through Ludo's chest. His eyes bulge with surprise and lose their focus within seconds. He slumps on his side, lifeless, with the prod thrust through his back.

"He would've never been a good agent," says Yasmina, standing behind him.

Their victory is short-lived. An army of Paragon agents are on their way, the thump of their boots thrumming in the corridor.

It's time to leave. Reading her thoughts, Yasmina nods at her and disappears.

Emily steps over the metal frame of the open door and it seals itself behind with a heavy whirring sound. She is back in *La Orilla*.

The appalling destruction of the restaurant gives the impression that an artist has let his madness run wild in his studio. Canvases are torn, carpets are stained with unspeakable fluids: a mixture of blood, saliva, alcohol, and food. Shattered glasses and wine bottles have spilled their contents, and the smell of fermentation clogs the air badly. Even the grand piano met a sad fate, completely ripped apart.

Quietly, Emily climbs down the few steps from the balustrade. Her feet wade through the liquid-soaked carpet and carry her to the scene that was supposed to be her moment of glory. Milo's corpse lies in a pool of thick blood that haloes his head. Emily crouches by his side, though deep down she knows he will not come back to life even if she willed it.

Did she hallucinate her fight with Ludo, her outfit changing —now back to her evening gown—and Yasmina's joining in her fight? It all feels like a dream. What if the hallucinations caused by the Syndrome are already taking their toll, making her even crazier than she ever was?

"Emily." She leaps to her feet, heart racing. Philip is back.

"Do you understand what this is all about?" he asks, coming from the private lounges. "Why they are so desperately looking for you?"

These are about the only constants since the art exhibit: the Paragon and Philip.

"Duke," she replies, the name taking on a meaning buried deep in her mind. "Duke Kay."

Philip nods, but Emily's suspicion does not waver. Something about the fact that he is always in the right place at the right time bothers her.

"Who are you?"

Emily almost regrets asking the question, feeling utterly stupid as soon as the words are out, but his face becomes serious. "You won't like what I'm about to tell you."

She stiffens, expecting a cruel twist of fate. Philip chooses his words carefully, "I'm what you're most afraid of." Emily bursts out laughing before his confused look.

"Try again," she scoffs without a trace of humor. "You know what? Let me do it for you. You're some Fairy under Duke's influence trying to control me. It's the only logical explanation in this ... large-scale hallucination. I would expect nothing less from a syndrome manufactured by the Paragon, but its lack of practicality is laughable. I am still in my right mind."

"It's a little more complicated than that."

"It wasn't a question," she cuts him off, impatient. "And I'm not afraid of you. Sorry to disappoint."

Emily turns away from him to prove her point, then surveys the scene pretending to find a way out of this mess. Was the centerpiece just a blank canvas? It doesn't make sense. And yet, this painting is the only one that miraculously remains untouched.

A dull roar rises with a reeking smell of heated metal that makes fermented wine the most fragrant perfume there is. The Paragon is closing in, she can feel it, even through steel, but what is she supposed to do? If the door of a gigantic safe doesn't get the better of them, nothing she does can stop them.

"You can't keep ignoring me, Emily."

"Why not? I've done just fine without you so far."

"You must face reality if you want to get out of this vicious circle."

"Reality?"

A wave of emotion overwhelms her. She sees herself sitting in an armchair near Duke wearing his smug smile. Everything comes back to her: Duke's last attempt to assimilate her into his mind-control program. As for Philip ... each time he is near her, it's like a fog is being lifted, her thoughts clearer. He accompanies her through this strange hallucination, for lack of a better term to describe this bizarre experience, but nothing says he is acting of his own free will. Could it be that...

"There isn't much to say other than that it's a lose-lose situation," she decides to answer to test Philip's influence. If he's on her side, maybe he can make himself useful.

"Why give up before even trying?"

"Duke has my memory sphere and full control of the Ark. Isn't that enough to persuade you?"

"He doesn't control us yet."

The hissing metal door is already melting, and Emily can only accept the inevitable. Her end is coming.

"There is no *us* in this mess," she stings. "Every time the Paragon caught you, you mysteriously escaped unscathed. How do I know you're not one of them? Or that this is not all your doing?"

Philip thinks for a moment. "What does your intuition tell you?"

Emily opens her mouth to answer, but suddenly a warmth spreads in her pocket.

The card. The North Star.

It is warm in her palm when she pulls it out, and something draws her to the blank canvas. Under Philip's watchful eye, she gets closer. She places the card in the center, remembering every sketch of the cards she drew after Philip's visit that day. She had felt this moment coming before it happened. Was that an intuition?

The door explodes in a bewildering din, and Emily lets out a cry of surprise. A flamethrower spits fire on the royal fabric of the restaurant which burns in a hellish storm. The flames devour the walls down to the curtains, and soon the thick smoke makes her eyes water. When she turns around, the card is no longer there, but the painting has been colored with acrylic paint. The North Star is clearly visible and gives off an odd presence. Emily brushes the craters of dried paint, and she desires only one thing: to leave this place.

And so, she disappears.

36

EMILY

Her memory sphere is here, nestled in a pedestal sitting in this somber place with darkness as its walls. It doesn't glow scarlet, but more like the embers of a slumbering fire. Even the smell of smoke from *La Orilla*'s furnace has made its way here, so it's only a matter of time before the Paragon locates Emily.

She startles. Someone's here.

She sweeps at the shadows to reveal Philip's silhouette.

"It's yours," he says with a nod toward the sphere, his voice echoing. "Take it."

"Not until you tell me how you got here."

Philip approaches the sphere, and his face turns a crimson red like he just stepped out of a steaming shower. The sweat beads on his forehead, his gaze lost in the thick curls of the globe. Leaning on the edge of the pedestal, he says, "Have you ever wondered what a Fairy really is?"

Skyler is the first who told her about it. He had been so shaken by this odd case at Med Bay. He hadn't been trained to fight it, and his helplessness was consuming him. He had flipped through the book Emily gave Gabrielle for her birthday, and the word Fairy had burned his lips. The rumor of these strange nightly creatures had spread throughout the ship which was always eager for some hot gossip. And then she had seen with her own eyes what the Syndrome can do when her prisoner Alexander Griffin went mad. His drawings were a carbon copy of the illustrations found in Gabrielle's books. They were those small-winged beings with an ever-changing appearance. Was it a coincidence? It's hard to say. Emily suspected that these beings could not exist, or at least, could not resemble those of legend. Who on the Ark had read or seen these illustrations anyway? One had to be fond of myths and legends, or deliberately search for them in the Archives, or, like Emily, get their hands on some ancient paper books on the black market…

"They all look the same for those who can detect them," Philip fills in her thoughts. "But for those afflicted with the Syndrome, only they can see their true form."

"An illusion."

"A way to protect themselves. When you know what they really are, there is no doubt about it. Why would anyone want to reveal their deepest secrets? You have been seeing them for an awfully long time yourself. Your sister Gabrielle in that hallway was one, your mother you've been seeing after she passed—"

"And you."

He doesn't deny her accusation. Emily has had enough of being anyone's puppet. First Duke, and now these Fairies—talking hallucinations? Fairies who pretend to be people she has known?

"All of you may be good at making children dream of a better world where anything is possible, but that doesn't explain what I'm doing here or why you're going to rob me of my life."

"Fairies have a magical connotation because they are ephemeral," answers Philip, who insists on dissociating himself from being one of them. "Because people don't understand what or who they are. Their appearance changes from one person to another, not because they have a physical body like ordinary people, but because they come from inside the person affected by the Syndrome. They are their weakness."

Her sister, her mother… Emily can understand. Her family is more important than anything, but…

"One of my weaknesses is you, Philip Farrell?"

She cannot help but laugh at this joke. Philip does not take offense, expecting her reaction.

She continues, annoyed, "Why does it have to be you? Of all the people I've ever known, you are—"

"The one you can't bear to see."

"It doesn't make sense," she says, shaking her head in confusion. "How can you—"

"Know what you mean, even before—"

"I don't want to say it." Emily fixes her gaze at Philip who stares back at her intently. They blink together, breathe with the same breath in a perfect synchronization that is beyond understanding.

The person she fears the most, the one who knows all her secrets, every last one of them.

Disbelieving, Emily whispers, "You are me."

Her other half, deeply rooted in her being, somewhere in her brain, and the very essence of her identity. Without her explaining why, the revelation blurs her vision with a curtain of tears.

"You never listened," says Philip's copycat. "I'm not here to judge you like others have always done. But if you don't trust me, I can't help you."

His words create a strange echo like he is talking directly to her inside her head. He has no aura that could tell her whether he is sincere or not, but deep down, her intuition tells her to have faith in him, if only for a moment. Yes, she is afraid of being wrong, of finding out that she is not the person she thought she was. But is that not what her mother had set out to do? Not only her mother, Violet too. To help the Archeans in their soul-searching, for life and its possibilities, be they good or bad, overwhelming, or even defying all logic.

What if he is right?

"I am what you could be if you gave yourself the chance. Philip Farrell represents that potential in you, Emily."

She could find her rightful place in the Ark, do what she really loves, build a family. Allow herself to dream without believing that this privilege is reserved only for others. Love herself a little more, if only to accept that she has lost her way in the past … and that she can change. But all these things will only be possible if she recovers from the illness killing her slowly.

"The Syndrome is not an illness as we comprehend it," explains Philip still mind-reading her. He is himself at the heart of this chaos of sensations, intentions, and emotions she feels. "It is a chance to commune with oneself. To merge the pieces of one's soul fragmented by the trials set in their way. The Flood was a turning point in humanity's history, a trauma rooted so long as it is not healed at its source. Redemption is necessary for it to happen."

"But people die from this disease, or they go mad trying!" she protests, conscious of the evil that inhabits her, always feeding a little more on her fear.

"Sometimes, facing yourself is the greatest test life throws at you."

Here it is, the great test the Creator has in store for them. It had to happen. The Flood was not just a passing event that one can simply survive and go back to life as it was before. It isn't a bad memory that can be easily forgotten. It is a much deeper change that must happen to adapt to this new environment. They have already crossed a point of no return.

These principles are not foreign to Emily, even if she does not share the Farrells' blind faith. But this way of thinking about it makes the experience more tangible, more real. It's a starting point that can be a stepping-stone in her healing process.

"What if I fail?" asks Emily firmly, her new understanding giving her an anchor.

"We're here together, aren't we?" Philip says this casually to be comforting. Emily hates to admit it, but he is the more resilient one.

"But is it always like that, with the others?"

"No," says Philip. "The memory sphere is used to create a lucid dream, a simulation, if you will, that makes the experience more accessible, less abstract, with more room to maneuver. Everything you experience here is in your subconscious."

Her change of outfit. Yasmina coming back from the dead. Violet, Catalina Garcia, Adeline White, Tom Harris, and Emily's dreams of becoming a famous artist. All this was the expression of her desires. As for Ludo and Philip, both represent some of her fears, on the one hand, for being betrayed and, on the other for facing herself. And then there was the Chapel, the memories of her repressed childhood.

"It doesn't guarantee a successful recovery, but ... it's good enough."

"But then why is the Paragon here?"

"Duke is trying to get into your mind to control it. If he gets his hands on you or worse, the sphere you're looking at—"

"He will win."

Emily chokes on the suffocating smell of smoke and her eyes start to seriously sting. She coughs hard and says, "What are we gonna do? Duke will get through my defenses. When we disappeared, the fire was burning down *La Orilla*."

"There's another problem."

"Another problem?"

"Emily ... we don't have much time left," he says with a rueful look. "This is the final stage of the Syndrome. We must decide."

The choice resonates in her mind: Either she gets rid of Duke, or she fights the Syndrome to realign her consciousness and her ego. No matter her choice, she loses. Her heart quickens as she realizes she's not coming out of this one alive. Before her eyes well up, Philip embraces her and a funny energy passes between them, both foreign and familiar.

"Do you trust me?" Philip asks, breaking off their embrace when Emily pulls herself together.

"Should I?" says Emily, then lets out a laugh.

"Well, it's not like we know each other that well," he says with a hint of sarcasm.

"Duke," Emily whispers, suddenly more serious. "Duke cannot get his way. He'll never stop."

The look of surprise on Philip's face makes Emily swallow hard. Did she make the wrong decision?

"We can try..."

"But there are no guarantees," adds Emily.

Philip nods slowly. He walks over to the large stained-glass window that appears before them. "This is where it all starts. Once you are inside, Duke will be aware of it, and his subconscious will try to root you out. If you follow this route, he will have to retreat from this place and your sphere will be safe."

"But it'll be more difficult to break through his defenses."

"On the other hand, if he stays, you will be able to navigate more easily in his subconscious, but the sphere will be at his mercy. In both cases, the risks are extremely high, and time is running out."

"But it's worth a try, isn't it?"

"If that is your desire, why not? You are the master of your destiny after all."

Emily smiles shyly, more aware than ever that Philip is her dearest ally. She approaches the stained-glass showing a commander before his battalion. The insignia of the Paragon shines with a golden color. And only then does Emily realize with dread that Philip was talking about her and not the two of them in his plan.

"Aren't you coming?"

She turns around, but Philip is no longer around. Panic overcomes her. They didn't even have a chance to say goodbye. Philip, of all the people she knows.

Emily sizes up the window to get a feel of its consistency, then summons the appropriate weapon: A fully loaded stun gun, like the one she saw those agents use in the restaurant during the first Paragon raid. She backs away to a comfortable distance, her heart heavy from leaving the world of her subconscious, where all her thoughts and desires can become reality.

The energy is collecting in the gun at lightning speed, and she takes her aim dead center. When the device is loaded to its maximum capacity, she pulls the trigger with a war cry.

The electric arc rips the air around her and comes crashing against the stained glass. Electricity ripples across the surface until the window collapses on itself in a discordant melody.

Emily discards her improvised weapon and marches right into the gaping hole leading straight into the subconscious of Duke Kay, leader of the Paragon and self-proclaimed Commander of the Amaranth.

37

SKYLER

The torches flare in the hollow cave stinking of sulfur. The air is dusty, and their coughing echoes loudly. Any attempt to conceal their location is vain.

Skyler can still feel Eliza's lips on his ear as they make their way into an old place of worship that—Skyler hopes—hasn't fallen into Ludo's hands. With the help of Rolf, Dan, and Derek, they managed to bring the families who were trapped in the clinic, but not all of them. Despite Skyler's vehement protests, they had to leave behind the patients on oxygen support and those who preferred to stay. Getting to the little temple was no easy task with a group of this size, and the tunnels could spit out a colony of drones at any moment. When they fled into the tunnels near the clinic under Skyler's orders, they encountered none. Could this be a sign that the battle raging in the dome is drawing all their attention?

Skyler naturally became the leader of the group as if sharing Neal's blood gave him this legitimacy. Dan and Derek are Mavericks and would be better suited for this task, but Neal must have spoken to them personally about this. Otherwise, they would be supporting the very tradition the Brotherhood was fighting on the Ark.

Rolf is making sure their group has everything they need by helping the mothers take care of their frightened children. When Skyler decided that they would go to the little temple instead of the residential area, Rolf offered to bring first-aid kits with oxygen tanks, in case they came across survivors during their journey. His sense of duty will make him a good doctor in the future.

The painted cave walls seem to be whispering as they pass with their torches casting shadows along the way. Parents, children, and even Skyler are still holding their breath. So long as the base is not safe, their life is at risk every second that ticks by.

"How did you know to come here?" mutters Derek.

Although Eliza has suggested they go to the little temple, there is no assurance that this place will be their safe haven. For now, the Creator is leading the way for them.

"People need to collect themselves," says Skyler. "This temple is big enough to accommodate as many refugees as possible and give us time to plan ahead."

"We can't stay. Fleeing on one of their ships is the safest way," Dan grumbles.

"Not until we have rescued the children. I've already abandoned patients at the clinic. I can't do the same with our future."

Skyler holds Dan's gaze as he finally gives a smile. "Stubbornness is a family trait, it seems."

The statues of mythical heroes and forsaken gods finally materialize in the darkness. Skyler has this feeling of being in the presence of something larger than himself again. His time spent here was a happy one when he reunited with Gabrielle and Dinah. He never thought he would return here with fear in his gut, fleeing a once-hidden enemy: Ludo.

And Tessa.

The pain is sharp when he realizes that this woman's lies

know no bounds. Not only did she borrow the Farrells' name, but she joined the Brotherhood knowingly—and made his brother fall under her spell!—so she could carry out a mission of destruction. Her betrayal is inexcusable. How many opportunities did she have to play fair with them? Skyler can't imagine how his brother must feel.

Will the Creator judge Tessa for all the evil she has caused? Will he offer her a way to repent despite her unforgivable sins?

"What do we do now?" asks Rolf, following Skyler like his shadow. They have reached the center of the temple where the outlines of a group of people are approaching.

"Who are you?" Men hold up torches that roar into bright flames, frightening the children, who begin to cry. Dan loads his gun, but Skyler stops him when he recognizes the voice.

"Dinah!" A gasp of surprise.

"Praise be to the Creator!"

Dinah Farrell emerges from the darkness, crossing herself, and instructs the men accompanying her to relax. They lead Skyler and his crew into the main room where over a hundred refugees are huddled. People talk on their way in with several of them coughing insistently. The air in the temple is cold and damp, and the aromatic incense can barely mask the acrid stench of fear that lingers.

"How did you know?" asks Skyler, who is at a loss for words.

"It's Uki," Dinah says, turning to the statue of a strange bird with outstretched wings, a hawk if Skyler's memory is correct. "She…"

Uki is sitting nearby, with a blank stare, as if her body were an empty shell. A trance?

"She came looking for me and urged me to bring as many people as possible to the temple. The Creator can manifest in mysterious ways and so I knew that he was trying to communicate with me through Uki."

Could the woman Tessa and Skyler rescued on the Sedna

have sensed what was about to happen? Or did she see something?

"Since then, she hasn't spoken a word," Dinah adds, apologetic. "The important thing is that we are safe and sound. What's the matter?"

"Uki was right. Someone is trying to destroy the Star," he explains.

"I was right to worry then. I tried to persuade them not to leave the temple, but not everyone shines with the same faith."

"We intend to evacuate. Do you know if there are other refugees?"

"I only know those in the temple."

"It's going to be hard enough with all these people," Dan cuts them off. "We can't take them all."

"The children," Skyler says emphatically. "Where are they?"

"Most of them are here," Dinah replies with a shy smile. "I usually hold daily activities for them, and I thought I'd create a scavenger hunt. They're over there."

Several of the children who came through the clinic are here, but Gabrielle and little Rose stayed with Chris at the camp, probably the safest place to be right now. Skyler breathes a sigh of relief. "Good. Are there any wounded?"

"Yes. Those who have been coming in sporadically for about an hour. I'll take you to them."

WITH ROLF'S HELP, they manage to dress wounds and explain the need for evacuating. Most of the wounded are lethargic, barely able to hold a conversation, and many have bad coughing spells which does not sit well with Skyler. It could be due to stress, but there must be something else to explain their condition. As soon as they are out of this place, Skyler will need to address this problem.

Dan urges him to make plans to leave fast, but for now, the wait is needed. Neal may return, and other children may join them. They will have to go back through the tunnels to get to the boarding bay, but with the looming threat of the drones, their odds of survival are too uncertain. If they were to be under attack, they wouldn't stand a chance.

Go to the little temple and kneel before the gods.

Skyler has been replaying Eliza's words over and over without figuring out their meaning.

"Where is the best place to pray to the Gods?" he asks Dinah as she finishes praying with a family hoping to find their child who has not returned from the *Skogenslofte* colony.

She looks at him curiously and, without a word, beckons him to follow her. They return to the shaft and its spiral staircase of polished stones. She leads him into a side corridor where he has never been before.

"The Creator has many faces that transcend time and space. He has many names, but His power is everywhere. This temple is no exception. Each of these heroes, for example, held one of His tears."

"His tears?

"When He created our world, the Creator shed eternal tears, for He was moved by the beauty of His creation."

"Are these tears some relics, like the ones the Ark's hunters salvaged?"

"They are immaterial, or so I believe. No one has seen them as such, but they manifest themselves through unique people who are their carriers. One recognizes these individuals by their feats and their life-changing actions such as saving one's people, winning a war, curing a disease. Miracles can take any form."

The Academy's teachings never mentioned these. Why did the Sanctuary not have a say in what they were taught?

"This is the first time I've heard of this," he says. "Even in the Archives."

"The story doesn't end here."

The presence of those timeless heroes is strong, and Skyler thinks about his brother's actions. Does changing the course of their Ark's history make him a Tearbearer? What about the commanders of the other arks? The Amaranth?

"How do you know all this?" he asks candidly, embarrassed by his ignorance.

"Is it not the duty of the Ark's priestess?" She holds back a shy laugh with her hand. "I still have to keep some mystery, don't I?"

"I must learn, then."

"You can ask me anything you want." She blushes, then quickly walks along the fourth branch of the star carved at the bottom of the shaft and into the room that opens before them.

"The Creator also shed tears when He realized how much humans had damaged His creation. A flood of tears, the premise of the Flood. There were cryptic messages in the years following the end of the Old World. It raised suspicions among the people that He might have sent His avatars to exist among us. Some have gone so far as to call them gods, but that is urban legend."

"Do you believe it?"

Dinah does not answer immediately and enters the corridor that leads to an inner room. "It doesn't matter what I believe, but the faith of the people. These unique monuments are an attempt to represent the avatars."

"Avatars?"

For each monument is painted a large circle that contains different curves that are unlike anything Skyler knows.

"In a foreign language. The people who used to live here, or rather built them, had knowledge beyond our understanding."

"How do you know that these are the famous avatars?"

"The name of this room: the Hall of the Gods. Let us pray, shall we?"

They kneel before the great monuments and Dinah says, "Remember our exercise from the last time?"

He breathes at regular intervals and asks the Creator to show him the way. He follows Dinah, and together they breathe rhythmically, leaving their fears behind.

Images of the past few weeks flash through him like watching his own memory sphere in a Nave. Dinah warned him that the Creator speaks mostly in images and, on rare occasions, through his Voice. Now, he sees.

The Refuge is compressed under the Ark's metal skeleton where people wait, slumped against the walls. They were abandoned with only death to save them.

The Sedna used to teem with life before the arrival of Thalassa. Uki healed her brethren suffering from the Disease. She was trusted and changed their lives. Then, the auditorium was filled with their corpses, their smiles forever gone.

Little Rose woke up from her coma, and her father Marko came. Many families were in tears to finally be reunited. Tears of joy.

The waterfall in the garden shone under the glare of the setting sun. Chris kissed him and disappeared almost immediately.

Skyler can feel himself jump into the present. In the middle of the snowy pine forest, Chris's face is wounded, and the pain of returning to the colony alone is unbearable.

Children are playing with the dogs near the wooden cabins of *Skogenslofte*. There is laughter and joyful barking, the promise of a future.

A gasp. Isn't that what Skyler has always dreamed of? He and his brother would always talk about it when they were kids. Allen would listen to him patiently while taking down some notes. This colony, they imagined it together. Built it together.

We will save them all. Our parents, our friends, and the people of the Ark.

Out of this prison and the confines of the ocean. The sun will dazzle our achievements, and the stars will shine for all those who have died.

Our children will never know the feeling of no longer belonging to this world that has rejected us.

Redemption will only be a painful memory of a past mistake.

From that moment on, the rules will be ours to make.

In a new world that we will have created.

With or without the help of the Creator.

The time has finally come, little brother.

Allen. Allen is talking to him.

Skyler's eyes snap open, and panic overwhelms him. He is almost certain to see Neal before him, but there is nobody here. He calls out to Dinah, but she does not answer, as if transfixed.

Allen's voice.

Skyler follows the echo of that voice which leads him back to the spiral stairs. He climbs them four at a time and even when he runs out of breath, he pushes on. Outside the temple, in the darkness-engulfed tunnel, Skyler grabs a torch burning at the entrance.

Allen's voice is pleading. But then, he glimpses a figure hunched against the rocky wall.

Skyler!

Allen's voice bears a warning that takes his breath away, but it is already too late.

Ludo's grin is unmistakable. Before Skyler can react, the warden raises his hand and bluish lights spring to life at each end of the tunnel.

Two, four, ten, twenty. He can no longer keep track of them.

Run!

Static noise. Skyler beats a retreat and throws the torch to the ground. The projectiles hit the walls of the mountain around him as he gasps for air. The string of steps blur in the semi-darkness. He should have kept the torch, but ... he misses a step. He tumbles down the stairs, and his body takes hit after hit until he falls into a hidden alcove.

A swarm of drones whirr inside the temple and soon enough, a choir of screams and shouts erupts.

Gunshots.

Someone is coming down, chanting in some unknown language. Ludo?

Skyler restrains himself from shouting out of rage as he bites his fist. His body quakes, and his thoughts are no more than a heap of disjointed feelings.

It's all his fault. He gave away their location, stupid as he is! He thought his brother was back. That he heard his voice! That Allen was calling him!

It seemed so real: His brother coming back from his battle, wounded, maybe even fatally. He would have needed emergency care.

But the voice was Allen's, not Neal's.

Skyler winces on his feet, intent on ending this once and for all. If Ludo or any of his drones find him, it will all be over. He can't live with that on his conscience. Nothing can ever forgive what he did.

This pain … this shame will devour him.

He is here! He should die with the rest of them! This is the price he must pay!

As he makes for the stairs where the drones are, he loses his balance and sinks deeper into the alcove until he hits a metal wall.

A door.

Another one of these goddamn doors!

And then, it hits him.

Eliza knew. That's why she sent them to the temple. This alcove must be connected to the Hall of the Gods, an emergency passageway, perhaps even leading outside the base. They could reach the colony, or better yet, the boarding bay! If he had figured it out before, they would have already evacuated, and Ludo would never have found them.

But why didn't Eliza just tell him?

HIS HEAD HURTS LIKE HELL, but Skyler wakes up anyway. As he was waiting for Ludo to leave for good, he fell asleep. His memories are but a blur, and when he tries to get up, he falls to his knees and throws up violently. A concussion. He should be happy he didn't throw his life away.

Propping himself against the wall, he descends the few remaining steps. His feet catch into something, and he barely has time to save himself from another fall to the ground. Mid-curse, he shuts his mouth at seeing a first aid kit. He throws himself on it and grabs an oxygen tank.

He can finally breathe.

The screams are no longer, and his dizziness is subsiding. He was intoxicated. Dinah!

With the first aid kit under his arm, Skyler returns to the room where they were praying, but the monuments are back to their stony contemplation. A pair of feet peek out from behind a statue. Dinah probably got up, but the toxin was too strong, and she slumped to the ground. He makes her breathe through the mask. But why did the gas leak not affect them before? Dinah spends most of her time in the temple.

Skyler sits next to her against the statue and lets the haze lift slowly. The bitter memory of his intoxication in the air ducts of the Gardens of Humankind flashes before him.

"What happened?" Dinah is awake.

"The gas," Skyler explains in a sluggish voice. "The concentration is too high in the temple, especially in these parts. If we'd gone any longer without oxygen, we'd be in the same condition as the patients at the clinic. There must be leaks in the mountain."

"This is odd. The Voice of the Creator spoke to me. It said…"

Dinah stops, then opens her eyes wide. She drops the mask and scrambles out of the Hall of Gods as fast as her wobbly legs can take her. Skyler goes after her to hold her back. No one must see. No one. No one!

She forks in the main hall of the temple and lets out a frightened scream before falling to her knees. Skyler freezes. It is too late. She saw everything. She knows what he did.

The temple is unrecognizable. A few carcasses of the drones are smoking on the ground, but the damage…

The statues are riddled with bullets and the place of worship is strewn with debris, swimming in a tide of blood.

The refugees.

The women. The children.

Dead.

They are all dead.

38

EMILY

How long will she be able to stay under Duke's radar?

Ever since she set foot on this alternate version of the Ark, with its dreary, endless corridors and stinking mold, the thought has been haunting her. It's hard to say where exactly she is on the ship. Maybe she's never been here before, since Duke literally has access to the entire Ark, like the Paragon headquarters, which is a true minefield. With every step she takes, she imagines a horde of Paragon agents ready to snuff her out on the spot, but so far, she's still alive.

She controls her breathing like Dad taught her during their secret after-school training sessions, pretending he is by her side on this suicide mission. Her magic tricks from earlier probably won't succeed as well here. But still, Duke had a hell of a time in *La Orilla*, and not just once at that! The destruction he caused was impressive, considering he was in Emily's subconscious. Well, she *could* have had much better control but for her lack of insight. If only she knew what was going on earlier, she might have turned the tables, but it's too late for regrets now.

There must be a way to have a greater influence on another

person's subconscious. Isn't that the mystery Duke has unraveled?

A tall, dark-skinned man with jet black hair she has never seen before comes around the corner, and that's when Emily finally knows where she is—the Alpha Division or rather, the Command Wing. The last time she was here, she was returning to the main part of the ship to stop the commander from leaving the passengers to their own devices before the Brotherhood could take over the Command Center.

The young man looks disoriented, judging by the way he scans his surroundings. Again, the glaring lack of auras is upsetting, but, of course, Duke could never see them, and as far as she knows his memories are no exception. He did mention their existence during his endless monologues in Emily's cell which means he might have seen them through the subjects he used for his experiments. This is a characteristic they all share, though Philip never bothered to explain.

Unsure whether this young man can see her, she hides in the dark, poorly lit corners, and stalks him carefully. At a bend, a much younger Duke surprises the stranger who shouldn't be walking around this part of the ship.

Duke doesn't wear the unnerving sadistic expression all psychopaths have. As Mom would put it: He hadn't deviated from his true mission yet. But his insufferable arrogance shows through his sneer and the curvature of his eyebrows, a trait the Kays have always shared. Some things never change.

"What are you doing here?"

Emily's heart drums, dreading that the question is directed at her. Fortunately, a rough voice answers in a tumble of foreign words.

"Is this a joke or what? Stop talking like a beast," roars Duke, burying his anxiety with a gust of anger.

The boy recoils, fear clouding his dark eyes as he searches for a way to flee like a trapped animal. Even Emily cowers under Duke's menacing tone. But then, he adds more softly, "What is your name?"

"Tajj," the young man says hesitatingly, his face wary, as he glances at the fire escape. "Tajj."

"Tajj? Which family?" asks Duke. He takes a step in his direction, then another. Tajj mirrors him to keep a safe distance between them while scanning for an escape route.

"No family."

"A Maverick, then. How did you get here without anyone seeing you?"

Tajj chooses this moment to take flight, but Duke clubs him preemptively. Tajj lets out a whimper, then, before he can crawl to freedom, Duke restrains him handily. His already well-built body for his age gives him an advantage over Tajj who seems to have grown up in less than favorable conditions. Now that he is closer to Emily, she can see Tajj's lean muscles and protruding bones. His eyes are not exactly dark, but a deep sapphire blue.

"My father will know what to do with you. Come on, get up!" Duke yanks Tajj by the arm, but his voice doesn't match the way he looks at him. He is fascinated by this foreign presence. Tajj's clothing looks nothing like what the Archeans or the Mavericks wear, more like a tunic. Could it be that Tajj … No, that's absurd. How could he? Yet the possibility seems too real. Duke is probably thinking the same.

Was Tajj born outside the Amaranth?

Emily hides at the last moment in a service booth, while Duke guides Tajj in her direction.

Duke almost caught a glimpse of her.

THE SERVICE BOOTH is not what it claims to be, but rather another memory.

The Kay's roomy cabin materializes before her. It is a

gracious apartment modeled on the pre-Flood mansions found on the Surface, with more plush furniture and useless trinkets than Emily can count. Relics from the hunts have found a home on chests of drawers set on a finely woven rug with oriental motifs, and ornate shrines display which Emily has only vaguely heard of at the Academy. She has a chill when she glimpses a collection of weapons on display. Their power lies dormant like wild beasts about to pounce on anyone who gets nearby. The two men standing beside don't seem to be bothered in the least.

Emily hides behind the imposing sofa that shouldn't be allowed to exist on a ship like the Ark. Its regal fabrics and upholstery are a joke to anyone in their right mind. How many cabins like the Bates's would be needed to hold a sofa like this and move about with ease?

The lavish life of the Kays disgusts her. Chris's growing up in such an environment is almost impossible to believe, but especially off-putting. What was he supposed to think every time he came to visit her in her hovel? To think that he avoided his cabin as much as possible, preferring to stay at the Academy after class, even if it meant sleeping there so he wouldn't run into his father! Emily could never understand.

"Tajj," Duke says in a more mature voice. He looks bulkier than he was. "I have something for you." The wristband worn by each Archean glints in his hand. "You can finally be free and live a normal life on the ship."

"Are you sure this is the right thing to do?" says Tajj in a sandy accent. Thin muscles cover his once bony arms, his face as delicate as ever and his eyes hypnotic.

"This is the only way."

"Everyone knows that I don't talk like them. They will always know."

"You have learned enough of our language to get by. You can always blame your shortcomings on the after-effects of a childhood illness. Don't worry. No one will dare ask because you will be working for the Paragon. I will be there for you."

"Your father—"

"Will have nothing to say. Do you hear me?"

Duke's eyes are bright with ardor. He embraces Tajj tightly, then cups his face in his hands, stroking his jaw with the tip of his thumb, as if he were admiring the most beautiful painting ever. *His* work of art, one that he has perfected over the years: a powerful secret for those who learn it.

"Nothing will happen to you so long as the Paragon is under my family's command. I promise."

Seeing Tajj is struggling, Duke places the wristband for him. It locks with a clink and Duke smiles like someone who's had a weight lifted from his shoulders. His fingers trace the edges of the wristband and the smooth skin around.

"Tajj… You never told me why you came to our Ark."

The mysterious young man leans his forehead against Duke's, closing his eyes like what he is about to say could break him, a wound that will never quite heal.

"You know I don't want to talk about it. Maybe one day. When I'm ready."

THEY ARE in an anteroom that looks like a private lounge in *La Orilla* with its couches, cushions, and curtains. Emily wonders if this is not the work of the designer that Mrs. Garcia hired. Oh! there is also some plant or rather a tangle of branches in a transparent waterless vase—that's new—but the leafy buds are petrified, desiccated to the point that a simple breath could reduce them to dust. She can't remember if she's ever seen any of those on her walks with Skyler in the park.

What if her memories are mixing with Duke's? As much as she could feel the Paragon's presence in her own subconscious, he must also feel her intrusion. She must be extra careful then. It's fortunate that the Kays display their decorations ostentatiously. It gives her plenty of nooks and crannies to hide.

Sitting in one of the armchairs, Duke's wife looks terrible. Clusters of bruises streak across her body where her uniform stops. Some of her hair has been sloppily shaved off like a peeled vegetable. The outline of an ugly scar on her skull can be seen in the harsh light, even from this distance.

"Charlie. You know how it works." There is no love in Duke's voice, but his authoritative tone, his voice not yet eroded with age.

"Why does it have to come to this?"

"I told you we would become a tight-knit family. But that requires her approval first. It's the only way the Kays will become the most powerful family the Ark has ever known."

"Power is worth nothing against the forces of nature. There are some things you can't control."

"Don't you want our son and our descendants to rule over the new Earth?"

"That was not a question, Duke."

"Anyway, none of that matters. After tonight, things will be easier."

Duke grabs his wife's arm stiffly and forces her to stand. She wears a stony expression, one that she has learned to use to hide her emotions from her husband. They both get into their sordid role of husband-and-wife walking side by side as if nothing had happened.

Emily follows them out of the lounge through a door on the other side. She wanders among the plants in the corner of the large living room where Laurene is waiting, younger-looking with shoulder-length hair.

"I hope it'll be worth my time," she says, sitting in a luxurious cream-gray armchair, legs crossed. "I didn't know your wife would be part of our little chat, Duke."

"Anything said in Charlotte's presence will be confidential."

"I have no doubt." Laurene swirls the ice in her glass mechanically, thinking. "We have to prepare for the war to come."

"Thalassa?"

"Among other things. Our enemies are many, and not only outside. Especially with the vermin on the lower levels. They should make themselves useful."

"The Incident we're planning should scare them for a while. They will be too busy retrieving the severed bodies of their cousins. This will give us enough time to implement the program without these rats sabotaging our experiments."

"They will come back. They always do."

Until now, neither of them has looked at Duke's wife, who is shooting darts at Laurene with her eyes like they share some troubled history.

"And the Paragon will teach them a new lesson they must learn or die trying."

Laurene gives a wry smile. "If it were that easy, I would've taken care of it myself. Do you honestly believe that only the Mavericks are the problem? The scale of this ... mutiny is such that conventional means will never eliminate this disease. What we need is a purge. And no one must be spared."

"If the Archeans were guilty of supporting the Mavericks in any way, the Paragon would know."

"I thought you were more perceptive, Duke Kay, son of Lance Kay who instigated the Furies' hecatomb. It's in your blood, but maybe you need a refresher."

She clinks her ring against her glass, and Duke turns pale.

"Carnal pleasures know no limits," she explains when Tajj walks across the living room with a sideways glance toward Emily's hiding place.

She holds her breath, but Tajj doesn't linger, despite the

gleam of understanding that crosses his face. He posts himself near the armchair.

"Especially for the unusual. That beautiful swarthy skin, those icy eyes, and this godlike body could make even a blind man shiver. But what does your poor wife Charlotte think? Her husband spends his free time exploring unknown lands, with their valleys and rivers open to the most adventurous."

Laurene leaps to her feet and caresses Tajj, who stiffens. He is the tallest of them all, and yet he could be invisible.

"Our son," says Charlotte, trembling. "Haven't you thought about his future? Would you rather love a stranger than your own family?"

"Charlie. Will you shut up?"

She struggles to speak, straining the muscles in her face, and a growl escapes from her throat. Laurene seems satisfied, while Tajj glares at Duke who's focused on Laurene.

"This Ark is just one cocoon among many," Laurene explains to Charlotte. "Sometimes, beautiful things can bloom, but weeds always have a way to flourish if left unattended. Do you know what I mean?" The question is directed at Duke resisting the urge not to stand between her and Tajj.

"There are other arks," he says, tense.

"You must know that the task ahead will have to extend beyond our Ark. Weed sprouts too easily."

"The Paragon will take care of it. With their minds under control, no one will dare step out of line."

"I sure hope so. I can't risk this program not being up to par. This new world cannot tolerate imperfections. How about we start now? A mother unworthy of the Kay bloodline, who has nothing to offer and is too stupid to know that her husband loves another has no place on this Ark."

"At least I never tried to kill my own child!" says Charlotte, while Duke seems to have lost his concentration.

"That's what sensible mothers do. Not just the mother of one child, but the mother of all. She protects the human race from an incurable virus that could spread. There is no cure for a broken genetic code, unable to adapt to our new planet now washed clean of all the misery it has suffered. You are unsuitable, as my child was."

She strides over to Charlotte and spits, "Raising a weak son is just an expression of your failure as a Kay guardian." Then, Laurene turns sharply to Tajj. "Don't you worry now," she says, kissing him on the lips. "He'll be all yours soon. Duke! Ask your wife to kill herself. Now."

"My wife?"

"Or would you rather get rid of our visitor too? That would be a shame." For once, Duke seems at a loss for words as he darts a look at Tajj and his wife.

Laurene sits and her excitement is disconcerting. She takes a good sip, then smiles amusedly. "I'm waiting."

Duke closes his eyes as if meditating. His wife moves toward Emily's hiding place and stealthily grabs a tool from a chest of drawers. She opens her veins without even blinking. Her blood spurts with her heartbeats, as Laurene and Duke watch her, unmoved. Emily repeats to herself that this is not real, that it is a memory of the most dangerous commander the Ark has known since the Flood. Not to mention, Laurene. How long will she rot in her cell if Duke is in charge?

Laurene makes sure the woman is truly dead by placing two fingers on her throat with a disgusted look. She jumps to her feet with renewed energy.

"I expected no less from Lance Kay's son. The Paragon has a bright future ahead."

Tajj chooses this moment to dive onto Charlotte and grab the tool to thrust it into Laurene's gut. A look of horror crosses Duke's face, and he shuts his eyes.

The sharp edge of the tool grazes its target without piercing, as if a puppeteer had decided to revise his act, dissatisfied with the way the story turned out. Tajj's hand whitens in his desperate effort to counter the invisible force that prevents him from regaining his hard-won freedom.

"My family, my brethren and sisters," articulates Tajj, his accent even thicker than usual under the strain.

"Hush," says Laurene by taking the weapon from his hands and tossing it on the ground. She takes in her arms a trembling Tajj seething with hatred. "You have a new family now."

Tajj kneels, tears streaming down his cheeks. Laurene strokes his head and lets him cry in silence.

"Out of curiosity, how did you … accomplish such a feat?"

Duke's answer doesn't come as easily—can he have any real feelings for anyone?—but he keeps his grip on Tajj who no longer seems able to fight back anyway. "With my limited resources, I trained Charlotte Harris via a cervical implant to map the neural network of her brain."

"Your own wife," says Laurene, taking a sip, looking mischievous. "Why her?"

Duke hesitates. Emily almost wants to answer for him. "Because she was the person who trusted me the most."

"You could have chosen your son, a younger subject, less … corrupted by this senseless life on the Ark."

"My son has a special affection for his mother." A smile ghosts over Laurene's lips as she takes a moment to appreciate the confession of a father who has sacrificed not only his wife, but the mother of his son.

"Do you think you can do it easily on a larger scale?"

"I have developed a simulation program that will simplify the procedure and will not require an implant to ensure a more natural and less invasive preparation of the subjects. I can show you if you like."

"Gladly. What about him? Does it work in the same way?" Tajj stares down, obviously trying to control his breathing as best he can.

"This is a special project."

"I love surprises," she exclaims. "Don't forget to keep me in the loop, but make sure not to damage him too much. What about this simulation of yours?"

So, the quarterly simulations were just a way to get them ready to be mind-controlled? After what Duke did to Dad, his own wife and…

A rustling near Emily startles her. She is face to face with Tajj who mouths her to keep silent.

The memory disintegrates in a maelstrom of light that gets sucked into oblivion.

THE ACADEMY. Emily hasn't been there in at least two years. In fact, since graduation. There's nothing to stop her from going back and reminiscing, which is what all the alumni do the following year, but Emily chose not to do like everyone else. The world that Yasmina introduced her to is too deep and dark to simply move on as if nothing ever happened. It takes time and a lot of willpower to escape the madness of the prisoners and cleanse her mind of all the atrocities.

"What did you learn in your history class today?" asks Duke faking interest.

"I don't want to go home with you," says young Chris, who is no more than twelve. "I want to go home with Mom."

"That's not how it works, and you know it, Chris. Don't make a scene in front of your buddies."

"I don't really care what they think. And you don't care either, just like anything you do that hurts others."

"You are a Kay, so act like one." Duke crouches in front of his son and speaks softly, "I want you to be happy. I really do. But you must want it from the bottom of your heart. Do you want to be happy?"

Chris nods weakly, sulking.

"Dad wants you to be the happiest person on this Ark too, but he's going to need your help. Without Mom."

"It's not the same."

"Some people don't even have parents, while you have the most powerful dad in the world. One day, he will be the next commander and you will follow in his footsteps. All your friends at the Academy envy you to death, even if they don't tell you so openly. And why is that? Because they are afraid. Afraid of the power you hold. You'll have everything you ever hoped for when you get older, whether it's on this ship or on the ground when we can go back."

Young Chris doesn't buy into these empty promises. But when he hears about the Surface, he's just another kid. He straightens up and opens his eyes wide, sucked into the biggest lie that keeps them alive, in search of a purpose.

"But for that to happen, you must trust me as much as you trusted Mom. And much, much more."

"Why did you wait until Mom died to change?"

Duke has a frozen smile, obviously uncomfortable. He glances around to make sure no one has heard anything.

"Mom once told me that if anything ever happened to her, it would be your fault because you didn't protect her. Is that true?" asks young Chris.

"I never got to spend as much time with you as I wanted. Your mother was very possessive. Maybe you don't understand it, but I tried everything to see you more often, but she always got in the way. She wasn't very nice to your father."

"Mom loved me, and she told me so every day. You never did."

"I love you Son, you know that."

"Then prove it." Chris slips through his father's grip and bolts down the hallway to where Emily is standing. Duke's face tightens and leaves after him with a stiff step.

"You'll pay for this tonight."

Did Tajj tell Chris what really happened to make him act this way?

While Emily was distracted, Duke came up to stare at her. Panicked, she races off in the same direction as Chris, with Duke on her heels. She expects at any moment to be picked off by some Paragon agent lurking in the shadows, but instead, she finds herself in the Refuge, near the passageway that leads to the airlock.

Duke is facing his son Chris, who's now Emily's age, amidst a convoy of people heading for the airlock. Without any convenient place for her to hide, Chris spots her, but he doesn't flinch, other than twitch his eyebrow. A crowd about to force their way out has gathered around them, and Duke pulls his son out of the throng.

"You weren't seriously planning to follow them," Duke snarls.

"Why not?" challenges Chris, who has grown more confident with time, his tone firmer and his posture more upright despite his father's scorn.

"They are our enemies."

"Everyone is your enemy, Father. This is not new."

"If you leave the Ark, I will no longer consider you, my son. Do you hear me?" Duke's grip is strong, the vein in his neck pulsing with anger. His otherwise impeccable face takes on a burgundy hue that Emily has never seen, not even when he was getting carried away in his delirious monologues.

"If that's what it takes to get you to leave me alone once and for all, so be it!"

"You are not aware of what you are saying!"

"When will you admit to killing mom, your own wife, to achieve your twisted ideals? Any son would want to forget his roots knowing that!"

"Who told you?" says Duke threateningly.

"Another person you sacrificed unfairly. It's natural coming from you, I hear. I don't need to witness another massacre led by my father."

Emily had no idea what Chris had been through. Why didn't he ever tell her? They were good friends. His aura never gave anything away, always all smiles and lighthearted. How could she have missed his terrible trauma?

"It's time to go," says Chris, stationed at her side without her even knowing he was there.

An alarm goes off and the passage is drowned in a crimson light, the color of blood.

Duke knows he has been infiltrated.

THE CHRIS in front of her is not really her Chris, but a part of Duke that could lure her into a trap. She has been wandering from memory to memory, unable to find a way to access the weak spot in his consciousness. This could be her only chance to find a breach.

She decides to follow Chris who takes her hand. They are transported to another place, where the metal walls become earthy like the trampled ground of the Gardens of Humankind. The ground is bloated with moisture, just like when the gardens are sprinkled early in the morning. But there are no plants, no trees, and not even the constant vibration of the Ark here.

Perhaps it is the lack of metal or the missing mechanical pulse that piques her curiosity. Her intuition tells her this alien environment shouldn't be in Duke's subconscious memories.

This place is not on the Ark.

Once her vision of this other world has stabilized, she asks Chris why he is helping her.

"Simply because we're friends. We always have been."

"You're part of Duke, you shouldn't—"

"Emily, the connection between your two minds creates a unique symbiosis that can merge your minds forever. This moment is crucial to what happens next. Neither of you will survive if this connection lasts too long. The capacity of the brain has its limits."

"You are my ally," she says, remembering Yasmina fighting alongside her against Ludo. "Did I summon you?"

"Your memories of Chris merged with Duke's and solidified my true self. I would never support my father's evil plans, and he knows it. It would contradict who I am, and that logic is encoded deep in our memories. There are rules to follow, even in this universe."

"I have to stop Duke," Emily repeats, focusing on what might be his weakness. "Any ideas on how to do that?"

"Locate his nexus, which controls everything. We are close."

"Easy then," she says encouragingly. "Find the nexus, screw it up, and we're off."

Chris nods and precedes her into this eerie place filled with wiring and electronic equipment. A strange vibration in the air is poking at her eardrums. Could it be from that big piece of metal glowing with a purplish light up ahead? It seems to be floating, towering in this massive cavern. She remembers seeing one of these natural structures in her Academy classes, which described how early humans harnessed the power of fire to protect themselves from the elements. These rocky caves allowed them to find shelter and organize themselves while the devastating storms raged outside. But Emily feels anything but safe in this gloomy place.

A tide of wires is attached to the luminous rock fragment and rains down on the earthy ground hooking itself into a weird contraption. The tangle is too thick to make out what it is exactly.

"We don't have much time," Chris presses. As if to prove him right, a burning sensation sears Emily's skull.

"My world, my rules," Duke says with a smirk. His loyal agents are spread out around him like a scythe ready to strike. "I don't remember giving you permission to come here, Miss Bates. I thought we might become good partners, you and I, but it seems that when you feed a dog too much, he wants to bite the hand of his master. That'll teach me for being too lenient."

"Emily!" shouts Chris and she understands what she must do.

This is the moment. She imagines the same feeling she had when she was facing Ludo. She has come so far; she can't let her chance to stop Duke slip away. Now that she knows his true face, she doesn't regret choosing to sacrifice herself.

Come.

The pain is so great that Emily thinks she is already dying. A hand rips something from inside her and she moans, bent in two.

"This has gone on long enough," says Dad at her side, wearing the Paragon uniform he would have worn the day he was crowned leader of Theta Division and the Ark forces.

Emily comes to her senses as she hears his voice, her father as exceptional as she has always imagined him to be.

"Nobody touches my agent," exclaims Yasmina, armed with an electric prod. "Not even Duke Kay."

"Another scum that has no place on the Promised Land," adds Sofia Reyes, swinging her timeless dagger.

"Never," completes Chris, who steps forward with a pistol from his family's shrine. "This world doesn't need a murderous father."

"On the contrary," Duke thunders. "The call of blood resonates with the Creator's desire to purge this world of the human aberration. Starting with you, my poor son. But don't you worry; Daddy is here to free you from this pain."

Duke closes his eyes and raises his fists. His army multiplies under his orders, ready to march on them.

"We have very little time to make this work," says Philip who materializes. "Come on."

The two of them take the muddy road leading to the foot of the monstrous installation, while their allies push back Duke's defenses as best as they can, in a thunderous din that makes the cave rumble. In their frantic race, Emily loses her footing after a blast shakes the entire structure, but Philip catches her in time. As they get closer to the center, Emily realizes with horror that the strange wiring is connected to a human being.

Tajj.

His body is constricted by all the wires that pierce through him, while he is half conscious. The most bizarre thing is the way his skin glows, the same purplish color as the fragment floating above their heads.

"Tajj is the equivalent of your memory sphere," Philip informs her. "You must destroy it."

"Yes, and he's not going anywhere," Duke says, threateningly. Somehow, he managed to break through the line of defense Emily had erected.

"I'm not afraid of you," retorts Emily, immediately getting into a fighting stance.

"It's a good thing I'm not either. This is my world, and you don't belong here."

"Yet here I am. You have exposed yourself by making this connection between us."

"It works both ways, Miss Bates." Philip bends over and screams, and the excruciating pain echoes inside of her. Her physical body flickers dangerously, like the poor-quality video that she was forced to watch from her cell in the Paragon headquarters.

"There's nothing you can do about it," Duke explains. "The

breach in your subconscious will allow me to control you completely. At last."

"You should listen to what your son has to say." The Chris from Emily's memories approaches, his sweaty features hollowed by fatigue.

"I was never the son you wanted me to be. You wanted to keep me close to you when I wanted to get away. Somehow, I dare to believe that you wanted me to be different from you. That I wouldn't make the same unforgivable mistakes."

"I've done everything for your sake," says Duke, whose breathing quickens. "Even if you don't understand it yet. This will all be over soon, once my army is complete."

"Try me. Your army isn't going anywhere," Emily says through clenched teeth.

The pulse gun Emily used to break through Duke's mind solidifies in her hand, and she aims at Tajj who has regained consciousness. Philip cuts the wiring hanging from Tajj's battered body. The Paragon agents disappear instantly. The fury contorting Duke's face is a sight to behold.

The pulse gun is charging dangerously as Tajj walks over to them.

"My biggest mistake was loving you," says Duke. Emily doesn't know whether he's talking to Chris or Tajj swaying on his feet.

"Dad, stop," says Chris. "It's over."

"If the Kays gave up so easily, I would never have become the Commander of the Ark, Son."

Emily had not seen the gun Duke kept hidden inside his uniform, but then a burst of gunfire erupts.

"I killed you once, I can kill you a second time. Tajj."

The expression of surprise on Philip's face worries Emily, who moves away from Duke. She loses her concentration, and immediately Chris disappears, as well as Yasmina, her father, and Sofia Reyes.

"Is everything okay? Philip! Answer me!" Emily has the horrible feeling to have lost everything.

Tajj bleeds himself out of purplish blood. He pronounces his last words in a gurgle, "I will always love you, Duke. For who you were and who you will always be in my heart. In this life and the next."

Tajj's body lights up with the same sparks as when the children in her memories vanished, and she knows that something terrible has just happened. Philip isn't answering her calls either. Duke's face is frozen in an expression of astonishment.

He kneels … and starts crying.

Philip's breathing resumes, the only encouraging sign in this lifeless world collapsing around them. The rock fragment has lost its glow, shedding its colors in a wild thunder.

"Emily," breathes Philip. "Duke is no more."

"How … how is that possible? He's standing right in front of us! We have to do something."

"There's nothing more we can do. Duke Kay has … destroyed his subconscious."

The leader of the Paragon, son of Lance Kay, and successor to the title of Commander of the Amaranth, has become a shadow of his former self, forever trapped in the world he has betrayed.

39

EMILY

The first thing Emily sees when she opens her eyes is Milo's face above her, frowning as he usually does when he is worried about her.

"Emily, tell me you're okay," he whispers, his warm hand nervously stroking her hair.

She almost feels like she's waking up from another coma. Milo was there too, as always. The memory of his death weighing heavily on her heart lifts immediately. Everything that happened in her mind was not real. At least not that part.

"I'm alive," she says in disbelief.

The emotions she experienced in the alternate reality wash over her in waves.

Seeing that she is coming to her senses, Milo helps her out of her chair. To Emily's relief, her memory sphere is still glowing before her. The crimson hues have given way to beautiful threads of gold swirling like the heart of a small sun, a tiny replica of the Sacred Fire. The yellows intertwine with the whites in a complex symmetry. Emily can hardly believe that this marvel, created by her best friend, has allowed her to live this intense and astonishing experience.

Flashes from her journey into her mind compel her to check on the psychotic Commander of the Ark.

Milo gives her the stability she needs to get to the chair where Duke is still lying. His eyes are open and moving in her direction, his pupils strangely dilated. His body doesn't seem to respond.

She did not kill him. Even if she had had the chance, she wouldn't have done it. Death only begets death. She didn't know what she was getting into by infiltrating Duke's consciousness, but her desire was to stop this contagious madness that could have caused irreparable damage to the entire Ark and their only hope of starting over on the new Earth. But in the end, Duke doomed himself, blinded by his forbidden love and his selfish motives. He is a prisoner of his own body, a fate worse than death. But Emily feels neither sadness nor pity.

This is what happens to those who stray so far from their mission that they are willing to snuff out the good part of themselves. Emily could have fallen into the trap too, but Philip helped her see through it before it was too late.

"Can he hear us?"

"I think so, but he can't harm anyone now," says Emily, staring into the irises of the most dangerous man on the Ark. "Something in his brain fried during the experiment. His own madness turned against him." Milo puts his arm around her to draw her closer to him, and she lets out a sigh of relief.

Sofia, who was busy tying up the last of the Paragon agents, comes to greet her. She has lost weight since their failed breakout attempt. Some of her hair has been shaved off like Charlotte, Chris's mother. Fortunately, Duke did not go through with his plans.

"How many Mavericks have been subjected to his experiments?" Sofia says with sarcasm. "The Promised Land can do without him."

"What should we do with him?" hisses Milo.

"We let him live long enough to realize that he was wrong about everything. Humanity doesn't need him. We can prove to him that we are stronger than he believes. His imaginary enemies will not get us, with or without his army." Emily speaks these words with blind confidence in her intuition. Maybe too much, even. But for now, she wants to believe. She hasn't felt this sense of security since Mom died. The world may not be so bad after all, so long as there are good souls to lead the way.

"How did you manage to break in?" Emily asks, her body aching like she's been training hard.

"You know I have a weakness for mechanics. Duke found out about it when I tinkered with something to stop the dormitory ventilation from waking us up at night. Nobody thought of that. It doesn't make sense not to be able to sleep after the insane workouts the Paragon put us through every day," replies Milo, with a hardened look.

Emily remembers the torture sessions that accompanied the training. "I know," she says, her heart heavy.

"I was right! The camera—"

"I've seen your training, your missions. Well, some of them."

"So, you know that Duke sent us to fix the Sacred Fire. He did his own investigation and saw us reinitializing the cores. He knew I was qualified to do it. And then our mission to extract the capacitor was successful, so he appointed me to install it on the Amaranth."

She remembers that voice now. Ludo is the one who shot Emily at the Sacred Fire, almost killing her in the process. Her induced coma certainly spared her from certain death. Had it not been for him, the events on the Ark would have played out very differently, but Emily keeps her thoughts to herself. There's nothing she can do about it anyway. She just wants to enjoy this longed-for moment with Milo, without a screen to get in the way.

"Sofia was doing good business with the Paragon agents. She

learned that Walker was part of a special team responsible for restoring the Ark. I arranged to meet with him about a bogus technical problem, and Walker warned me that Duke was preparing a special experiment for you. Walker worked with Sofia to get the details and lead us to you. By the time I arrived, it was too late. You were asleep and I thought…"

His eyes are wet, like when he spoke of Evelyn and her tragic story. Emily knows how much he loved her. To be able to count so much in his eyes warms her heart.

"Thank you."

"If I could have—"

"There was nothing else that could've put a stop to Duke's plans."

"Maybe," he says, unconvinced. "But we've lost too much."

But at least they didn't lose each other.

A wave of disappointment overwhelms her when she realizes that Philip is not here. The North Star card, the object that brings her closest to him, is still in her pocket. Emily feels she understands Violet better when she talks about the Creator and her way of communing with Him. This card reminds her of the importance of loving and listening to herself, or else she runs the risk of losing herself forever. She doesn't intend to go back in that direction.

The Mavericks who accompanied Milo and Sofia take out Duke, or rather drag him out, along with the Paragon agents who seem to wake up from a nightmare.

Emily really did it. By taking down Duke, she dissolved the psychic link he shared with his army. Her intuition told her that the strange wire installation attached to Tajj represented this psychic link. The agents in the simulation had disappeared when Philip had severed the wires to free Tajj. Not only will Duke never control Emily, but he will also never control all those who had been forced to submit to his twisted mind again. They will go back to being human again instead of war machines. Perhaps the Paragon could return to the nobler calling of old, the same precepts that Dad wanted to push for if he had had the chance to become their leader. For now, Emily doesn't know who will replace him. She can't wait to break the news to Chris if they're lucky enough to find him. Without his father to use him as a pawn in his game to exploit the weak, perhaps Chris could reconnect with his innate talent as a leader.

"You go first," says Emily, who stays behind.

She returns to the sphere, its glare both hypnotizing and terribly intimate, now that she knows what it holds. She takes it in her hand gently, and she is surprised by its radiant heat. She finds the box Duke used to carry it and places her sphere inside, the pad crinkling neatly under its weight. How can something so small be so powerful and mysterious at the same time? Skyler will never cease to amaze her.

Emily clamps the box with a sigh of relief and the feeling that this object is her most precious possession. She won't ever let anyone get their hands on her sphere again. She has had her share of mishaps, both terrible and unpredictable, and destroying the sphere for her peace of mind remains a possibility. But before making such a decision, Skyler should know about it. He is its inventor after all.

THE ARK IS BACK to its normal pace of life with the Sacred Fire pulsing through the ship. The Brotherhood members who stayed behind after the exodus to the refuge base—Milo filled her in on everything she missed—have regained control of the Ark. As for the Paragon agents, they obey under the leadership of those who had pledged allegiance to the Brotherhood before transferring to the Refuge. There is much to be done before the ship returns to the order Commander Hawk had established, but they are on the right track, and that alone makes them happy. They are all working toward a common goal. Within a week, they should reach the North Star. The name did tickle Emily's mind, and she wondered if Philip had deliberately chosen it for the card and if the two were somehow connected. She may never find out, but she will conduct her own investigation when things settle down.

For now, this special evening in *La Orilla* is her priority.

She swallowed her pride and approached Catalina Garcia to host a special dinner. Mrs. Garcia is not the snobbish, off-putting owner Emily imagined. In fact, Mrs. Garcia doesn't care much for the whole reputable family thing, much to Emily's delight. Perhaps the events of the past few weeks have mellowed her. After all, Emily isn't the only one who's been through some very trying times. Each surviving soul is the hero of his or her own story, and Emily doesn't pretend to know the details. She can only show a deep respect for those lucky enough to live another day.

Who knows? Maybe she'll find the courage to present her art to Adeline White. But first, she needs to refine her technique with Professor Paradis at the Academy. Emily is still considering whether to take her up on her offer to have private lessons. She can already imagine the crowd massing in front of her paintings, right here. Having her own art exhibition is one of her deepest desires she has ignored most of her life. The Philip of her subconscious would approve of her decision.

As Emily prepares her surprise for Milo, she can't help but think about what happened to the Syndrome. Didn't Philip tell her she had to make a choice?

"I told you to trust me," says Philip, who got into the restaurant, even though she said not to let anyone in.

As always, he managed to find a way around to get to her. For once, his presence doesn't bother her.

"You're always full of surprises, aren't you?" she replies.

"Surprises make life more interesting, don't they?"

"That's true," admits Emily. "As long as they're good, of course."

"Isn't that the point of a surprise? You never know until you find out."

"What exactly are you getting at?"

"I hear you're going to be very busy tonight," he says, putting his hands behind his back and winking at her. "I wouldn't want to interfere with your surprise for him."

"Do you…"

Emily doesn't finish her question because Philip is already gone.

She thinks she already knows the answer to her question, after all. Does Philip really exist? He does and he doesn't, depending on how she sees him. But one thing is sure, Emily is real, and feeling whole, more than ever.

She feels lighter since she woke up, like the Syndrome is but a distant memory. Something has changed inside her for the better.

This time, Milo makes his entrance. Once again, she wonders why no one told her before letting him in. She hasn't even finished lighting the candles!

Emily gives him a heartfelt smile as he steps off the railing, dressed in plain clothes. She didn't tell him the reason for their meeting, only the location. As soon as he realizes the setting of the place, he looks embarrassed. Emily still forgets sometimes that he grew up among the Mavericks, and he has never set foot in *La Orilla*.

There are so many things she would like to talk to him about. She'd like him to tell her about everything that happened while he was trained as a Paragon agent, the mission he led on behalf of Duke, where his burns came from, what happened to the others, including Fiona. While she doesn't care about her rival's fate, she knows that Milo does. Their history dates back a long while, and anything that might affect Milo matters to Emily, naturally.

"I'm glad you came," she says.

"You should've told me."

"It wouldn't be a surprise, otherwise," she says, echoing Philip's words. "I hope you like it."

"I like everything about you," he replies with a smile that highlights his freckles in the dim light. "Since I met you."

His words send her right back to the Ark's prison, and her good mood vanishes.

"Sometimes I can't understand the horrible beginning of our story," she says, her remorse still heavy in her heart.

"You've changed so much since then, Emily," Milo says with a sincerity that moves her. "We carry our memories like a collection of scars. There's nothing we can do to erase them, but they help us discover who we really are. Of all the people I know, you are the only one who has achieved that."

Emily returns a shy smile as she takes the time to absorb what he has just told her.

"It's only because you keep saving me every chance you get," she answers after some thought.

"Because it's worth it," he answers without hesitation.

Milo places a kiss on her lips that lasts only a moment but warms her heart like the sphere she held in her hand.

"For a long time, I believed that fate had already decided on my life before I even tried changing it," she says, feeling herself gradually opening up, her fear of being judged gone. "A ready-made mission that I had to follow. Now I see that I was wrong. Everyone I've met is filled with surprises, especially you, a Maverick. And myself, someone I'm struggling to understand, someone I thought I'd known all my life, but who is so foreign to me."

She swallows hard at this admission before adding, "Milo, I'm scared."

He gives her a look filled with respect and empathy that calms her, a feeling she is starting to enjoy.

"You're still in shock," he says, and she doesn't see how he could say it any better.

Milo takes her hands, and his aura pours warmth and comfort into her.

"But despite this fear, I know I'm on the right track," Emily continues. "As you said, my memories are just that, memories. They don't define me."

She offers him a cup that she prepared for their evening in *La Orilla*. She even managed to find the violinist who has miraculously survived the events since that evening that she spent with Skyler. The violin fills the restaurant with its magic, and Emily can already feel its effect.

They clink their glasses, and Emily takes a sip that burns her mouth. Milo, on the other hand, puts the cup aside and, as soon as she finishes, takes her by surprise with a fiery kiss.

Emily responds with equal force and puts down her cup while groping for him.

After their languid kiss, Emily's eyes fall on Milo's neck, where she places another kiss. She thinks she's left a mark, with a shape that reminds her strangely of one of Philip's cards. She wants to take a better look at it and wipe it off, but a familiar presence ruffles her skin.

"You weren't supposed to kiss, but I guess you got what you deserved," Fiona says to Milo.

Emily leaves Milo's embrace and watches Fiona, who has dressed for the occasion in a garment that does justice to the natural color of her aura. For a moment, Fiona's image splits, and Emily leans on Milo, who barely catches her. The next moment, her legs buckle.

"I always thought our future was bound, Milo, until that Emily Bates upended our lives. She is the source of all our problems, and I couldn't let her live. Whether or not she took out

Duke Kay, it doesn't change what she did to us. And you were stupid enough to fall for her. I didn't want to lose you. Truly. But it's too late now. You'll be with her forever like you wanted."

"Fiona," Milo mumbles. "You've lost your mind. What have you done?"

Emily's vision blurs, her thoughts are a confused mess.

"What I had to do," she answers, trembling with rage. Or pain? Emily couldn't tell.

"What the hell was going through your mind, Fiona?" roars Sofia with hurried steps. "I knew someone had gone through my bag, but my own daughter. It's beyond me."

"As you've told me so often, I'm just like my father in every way," Fiona simply replies, sniffling.

The burning sensation in Emily's mouth spreads down her throat and throughout her body like when *La Orilla* was on fire. But this time, her body is burning from the inside.

One last image permeates her mind: Milo's face against the ground. Milo is looking at her, his pupils dilated, his hand stretched toward her, a tear on his cheek.

40

SKYLER

The passageway next to the Hall of the Gods leads to the bay. If Eliza knew such a passage existed, why didn't she just tell him? They could have evacuated. They could have saved everyone.

Sedated by his remorse, Skyler searched the little temple with Dinah's help to look for survivors. She doesn't know it's his fault the drones located them, because he can't find the courage to tell her. It would be like confessing his sin to the Creator himself. Skyler wonders if He had a hand in this abomination. During his prayers, was it Allen he heard or his Voice?

"Unbelievable. They were here all along!" Dan emerges from the Njord throwing a dark pile glowing under their torches. "That damn armor."

"Definitely foreign," Derek says, feeling the makeshift bandage Skyler put on his shoulder as he examines the gear. "That could've changed everything. Why didn't Tessa share them with Oslo's guards?"

"That's what traitors do."

No one has an answer to that. Derek and the priestess help the handful of survivors board the Njord. Each of their tired faces is imprinted on Skyler's memory. None of them know he is responsible for their tragedy. He brought whole families to seek refuge at the temple and now, their loved ones, their children are riddled with bullets or crushed under shattered rocks. Without the Brotherhood to get rid of these drones, they would have all perished.

Skyler boards the ship next while Dan collects the armor and puts them away in the open metal locker where he found them. Just before embarking, Dinah signs herself, her glance fixed toward the dome.

"Skyler," she says with a frown. She caught him putting on a breath-crushing armor to remind him of what he has done.

"I have to do this," he says, making sure the others are already inside. "Please."

The priestess watches him for a while, then finally nods. Skyler exits the Njord and rushes through the secret passageway, praying for them as Allen's voice guides him.

Not so long ago, Skyler got here by chance. Now, the flame of his torch creates a macabre dance on the inoperative equipment. The presence he felt last time doesn't manifest itself, but the stifling heat would be reason enough to turn back.

The same voice that called out to him during his prayer before the avatars led him here. Allen wanted him to come to the reactor.

"We need some light in here," Dan grumbles, yanking Skyler's torch away. He came alone, wearing the augmented armor.

"How did you know?" asks Skyler, alarmed.

"I leave you alone for a minute, and you decide to be a jerk. This is no time to be reckless. You're our only doctor on board."

"What about Chris and the kids? We must go get them," says Skyler.

"It's too dangerous," Dan cuts. "We must leave now. We'll come back when we're sure there is no more danger. There is no guarantee that Ludo's schemes will stop here."

The whirring of a system kicking back to life startles them. The neon lights flick on one by one with the distinctive sound of sparks crackling in the bulbs. As the room lights up, the outline of a central reactor fenced off by a ramp appears. They are in a large glass control room with reinforced doors looking out on a large bottomless pit dug right in the center. The large window that should protect them from the radioactive fumes has a gaping hole in its center and the place gives off a nose-wrinkling smell of gas, soil, and something Skyler cannot identify.

"If I were you, I'd put out that torch, unless you want your intestines to soar ten thousand feet into the air." Ludo is leaning against the console like an invisible shadow. Has he been standing there all this time without Skyler noticing? Was he Allen's voice?

None of his drones are keeping him company this time, and his armor is damaged.

Neal failed.

"I guess the gas leak was your doing too," Skyler says, keeping his composure.

"This is just an unfortunate side effect of my more-than-successful discoveries."

"Why go to such lengths to eradicate your own species? How is this reasonable?"

"The Executioners do not question or challenge the will of the Gods. They execute."

Skyler can almost feel the sharpness of his words cutting through metal. Dan reaches out to his holster, his hand stroking the butt of a concealed weapon.

"Leave the North Star out of this mission," says Tessa who comes in, gun leveled at Ludo's head. The bastard feigns surprise with a mocking face. "My uncle never ordered you to destroy every living thing. He may be crazy, but not *that* crazy."

"All this would never have happened if you had shown up at the Sacred Fire as planned," says Ludo, with a serious, dramatic air. "Consumed by its eternal flames, the Amaranth would already be nothing but a pile of rotting scrap metal in the Great Ocean's abyss. But no! Instead, you sent this Brotherhood to do the dirty work for you. It's a shame I could only shoot the girl. I was only getting started purging that Ark before I was spotted."

"Emily," Skyler lets out through gritted teeth. After discovering the Commander's code, he remembers saying goodbye to his best friend as she and Milo set out to the Sacred Fire. "So, it was you."

"Do you know her?" asks Ludo, licking his lips. "You can tell her that I'm eager to finish what I started. If she ever wakes up, that is."

He reveals his teeth gleaming with a metal prosthesis, and Skyler is struck with horror: The beastly holograms of the Academy aren't so far from reality after all. How can anyone be so unhinged and devoid of empathy? He must be suffering from a severe form of the Fairy Syndrome—that or an advanced form of psychosis.

"These little gems will make for the most beautiful fireworks this planet has seen since the Flood," says Ludo, revealing the inside of his armor strung with rows of black grenades. "As a bonus, you get a front-row seat on the Promised Land to watch them from up there."

Ludo grabs one and presses it against his cheek, so that if Tessa dares to shoot him, chances are she will hit the strange grenade too. Tessa's grip on her gun weakens torn by the choice she must make. Ludo takes the opportunity to move closer to the reinforced door that leads to the reactor bridge.

Dan decides to play the hero and throws himself on Ludo which turns out to be sheer madness. Ludo's eyes roll with pleasure as he bites Dan who screams in pain, his blood flowing profusely. In the scramble that ensues, Ludo throws his black grenade through the yawning glass overlooking the reactor shaft, and Skyler feels his heart fall into the abyss.

He sees his brother Allen drop into the depths of the Ark, his face marred by astonishment, but this time, Skyler leaps through the window to catch him, hand outstretched, time holding its breath as their lives are about to be decided.

The shock is so brutal that Skyler loses all notions of gravity, the blood rising to his head. His breath returns after a few seconds, his hand firmly holding Allen as he floats in the vacuum of the reactor shaft. Skyler will not fail this time, even if he loses his life. This will be the redemption he has longed for all these years. Everything he ever accomplished was for this fateful moment.

Allen talks to him in his timeless, younger, more confident voice. His real brother.

"You have to let go of me."

"Never," Skyler replies with a strained voice that echoes down the abyssal shaft. "Can you hear me? Never!"

"This is how it must be, and you know it. You can't accept it now, but one day, you will understand why. The Creator has his reasons for doing what he does."

"I won't. I can't!" shouts Skyler in a drunken rage. "If I have to defy the Creator himself to keep you, I will."

"I will always be a part of you when you face the Creator's wrath."

Someone runs down the stairs onto the bridge. Skyler is floating above the chasm of the reactor, hanging by his uniform that caught in the barrier. Allen is still hooked at the end of his arm. Then, gravity shifts, and Allen is sucked into the darkness.

There is no scream. There is no noise.

"Allen, Allen," stammers Skyler, confused, slumping to the floor in a daze.

"Get a hold of yourself, Skyler! Your brother isn't here. Look at me!" Tessa cups his sweaty face while Skyler's hand is firmly clasped around the black grenade that he risked his life for.

"It was Allen," he repeats as he crawls to the edge of the reactor shaft, Allen's face etched in his memory. "He was there, he was there! The Creator stole him from me a second time!"

"Skyler, he's not here. He was never there. Please, please, please!"

An ominous, throaty laugh echoes through the reactor room, drowning out Tessa's pleading voice. Ludo hobbles toward them on the bridge, his armor open with the other grenades. Tessa stands on her feet, leaving Skyler by himself against the railing with the black grenade.

"It's not over yet," Ludo hisses. He sniffs around like a beast, the veins in his neck throbbing with strain.

For every step Ludo takes, Tessa aims with uncanny precision: First, his legs, then two clear shots for each arm. He collapses before he has time to throw himself into the shaft. With superhuman strength, he crawls with his fingers twisting against the metal of the bridge. Tessa crushes them under her boot, then kicks him in the face with a loud crack.

Ludo licks his own blood pouring from his nose and still manages to show his chaos-hungry grin.

"Hide as much as you want, you'll never be safe," Ludo articulates half-consciously. "More Executioners will be sent now that Thalassa knows your location. They know about the Ark too. It's only a matter of time."

The shot comes clean through his head, and his lifeless carcass slumps against the ground. Tessa stares blankly, her pistol still raised long after.

Skyler watches her struggle against a pain he knows all too

well. He rises to his feet to join her and puts his hand on hers, slowly lowering her arm.

"What have I done?" cries Tessa as he wraps his arms around her, feeling her pain shoot through him.

"The right thing," Skyler replies, feeling the doubts he had about her dissipate. "Even if it means sacrificing a part of yourself."

She sobs and drops her gun like it is a burning sun. "I never wanted any of this."

"You made it this far. You made the right decision for all of us."

"Nothing can excuse my uncle or these selfish gods. I should've known better."

"The Creator always finds his Way to be heard," says Skyler with a bitter taste on his tongue. "It is up to us to tell the truth from the lies."

Tessa does not answer, tormented by her betrayal to her own kind. He decides to break their embrace to give her some space.

Dan groans, his head lolling to one side, while staunching the blood from his neck with one hand, and Skyler rushes to dress his wound with a torn-off piece of clothing. As Tessa disarms the grenades on Ludo's corpse, Skyler finally notices that Ludo had smeared his face with Dan's blood, making him look like some divine fanatic.

What if he was one of the Creator's envoys who came to do His dirty work?

It is because of Him that the refugees are dead, so is Dan's bleeding out, and so is Neal's death in the fight against Ludo. The game the Creator is playing is all too clear to Skyler now.

This is what Eliza was trying to tell him, this obsession of the Brotherhood. This Promised Land is none other than the place where this unjust Creator is enthroned, ready to pick the dead, shrubs that he so carefully grew and then abandoned.

He sent an incurable disease to eat away at them from within, blackening each of their leaves, their branches, and the trunk down to the roots. He watched without lifting a finger, for there is as much destruction in a Flood than in deciding to sit idly by and watch.

Letting death take its claim with a clear conscience, without even trying to stop it, is as sickening as using one's strength to kill willingly.

This world is ruled by a merciless Creator who plays with them.

Skyler can sense it: Something in him has changed. Allen's presence, or what happened to Neal, is somewhere inside him, breaking the fetters of the Creator who wants to keep his secret safe from the living. Allen has revealed to him what the Creator's true face is and what evil plan He has for them all.

Even if the Creator has decided to chain Allen in his eternal realm, Skyler will do anything to bring him back—even if it means rebelling against Him and the evil gods who assist Him.

It is time to end the infernal cycle of death.

END OF BOOK 2

ALSO BY DAVID M. SNOW

Flower of Memory

Amaranth

ACKNOWLEDGMENTS

First of all, I would like to thank Pascal Raud, my outstanding and brilliant and fantastic — did I say that already? — editor. He is not only a mentor, but also a friend who always knows how to push the limits of a manuscript and this book is no exception. It's a joy to have someone like him who can read my mind and put the right word on my sometimes foggy ideas. He has the best mist blower I know (and a whip to bring me back to order if I'm lazy!). His suggestions have greatly improved the flow of the story, and each manuscript he comments on with great care is better than the previous. Now it's my turn to challenge him to write his first novel. Get ready!

My best friend Kim Archambault for all our discussions that rekindle my desire to write even in my moments of self-doubt. Not only can she listen like no other, but she has a contagious passion for writing. There is no better partner to bounce ideas for stories that take unusual turns.

The copyeditor of this book, Heidi Ripplinger, who polished this piece with her insightful comments and clarity.

Special thanks to my parents for their unfailing moral support. They have always believed in my projects even when I no longer believed in them.

My partner for not judging my blank stares and hours of isolation while I write.

Thank you, my readers, for inspiring me to be a better novelist and allowing me to create stories to share. Without you, writing would be meaningless. I'll see you again for the last book in this series (but probably not in the Amaranthverse)!

David M. Snow

ABOUT THE AUTHOR

David M. Snow is a science-fiction and fantasy author for adults. When he is not busy reading with a cup of green tea, running 5km, looking up new words in the dictionary for hours on end, or learning Mandarin, Tagalog, Japanese or Korean, he sits down with his MacBook Pro and types his next novel in a frenzy.

With a Master's in Applied Linguistics and ten years of teaching experience, he is also a linguist, polyglot, entrepreneur and teacher. After living in China for several years, he is in search of new places to explore.